# DESIRING DARKNESS

# DESIRING DARKNESS

NELLY ALIKYAN

DESIRING DARKNESS

Copyright © 2022 by Nelly Alikyan



Published by Innocent Sinner Publishing LLC

Find me:

https://nellyalikyan.com

Copyediting: Katie Wismer [https://www.katiewismer.com]

Cover Design : Maria Spada [https://www.mariaspada.com]

ISBN: 978-1-956847-06-2

First Edition: November 2022

10 9 8 7 6 5 4 3 2 1

*To my future Hunter.*
*I hate you.*

**Whittle Magic Series**

Alluring Darkness

Beholding Darkness

Claiming Darkness

Desiring Darkness

**Catchers Series**

With the Flames Catching Midnight

With the Rains Catching Dawn

With the Ice Catching Twilight

With the Storms Catching Dusk

With the Winds Catching Sunlight

With the Ashes Catching Daybreak

# ALSO BY N. ALIKYAN

Buttercup Baby

Promise of A Lifetime

PROLOGUE

Miradora fell fast through the pits, but nothing mattered to her. Not the possibility of hitting the hard ground or the flames surrounding her as she fell or even the skips of her heart at this endlessness. Nothing but the fact that she was that little bit closer to her mate.

She hated that man. Hated him for being the villain. Hated him for every awful thing he'd committed. Hated him for ruining people's lives. Hated him for ruining *her* life, for making it so she could not live without him. Hated him for what she'd had to do to get back to him. Hated him, most of all, because she loved him.

She hated that she had never needed to hear him say it back to know he felt the same way. Hated that when the High Priests surrounded him and he realized there was no way of getting to her, he stood there and met her gaze. Hated him for telling her in those last moments before he was sent into the unbreakable, unbearable prison that he loved her.

The depthless pits ended with a bone-shattering landing on dirt grounds, but because this was Hell's Gate, no real injuries would be acquired.

Miradora was on her feet in an instant, needing to know

she'd done it and come back to her mate. She needed to meet his beautiful black eyes again.

She was at the edge of the cage she'd fallen into, the flames beyond it enticing and the endlessness beyond that everlasting. She turned in her spot, and her heart stopped when she came face-to-face with the man standing at the other end of the rounded cage.

Her demon.

Her mate.

Her forever.

"Adramalech," she breathed, unable to believe it herself that she was there.

His gaze was hard, jaw grinding.

"I cannot possibly have been in here so long as to hallucinate." He spoke like he was talking to thin air. "Hell's Gate cannot conjure up apparitions, and I cannot have already lost my mind."

Miradora almost crumbled in her spot as she shook her head. "You're not hallucinating, my savage beast."

His breath caught at her use of that nickname she'd given him, and his head slowly shook as those beautiful eyes watered. He wouldn't allow himself to believe it was her.

Miradora took a single step forward and raised her hand. "Touch me and know that I am real, that I am truly here."

He took a large gulp, then took a tentative step forward. Then another and another until he was finally before her.

His hand shook as it reached out to touch the one she still had up. When their fingers brushed, his entire body shivered. "Miradora." The whisper left him like a prayer.

"My love."

His breath froze as he took a final step forward so they were only a foot apart before dropping to his knees.

Miradora's hands moved immediately to get lost in that black hair that touched his shoulders, and her eyes closed on a relieved sigh. "Adramalech, my love."

His hands grabbed her hips roughly, almost painfully, as he leaned into her torso and laid his head to rest like he was praying to her. "My love," he mumbled against her stomach, leaving trails of light kisses everywhere.

In that moment, Miradora didn't care about all of the awful things she'd had to do to get to him. She didn't care about all the innocent lost lives because she knew she would've burned all those villages in order to get him back. She dropped to her knees before him and brushed her forehead against his, breathing in his breath.

When she kissed him, his lips took her savagely, his tongue unwilling to wait for permission to conquer her. It was invigorating.

Then he abruptly pulled away and held her face in both his hands, his eyes crazed with realization. "How did you get down here, Miradora?" His fingers curled with fury. "You cannot be stuck here too! I will not allow…"

She softly brushed his jaw with one hand as the other played along his chest. "I have done a lot of horrible things, my love, but I would do them all again to be with you. We won't be staying here. I'm going to get us out the same way I got myself in."

His gaze searched hers for long moments before he leaned forward and whispered against her lips, "I trust you."

Before she could respond, his mouth was on hers again, savage hunger for her winning over his need to be out of the prison. His hands ripped at her dress as she tugged on his shirt, not strong enough to tear the material apart, but needing him naked as desperately.

Their clothes littered the dirt grounds of the cage in record time before he laid her over them and kissed his way down her body. As much as she'd missed his tongue and fingers in their separation, she needed him inside her. She needed to stare into those eyes and know with finality that they were back together.

She tugged at his hair to drag him up her body and line his

cock up at her entrance, and clung her legs around his waist, begging for him to enter her.

He slowed as he filled her, then paused, his fingers tracing her face in wonder as he stared into her eyes. "How did I get so lucky with you, my love?"

Miradora wiggled beneath him, needing him to move. "I love you, Adramalech. I believe myself lucky to have you every moment I'm breathing."

He finally moved, thrusting into her slowly. "And I you. I have fallen in love with you, Witch."

Entry #1

Mama keeps telling me they're only stories, but she doesn't know that I know. They're not only stories.

They're the supernatural.
And I will be their God.

1

It didn't matter that she now accepted them, it was still annoying to Camilla that she smiled so warmly when she watched *that* demon kiss her sister. Thankfully though, this time the act was done less obscenely given they were in front of their entire family, specifically her parents.

Camilla still saw a bit of tongue though. She doubted Hunter could've refrained if his life depended on it.

And especially not on his wedding day.

A hand slid around Camilla's shoulders, and she stiffened as a breath hit her ear. "You like that, princess? My tongue would be happy to do the same to you."

Camilla exhaled slowly and kept her loving gaze on the middle Whittle as that kiss extended longer than normal. Apt, considering they weren't a normal couple.

That breath tickled her ear again. "When they go off to *celebrate*, why don't we do the same?"

Camilla ground her teeth this time and let her elbow do the talking as it jammed into Kai's gut.

Then a small bouquet of flowers was thrown in the bride and groom's direction and hit Hunter square in the back of the head as Warren yelled, "That's enough, asshat. Her father's here!"

Camilla held in her giggles and clapped with the others as Maya and Hunter finally broke from their embrace, staring into one another's eyes and smiling brightly. It was clear Hunter wanted to shadow them away immediately and have the most passionate night of their lives with his mate.

But Camilla's smile still softened at the way they stared at one another. The look on her sister's face that had never been there before made Camilla happy. But the look Hunter gave Maya, the devotion and adoration clear in his eyes, past his need to get her undressed, was what really melted Camilla's heart. He was gross—that went along with being a full-blooded demon more than anything—but he showed in a simple look, touch, kiss to her sister how much his entire world only held her.

The wedding wasn't needed. It didn't tell them anything more than the mating rings had, but it was something small that Maya had wanted to do. To make it feel more official to her since she'd grown up without the knowledge of the supernatural world and their matings—though only werewolves and demons had matings.

So, now they were mated and married.

Maya had even gone for a beautiful silk, white dress, her hair tumbled down around her shoulders in dark waves and two small strands slipped back in braids. She looked radiant, and that smile bright on her face made Camilla happier for her sister than any ill-willed feeling she could ever have for a demon.

Hunter's ever-insistent, gelled-back brown hair along with his immaculate—and if Camilla had to guess, ridiculously expensive—tux somehow made him look elegant and causal all at the same time.

As Camilla rose to her feet with the others around their beautifully flowered backyard, that breath hit her neck again.

"You're quite tense, princess. Maybe we should skip the cake. I can take you up to the room now and enjoy my own dessert."

Camilla's core tightened at the thought, but she wiped it out of her mind immediately as she jammed her elbow even harder into his gut and turned from him.

She followed the group, which consisted solely of the Whittles and Delvauxs, plus Kai who had invited himself, to a small table that had been set up for their nibbling enjoyment. They may have been in the middle of this *situation* with Jenkins and Selin, one after Hunter and the other Maya, but they would get their deserved day. Everyone would celebrate their love.

Because that's exactly what it was between Camilla's most beloved sister and that heartless monster.

Everyone took their plates and began filling as Camilla stood off to the side. Her parents kept staring into one another's eyes like it was *their* wedding day. Harry and Vera giggled together as they laid on more food. Augustine smiled at Maya like he was happier to have her part of the family than either of his sons—which his greedy ass probably was—and Warren and Kai goofed around.

Camilla tried to push aside the twinge of annoyance that the two of them were friends when an arm landed around her shoulders. "Well, well, well, Little Sister, is that wide grin because I'm officially your brother now?"

Camilla tried to fight the grin, but her lips twitched up at the demon anyway. "You were always my brother. That *is* how mating works."

"Yes, but I've come to believe a wedding makes it feel more real for you lot raised in the human world."

"I still don't like you, Delvaux."

He winked. "Don't kid yourself, Little Sister. You're obsessed with me."

"Maya," Camilla called out. "Your *husband* is bothering me. Again."

Hunter's eyes flamed at the term as a smirk graced his

features. "You think I'm afraid of *my wife?*" His eyes flamed up even more at those last two words.

"Yes the fuck you are." Maya's voice came from beside them, and Camilla jumped a little to find her on Hunter's other side.

Hunter chuckled and threw his other arm over her shoulders. "Are you having vivid dreams again, love?"

"You don't have to act macho, baby. All men are afraid of their wives." Maya's arm wrapped around his waist, and Camilla began to feel a little uncomfortable still on Hunter's other side.

"That's because not all men are mated." A low grumble left him with the words.

Camilla cleared her throat as Maya said, "But all men fear sex getting taken off the table."

"Okay!" Camilla threw Hunter's arm off her and watched it naturally fall to Maya's waist. "I've heard enough."

Before she left, Camilla heard Hunter as he leaned down so he shared breath with his wife. "You're right, love. I am afraid of my wife. Terrified, in fact."

Giggles followed Camilla as she walked away from them and stopped before her family, who were looking on to the couple with pure endearment. She turned back to see them cuddled up, dancing to a song playing in the background as they whispered to one another in their own little bubble.

"Well, now I can vouch for sure that brothers are annoying," Camilla said with a big, bright smile on her face.

---

When Vera was awoken the morning after her sister's wedding, she was annoyed to find it so early.

Rather than cuddle her into his chest and go back to sleep like a normal person, Harry urged her to get up and follow the smell of freshly made French toast coming from the kitchen. It smelled delightful, but Vera was so unlike her middle sister and preferred to sleep in.

"Come on, sweetheart." Harry kissed her temple a hundred little times. "Up. Up. Up."

She groaned and finally pulled herself up but refused to get changed as they headed down to the kitchen where her father, who was so very like the middle Whittle, made breakfast while her mother and Kai talked over their cups of coffee. Even Camilla was up, and not in the miserably-wants-to-go-back-to-bed way that Vera was.

"How are you so awake?" Vera asked her as she poured herself a cup of coffee to the brim.

Camilla glared at Kai as answer.

Kai merely smiled to Vera cheerfully. "I was excited to tell your sister a little story this morning."

Camilla threw a mandarin at him. "He woke me up, then sat at my bedside as I tried to go back to sleep and rambled on about the *meticulous process of cutting grass.* I've been up for over an hour, and I didn't even need the coffee."

"You mean creamer, in your case," Harry joked and received a death glare from the little Whittle in return.

Vera tried to suppress her smile as Kai enjoyed the moment far too much. Their little friendship—though Camilla refused to call it so—was so very different than the one Camilla had had with Warren. Vera believed it to be the better one for the youngest Whittle.

Even though the youngest Whittle would disagree.

"In any case," her mother broke in, obviously trying to suppress her own amusement, "I'm glad you are all awake now. With the excitement of the wedding behind us, let us focus on a different aspect of Hunter and Maya."

Vera's grin fell as Harry handed her a plate of her father's delicious breakfast.

They'd spent the last week since finding out about Jenkins trying to distract themselves with this wedding. They'd known it would come to an end quickly, but it had been a blissful, much needed break to Vera.

Now, it was time to focus on the real problems they had, and ones that weren't necessarily against the entire supernatural world—though if Jenkins came to power, it would be detrimental to the whole of them.

But for the time being, he was simply after Hunter for the specific demon's ability to hold an unlimited amount of power.

And with Grandmama—Selin's—faerie dust magic, he would be able to transfer into the demon's body and take all his stolen powers for himself.

All he had to do was help Selin kill Maya first, her final and most prized victim.

Any way the situation turned, both Hunter and Maya were in trouble, and Vera didn't like that at all. Even the part that only hurt Hunter, and not only because it would destroy Maya, but because she'd grown to like the man in her own way.

"The one that's going to make you a grandmother in nine months?" Kai asked, then looked down at the invisible watch on his wrist. "They've probably consummated at least a dozen times by now."

Again, Vera had to suppress her grin as a mischievous glint shined in Kai's eyes.

"Can you at least pretend to be a little respectful?" Camilla grimaced at him, then turned to their parents. "Selin and Jenkins?"

Loretta nodded. "I've already sent out a mass alert to the other covens about Jenkins' plans. Some of the more powerful may want to meet to discuss things further. I sent another to the species heads so they can pass the information along to their people. The response is as angry as you can imagine, but at least they know that there may be a threat to the supernatural world now."

"But Selin first," Bishop answered. "She's the more immediate threat since Jenkins needs her death for his plan, so he'll wait longer."

"So what? Selin first?" Vera asked as she swallowed the

French toast that she couldn't argue was worth waking up this early for. "We'd have to use Maya as bait, and even if we were okay with that, her mate wouldn't be."

"It scares me too," Loretta said forlornly. "Because Selin doesn't strike me as the sort to talk out her plans. She'll strike when she has the chance, and we can't take that risk with My. But what other choices do we have?"

"Not getting the originals involved at all." A new voice entered their kitchen.

Augustine Delvaux, father of her new brother-in-law and patriarch of the powerful Delvaux line, took a plate and invited himself to their breakfast.

"The originals?" Vera questioned.

"Hunter and Maya," Harry said in consideration as he watched Augustine closely. "But if not them, who?"

"And how?" Camilla added.

"Transfiguration potion," Kai answered, then turned a snarky comment on the youngest Whittle and pinched her nose like she were a child. "You *are* a witch. Or do you forget that high up on that pedestal, princess?"

Camilla huffed out a sigh of frustration as Bishop said, "That's true. We don't need to involve them at all. Maya will remain safe and out of harm's way."

"But that still leaves someone here getting killed, and hello" —Vera mimicked sarcastically—"I'm still not okay with that."

"Don't worry, sister." Kai threw a loving arm over her shoulders, so unlike how he was with Camilla. "I've transfigured so many times, and no offense to the others"—he threw a wink in her direction—"I'm also the fastest. I can port out before she kills *Maya,* and we can get her."

"Oh you!" Camilla's lips tipped up into a wide, creepy grin. "Oh, you're the least of our concerns. *That* we can be okay with."

Her happiness at using him almost reminded Vera of the time she'd been equally as happy to send Hunter into the room full of witches that had almost gotten his soul sucked out. And look at them now—Camilla loved Hunter even though she'd never admit it. He was truly her big brother.

That smirk Kai made almost exclusively to frustrate Camilla appeared. "Don't act strong, princess. I'll come back, and you can kiss my booboos better. I'll make sure to get especially hurt around my c…"

"That's enough!" Bishop growled, and Vera barely held in her laughter. She was surprised he always let it go on so long.

"Not to mention, he's called the Demon Warlock for a reason," Harry added, more fascinated with his French toast than Kai's safety as he shoved Kai's arm off of Vera's shoulders and brought Vera in for a kiss on the cheek.

"Well, let's see how that works before we think of what to do with Jenkins," Augustine finalized as he was handed a cup of black coffee.

2

Bishop didn't want to let go of his wife as they landed in the middle of the Czech Republic.

Their old stomping grounds were as beautiful now as they had been almost three decades ago when he and Loretta had left the coven for the North American territory. The abundance of art nouveau architecture brought Bishop back to the many times he and Loretta would sneak off together into one of these beautifully constructed buildings.

"Bishop, we are here for a reason." Loretta tugged on his arm to release her.

His lips tipped up on one side. "I can't help but remember how much fun we had here."

She caressed his cheek. "I know." She stared up into dark brown eyes that his two older daughters had inherited, then kissed his lips softly. "And when this is all over and our girls are safe and happy, we can come back and have that fun again."

He grinned. "Promise?"

"Snesl bych ti modré z nebe." *I would take the blue from the sky for you.*

"I'd do anything for you too, my love." Bishop kissed her a final time before releasing her.

He took her hand in his as they moved through the streets for the small alley that would lead them to a building with a door that worked almost like a portal. It would send them to the Wittlieff Coven—their original coven. Whittle had only been created after they'd moved to America.

Moving through the door and portal was simple. It was comparable to anyone walking down their street to get to Whittle House. Getting inside the coven would be the more difficult part, as getting into Whittle House was.

The portal sent them through to a vast land of greens, the buildings to their right not even filling a fifth of the space the coven owned. It had always been Bishop's favorite part of this coven he'd been lucky enough to come to—the greens.

So much space to run. He and Loretta had also had plenty of fun out here.

"You're falling into nostalgia again, my love." Loretta's soft tone brought him back.

"I cannot help it, dear." He watched her. "I am quite obsessed with you."

"Which only means we must fix these issues sooner so that we can go back to the life where you chased me around greens and had only your attentions set on me." Loretta watched him like she wanted to rip his clothes off out there in the middle of the greens.

The fact that they were in the line of sight of the Wittlieff Coven was the only reason Bishop pulled away and finally turned to the buildings.

As expected, as they got closer, they were stopped about twenty yards out.

The barrier shook, telling the coven that unwelcome guests were on their lands. The unwelcome being anyone who wasn't part of their coven.

And because they'd moved to America and changed their names—which had been done for the Wittlieff Coven's safety—

they were no longer members of this coven both he and his wife loved dearly.

It took less than a minute before they were greeted by three people.

The warlock who took over as head when Bishop had fallen in love with Loretta—Jakub.

The woman heading the Wittlieff Coven, a promotion she had gotten almost ten years ago, and his old best friend—Anna.

And most painful and amazing of all, Loretta's mother —Adela.

None of them looked pleased as they stopped beyond the shield that protected their homes, but it was Anna who scoffed. "Word had come that you two were, in fact, not dead."

"You have heard correctly," Loretta answered, her tone even and soft.

Bishop's heart pained for his wife whom he could tell was hurting by her mother's inability to look at her. Most of Adela's attention was on Bishop, and it wasn't the most inviting sort.

"What is it you want here?" Jakub asked. "You have created your own coven now."

"We have come only for information," Loretta replied, hiding her emotion perfectly.

"You copied our coven book into one of your own when you left. You have all the information you require," Adela bit out.

Bishop didn't doubt that it had pained Adela the most when he and Loretta had packed up, taken their own version of the coven book that the supernatural world wanted more than most, and left.

Loretta swallowed but remained poised. "We require information about Bishop's ancestors." She met her mother's eyes, and Bishop hated how unwelcoming they were. "It is for your granddaughters."

Adela's gaze narrowed, and it was clear she wanted to know more. As angry as she was at the two of them, she would never punish her granddaughters for it. Granddaughters she was never given the pleasure of meeting.

"Are you aware of the story of Adramalech and Miradora?" Bishop asked.

Adela looked hesitant to say anything before finally giving in. "It is deep in your ancestors. Before mixing with the African tribe, your lot were in the Hellas—Greece."

Jakub and Anna watched her carefully, like they were learning this for the first time as well, before they turned back to Loretta, and Jakub asked, "What does this have to do with?"

"Are you aware of the power Miradora used to get Adramalech out of Hell's Gate?" Bishop asked Adela instead of answering Jakub.

"Of course," the older woman bit out.

Loretta stood tall, but Bishop could see how nervous she was, could feel the tightening of her hand in his. "Your second granddaughter has mated to a demon."

Adela breathed carefully, analyzing. "I am aware. I hope her all the happiness. Demons can be some of the most loving people once they find the person worthy of such affections."

"I'm glad you think so," Loretta opened. "Because like Bishop's ancestry, Maya would do anything for Hunter."

"What do you mean by that, child?" Adela's tone grew demanding, her eyes darkening like she was figuring it out.

"Maya has Miradora's magic, Mother. A far more powerful version of it."

Adela gasped as her gaze widened, and both Anna and Jakub at her side shot their gazes between mother and daughter to try to catch on.

"She would do for Hunter as Miradora did for Adramalech, Mother," Loretta finished. "Ravage the earth."

Camilla was seated in a different spot than her usual, somewhere in the middle of the lecture hall. And she was nervous about whether she'd be seeing Jenkins or not in her first literature class since he exposed himself as the man after the supernatural world.

She was rewarded with the answer when a professor she recognized as the lead of the literature department moved to the front and began messing with the projection in order to put up that a change had been made with professors. Camilla wondered what had been told to the school for Jenkins to get out of it. She wondered if he'd even bothered telling them anything. She doubted it.

Before she could think for too long about it, the doors to the front of the lecture hall opened and Warren walked in and met her eyes, a smile wide on his handsome face.

Camilla smiled back before she realized that the smile had been the result of a joke made by none other than the bane of her existence.

They both moved to her, taking a seat on either one of her sides, as Kai grinned sweetly at her. "Princess."

"*What* are you doing here? You're not a student!" she hissed his way as her elbow met Warren's gut when she noticed how much amusement he found in her current situation.

"After saving you from going on a date with that psychopath last time, I think you should be happy to have me here. A princess does need her guard."

Camilla turned to Warren. "I thought we broke up amicably. Why would you bring him?"

Warren laughed. "He would've come whether or not I brought him." He looked over Camilla's shoulder to his friend. "In any case, doesn't look like Jenkins is gonna show up, so you may not be needed."

Needed? Like he was actually there to protect her rather than drive her to jump off this fucking building.

Instead of chastising Warren for his use of that word, Camilla turned to the warlock at her right. "You heard the man. Leave."

That ever present, and more annoying than Hunter's, smirk made its way up. "No."

Camilla went to argue, but class started, and all quieted down for the new professor to explain the situation at hand and how they intended to move on with the class.

As Camilla ignored the warlock, Warren leaned in close to her ear. "They're changing the curriculum. All of Jenkin's lectures and readings were related to magic, old tales and all."

Camilla scoffed at the reminder. "Now we know why."

"It can still help us. If we focus on the old syllabus and go through what Jenkins still had planned, we can see what he was planning all along. He knew we were in his class, knew you were here. He probably enjoyed putting all the hints right in front of us and watching us walk right past them."

"Get me a copy of that syllabus," Kai whispered toward them, never breaking his stare toward the new professor.

Warren nodded even though Kai wasn't paying attention. "You can catch up while we read on." Warren turned to Camilla. "If you think of anything from the first half of the semester we could look deeper into, let me know."

She met his hazel eyes and was momentarily transported to the beginning of their relationship and how in love she'd been with those eyes, so intelligent and caring and accepting. So perfect.

Camilla nodded numbly and turned back to the lecture.

As she watched the new professor—Atkinson—switch slides on the PowerPoint, she whispered to no one in particular, "I'll also send the slides from the past lectures. I had them all pre-downloaded. We can see what Jenkins wanted emphasized from the stories. A lot of his ideas were based around power. I can only imagine how much he loved rubbing it in our faces without our knowledge."

"Anything else?" Kai asked. "Any notes you took of things he said in lecture rather than presented as a slide or in a reading?"

Camilla felt Warren shrug to her left. "I don't know. I'll send my notes anyway."

"Me too," Camilla added subconsciously.

Though she tried to pay attention to Atkinson, Camilla's periphery latched onto the man to her right and wouldn't let go. He was watching the lecture intently, almost like he was analyzing the way the professor talked, walked, and looked. The way he positioned his movements and smiled at any slides. Like any minuscule thing could give the man away.

"Is there something about him?" Camilla leaned into him and whispered, hating to admit that he *had* been able to tell something had been off about Jenkins.

Again, the warlock didn't look over to her as his lips tipped up into that cocky smirk. "No. I'm just interested in literature." He turned toward her, and they shared breath only an inch apart. "Thought you were too, princess. Want someone to talk to about lit?" He winked, and when she didn't say anything or move away, his eyes softened on her. "But I'm glad you finally see my skill, princess."

Camilla inhaled deeply, getting lost in his woodsy scent as her gaze latched onto *his* hazel eyes, mischief and something else now staring back at her. She pushed back into her seat, taking the warlock's stead and actually paying attention to the lecture. Especially considering she *was* a student.

But she could feel his eyes on her for long moments before he finally turned back to Atkinson.

3

incent Heisenberg was a twelve-year-old demon with a primary power that made him a strong ally to Hunter. The fact that he was a Heisenberg really faulted him, but even the kid hated that bit.

Hunter appreciated in that moment that Dragen wouldn't have trained his son because of his belief that astral projection was Vincent's primary power, and that was one of the things that made the man a complete idiot. Even if astral projection had been the kid's primary, anyone could be useful and needed training.

But it also meant that everything Hunter taught the kid would make him a stronger ally since he wouldn't have his father's absurdity in his head. Vincent would be someone Hunter could use in the future when needed. Considering their current problems with Jenkins, his powers might be needed sooner than Hunter would've planned.

And after the kid helped, Hunter would be ready to return the favor. Especially when, in the future, he left his family—or hopefully killed and got rid of the fuckers—Hunter could help him with that.

As he moved the kid through his father's dungeons, Hunter

was glad to see that he was unaffected by what he saw down there. So he was more like Hunter than Warren. Hunter had assumed since he was a full-blooded demon, but he hadn't been entirely sure.

So maybe the kid's affections for the fish were more similar to his affection for his witch than he'd thought—uncaring for anyone else but her. If he'd found his mate so early on, he was a lucky man—though when the lust hit him in a few years, and Bella still wasn't ready, little Vincent might not believe himself the luckiest of men.

Hunter stopped in front of a cell of a demon who had made some kissing noises toward Maya the last time they'd been in the dungeons. As much as Hunter had wanted to hurt him for it, he couldn't kill all the fuckers who said something toward her. They'd have no one left in these dungeons if that were to happen.

"Ready to play?" Hunter teased into the cell.

The demon within only gave a crude grin in return, getting up on his grubby and dirt-stained legs. He smelled like shit, and parts of his trousers were covered in his piss and shit, but Hunter didn't give a fuck about that. He was a prisoner, not a guest.

Most of the prisoners were demons, so when the opportunity came to be let out, even if only to be used as target practice like when Hunter had tried to train Maya's power, they got excited.

Hunter grabbed for the man's collar and pulled him down the corridors while the other prisoners catcalled, each one wanting a chance to be let out and have fun. He'd go for them later too, pick one at random. That's what he normally did.

Hunter threw the prisoner in the middle of the open space at the edge of the cells, the spot he used for these trainings most of the time so he wouldn't need to take the prisoners out of the dungeons.

Then he turned to Vincent. "Let's see what you have, kid."

He'd already mentioned he was completely untrained and the only times he'd truly used his skills were when he needed to—namely, when Bella was in trouble. It was another factor as to why Hunter knew they were mates. Vincent's magic was reacting to Bella, protecting her. Had Hunter not been so in control of his powers when he met Maya, his would've done the same.

Vincent took his position, but he looked serious, not nervous. He didn't have the pride dwindling down on him like caring creatures would. This was a training for his advantage. He knew he was nowhere near Hunter's power, and he wouldn't try to act like it—he would take direction and make himself greater. He could protect his fish, which was his main priority, a fact he hadn't been shy about mentioning when Hunter had talked to him before bringing him down to the dungeons.

Biokinesis, the internal bleeding of one's organs, wasn't a visual power, so all Hunter would be able to see was the prisoner's reactions. He wanted to see that before he partook in his next step.

The demon stood there with a cocky grin, eyeing Vincent like this was a joke and the kid couldn't do a thing. It took a moment, but Hunter then saw the slight twinge the man had to his right side. Just a single, minuscule flinch, but one nonetheless. Then another one before his hand fisted and his eyes darkened on Vincent.

After another moment, the prisoner growled and charged for Vincent, who remained unmoving and staring at the man. Hunter could see the man's pain on his face as he ran for the kid, and he struck out his fist to knock the prisoner in the face to stop him.

When the prisoner fell back, Vincent took a small step back, indicating to Hunter he'd stopped, and waited.

Hunter then moved for the prisoner and forced him to open his mouth by holding the man's jaw open and shoving a vial into his mouth, making him swallow.

Hunter released him when he stopped trying to spit it out, coughing as he gave Hunter dirty looks. A minute later, the prisoner's insides were visible for Hunter to see. He would be able to see what Vincent did. They would all be able to see it. Vincent, too, for the first time would be able to *see* what his powers did to the victims.

"Go again."

The prisoner narrowed dark eyes on Vincent and rose to his feet as Vincent took his stance, and slowly, Hunter saw the kid's power take effect. Blood was slowly filling a lung, then flowing back out, playing with the man's breathing. It was visibly untrained, but still a powerful magic.

When the prisoner charged for Vincent again after witnessing what he was feeling, Hunter knocked him on his ass again, then smirked toward Vincent.

"Let's get you trained, kid."

***

Maya knew Bella loved seeing her sister, and especially loved seeing the way Alloy treated Brynn, but it was obvious the kid was distracted. Vincent was having his first training session with Hunter, and she had argued long and hard about being with him for it.

At the end, it had been three against one with even Vincent arguing against having her there. Maya knew it was because he wanted to train his powers without the distraction of having her around before adding that to the list as well—the way Hunter had his entire life before meeting Maya—but it was also a bit of pride. Full blooded demons didn't have pride, but when it came to specific things, like showing up for their mates, they were annoyingly prideful.

And though Vincent and Bella weren't "officially" mated, it was an unspoken knowledge of their relationship. They were still young, literal children, but in a few years, they'd be wearing rings made of their blood too.

Maya laid a hand to Bella's thigh as they sat on one side of the table in Brynn and Alloy's private beach house as the couple whispered to one another on their way to bring snacks and drinks to the table. "Relax, Bell. You're gonna have them asking questions."

No one else knew about Vincent. Not even her sister. She wanted to tell Brynn but hadn't been able to in the past.

Bella met Maya's gaze with a worried one. "I can't help it."

"He's going to be fine. Hunt isn't going to let a thing happen to him. If you see bruises, it's just training."

Bella froze. "Bruises? Why would he have bruises? It's magic training. Powers. Why would he get bruises from—"

Maya moved her hand to the mermaid's shoulder. "Bella. Relax. Hunter's going to get him trained in combat too. There's no way Vincent won't ask for it. He's going to want to know how to fight, all demons do. But he's especially going to want to know in order to protect you. Any bruises will just be training. I get them too. Hunter won't let anything happen to him."

Bella slouched. "You probably think I'm ridiculous. I'm only ten. I shouldn't worry so much about a boy."

Maya smiled. "Not ridiculous, a little jealous. I can only imagine what it would've been like having Hunter in my life growing up. You're lucky." Though Hunter was six years older, so maybe growing up knowing him wouldn't have been the best of things.

Before Bella could say anything, though there was a thankful look in her eyes, Brynn and Alloy set plates and cups on the table as Brynn asked, "Why's she lucky. What're we talking about?"

Maya was about to come up with something to say when Bella squared her shoulders. "Demons. Our demons."

She treasured Vincent so much, was so secretive about him, it was nice to finally see her trust another person with the relationship. It had been easier with Maya because of her similar relationship, but Brynn was her sister and also in a cross-relationship, so Maya had no doubts she'd be supportive. Even if this was with a demon, and most every species hated them.

"What does that mean? Our?" Alloy eyed her with a cheeky glint in his eyes as he leaned back in his chair and threw his arm around Brynn's chair.

Bella swallowed. "Maya's demon, Hunter. And…and my demon." Then quieter. "Vincent."

Both Brynn and Alloy sat up straighter, eyeing between the two of them before stopping on Bella as Brynn asked, "Vincent…?"

Bella nodded but said nothing more.

Then Brynn's eyes were on Maya as she asked multiple questions without a word uttered.

Maya met their concerned gaze with a warm look in her eyes, hopefully easing them. "He's twelve, also a child."

They both seemed to deflate with that. Then their eyes moved onto the other question.

Maya turned to look at Bella for that. This was her relationship, and though Maya knew the answer, Bella needed to answer it. She was a smart kid. She would be able to read the question from her sister and brother-in-law just as well.

After a moment, Bella met both of their gazes. "Not officially. It's not like marriage, so we don't have to wait until we're eighteen, but demons are said to wait until they're older to make it official. I think it's a providing thing. He would need to be older to be able to."

"You're the only other heir, Bella," Brynn finally said. "And demons are already mass-hated. There's going to be a lot of pushback when it comes out. Are you ready for that?"

Bella looked down to her fidgeting fingertips on the table like she was ashamed—and because she was a caring creature, she probably was a bit ashamed for her answer. "I would do anything for him."

Brynn stared at her sister wide-eyed for a moment, then met her gargoyle's eyes. Then they both broke out into large grins and leaned into one another, laughing and kissing in a private joke.

"What?" Bella sat up straight, apprehension still rolling off of her.

"Nothing, nothing." Brynn faced them again, still giggling as she fell into Alloy's side.

Then Alloy wiggled his eyebrows, teasing Bella. "So when do we meet this demon? I cannot wait to see the way you beat red around him, Bels."

Maya laughed as Bella fell into herself, already turning crimson.

When she met Brynn's eyes again, there was still amusement there, but it also held a serious undertone. Maya read it clearly —was he good to her?

Maya nodded, a small smile lifting her lips at the memory of Vincent throwing Bella into the pool because of his desperate need to get her in water when Selin had kept her body dehydrated—a killing move for mermaids.

Brynn mirrored her look, then sighed. "I guess the plan's simple then—let's get rid of these psychos after the supernatural world. I need my sister and her mate to have their chance. I cannot wait to end up as the 'good' child."

Bella laughed into her arm she was hiding behind as she threw a cherry tomato at her sister.

4

It was Maya's first official dinner with the Delvauxs.

As a Delvaux herself.

Though she'd been part of their discussions in Augustine's office plenty of times and they'd shared dinners together, it had never been just the four of them. And though she knew it should feel more intimate and awkward, Maya felt entirely comfortable around the three men.

"An official Delvaux now, Daughter, that you've joined us for this dinner." Augustine's eyes shined down at her to his right.

Hunter had given her his seat directly beside his father and put himself on her other side. He said she deserved a higher position, but Maya knew he'd also done it so she wasn't left open on any side. This way, she had Hunter to her right and Augustine to her left. Not to mention, Warren right across from her.

Maya knew by the simple look on Warren's face that he saw her as a sister and would truly do anything for her, including protect her with his life. The complete opposite from where his actual sister, Colette, stood.

Maya refrained her eye roll. "I'm so honored to be invited."

"I know." Augustine took a sip from his drink as if she'd been serious, then put it down with more authority. "We normally do not pass the time with pleasantries."

"Didn't expect you to start now." Maya brought a small bite of lamb to her lips, suppressing the moan at the pure deliciousness of the meat.

Hunter's hand squeezed her thigh, and when she looked over, she could tell he knew how much she was enjoying her meal. Unsurprisingly, given they had the best chefs employed within the patriarch Delvaux's manor.

"Let us begin with the most important of matters—your extraordinary little power."

Maya quirked a brow at him. "I think you mean the most important matter is the fact that a psychopath is after your son for his ability to store an unlimited amount of powers."

"To you, maybe, but to me, that portal is the most important."

This time, Maya didn't suppress her eye roll.

"And to me, the fact that Selin is after you is most important," Hunter added.

"Awesome, so we're all focused on different things."

"Not entirely." Augustine's lips twitched up. "Both my son and I are concerned with you, dear daughter."

Maya looked to Warren. "Please tell me you're on my side."

Warren gave a small smile and a shrug. "Sorry."

"Seriously." She scoffed. "Which one?"

"Hunt, of course. You can ignore Father. I normally do." He winked when she scowled. "You're my sister now, of course I'm more concerned with your well-being."

"Hunt's your brother. By blood."

"I like you more."

"We all like her more," Hunter interjected, his fingertips running soothing circles on her thigh.

"Fine." She took another bite of the lamb because it was too good to leave sitting on the plate. "You all like me more. Which means my wants should be met. And I want Hunter protected and safe against that pyscho."

"Relax, Daughter." Augustine played with his cup. "There is no doubt Hunter will be protected. How else are we meant to keep you sane and around with that power of yours?"

"Oh, shut up, you old man, you know you like me for more than just my power." Maya took her own sip from her cup, water for her. She'd never been a fan of alcohol.

Augustine tsked with a wide smirk. "That's the man to your right you're thinking of."

Maya allowed the small eye roll as she looked over to the man at her right and felt the smile involuntarily make its place on her face. "Is that so?"

Hunter leaned in and whispered low so only she could hear. "Undoubtedly. I have a rather large fondness for the way your cunt clenches around my cock."

She narrowed her eyes but didn't break her stare.

He leaned in closer. "And that mouth—the way it sucks me, yells at me, punishes me."

She bit her lip to keep the grin at bay as she read just how much he loved her in the way those black orbs of his shined. He didn't have to say it. She never needed to hear it to know how true his love was.

"I hate you," she whispered against his lips.

His lips pressed softly into hers. "Good."

Maya allowed herself another moment in their little bubble before turning back to the family. "Now, back to important matters. How do we keep Hunt safe from Jenkins?"

Warren shrugged. "My answer still stands, My. If we keep you protected, then Jenkins doesn't get the remnants of Selin's power and cannot go after Hunt. Father's side stands too. If we focus on your power, on controlling and strengthening it, you're more protected, which leaves Hunt even more so."

Warren's grin grew a little as he looked over to his brother, and Maya knew without turning that Hunter was annoyed they were speaking of him like that. Like he *needed* protection.

She also knew, as much as he'd help train her to protect herself, he'd never allow a situation where she needed to protect herself against Selin if he could help it.

And now with Vincent's allyship, he would even put the kid in danger long before anything happened to her. She would need to make sure that wasn't an option as much as possible.

"Fine. We can train my power." Maya threw a glare in Augustine's direction. "You win."

He smirked. "Never doubted I would."

"Look at the positive, Maya." Warren looked almost giddy. "You can practice on our father, Mr. Know-It-All Extraordinaire."

Augustine's eyes widened as he no doubt remembered what her power could do before he schooled his reaction and met her gaze. "As long as it'll train up your power."

Hunter chuckled at her side, deep and inviting and oh so sexy. "I think he's a little scared, love."

Maya grinned innocently in Augustine's direction as she cut herself another piece of lamb. "Is that so, Father?"

"Oh, shut up, the lot of you."

Hunter's chuckle was soft, but Maya and Warren laughed unabashedly at his reaction.

---

She could feel Harry's eyes on her as she focused on her fingers gliding over the piano keys. He'd told her before he found it fascinating how passionately focused she became when she watched her own fingers move across the keys. He'd even said he could see the passion when she closed her eyes and let her fingers move of their own accord.

Normally, Vera was so engrossed in her art she didn't realize she was being watched. But she knew he was beside her now, and her body reacted to all the attention it was receiving, heart hammering with giddiness.

Harry's breath hit the bit of skin below her ear as he whispered, "You're breaking from my song, sweetheart."

Of course she was. With how excited her body was at having him by her side, it was difficult to play something of anguish when she felt the complete opposite.

"You're distracting me," she whispered as his fingers danced on her thighs, so high they were barely touching, and yet it took every bit of her to control herself.

Harry was straddling the bench so when he leaned in, her side brushed his chest, and he chuckled at her shivers.

And stopped touching her. "I'm sorry. I'll just remove…"

"No!" She stopped playing immediately and reached for his hand to place firmly back on her thigh. "Don't ever stop touching me, Harry."

His hand expanded before relaxing over her thigh. "As you wish, love." He landed a delicate kiss to the spot behind her ear. "But only if you continue playing."

Vera's breaths came out louder as her fingers found their way back to the keys. "You know I won't be able to keep to your song if you keep kissing me."

He kissed her again on that most sensitive of spots. "Shall I stop?"

Her head shook as she said, "Yes."

His chuckle tickled her ear, and her hips involuntarily moved. "Your words and actions are so very different, sweetheart. And I've always been told to listen to actions over words."

"Bad advice." Her eyelids fell closed.

He kissed that spot again. "I don't know. I've been alive a long time."

"But you've never felt for anyone the way you do me. You have a learning curve, old man." Her voice was still breathy, eyes still closed, as her fingers played that beautiful melody.

His hand moved from her thigh and wrapped around her

waist to pull her into the spot between his legs. They were meshed so close, her knees hit the piano as they fell over his thigh.

Vera's eyes shot open, and her fingers stuttered on the instrument. "What're you doing?"

Harry held her face softly. "What exactly do I feel for you, oh wise one?"

She caught those hazel eyes and melted as she stopped playing and whispered against his lips, "You see me as the most beautiful creature in the world. You hear my voice and your heart jumps. You smell anything that smells like me and you get excited. You cannot think about a piano or the music created by one without thinking of me. You take every difficult day because you know you'll fall into bed with me at the end of it and all will be better. You love me."

His gaze jumped from her brown ones to her lips and back again. "Are you sure Camilla has the mind reading power?"

A small smile twisted Vera's lips. "I only imagine you feel for me as I do you."

"You're wrong." His lips brushed hers. "I feel for you more than you me. I feel all those things you said with the added need to protect you at all costs. With the added need to be by your side at every moment, even when you'd rather be alone."

Vera laughed against those lips she loved so much. "You're right. Maybe you love me more."

"Oh, I definitely love you more."

Harry kissed her slowly, but filled with so much passion, he was regretting not having locked the door behind them when they'd come into the room.

And especially so when a throat cleared behind them.

They pulled apart to see her parents standing by the door, watching them.

Vera tried to pull away, but Harry kept his hold around her waist and kept her pressed into him. "You're not going anywhere, sweetheart."

"If you'd like some peace from him, sweetheart"—Loretta's use of the term a far cry from Harry's—"just burn one of his little suits."

Harry narrowed his gaze on the woman. "That wasn't funny when you did it thirty years ago and it's not funny now."

"I don't know," Bishop said as he eyed their position on the piano bench. "I find it rather entertaining."

Harry smirked at the man and dropped a kiss to Vera's shoulder. "Do you?"

Vera was the one daughter Bishop had personally raised, and so Harry understood that though he loved all three of them, he held a special connection with Vera. He also understood it made Vera blush deeper when her father eyed them in situations like their current one. He normally wasn't an ass about it, but in moments like these, Harry joined Hunter in the category, holding Vera closer and playing with Bishop.

Vera tried to push away, but he held tight as Bishop growled, "Watch it, Harrison."

Vera giggled again as her mother looked them over fondly. "We wanted to hear you play, Vera. Your father's always told me how lovely you play. Better than me, apparently."

Harry stopped teasing and released her enough to give her the required space to play. "She's enchanting, Lore. You'll love it."

Then there were moments like this when the real Harry, the sweet one who praised the grounds she walked on, came out, and Vera was mesmerized all over again. It was moments like these that she knew her father saw more, that showed her father how much Harry loved her.

Vera's heart skipped as she caught Harry's gaze a final time, then turned to her hands on the keys. "This is the new song I've been writing for Harry."

All her songs were for Harry at this rate.

5

She'd been excited for the Delvaux family dinner, but Maya had put her foot down when Hunter offered her the chance to come with them on a business trip. She said she didn't care for whatever crap they did on these trips. Though he was glad it meant she stayed safe at home, drawing another commission, Hunter was a bit upset she hadn't come. He could imagine how sexy she'd be walking between them, the leader of their pack. Because as much as his father liked to think himself the patriarch, Maya had the man wrapped around her little finger.

Hunter was also glad to exclude her this one time because she wouldn't exactly be happy about the type of trip they were on that day, but he was determined to convince her to come at some point. This particular type of job Hunter would never want to bring her on. Her caring heart wouldn't be able to handle it. It was why Warren hadn't shown up—this wasn't a 'moral' job. No ethics about it. This was all about the money and not something a caring heart could easily accept.

"I'm surprised your mate didn't stop you coming," Augustine remarked as they strolled down an alleyway in suburban Los Angeles.

"My mate knows most of the money comes from things she wouldn't approve of." He was a lucky man to find a mate who accepted him fully.

"She doesn't care that you're going to kill a completely innocent family for a payday?" Augustine asked without an ounce of belief.

Hunter smirked. "She doesn't ask for specifics about these." They jumped the brick fence to the backyard of said family rather than shadowing in. It was more fun this way. "But yes, if she knew, she'd be upset. But still, she wouldn't stop it."

His pocket vibrated as they moved up the yard toward the house. *What if I told you I'm so wet right now, we're going to have to get all new furniture in your study? Would you come home?*

No, she wouldn't stop his trips.

But she would distract him from them.

*I've told you before not to tempt me on trips, mate. I intend on keeping my word.*

*I'm in your office chair. It smells like you.* Another text. *My legs are spread on your desk so my fingers can have their fun.* Another. *I'm already dripping onto your leather chair.* Another. *Mmm, just imagining your cum dripping out of me and onto this chair made me come so hard. What should I think of next?*

Hunter growled and closed his eyes to try to block out the vivid image that text created. He put his phone away as it vibrated again, not giving her the satisfaction of getting to him any more than she already had.

Augustine's amusement was large as he watched on. "The mate?"

"Is a dead woman," Hunter growled and didn't look at his father as he marched into the house, another vibration coming from his trousers.

He wondered if she knew getting him strained so much would only make him more ruthless in his killings. But maybe that was part of it—this way the deaths would be swift.

The job was a simple one—the Delvauxs worked by taking requests.

Though they normally came from other demons, from time to time, they got requests from other species. And even more rare, but still a commonality, they'd get a request from a human —one who knew of the magical world, or more specifically of demons, and thought he could take advantage of the information. Normally politicians and mobsters.

They thought they were summoning the demons they saw in those hocus pocus movies.

It didn't matter to Hunter as long as they got paid.

And no matter how ruthless the human, no one ever attempted to swift them.

This time, the victims would be a family of the rival to a mob. Their little employer had wanted to hurt his rival in the worst way he could think—killing the only relatives with no evidence pointing back to him.

Because they were demons, they'd leave nothing behind.

Another vibration came as Augustine joined him in the house, the sound of the children upstairs and the parents in the kitchen distinctive.

"Which would you like?" his father asked.

Hunter was about to give the same response as always—it didn't matter—when he paused.

He'd never been opposed to killing children. Had done so on many an occasion.

But he couldn't do it. Couldn't get himself to move in their direction.

"I'll take the parents."

Augustine narrowed his gaze, obviously wanting to know the reasoning behind Hunter's direct answer this time, but said nothing more.

Hunter didn't wait around to see if he would question it before moving to the kitchen.

The family they were after were the rivals' brother, sister-in-law, mother, and his three nieces and nephews. The only people the man had left in his life.

And they were worth a pretty penny. Killing innocents was always worth more.

Hunter turned the corner into the kitchen, knowing his father was making his way upstairs even though he didn't make a sound. When the three adults standing around the island laughing saw him, those smiles dropped.

Another vibration.

The man pushed the two women behind him as they screamed, but Hunter didn't react to it as his head tilted to the side. They screamed even louder when the screams of their children reached the ground floor.

Because his mate was such a bleeding heart, Hunter shadowed to each one, beginning with the grandmother, then the mother, then the father, and snapped their necks. Swift and painless. Maya might not have been around, and she might never hear of this, but Hunter still felt the need to do as his mate would like.

Another vibration.

This time, Hunter pulled his phone out to a slew of messages.

*I chose an image of you in that lazy lounge while you pump your cock. You're moaning my name of course.*

*It's rude to ignore your mate in her time of primal need, Delvaux.*

*Come home and put that tongue between my legs, baby. I love that tongue.*

*You're ignoring me. Fine, I'll stop. For now.* Winky face.

Hunter stared down at his phone for long minutes, his entire focus on the name in the contact section rather than the messages. His mate and entire reason for being.

Maya, Maya, Maya.

He still remembered the first time he'd heard that name. It'd been such a shock to his system, he'd momentarily thought she'd somehow cast a spell on him, somehow believed

that the newbie witch before him had magically outmaneu-
vered him.

He remembered saying her name for the first time. The way
it had felt on his tongue, and how hard he'd gotten each time
he'd voiced it. He remembered the way he'd growled that name
that very night when he'd gotten home from the forest and
stroked his cock. He remembered the mind-shattering orgasm
just saying her name had gotten him. It was nowhere near truly
touching, tasting, fucking her, but it had been an out-of-body
experience for Hunter at the time.

Hunter felt his father enter the room after some time but
couldn't stop staring at the name.

His eyes hovered down when a final message came. *I found
your photo albums. You were a cute baby. We're going to have cute
babies.*

Hunter's heart skipped as his lips tipped up involuntarily.
His Maya.

---

C amilla didn't know how she felt about this ridiculous plan
they had to turn Kai into Maya in order to finish off
Selin. If it worked entirely in their favor, it would be an easy
problem fixer.

But Camilla had a feeling it wouldn't be so simple.

Selin had come this far. Camilla couldn't see her doing so
without learning how to protect herself and knowing when she
was being played with.

And if it wasn't going to be so simple, Camilla didn't see why
they should be risking Kai. Not that she cared for him, but she
could admit that he had skills that could—and have been—useful.

Plus, Maya wasn't aware of the plan, and if something were
to happen, she'd be angry. And recent events had shown Maya
angry. It was a scary picture.

Scarier than truly angry Hunter. A sight Camilla could still conjure when she thought of Hunter shadowing into the house and slamming his sister into the ground for threatening the air that Maya breathed.

But alas, her family decided to turn Kai into Maya anyway, and she had no grounds to refuse the plan.

The part that truly angered her was after deciding on the plan, they had unanimously and promptly forbidden Camilla from going with them, a demand made especially by both Kai and her parents. Apparently, her non-active powers put her in the useless category even though she could beat all of their asses in hand-to-hand combat.

Instead, she stayed back with her father and looked at the events transpiring through a small screen that was linked to a tiny camera attached to her mother's shirt. They'd all, aside from Kai, be invisible, so she couldn't see them, or any other magic, but still, Camilla watched on.

Her leg jutted as she and Bishop sat on the couch and she held the screen before them.

Bishop's arm fell over her shoulders, and he brought her into his side. "Be calm, sweetheart. He'll be fine."

Her leg froze. "I'm not worried for him. I'm worried for the others. And Maya if this doesn't work."

"Okay." He kissed her crown, and she could feel the smile on his lips. "Well, they'll all be fine. Your mother's not going to let a thing happen to them."

The camera footage showed them in the mess of the rubble the blown-up warehouse had left behind. Kai had suggested a slightly dark magic to call upon Selin, and because he was the Demon Warlock, no one batted an eye at the suggestion. They all simply ran with it.

Kai looked so convincingly like Maya that Camilla actually thought this might work.

Being that the others were invisible, Camilla couldn't see

where they stood, but still, her heart raced with the thought that any of them may be severely hurt.

"You should've gone with them!" she urged for the umpteenth time.

Bishop chuckled as he kissed the top of her head. "Harry will be able to heal them fine, and Kai's warlock abilities will self-heal. And if anything, I can port there in moments. I needed to stay by your side. It's more important to your mother and me to keep you and your sisters safe."

"But…"

"But nothing. Harry won't allow a thing to happen to Vera, Maya's with Hunter, and you're left alone. With Kai being our actor, I needed to stay with you. When you become a parent, you'll understand."

Camilla was about to argue that Kai had nothing to do with her safety when the unbelievable happened on the screen and Selin showed up.

She looked more fragile than before, but Camilla wasn't sure if that had to do with the fact they were looking through a camera. She'd always been old since getting resurrected, but now she looked more like she was coming unto death's door. Was it magic that couldn't transfer through cameras that made her look so?

Camilla didn't have time to think of it. Now for the most nerve-wracking part of this entire scheme—transfiguration only affected appearance. Kai would look and sound like Maya, but his powers would be his own. No darkness. No fire. No portal.

"I'm surprised you came alone. Won't Mr. Boss Man be upset you ran away?" Kai asked, lilting his tone in the same way Maya would.

Selin chuckled. "I only came to see the production. What have you to put on for me?"

"Meaning?" Kai quirked a brow.

Selin moved closer to him, and Camilla wondered why no

one was trying to trap her when the reminder that magic couldn't be seen through a camera came back to her. If Selin had anything around to protect herself, Camilla wouldn't be able to see it through the screens.

"You expect me to believe you, *Maya*, would come here without your mate?"

"You expect me to put my mate in the line of danger?"

"Fair point," Selin conceded. "But again, I must remind you, I've been waiting for this moment for a millennium." She was within touching distance to Kai, but still, no one moved against her. "You do not truly believe I went after any of those I killed without knowing with absolute certainty they were the right ones, do you?"

There was movement with the screen, and Camilla knew her mother was trying to get closer to Selin.

It looked to be failing.

Kai quirked his brow in that annoyed way Maya did when she wanted people to get to the point. "Meaning?"

"Meaning, dear child, you play her quite well, but I am not so gullible as to believe you are her."

"That faerie dust finally beginning to affect you mentally?"

Selin's laugh was both condescending and amused. "Okay, Maya, why don't you set me on fire then? I won't fight back."

"You know"—Kai tilted his head like he was assessing the old woman—"this is why the villains always lose in movies—they go on and on and give the heroes enough time to complete whatever it is they need."

Selin sighed. "Rest assured, child, when I get my hands on Maya, I will not be waiting any longer. The sooner I can rid her of this world, the sooner I can be back to my family."

More movement and more failure came from Loretta's part. Undetectable magic for sure.

"Can't you be back to your family without ridding me of this world?"

"No." Selin looked more annoyed now that Kai as wasting

her time—and not giving up that he wasn't, in fact, Maya. "My millennium waiting for this vengeance will only get me back to them if all is completed. Maya must die."

"Shame I'm not going to. My mate would never allow it."

Selin's sigh was more frustrated now. "You may not be dying now"—a mix between a bat and a piece of dry wood materialized in her hand—"but you are grating on my nerves, dear child."

She didn't allow Kai the moment to process her words before the wood in her hand went flying and knocked right into Kai's head.

Camilla shot straight up as she held the screen still, not wanting to miss a second of what happened.

Blood splattered towards the camera, and Selin was gone all at once. Kai didn't fall straight down, so Camilla had to assume someone caught him since the invisibility potion they'd made was strong and still hadn't let up.

She knew she was right when a glow came from the space around Kai's head to clean up that wound because it would work faster with both his and Harry's warlock powers than just Kai's unconscious one.

Then Harry's voice came. "The wound is healed, but I need to wake him. He'll have a concussion for sure, and there's nothing any of us could do about that."

6

*M*aya was shocked to see her entire family up when she entered the kitchen at the ass crack of dawn. She'd gone to bed early the night before after her bath, so she'd only felt the light kiss of Hunter's lips on her temple before he nestled in beside her.

This morning, she had a craving for one of Vera's special chocolate croissants she'd seen her sister making the day before, so Maya had left the bed quietly to make sure Hunter got the rest he needed after his trip. Albeit he was normally more elated than exhausted after those things, Maya wanted him to rest. She shadowed to her family home for the pastry with every intention of quietly moving through the still sleeping house before returning home.

So she was shocked to see everyone already there.

"What the hell is going on here? You guys do realize it's early and most of you hate mornings."

"Trust me," Kai said with an eye roll, "if they allowed me, I'd be cozy in bed dreaming of your sister riding—"

"I'll make that concussion worse, Kai, I swear I will," Camilla seethed from the other end of the kitchen where she sat on the counter.

Maya's brows furrowed as she moved for the covered batch of pastries. "How'd you get a concussion?"

She picked out the delightful croissant as her husband walked into the room.

*Husband.* She still wasn't used to that word.

"You know I don't like it when you leave our bed, love." His gaze dropped to the pastry in her hand.

Maya smirked and grabbed two more, then moved to the microwave to warm them. "Sorry, baby."

Hunter kissed her head and held her back to his front as the microwave beeped and Maya pulled out the heated goodness.

"You know you could've warmed that with your fire." His voice rumbled behind her.

"Shut up." She stuffed one into his mouth and took another for herself before turning back to Kai. "So why do you have a concussion?"

He shrugged nonchalantly. "I was hit in the head by a psychopath. And warlock powers can heal everything but a stupid little concussion."

Vera scoffed. "It is not little. She smacked the shit out of you."

"Who smacked the shit out of you?"

Loretta sighed. "He used a transfiguration potion to turn into you and dark magic to lure Selin out. Unfortunately, the old woman knew immediately that it wasn't you."

"Are you guys insane?" Maya froze in her spot, hating that they were putting themselves in harm's way because of her.

Camilla gave her a snarky grin. "Your husband's father suggested it. We just used Kai as bait."

Maya sighed and took the last croissant she'd warmed as she moved for Kai, wanting to get a better look at the wound. "Didn't work at all?"

"Well, no, it wasn't a total failure," Harry answered. "We did learn that she can only return to her family if she kills you too.

Anything short of dying before finishing her revenge will not send her to them."

The information sunk into Maya as she stared at Kai's head. From the tidbits she'd learned of Selin, Maya couldn't blame the woman. If she were in the same position, Maya could imagine doing anything—killing anyone—to be reunited with her husband, children, and grandchildren. In a way, Maya empathized with Selin.

If it weren't Maya's life on the line, she might have been able to play devil's advocate a bit too.

There was no visible wound on Kai, and when Maya touched his head, she felt nothing significant, so the healing had done its job.

She took another bite of her pastry and slowly chewed to allow herself time to get rid of these feelings coming up for Selin. Sometimes, Maya hated that she looked at all sides of a problem. It would've been so nice to conclude Selin as the villain with no real motives.

Like Jenkins.

Finally, Maya turned back to the others and leaned into Kai's chair. "Don't really think that's good enough information for almost getting Kai killed."

"Matter-of-fact, I think it's way more than expected," Camilla snarked.

Hunter nudged Camilla's leg. "Oh, stop, Little Sister. We all know you pick on those of us you adore most."

"I still don't like you." Camilla glared in his direction.

Hunter winked. "Ditto."

"In any case, we now know nothing short of truly getting to Maya will stop that woman," Bishop stated. "And after today, I don't believe anything short of Maya will lure her out again. She knew immediately that it was a transfiguration. In order to kill Selin, we would need to use Maya as bait."

"Not happening," Hunter barked in his direction while his eyes remained on Maya.

"I wouldn't allow it myself." Bishop tried to stifle his eye roll, but a small one still made itself present. "It's just a conundrum that my ancestors brought upon her, and I cannot figure out how to get around it."

Maya's gaze shot to her father as her eyes warmed. "This isn't your fault. The powers I got because of your ancestors make me who I am, and I love them. I wouldn't change my position."

"No." Hunter caught her attention again. "But he's right. We need to get you out of harm's way."

Maya rolled her eyes at her mate this time. "Lest you forget, we also need to keep *you* out of harm's way."

"You're more important." There was no humor in the way he said it. He'd do anything to keep her safe.

"Amen," Camilla remarked by his side.

"Well, to me, you're more important. Not to mention, to the whole of the supernatural—and probably human—world. So, definitely you, baby. Plus, you always give me everything I want."

His lips twitched up. "I've spoiled you a bit too much, wife. Allow this to be the only thing you won't get."

Maya's vision faded to all but the man across the room from her. "I like it when you call me wife."

Hunter's eyes flamed as he smirked.

Bishop interrupted with a throat clearing before Hunter could say whatever inappropriate thing Maya knew was ready to fall from his lips. "The lot of you sure forget that I'm their father, don't you?"

"The lot of us?" Harry asked, affronted. "I'm the complete gentleman."

"Thank the lords," Bishop whispered, then caught Harry's eyes. "I raised Vera. It'd be far worse to hear these things about her."

Maya wanted to pay attention to her family, but the way

Hunter watched her made her blood boil, the flames within her begging to make an appearance. To mix with his.

"Oh, we hardly say a thing," Kai sang as he lounged back in his chair.

Bishop's gaze narrowed. "You're the worst of all."

Kai's grin turned cunning. "What can I say, old man? Your daughter enjoys my foul mouth."

Camilla grit her teeth, but instead of responding to him, she reached out and caught her father's shoulder. "Don't worry. I'll make the concussion worse later when no one's around to help him."

Again, Maya was too caught up in her mate to pay the others too much mind. Hunter's eyes glinted like he knew the effect he was having on her. By the need coming to her through the rings, she knew he could feel her desires the way she felt his. Not to mention, his heightened scenting would detect exactly what she wanted.

Bishop laughed to Camilla. "That's my girl."

"What I'm hearing," Hunter interrupted, "is that the conversation regarding my *wife* is over?" His eyes blazed with the use of the word.

"Yes, yes," Loretta answered, amusement for all that was happening within her kitchen clear on her features. "When we learn more, you'll be the first to know."

"Good." He pushed off the counter and stormed over to Maya. "Now, if you'll excuse us"—his grip around her neck was strong as he slammed her into the wall—"I've got a wife to teach a lesson to."

Maya couldn't hold back her joy as she remembered his threat the last time she'd distracted him while he was on a business trip. She'd been asleep when he'd returned home last night, but she was hoping he'd still deliver her punishment.

7

---

Their tongues were fighting before their shadows landed back to their manor.

Hunter pushed away and ripped his shirt off. "You know where this is going, love?"

Those cunning lips twisted into a smirk as she eyed him, waiting. Acting innocent.

He gave an unamused, rough laugh as he grabbed her around the throat again and pushed her back until they hit the bed. "I can only be glad you were asleep last night. That gives me all day rather than a simple night to punish you."

"You wouldn't dare keep me wanting so long."

He ripped her shirt in two. "I don't think you're prepared for how much I intend to play with you, love." He gripped her jaw to make sure her gaze didn't waver. "Now finish undressing and lie back before I decide to not allow a single orgasm."

A fearful inhale gave away her anticipation as she pushed away from him.

He watched as she lay naked in the middle of their bed and smirked as he pulled out his chain cuffs.

Her eyes widened, but he read her desire in them.

He tied one to either end of his four poster, then attached

the long cuffs to her ankles, spreading her completely on the bed. He licked his lips as he eyed her up and down slowly.

"Enjoying yourself, baby?"

He tsked. "Not yet."

He moved for her arms, clasping them together above her head and attaching the final chain there so she was completely at his mercy.

She breathed heavily as she asked, "Now?"

His breath tickled her lips as he answered, "Absolutely."

Her gaze shot from his eyes to his lips, then back again with impatient insistence.

"Is there something you'd like, wife?"

Her hips shot up at the term. "Fuck me," she moaned, and in a breathy whisper, added, "my mate."

He growled, the term having the same effect on him as wife had on her. "Behave, love. I really need you to come in my mouth, but that can only happen if I allow those orgasms."

"Fucking asshole," she grit out just before he clashed his mouth to hers.

Their tongues fought for dominance. She bit and pulled on his lower lip as her hips thrust higher for the chance to meet with his.

He laughed at her aggression before diving back into her mouth. "I miss this mouth every time I'm not kissing it."

When he pulled away with a wide grin, she gave him a genuine, happy smile at the sentiment which paused him in his antics. He couldn't help but stare down at her beauty.

His thumb softly caressed her cheek. "You're absolutely beautiful, my mate."

"I love you, Hunter."

His breath caught. There was that infernal word again —*love*. He still didn't understand it. Couldn't fathom how people knew themselves to feel this thing that was falling in love. It wasn't a fated thing like his mating, so how did they know?

She stared up at him another moment, like she knew he needed the time to take her in. To take in what she'd said.

And instead of waiting for a response as humans so often did, her face twitched with a mischievous grin. "Now, we both know you'll give me whatever I want." Her brow quirked in a challenge. "And I want my orgasms. I want *your* orgasms."

He kissed her softly as the laugh bubbled out of him, then he made his way down. Her jaw, her ear, down her throat, over her shoulders. Every little bit. He didn't want to miss a moment of her.

His wife.

His mate.

His Maya.

He kissed down her chest, taking his time making it around her nipples, but making sure to ignore the peaked nubs begging for his tongue.

He kissed the valley between her breasts as his hand found its way to her cunt, sliding through her folds. "Mm, so wet for me, *Maya*."

He kissed her again, finding joy in the way she tried to push her chest into his face and her hips into his hand.

"Now," he kissed her breast again, slowly making his way to the peak, "what is it you were saying about giving you what you want? I seem to remember promising to have you peaking."

"Don't." She breathed hard as her hips thrust into his fingers slowly filling her. "You." She moaned as his two fingers filled her and his thumb played over her clit. "Dare." Her head fell back as her eyes fell closed.

He laughed into her skin. "What kind of man would I be if I didn't keep my promises, love?"

"My favorite man," she gasped as she squeezed around his fingers.

He kissed the dip at the bottom of her throat as he pulled his touch away completely and listened to the frustrated groan leave her. "No, no, love. I'd never break a promise to you."

She narrowed her gaze on his smirk as he dipped his mouth to that peaked nub and finally took it into his mouth, squeezing the sheets between his fingers to keep his slow pace. As much as he loved torturing her, it was an equal torture for himself.

She fell back with a breathy moan as he gave his special attention to his two favorite girls.

He switched between the two, taking his time and delighting in the sounds that passed her lips. He loved how uncensored she was in their time together. How completely she gave herself to him.

And how frantically she thrust her chest up, knowing she was so close to the peak, all he had to do was give a few seconds' attention to that nub between her legs.

So instead, he pulled away entirely and held himself up as he watched her catch her breath and glare at him.

"How is it possible that you taste better every time?" He kept his tone nonchalant to irritate her even more.

"Sometimes I regret not listening to my sisters and leaving you."

He barked a laugh, unable to contain himself. "We're mates, love. You would've burned the world down to get to me." He kissed the valley between her breasts. "And I would've delighted watching you do it."

"Sometimes I don't like how confident you are about us."

His chuckles subsided as he kissed the valley again. "Behave, Maya, and I'll get you that orgasm."

"I'm sorry," she growled and pulled on the chains, "*Liar.*"

He kissed just beneath her breasts. "I've never lied to you before, my mate. I said I wanted you to come in my mouth. You didn't think I'd let it happen before then, did you? I want it all, love."

She grit her teeth. "Then get between my legs, Hunter. Now!"

"Feisty, little mate."

He kissed her navel. Then again and again, feeling no rush to continue south.

"Speed it up, Delvaux," Maya ordered as she strained her neck to look down at him.

"I'm just saying hi to those cute babies we're going to have."

She pulled on the chains, and a chuckle left him. "Hunter, please."

"Mm." He kissed her hip bone and let his facial hair tickle her as he moved to the other one. "I like when you beg me, love."

"That's because you're a sadistic ass," she seethed.

He tsked a few times, his grin pressed into her skin. "That doesn't sound like the way you speak to someone when you want him to devour you."

"I hate you." Her head fell back as her hips strained to push his mouth to the exact spot she desired it.

"I'm counting on it, love." He finally kissed the apex of her inner thigh. "If you didn't hate me, I'd have nothing to live for." He finally kissed her cunt, softly. Nowhere near the way she desired.

She growled. "Delvaux."

"Yes, Delvaux?"

"Please," she screamed, a mix of a pleased moan and a tortured groan.

He laughed. "As you said earlier, I give you anything you desire. Your wish," he finally dipped his face between those legs kept spread for him by the chains around her ankles, "is my command."

She was completely drenched for him and soaked his face the moment he allowed himself to feast.

She was so sensitive his tongue only teased her clit a moment before she was stiffening and he was pulling away to a desperate cry.

When she seemed settled enough, he dipped back to her opening and delighted in the way his tongue fucked her and stole every drop it could muster.

Her cries and pulls on the chains were so harsh, Hunter finally took pity on her and licked up her folds and suckled on that little nub. She clenched and cried out almost immediately as he dropped his mouth back down to catch every bit of what she had to give him.

And though he loved that the chains kept her spread for him, he missed the way her thighs normally suffocated him in this moment.

When her body calmed and he'd licked as much as he could, Hunter rose to his knees and wiped the excess of her taste off his stubble.

His cock was so hard at that point, it was straining and wet from the pre-cum that soaked down it.

He fell over her and kissed her gently, letting her take in her exquisite taste as he lined his cock up to her opening.

Her cunt squeezed his cock so tightly while they kissed, he almost came from the single thrust. "You almost made me come, Maya."

She laughed as she tugged on his bottom lip. "Please do. Fill me, Hunt."

He groaned but played with her still. "I think you deserve to wait a bit longer because of that little stunt, Witch."

He knew she wanted to argue with him, but her head fell back as he thrust hard.

He sat up to his knees so he could watch her as he fucked her. So he could watch those perfect girls bounce with every deep thrust he made. So he could watch Maya's eyes roll back and her voice crack as she fought the chains that restrained her from holding his body to hers.

When her body began to tighten and she cried his name, Hunter pulled his cock out and stopped touching her. Deprived her of that orgasm that was going to crash into her.

Genuine tears rolled down her face as she looked at him with pure hatred. "I'm going to kill you."

He merely grinned as he watched her body calm but didn't allow it to settle all the way.

When she still spasmed with sensitivity but was gone from the almost high, Hunter finally moved with the glare of his mate on him the entire time.

He unclipped the chain around her ankle. Then the one around her other ankle.

And brought them both to his lap to massage for a moment.

He saw that kind nature of hers seep through the hatred as she watched him.

He kissed each ankle softly, knowing the way she'd been pulling would leave bruises.

Then he lined his cock up to her entrance again and pushed her thighs down so her knees hit her chest and thrust hard and deep.

They moaned in unison as he seated himself to the hilt and paused.

He took in her beauty again, then moved to unclip the chains from her wrists.

Hunter brought each of her wrists to his lips and kissed them fondly before letting her fingernails take root in his hair and at his shoulder. He already anticipated the marks she'd leave him.

And resented the way his body would heal those slight indications of their time together. He wanted them to scar, wanted the permanent reminder of their time together.

"Fuck me, Hunter." Maya's nails raked down his back. "Show me whose mate I am."

His signature smirk took its place as his body involuntarily listened to his mate's demand and fucked her.

Her hips matched his thrust for thrust. He tasted her mouth as their bodies came together again and again, and he was thankful to all the lords when she clenched around him, then came before either one of them could process it.

She screamed so loud Hunter genuinely heard the crack in her voice as his own finish came.

It almost felt as much as their first time. Part of him thought it was more than their first time.

He felt it seep out of her while he was still in her as his forehead fell to hers. "Think you'll behave now?"

She chuckled. "I think I'm going to be the baddest girl you've ever met." He laughed with her as she cradled his face and whispered against his lips, "I want more."

"Good. Because we just got started, love."

## 8

"Considering it is you and your mate that are being targeted, Son, do you not think it wiser to spend the day getting rid of the threats rather than hidden away at your manor?" Augustine let the drink dangle from his hand as he lounged back in his seat in his office.

Hunter smirked, taking his own drink to his chair as Warren brushed over books scattered in their father's office book-shelves. "Contrarily, if my mate allowed it, I'd lock us in that manor forever so I can die gorging on her."

"Allow the rest of the world to go down as long as you get your cock wet, right, Son?"

"Without hesitation." Hunter leaned back in his seat, the memory of Maya beneath him coming back to him.

Every gasp.

Every sigh.

Every delicious moan.

"Would you stop getting yourself hard and pay attention to the problems in your life?" Augustine said in the authoritative tone he only ever used when he was annoyed with Hunter. "It *is* your mate in danger."

Hunter grit his teeth. "Don't worry, Father, I never forget when there is a threat against my mate."

"So, what do you intend on doing about it?"

"I'm going to rid of the problem, of course."

"Kill Selin?"

Hunter stared at his father as if there'd be another way.

"Don't you think if it were that simple, we would've already done it?" Warren jumped in without turning to face them. "Plus, Kai's little stunt showed us Selin won't fall for anything but Maya."

"And as Maya's mate, she'll take delight in trying to hurt my mate by hurting me." Hunter stared into the fireplace, into the power that both he and his mate shared. "Just because I spend my days delighting in her does not mean I do not spend every other second of my life thinking about keeping her safe."

Warren finally turned to them, his features hard, making him look so much more like their father as he met Hunter's gaze. "Maya will kill you if she finds out you're on a death mission."

"She'll get over it."

"After the last scene, I really don't think so," Warren argued.

*I make you this bond today the way I made you the mating one weeks ago. A bond, meaning the two of us joined together, that we are in every decision together up until the very basis of your safety, because, love, I don't care how much you hate me for it, if your safety is on the line, past simple threats, but really put on the line, I will not hesitate to kill myself to save you.*

Maya would understand.

"I'll have to agree with my youngest now, Hunt. She's quite the fearsome thing to behold," Augustine added.

"We promised each other that everything up unto the other's safety will be discussed together. When it comes to her safety, she knows I'd do anything to ensure it. She'll be upset, yes, but she will get over it."

His mate would understand. She'd be enraged, but she would know why he did it.

"Hunt," Warren tried.

"Hunt nothing," Hunter interrupted. "I have my own family to protect now. And as much as I hate thinking of anyone else around her, I trust you to keep her safe if and when I'm not around."

"Hunter…" Warren tried again.

"You fight it, War, but you are a demon. And I know that if you needed to, you would let the demon half take over. *You would protect your family.* Maya is your sister. I *trust* you to keep her safe."

"Tough luck making that happen when she kills me for allowing you to do whatever dumb thing you have planned." Warren grimaced as he turned back to the shelves.

Augustine quirked a brow. "Assuming you have a plan?"

Hunter shrugged. "The moment Maya jumped into my arms in front of that dilapidated warehouse, I had a plan."

"She'll hate you, you know."

*I love you, Hunter.* "I know."

Augustine finished his cup and settled it on the small table beside his chair before leaning forward. "Now that we're clear about all that, what're we doing?"

Warren's head snapped. "Are you insane? You can't encourage him!"

"I want this threat off of Maya quickly as well."

Augustine turned to Hunter as he finished speaking, and Hunter caught a look in his eyes that said he knew something. Hunter had wondered if his father would pick up his change in behavior. He'd done so when Hunter had first met Maya.

And with the look they shared now, Hunter knew the man had picked up this bit too.

"I'm going to offer myself." He finished off his drink. "To Selin." He placed it on the table beside his chair. "Your assistance won't be required."

"It is my family too, Hunter." His tone was firm, authoritative.

"I know," Hunter replied calmly. "But I cannot risk something happening to you too. I need you around to protect her. I need both of you to protect her."

"You don't need to ask us to do that, Hunt," Warren spit out as the anger in him grew. His hazel eyes turned darker, almost black, and he looked exactly like Augustine as he slammed the shelves and turned back to them. "Dammit, Hunt! That girl loves you. You cannot do this to her."

Hunter looked into the flames again, the image of Maya lying in bed and smiling up at him clear before him.

He stared for long minutes, not wanting to wash away that beautiful look on his mate's face. But then he turned back to his brother who stood across the study, breathing hard out of frustration.

Hunter slowly rose from his seat and moved until he was before his little brother. He clasped the man's shoulder as he said with nothing but pure honesty, "I want nothing more for you, War, then to find a mate of your own. I want you to have these feelings, these things that I always ridiculed. I want you to obsess over her, to hate her, to possess her. I want you to find the woman you cannot breathe without."

"Hunt..." Warren whispered.

"And when you find her, you'll hate yourself for hurting her, but it'll be more important to keep her safe than whether or not you get hurt." Hunter let out a breath. "I need to keep her safe."

Warren's jaw grit as he looked away, the edges of his eyes lined with water, before he turned back to face Hunter. "She's my sister. I'd do anything to protect her, Hunt. But you're also my brother, and I need to protect you."

A small smirk lifted on Hunter's lips. "I thought you hated me."

An even smaller grin lifted on Warren's. "I do. The same way Maya does."

Hunter's face twisted in a grimace. "Definitely *not* the same way Maya does."

Warren wiggled his brows as the grin grew. "Oh, I don't know, Brother."

***

It had been surprisingly easy for Harry to fall back into his friendship with Loretta and Bishop. Even while he was in love with their daughter.

He'd been worried it would be too difficult to manage the two relationships, but somehow everything had worked perfectly. He knew the couple's acceptance of his relationship with their daughter was the leading factor as to why. Not for a second had they been anything but supportive of the way Harry and Vera felt for one another. Though Harry had been best friends with Loretta, he hadn't been expecting that. He'd surely thought a bit of resistance would have surfaced.

But none of that had happened.

He had a feeling that had to do with the fact that they'd missed out so much of their daughters lives, and now that said daughters were grown, they just wanted to see them happy. And Harry hoped with every fiber in his being that he made Vera even a fraction as happy as she made him. He assumed by the way her parents watched them with warm gazes, he did.

But still, he'd been expecting a bit of resistance. He was becoming far too accustomed to this acceptance.

So when they were called by some warlocks from a few different covens to talk about matters of the supernatural world —especially now that news of Bishop and Loretta being alive had come out—it felt natural to hold Vera's hand as they ported out. To continue holding her hand after they landed.

The two of them, her parents, and Kai at Camilla's side landed in the far side of the community gardens in the Midwest. Kai still annoyed Harry when he made comments that might make Camilla uncomfortable, but he was an asset, so Harry hadn't fought his insistence to come along.

Plus, Harry hated to admit that as much as he wanted to protect his youngest of sisters from the man, he could tell she enjoyed the Demon Warlock's presence by her side. Even if she would never admit to it.

There were four warlocks and three witches waiting for them when they landed. Two of the witches and a warlock were from the Lennox coven, the other witch and another warlock from the Riddler coven, a warlock from the Wremon coven, and the final warlock from the Loman coven. All of which were from covens dispersed within the southern parts of the Midwest.

"Hello." Bishop moved forward as the head of their group. "Nice to see you lot."

"You too, dead man," the Wremon warlock said, but it didn't sound like a tease. Many of the covens had been angry to learn of Bishop and Loretta's fake deaths—a fact, Harry assumed, had to do with the fact that the couple had always been the buffer to demons when the other covens didn't want it. 'Dying' had put that responsibly on these other covens.

Harry's hand tightened around Vera's as he prepared for the reasoning behind this meeting and caught the Lennox warlock take notice.

"What is it we can do for you then?" Bishop was aware that some of these covens didn't necessarily like theirs for mixing with demons. Good thing they weren't aware of Bishop's ancestry and the possibility that his entire line was part demon, even if that demon blood had died out in all these years.

"We need to discuss that daughter of yours," the witch, Hanna Lennox, said.

Bishop's lips twisted into a fake grin as he spread his arms. "Which one? I have two with me today."

The Lennox witch sneered. "Unfortunately, not the one we want."

"But if you'd like, we can certainly discuss what to do of your situation," the Loman warlock added as he glanced over Harry and Vera.

Loretta's chin jut out. "And what situation is that?"

"The family warlock is sleeping with his charge. Do not pretend it is not sickening to you. It is your daughter he's degrading."

Harry stood taller and felt Vera shrink behind him. They'd been lucky not to receive too much more than a few odd looks so far, but he hadn't been foolish enough to think that they would be accepted.

He hated it. Hated that Vera already had these insecurities because of the lonelier life she'd led growing up and being the 'new' sister in her family. She didn't need people judging her, staring down at her with vile contempt, because she chose to be with him.

To be fair, had he been an observer, he could understand their misgivings. But finding out that the witch only became the warlock's charge a few months ago should clear that up. He hadn't raised her.

Unfortunately, most didn't care about that detail. The only acceptable relationship between a witch and a warlock was one where the warlock was from a different coven—whether they met at some event or he came for a short visit to her coven, met, and decided to stay with her. But between them, these covens only saw a warlock in love with his charge. Disgraceful.

Simply put, Vera had been Harry's charge, no matter how short the time. This wasn't a situation like Bishop and Loretta where Bishop had been a warlock in the family but had already been with the African coven when Loretta was born. She hadn't been his charge. He'd gone back and forth between the Wittlieff coven in the Czech Republic and the Atolla coven in Nigeria, but he'd never had his own charges. And he'd only come back to the Wittlieff one when Loretta was already old enough to catch his attention.

The same thing had happened between the witch and warlock from the Riddler coven standing before them.

Those were acceptable relationships.

Harry was so lost in his thoughts, he barely heard the warlock add, "...he's sullied her body."

"Have we forgotten our manners?" Kai spoke with the superiority of a demon, but Harry could see the fire behind his eyes. He didn't like the comment any more than the rest of them.

And though all those before them tried to feign indifference to Kai, Harry saw the way they shrunk into themselves a bit.

"One with her own warlock. One with a demon. And one with the Demon Warlock," Hanna concluded to Loretta and Bishop. "You two must be so proud."

"We are delighted with each of their choices." Loretta added a hint of superiority to her tone as well. "Now, what of our middle daughter would you like to speak of?"

Harry had been expecting these conversations to happen after all the North American covens were made aware of the threat of Jenkins, but it didn't mean he wanted to be there for them. It didn't mean any of them wanted to be there for them.

"She's with the demon," the Lemon warlock said.

"You're observant," Kai muttered.

"You're a waste who deserves what his coven..." the second Lennox witch started.

"You need to watch your tone," Camilla sniped before the witch could finish.

Harry was surprised with the bite to Camilla's tone and the hatred in her eyes. She was normally more accepting, especially of other witches.

But as he glanced between his youngest charge and the Demon Warlock, Harry knew Kai had told her of his past. He knew that though she claimed to hate him, Camilla was protective of Kai.

Mark, the Lennox warlock, quirked a belittling brow at Kai. "Allowing the girlfriend to fight your battles now?"

Kai smirked. "Don't worry. She'll be rewarded properly."

They all grimaced, and even Harry had to fight the eye roll at Kai's insinuations. He had no idea how Bishop handled it. Harry hated hearing about the possibility of their sex life. There was no way Bishop enjoyed hearing about any of his daughters' sex lives.

Bishop brought everyone's attention back to him. "For the final time, what of our daughter?"

"She married the demon. The one who's being hunted," the Lemon warlock stated.

"Fucked up part of this is I would've loved to see that man go down," the Riddler warlock spoke up for the first time.

"But unfortunately, if he goes down, we may all," the Riddler witch continued. "We need to know what is being done to take care of the situation."

"We assume your daughter has deluded herself in love and won't allow anything to happen to him, so we can all go home and forget about it? Your family's problem?" Mark commented, and it sounded almost hopeful even though they all knew the answer.

"You are correct that Maya loves him. And will protect him, whatever the cost," Loretta answered. "Unfortunately, he would also sacrifice himself for her, and that's our biggest worry."

"So how do we stop it?" the Riddler warlock asked, looking annoyed at the insinuation that a demon could love.

"Help us kill the man after our son," Bishop answered simply.

Harry froze at the comment and felt Vera do the same. Loretta and Bishop had always accepted Hunter, but Harry had never heard them use that term to describe the man. Surely, being married to their daughter made him their son, but it was still not something Harry had expected to hear.

The entire group of them watched, but no one spoke. Harry wasn't sure if they were taking in the fact that Bishop had just called a demon his son so nonchalantly or if they were considering whether to help a demon. These four covens were the most powerful within their grouping of the Midwest, and they held guidance over most every coven in the Midwest and South, so their allyship would be of great help.

Finally, the Wremon warlock said, "We'll see what we can do."

And they were gone. One by one, each coven's representatives ported out.

Harry finally allowed himself to turn to Vera. He took her face in his hands and made her meet his gaze. "Don't listen to them. There's nothing wrong with us. I didn't raise you."

He knew Vera's past with not feeling accepted and not having anyone in her life to rely on. Especially after Bishop had 'passed.'

"I know." Vera gave him a light peck, but her tone wasn't all too convincing. "I know there's nothing wrong with us. It just… feels…" She looked down, then met his gaze again. "I can understand how Maya was feeling. And we're lucky. We don't get much of it. I just…it sucks. And I feel awful to have done it to Maya."

"I know, sweetheart." Harry leaned down for a chaste kiss before bringing her in for a hug.

He looked over to the others as he held his witch and caught Bishop's gaze. The man gave him a nod that said he approved of their relationship, and it was all Harry needed. It was the most important thing.

Moments after the following silence, Camilla turned on Kai like she remembered she hadn't countered that she was his girlfriend. "I still don't like you."

Kai smirked as he eyed her up and down. "I still love dessert."

9

"You still have that pocket watch I made your mate?" Zathrian asked Maya as they stood around his shop.

Maya pulled the pocket watch out of her trousers and let it hang from her hand. "I always have it on me."

Hunter stood at the other end of the workstation room, playing with some knicknacks he was probably going to buy for the mansion, when his gaze shot up to watch her holding the piece. He loved that she carried it with her, and it made Maya love doing so even more. Though she didn't do it for him. She did it entirely for herself.

Especially after being in the warehouse with no way to get to Hunter. Having the pocket watch had been settling. Even though they had their rings, this was the first thing he'd given her, and Maya cherished it to depths she couldn't explain.

Zathrian took the pocket watch from her hands and smirked at the way her body stiffened and she had to force herself to refrain from jumping at him.

"How'd you know I had it at all?"

Zathrian shrugged. "When I made it, I had a feeling it would be given to his mate."

Hunter quirked his brow from the edge of the room. "When you made it, I didn't know Maya. What made you think I'd ever have a mate?"

Zathrian's smirk twisted up before he tried to fight it down with a grin. "I grew my status with the demons by knowing things, Hunt. I saw the way you were good on my mate, my witch. I knew you would have a witch."

"Yet you were shocked when I came around?"

Zathrian's smirk jumped back up. "Just because I knew it doesn't mean it wasn't shocking, My. Hunt with anyone would've been a shock, whether I knew you were destined or not."

That thought still made Maya happy. She loved that Hunter had never been seen with another woman. She was the one and only person he had ever been public with, the only one who mattered.

"So what do you need with it?"

"Nothing particularly," Zathrian answered as he opened the watch and leaned over the table to show her the clock. "I wanted to show you this. You see behind the hands, those shimmers that look like they're bouncing and disappearing?"

"Yeah." Maya loved that part. Sometimes she opened the pocket watch and stared at them disappear and reappear, bounce around and play.

"That's an element against dark magic. Knowing Hunt was going to give this to his mate, I put it in there."

One glance in Hunter's direction had him rolling his eyes. He obviously didn't like how perfectly Zathrian had read him. But he was paying less attention to the knicknacks now and more to what Zathrian was saying—anything to keep her safer was always his top priority, and the fact that he'd given her something without knowing it probably made him happy.

Acacia placed their teas at the end of the table, one cup for Zathrian and one for Maya and Hunter to share. They'd done so since the first time they'd been pulled out of Hell's Gate, and Maya still loved sharing with him.

"Zath keeps trying to make me something to carry too, but I don't like carrying that stuff. Or wearing anything other than our mating rings," she huffed as she took a seat on one of the stools around the workstation, her belly bigger every time they came around.

Zathrian rolled his eyes now as they all laughed. "Anyway, I can put that same magic into daggers and any other type of weapon. I can make you special weapons to fight whatever dark magic infested thing Jenkins tries to send your way."

Maya smiled. She knew he felt guilty for not being able to physically be there, but he wasn't about to leave his pregnant mate and possibly get hurt, and neither Maya nor Hunter would ever ask him to do so. But he was still trying to help in any way he could, and Maya loved that about him.

"Thank you, Zath," she said softly.

"Yeah," Acacia said even softer, seductively. "Thank you, Zath."

Zathrian handed Maya back the pocket watch, then picked up one of three designs for a dagger, but his dark gaze hovered to his mate.

As Zathrian went to explain the difference in the daggers he could make, Acacia said, "It makes me so hot when you're sweet like that, baby."

"Stop it, Acacia," he growled and tried to keep his gaze on Maya.

Maya met Hunter's black eyes from across the room and bit back the grin that was fighting to make an appearance.

"Oh, c'mon, Zath. I'm just saying you're such a good demon. Good demons should be rewarded. I think I need to feed you your favorite dessert. What was that again?"

Zathrian growled so low and long, the workstation vibrated.

Maya and Hunter laughed as Acacia moved for her mate and

licked up his neck, grabbing for his hand. "They can look at these on their own, Zath. Let's go to the back."

Zathrian's eyes twinkled, and the demon—and simple man— in him came out as he dropped everything he was doing and lifted Acacia into his arms, already sucking on her neck as he moved for the back, her moans echoing into the workstation.

Maya laughed as she watched them leave, so distracted she didn't know Hunter had moved until she felt his hands on her hips.

His breath was hot on her neck as he whispered, "Now why don't you get up on the workstation and let me ravish *you*, love."

---

Vera's punches weren't as strong as her little sister's, but she still swung at the sandbag in the middle of the empty boxing space at the school gym. She'd taken Camilla's I.D. and snuck into the gym in order to get some tension out of her body.

And hadn't told anyone she was there. Not even Harry. She needed this time.

She needed to think about it all, about Harry.

He was her warlock. She was his charge. It was looked down on, and Vera could understand parts of why so, especially if he had raised her.

But he hadn't.

Yet, still, everyone looked at him like he'd groomed her to be his personal toy. They stared at her like they felt sorry for her, but also like they were disgusted she was playing along with her warlock's games. They made her feel small. Smaller than she had before finding out she was a witch with a family. Smaller than all those times she'd felt too lonely and all she desperately wanted was one person to love her.

She had that now.

Had many of them, but Harry loved her differently.

So why couldn't she stop thinking about the way those covens looked at them? Why couldn't she stop thinking it may be simpler to not have to deal with that? Would it be simpler to let go of this happiness? Was she right in choosing him or had she seen a beautiful man—a good man—and instantly wanted to grow closer to him?

She punched at the bag. Three as hard as she could muster to stay off the tears that wanted to form at any thought of leaving Harry. He'd given up his immortality for her—a warlock's greatest show of their love and devotion. How could she consider that he didn't love her?

How could she consider herself? She knew she loved him. Even never having felt it before, Vera knew this was the love her parents had for one another, the one her sister had with her mate.

But her parents never had to be put under this scrutiny. Even if anyone didn't like their relationship, it was for personal matters, not the fact that they were witch and warlock from a same—semi-same since Bishop hopped around covens so much—coven.

And Maya had her mating with Hunter that made things extremely different with her. Maya was destined, in this life and in every other, as their mother had proven with dying eight times, to be with Hunter. Not to mention, Maya had a colder heart than Vera did. Though Vera knew it would've hurt her sister every time the family went against her relationship, she'd always been able to hold her own, be stronger. Vera envied her sister that.

She needed that now. To be strong for Harry.

He was the best man she had ever met, yet she couldn't help but think about whether a relationship with him was worth it.

Vera punched at the sandbag again. Harder each time, wanting to bruise her padded knuckles.

How could she be questioning this relationship? She didn't deserve him or any of the love he showered her with.

Vera gave it her all before the tears watered her eyes and she fell into the hanging bag. She laid her forehead to rest on the bag as her arms rested caged around her.

Harry was the best of men.

Harry was her man.

Harry was hers.

And she wouldn't ruin it. He deserved every fiber of love she could muster, and that lonely part of her that still made an appearance, because a lifetime of feeling unwanted couldn't be wiped out by a few months, would have to find another way to get to her.

She couldn't lose Harry.

"There you are, my girl." Her father's voice pushed through the white noise around her.

When Vera turned to face him, sweat falling off of her in puddles, she knew he would be able to read how helpless she felt at the moment, though the tears were gone from her eyes, determination to keep Harry having washed them away.

He spread his arms wide. "Come here."

Vera didn't hesitate in moving for her father's embrace. Cuddled in his arms, she remembered Harry. She remembered how much both her parents, but especially how much Bishop, accepted her relationship with him.

So maybe their relationship definitely was the right one. They loved each other, right? No matter how taboo everyone else tried to make it seem.

"You're drowning in that head of yours, V."

She hugged him tighter. "I know."

"Why doesn't Harry know where you are? Why aren't you picking up your phone?"

"I needed to think."

"About?" When she didn't answer, he gave an amused scoff. "Do not let others get into your head, Vera baby. I've known Harry a long time, and I've never seen him so out of his mind as he is now searching for you."

Vera finally glanced up at him, hating and loving that he'd always been able to know what she was thinking. "Do you have Cam's mind reading too?"

He laughed and kissed the top of her head. "No. You're just my little girl, and I know how lonely you were growing up. I know I had a large hand to play in that when I left you. It kills me, but do not begin reverting back because of those covens. Harry loves you. And you need to talk to him about any insecurities."

Vera sighed as she simply stood in his embrace, then suddenly pulled back. "How'd *you* find me?"

Bishop only laughed and winked.

## 10

*C*amilla didn't know how or when it had happened, but Kai's appearance in the astronomy tower didn't bother her anymore.

It was her place to think and relax. To give her body and mind the time it needed to recharge.

And she had a feeling Kai used it for similar reasons.

But more importantly, he never took away from her reasons for being there. He never made those inane comments that made her want to smack him over the head; never made any innuendos or advances; never did anything that would make her resent the place. He allowed, and respected, her need to take the time away in this tower.

As much as she despised him, she appreciated the fact.

And more surprising than anything else was how much she didn't mind his presence. How much she didn't mind that his following her around should bother her, but it didn't. How much it didn't bother her when he watched her silently. Or when he ignored her to stare out at the skies as she watched him.

How much comfort she found in being at the top of the astronomy tower with him.

"You're staring."

They were lain out on a blanket in the middle of the tower with another thrown over them to keep warm in the breeze.

"We need to get you a last name."

He laughed through his nostrils. "Why's that?" He didn't turn to look at her as he said, "The only thing a last name ever got me was pain."

She rolled her eyes, then went back to watching him. His every feature. Attractive, for sure, but his irritating habits really took away from that.

"What was Nico's last name?"

His breath caught for a moment before he spoke. "Sinclair. Nico Sinclair."

She didn't say anything to his response. Didn't even know why she'd asked. She found time and again the need to learn small aspects about him, and when it came to Nico, she was especially curious.

And he didn't mind telling her. She'd asked to make sure she didn't continue to bring up a sore spot—because even though she didn't like him, she didn't want to intentionally hurt him— and he'd only stared down at her with shining eyes and told her to ask him anything.

She sighed. "I need something to call you when I'm angry. Which, realistically, is most of the time I'm around you." He laughed as she added, "You need a middle name too. It's far more effective if I call you by a full name."

"What's your middle name?" He finally turned to meet her gaze.

Her face twisted down. "Georgette."

His twisted up. "Why the glum face? That's a beautiful name."

"It sounds like a guy's name."

He bit his lip to fight the grin, but it didn't work as he knocked his forehead against hers. "How about this—my middle name will be George. Now you only need to find that blasted surname."

She rolled her eyes and turned away from him to look up at the sky. "Ha. Ha. Very funny."

"I'm serious, princess." He knocked his shoulder into hers this time. "If you'd really like, we can make my middle name Georgette too."

She tried to fight her laugh as she shook her head, but it was a losing battle. "I really don't like you."

"Ditto, princess."

She turned back to face him. "And I really don't like when you call me princess."

"Liar," he whispered to her, gaze shooting down to her lips before he turned back for the skies.

She turned back too, her heart racing a little for a reason she didn't understand.

They were at the tower for a reason—she wanted time to simply think. About her sister and now new brother. And her other sister and basically other brother. About her ex-boyfriend who would officially forever be part of her family. About said ex-boyfriend being really good friends with the warlock by her side. About her parents being alive and amazing.

About…life.

And how insanely different it was from what she'd pictured only a few months prior when she was a human living a life without the supernatural. Even different from the life she'd planned after finding out she was a witch and wanting to keep her human life.

She didn't want that anymore. Couldn't fathom a life without magic. One that was so mundane as living in the human world.

As she allowed herself to relax into her thoughts, her eyes fell heavy with the need to rest under the beauty of the skies and the perfect breeze around them.

"What're you thinking about, princess?" His voice sounded far away and right by her side all at once.

Her eyes fluttered closed as she said, "I'd like to go to Scotland."

———

Maya wasn't too sure about heading to Hayes's without Hunter given the wolf's last warning, but he wasn't answering his phone. A quick search through the rings told her he was at the manor, so she could only assume he was doing something to surprise her.

But Hayes had sounded serious on the phone when he'd called to ask for a meeting. Plus, the man understood her position as a mated woman so she wasn't worried he would try anything.

So Maya took her parents, and they ported to the North American wolves territory, Hayes waiting out for them before the cabin. And to Maya's shock, Felix and Juliette were by his side.

"What happened?" For some reason, seeing the couple there made her panic slightly.

Hayes turned his rigid form and serious eyes on her, then froze. He stared her up and down and inhaled before his gaze landed on her midriff, then snapped back up. And he just stared at her with a narrowed gaze.

Maya sent furrowed brows in Felix's direction and watched the male do the same thing as his leader. Strange.

"What. Happened?" she asked again, losing her patience.

"Nothing," Juliette broke, giving her own odd look to both men. "We just wanted to talk to you."

"And your mate," Hayes finally broke. "Where is he?"

"Preoccupied," Maya stated with authority.

Hayes rolled his eyes. "You know a great many creatures do not like your mate. They may side against him merely out of spite."

Maya narrowed her gaze now. "Is that why you called? Because you can take one thing to your grave, and that is that I *will* protect my mate."

The lightness Maya was used to seeing in the leader's eyes came back, and he turned to meet Felix's gaze, a knowing look sent between the two. "Feisty."

Felix smirked. "Hunt handles her mighty fine."

"As much as I love hearing about my daughter's sex life," Bishop interrupted. "What is this about?"

Hayes turned to Bishop, and the authoritative leader came up, strong and feral. "Word is spreading rather quickly about the dead halfies and the psycho human trying to make himself the ultimate power king. Most creatures may not like witches and demons for their superiority, but they can accept that those are birthright powers. No one wants a human to have any."

"Okay." Maya elongated the word.

"Of the other creatures, I cannot speak for, but the wolves will help you. Meaning, we need to know what is going on."

"And you know our Ragtag House is going to help," Juliette added.

Hayes met Bishop's gaze again. "You're a seasoned warlock. I presume you know the most."

The other creatures weren't as powerful as witches and demons or as strong and fast as werewolves, so Maya wouldn't want to ask them for help either way. Asking the wolves for help already felt like too much.

"As a matter-of-fact, we all know as little as the other," Loretta answered. "The man's been killing for months and harvesting powers. Hunter can hold an unlimited amount—a rarity amongst Powers—so he needs Hunter's body. The woman from the storybook that was brought to life with the halfies' help, he needs her faerie dust to transfer into Hunt's body."

"The most we've been able to pick up is why that woman from the storybooks, Selin, was after Maya." All three pairs of eyes shot to Maya. "It has to do with my ancestry, but we do not know much more than that. And it still doesn't have to do with Jenkins and his need to possess all that power."

"She's after you too?" Hayes ground out.

Maya shrugged. "The witch that got her family killed was our ancestor. Apparently, I hold that witch's power, so I'm the last piece to the retribution. Then I believe she'll die, and the faerie dust will go to Jenkins."

As Maya stood there, she felt odd in her own skin. She didn't know what it was and tried to ignore it as the wolves watched her and spoke.

"Ancient faerie dust was far more powerful than what it is today," Juliette informed. "It could be what's kept her going all this time. And with it, possibly help this Jenkins man become the closest thing to immortal too."

Hayes grimaced. "Even worse than a human with powers. One who will yield that control for hundreds of years. And maybe find a way to make himself fully immortal so it's the rest of time."

"With this man's determination, I do not doubt he would find a way," Felix added.

Hayes shook his head, obviously in thought. "The wolves will be at your aid."

"We cannot ask the wolves to put their lives down for our family," Bishop said exactly as Maya had been thinking.

"You are not asking," Hayes reassured. "They're offering. I would not force my tribe to protect anyone. They wish to do so, if only for the safety of the supernatural world. They have mates they need to protect too."

"With all of us, we should be able to protect Hunter from Jenkins," Felix finished.

"And definitely Maya from this Selin," Juliette added.

"Yes, yes. In any case, we're less worried about Selin actually getting Maya, and more about Hunter putting himself in danger to protect her," Loretta voiced.

No one argued with her there, wolves being the most aware —even if they'd never gone through it, like Hayes—of the protective instinct that came with mating.

But her mother's statement froze Maya to her spot. She tried to calm herself, but an unsettling realization started to creep in.

Maya checked the ring again—something she'd told herself she wouldn't do but couldn't help—and couldn't feel him any longer. His presence wasn't within her anymore.

Had this been what she was feeling before? Now that she searched for him, she realized how empty her body felt. In the few short weeks she'd been wearing the rings, she'd grown accustomed to the feeling of Hunter in her veins.

Maya relaxed, knowing this could very well be part of whatever surprise Hunter had planned for her. That had to be it. Her emotions had been out of whack recently, and she would not allow herself to overreact over this situation.

Instead of allowing emotion to take over, Maya focused on her breathing as the others huddled over to Juliette for a taste of some apple strudels she'd made, still discussing the events of the past and every detail the wolves and Ragtag House may need to know. Maya wanted one too, but she needed to calm herself first.

Hayes stopped beside her and crossed his arms before his chest as he watched the others. After a moment, he broke their silence. "Congratulations, by the way."

Maya came out of her concentration and was about to thank him when she realized she had no idea what he was talking about. "For what?"

Hayes turned his attention on her, and from the looks of it, analyzed her expression. Maya didn't think he found what he was searching for.

"You said that mate of yours has heightened smell, right?"

Maya's brows furrowed deeper. "Yeah, so?"

Again, Hayes analyzed her before settling on his decision.

"Nothing. Just congratulations on the mating. I don't think I said that before."

Maya had a feeling that wasn't what he was congratulating, but the look in his eyes said he wasn't going to tell her anything more. So in the same way he always trusted her, she would trust him with this.

When Maya turned back to watch her family, she could feel Hayes's stare on her. But all she could think about was the fact that she still couldn't feel Hunter.

11

---

$\mathcal{L}$oretta had been upset to be sent away after visiting her mother and her old coven the last time, but she understood their need to think about things. She understood the coven's need to learn the story of Miradora and Adramalech on their own and know exactly what they would be getting themselves into if they helped.

But getting the call that they may return to the coven grounds in order to learn more about Bishops's ancestry had been reassuring. As much as her mother hated her for leaving, Adela would never fault her granddaughters for such a thing.

So after leaving Maya to shadow away and bidding the wolves and the leaders of the Ragtag House goodbye, Bishop ported them to the Czech Republic where they took their door portal to the Wittlieff coven grounds. The barrier was down for them when they arrived to the coven's territory, and Loretta got smacked with a sense of familiarity and nostalgia as she walked past the buildings she grew up around.

She and Bishop moved for the one at the end of the small street that resided as a meeting ground for official matters or for times they had trusted guests to entertain.

Loretta's mother, the coven head Anna, the head warlock

Jakub, along with three other coven warlocks, three witches, and two elders were the only members within.

Loretta felt their stares like a burn to her skin, but she tightened her hold on Bishop's hand and continued on as if she wasn't bothered.

Bishop led her to two chairs pulled out for them before the others and placed their entwined hands on his lap as they took their seats. His thumb ran reassuring circles on her hand to remind her that all would be all right, and Loretta loved him a bit more in that moment.

"We are glad you called," Bishop opened.

"It is not my granddaughter's fault she wasn't given the opportunity to grow with her coven," Adela stated. "Nor is it her fault that this power is upon her, though that bit wouldn't be anyone's fault. It is in fate that she mate with her demon, and in turn, hold the magic needed to protect said mate."

"Adela, Milena, and Iva have told us what they know of Bishop's past," Jakub continued, referring to the two elders. "From what we can understand, it is a line of intense passion between mates."

"Yes," Adela stated, an almost judgmental eye brushing over Loretta and Bishop. "The ones that would truly burn down worlds rather than merely threaten it."

"That sounds like our Maya." Loretta tried to lighten the air given the seriousness of their situation.

That also sounded like her and Bishop. They may never have burned down the world, because their daughters were on it, but they had been ready to die together.

"And our Hunter," Bishop added. "They are, in fact, the reason we faked our deaths."

"Yes," Adela called coldly. "Another matter a mother should be proud of. Learning of her daughter's death hadn't been enough. Learning it had been faked nearly shriveled me up."

"It wasn't." Loretta couldn't look at her mother, so she let her gaze fall to her hand in Bishop's. "Faked. I died eight times. The next, I won't be able to come back from."

Gasps came from all around her when Milena's voice came. "You have the cat's lives?"

"Yes," Bishop answered. "And in every one of her deaths, it was because of Maya and Hunter's mating that she perished. She finally told me the last time around, and I couldn't allow this final one to stick."

"What do you mean, it was because of Maya and Hunter?" Adela finally voiced some concern.

Loretta looked up to everyone in the room before meeting her mother's gaze. "Maya is the most loving little girl, always has been. She has a different way of showing it, seems colder and more blunt, but she's soft on the inside. She is protective and caring and amazing."

Adela's lips twitched up, and it was clear she was reminiscing on a past of spending time with her granddaughter she was robbed of.

"But she is also passionate. And leans toward the dark side, not only in her magic, but her natural way of being," Loretta added. "They mate in every life I've lived and every life to come. That would never change. But the way their relationship develops is different in every one."

"Not much is known of Miradora, but it is said she betrayed a great deal to get to her Adramalech," Milena stated. "She pained for those she left behind, but she couldn't live without Adramalech. And she couldn't allow him to perish in Hell's Gate."

"The first time I died," Loretta looked back down to their conjoined hands, "Maya had met Hunter for the first time, so very different than how they met now." Although it had led to unfortunate circumstances, Loretta still smiled at the memory of how giddy that Maya had been. "I had hidden the supernatural from them for most of their lives, but I had just shown it to them, told them they were witches. We—Maya, Camilla, and I—were in a forest off the state of New York that creatures frequent for ingredients when Hunter showed up. It was a casual bump in the woods as the girls were practicing their magic, but Hunter and Maya locked eyes over the flames she had coming from her hands...

"Hunter was the utter gentleman, apologizing for his family —which I have no doubt was done so we'd know how to find him again. Maya didn't outwardly show her excitement, but I could see in my baby's eyes how much she wanted to see him. So I found Delvaux Manor, and we went to them. I think what went wrong that time was their love grew like a wildfire, obsessive and crazed. They didn't fall for one another, rather, they clung to the crazed idea of being together. It wasn't pretty, most everyone was in jeopardy of dying, but I went first. Not by either of their hands, but because of them. When I came back for another life, I remembered it all, but we were back to a time where the girls didn't know they were witches, and so Maya didn't know Hunter. The second time they met, I made sure to keep their relationship more stable, but it still blew out, crazed."

Loretta met her mother's gaze. "It is not like that now. I think their meeting in a time when Maya didn't know much of the world and believed he could have something to do with my death kept her guard up around him. Without having me to run to, she had to be more on the defensive, if only to protect her sisters. Especially considering Harry had been with you lot before then, so he was also learning the American territory. This time, Hunter and Maya grew to trust one another, to want one another for conversation as much as for the sexual release." Bishop twitched by her side, and she knew the talk of his daughters' sex lives was disturbing to him. "They would do anything to protect one another. Mates in the true meaning of the word."

It was silent for a while before Iva added, "Miradora pulled Adramalech out so they could be together. So they could rule Hell together. It wasn't for the control of the people, but for the chance to be together, no matter what they had to do. A true meaning of the word for them as well."

"We worry for their safety now," Bishop finished. "Because Hunter is being hunted for his ability to hold an unlimited amount of magic in his body. Maya will go down to save him."

"Or take everyone else down for him?" Anna added.

"The more we learn of the original pairing, the better we may be able to help them now," Loretta finally finished the reasoning behind their visit. "Anything about Bishop's past we do not know?"

"Nothing that we have kept from you," Milena said.

"But I may be able to contact someone who will know more," Adela added. "For my granddaughter."

---

*I can't feel Hunter's ring. Where is he?*

Warren stormed through his father's manor knowing damn well that he wouldn't find his brother. The fact that Maya had texted meant he wasn't at their manor either.

Warren scoffed. The asshole had actually done it. Warren knew it without a doubt.

And still, he stormed the manor in hopes that he'd find his brother playing a game on his wife. Infuriating the little minx in order to get a *very* heated angry-sex-to-make-up-sex night.

But that wasn't Hunter. Not when Maya was in real danger, at least. He wouldn't make her worry with the problems they were facing.

In the future, when all their problems were taken care of— when Jenkins and Selin weren't after them—Warren knew Hunter may do it.

But not now.

Hunter wouldn't put Maya through so much worry.

Not unless he needed to.

Warren slammed open the door to his room as a last resort

after having checked the whole of the manor—and gotten some fearsome, wide-eyed looks from the other demons around when he'd ravaged the place.

He growled as he paced within his room. "Hunter, you fucking idiot!"

Warren ran his hands through the light curls on his head as he tried to imagine what dumb ideas Hunter had when his gaze caught to something on his bedside table.

He never left anything on his nightstand.

When he walked up to it, Warren found the ring Maya was missing the feeling of and a letter folded with a sheet of paper over it.

*Use your anger at me to keep my mate safe.*

Warren exhaled sharply as he opened the letter and read the contents left for Maya. He squeezed his eyes hard as he readied himself to give it to his new sister. One whose emotions had been askew as of late.

And now Warren knew why.

He paced again, unable to keep still as the anger within him grew. He scoffed as he thought of the words his brother had left him. Of course Warren would use his anger to keep Maya safe. As his sister, and now the mother to his future niece or nephew, she'd walk only the grounds that the Delvauxs worshipped.

"Hunter, you fucking idiot! Out of all the goddamn things you could've done." He put the words out, but they weren't enough.

Warren threw the letter and ring onto his bed and screamed, needing to release the tension somehow.

Then, without knowing how, he was before the wall by his desk and there was a hole in it, the edges quickly melting from his power, then cooling to mold a dark liquid. "You fucking ass." Punch. "She loves you." Punch. "She's carrying," punch, "your," punch, "fucking," punch, "child." Punch.

He seethed as he paced the floor again.

How was he supposed to do this? How was he supposed to

look into Maya's heartbroken eyes and tell her her mate was on a suicide mission?

Warren paused in the middle of his room and focused his attention on his breathing, knowing he needed to calm down before he tried contacting Maya.

Because he needed to tell her.

As much as he hated it, with the baby, Warren couldn't allow the stress of not knowing to weigh on her.

Though he doubted the stress of knowing what Hunter was up to would do her all that much better.

He stared at the holes in his wall, the molten bits around the edges that his melting had frozen over, and thought of his big brother. "Hunter, how do you make it possible to hate and love you so much? You don't deserve any of it, you fucking ass."

Warren calmed himself, breathing in and out for a long time before he moved for his bed and the two pieces he'd give to his new sister—the letter that explained his disappearance, and his ring.

The ring that connected them without magic or technology. The ring that worked as a tracking mechanism, and therefore, Hunter would've made sure to leave behind no matter how much it pained him.

The ring that symbolized this—his mating. So rare for a demon, yet so powerful.

The phone only rang once as he stood there. "My room. The manor."

Not a moment later, not only was Maya in his room, but the whole of her family. The whole, which included his father. Warren had no doubt they had been trying to keep her calm.

And he hated that he would take that away from her.

Warren caught his father's stare and received the small nod that said he picked up on what had happened the moment he heard Maya couldn't feel Hunter through the rings.

Warren numbly moved to his sister and hated how scared

she looked. Maya never looked scared. She was the toughest person that walked this earth.

He slowly lifted the ring and watched the way her jaw grit and she strained to keep her eyes dry.

Warren cleared his throat, then handed her the letter.

## 12

$S$he couldn't take the ring.

But she had to take the letter. Had to know what he was doing. Where he was. Had to know he would be okay.

Her hands shook as she unfolded the paper and found Hunter's jumbled and beautiful handwriting on the page.

*My bleeding heart,*

*I think in all my years within the demon world and my time in Hell's Gate, I've felt all forms of torture. But nothing would hurt me more than losing you or the family we're building.*

*If you're thinking you hate me at this moment for my decisions, know that I hate you more for coming into my life and destroying everything I'd built. And yet, the destruction you've caused to my world has led to this.*

*To you and that little one.*

I'm thankful to you for it, my dark, impossible thing.

So know that this is unto not only your safety, but that of our child's, so the vow has not been broken, my mate. I will protect you and come home to our family.

But know that my conceit only moves so far, love. I will rid Selin of his world to protect you, but if in the process, I'm taken from you, take care of our little one. You'll have my father and brother at your service. You'll want for nothing.

Do this for me, love, and bring our child into the world. Show the world what horrors we'd bring to this earth. Show the world what beauty we'd bring to this earth.

I need you to continue on and to continue to destroy this world for a long time to come. With or without me, my mate.

Yours

The tears were freely falling down her cheeks, but Maya hardly felt them. All she could do was move one shaky hand to her stomach.

The letter fell from her grip as she stared off into space and remembered it all. The way he kissed her stomach the last time they were in Hell's Gate. The way he placed a possessive hand over her stomach when they faced his sister. The way he kissed her stomach the other night and referenced the cute baby they made. The way he always spoke to her stomach.

Even the way he watched her, treated her, cared for her had been different. He smiled every time she ate a little more than customary. He calmed her irrational emotions, kissed them away and never faulted her for acting insane.

*You said that mate of yours has heightened smell, right?*

He'd been able to smell it the way both Hayes and Felix had scented it on her.

And instead of freaking out, he'd simply watched her with so much adoration. All because she'd been carrying his child for who knew how long.

And he'd known.

The fucking ass had known, and he wasn't around for her to smack and kiss all at once.

Because they were having a baby.

She was having his baby.

They would be a family.

Then the letter came crashing back to her, and the white noise around her turned too loud too quickly. He wasn't there.

He wasn't there.

She needed him.

"Maya," Vera's calming voice came to her through the fog. "You're pregnant?"

She barely heard her voice as she stared off at that image of her and Hunter and the baby in his arms. "I guess."

"You didn't know?" Camilla asked softly.

Maya came back to this dark room that Warren used when he stayed at his father's manor. She needed to get him a room in her manor. He needed the location to it too.

She shook her head slowly, both processing this new information too quickly and in slow motion.

"Did you?" Warren turned on his father.

"I guessed," Augustine, and shockingly, Kai answered.

Maya noticed the glare her little sister sent the Demon Warlock before focusing her attention back to the letter.

Maya turned to Warren and held out her hand, still finding words too difficult to compute.

He stepped up and cradled her jaw as his other hand deposited the ring into her hand. "We're going to find the jackass, Maya. And we're going to get him back. Alive."

Maya leaned into his chest and just let the soft rise and fall of his chest lull her. As his brother, Warren was the closest she'd get to feeling Hunter's heart beating beneath her at the moment.

She thought back to the other night. To the way he'd stared down at her so lovingly, she hadn't been able to stop the words from slipping from her lips. *I love you.*

The look in his eyes had told her how unsure he was with the meaning of those words. But at the same time, she'd seen in those black depths how much he felt it too.

Read it in that blasted letter.

Knew it in the sacrifice he intended on making on her behalf.

And their child's.

She finally pulled away, only enough to face Augustine. "What do you think?"

He'd be honest with her. The best part about demons not feeling the way everyone else did was that they didn't believe in sugarcoating. Knowing the truth, though it may pain or anger a person, was always better.

"We won't rescue him, Maya. You won't rescue him. At least not physically."

"Father…" Warren tried to silence his father, but Maya stopped him with a soft touch to the chest.

Augustine stepped up to her. "He's your mate and damned annoyingly stubborn when he wants to be. Rest assured, he will make his way back to you." He touched her fondly. "We'll find him. But nothing will stop Hunter from killing that woman and bringing himself back to your arms. He needs to do that as much for himself as for you. Even more so for himself."

"I can't live without him." It was all she could muster.

His thumb soothed her cheek softly before he pulled her into his chest so she was almost cradled between the two remaining Delvaux men. "I know, darling."

13

elin and Jenkins had a thing for warehouses.

Hunter wasn't sure if that was purely one's preferences, but he had a feeling Selin, at least, preferred them. Something about the secludedness of them and the way she had been alone at the top of her mountain made him believe she hated being around people more than because of the annoyingness of the general public.

The fact that she'd been resurrected in a warehouse and held both him and Vincent and Bella in one helped support that idea.

Realistically, Hunter didn't care. As long as he wasn't thrown into a warehouse as he played with the woman after his mate. Those places were annoyingly stifling.

He was in the woods, too far out for any of his family to get to without shadowing or porting. And thankfully, a spot Maya didn't know of that Hunter had enjoyed using in the past to play with his prey.

He'd set it up years ago, in his older teenage youth, in order to create a chase. To listen to the cracks of branches beneath the prey's feet as they ran and to breathe in the fresh air as he readied himself for a bloody death.

It had been exhilarating. Hunter forgot why he'd ever stopped.

He was giddy now with the anticipation that always came when he was in these woods. But he had to settle that excitement because this wouldn't be one of his chases.

Selin wanted him as much as he wanted her. She wouldn't run.

Hunter's true tactic here would be to play her down just enough to see if he could get any information out of her about Jenkins before ripping her body apart. Because as much as he didn't care for his own safety because Maya was currently in danger, when Selin was gone, Jenkins would remain a danger to Maya, if only because he wanted her mate.

As Hunter moved through the familiar woods, the earth crunched beneath his steps as his flames scurried after his feet, leaving ashes beneath him.

The same dark magic Kai had used to contact Selin for his ludicrous plan to pretend to be Maya was in motion. Except Hunter made sure to let the old woman know exactly who she would be meeting with. He made sure Selin knew she would not be getting her hands on his mate.

He knew the insinuation that she could not get to Maya, could not get back to her own family, would drive her crazy enough to come to him. If only to prove him wrong.

Because she was part of the caring creatures by nature, no matter how coldly the years had treated her as she waited for her vengeance. As a caring creature, pride prowled through her in a way it didn't in demons. Made her easier to play with.

Demons only felt the pride that ate away at caring creatures in situations. Like when he'd been in Hell's Gate the first time and *Pride* had been at his ear—it had been the pride of wanting to show his desired woman that he was worthy. Like when one ruling family kills or tortures to show the others where they stand—it was the pride of being a ruling family, thus not showing an ounce of softness in order to continue holding power.

But the pride that came so easily to the caring? The one that insisted proving oneself to strangers? That was completely lost on demons.

Thankfully so. It was a completely ludicrous way of going about life.

As Hunter moved through the woods, the crunch under his feet every few steps, he listened to every one of his instincts. So when Selin showed up, hidden behind a bark so large three of him could hide behind it, Hunter knew.

"Aw," he mimicked. "Are we scared, *Grand*-mama?"

Her laugh trickled to him, no fear within it. "You demons need to learn to wash away your conceit."

He respected that she was an attacker rather than a talker. Respected that she wasted no time in throwing one of those marbles he'd found their particular group fond of. Warehouses and magic marbles.

Hunter shadowed away leisurely, already lounging against another tree as the spot he'd been standing blew into smoke. He wondered what was in those little marbles. The old woman knew of his flames, knew heat wouldn't bother him.

It must be the same type of acid she had attempted to kill Maya with in that warehouse.

Hunter wasn't sure how many of those marbles she had, but had to guess no more than a couple handfuls. Then she'd have to rely on her faerie dust to keep her going, though Hunter doubted it would do her much good against all of his magic.

"That's an interesting little magic you have there," he said as he shadowed away from another marble. "Interestingly made. I presume the spells are laced into the potion that's stored within the marble?"

Dark magic.

He'd known it the moment he'd seen them with marbles. The much easier and exciting of magic, yet by far the most dangerous. He wondered what they'd sacrificed for these marbles. Probably all the bodies they'd collected.

"Maybe if you had a more interesting mate, I could show you how it was done and you could have your own fun," Selin responded in a bitter tone she attempted to mask but failed at miserably.

Hunter chuckled. "I prefer using my own magic. Though I would be curious of the spell, if you're so willing."

"Give me what I want, and I'd be happy to give it to you."

Hunter chuckled again as another marble came his way. He was sitting on another tree branch, leaning lazily on the bark, when he said, "I have the most interesting of mates."

"And useful too, huh? Her control of Hell's Gate will not only keep you in ruling family status but will make you the ruling monarchs of the supernatural world."

He shrugged. "If she wishes to be queen, she shall be queen."

"You speak so like him. Adramalech was a ruler with Miradora at his beck and call, and he still bowed down to her."

Adramalech and Miradora, Maya's ancestors and the reason Maya was being hunted now. But also representative that Maya may have a bit of demon in her, even if it had faded in all the years to such depths that it was indiscernible.

"Mates have a tendency to do that, we do."

"The fool was in love with that *witch*. The way you are now. It is pathetic. As a demon, both you and he should see that."

Hunter sighed. "I do not know why everyone feels the need to speak of love. It is a non-demon need, I suppose." He shadowed as another marble came his way, and he landed right before her. "What do you think, Selin?"

Close as he was, her jump of fright was even more entertaining.

As he eyed her, Hunter realized how frail she looked compared to the last time he'd seen her in front of the warehouse. Then, she'd looked like the first time she'd been brought back by the halfies—like the faerie dust was helping her remain any way she wished.

Now, she looked to be deteriorating.

Hunter's smirk grew.

Maya may have been angry when he'd made a deal with Selin to kill the elf she was after for Maya's safety. Now, he was gladder than ever that he'd done it. Because Selin had promised no harm would be done toward Maya, by her or her halfies.

And she'd broken her promise by trying to kill Maya in that warehouse. Since that day, Hunter had wondered if the dark magic they'd made their deal over had begun taking its effects. He saw now that it had and supposed it the reason behind Selin's worn down patience to kill Maya quickly. She was deteriorating before him, her normally old skin shriveling slowly.

That, and being that Maya was the final piece to her puzzle, Hunter was sure Selin was prepared to be over with it all. He knew that Selin would no longer care for whatever deal she had with Jenkins since he hadn't upheld his part and made sure of Maya's death.

And he knew Maya empathized with her. He knew Maya felt badly for Selin's loss of her family and her need to return to them.

Hunter didn't feel the same as his mate, expectedly so, but he knew Maya did, even if she never voiced her thoughts. Hunter didn't need to hear the words from his mate to know them to be real.

Still, as poorly as she felt for her, Maya wanted Selin dead. And Hunter was known to give his mate anything she desired, even if ridding of Selin was more Hunter's desire than his mate's.

"Drop another marble. I dare you." His grin grew, knowing the proud creature before him wouldn't risk her own life before she had her full retribution completed.

She stared up at him defiantly and did as he expected—

dropped a small one behind herself to open one of those portals she used to move around, then another at him.

He shadowed before it could make an impact but still enjoyed her attempts. "This is fun." He shadowed behind her new position at the other end of fallen trees and had a hand in the pocket she pulled those marbles out of. "But I think we should make it more entertaining." He threw the marbles all out ahead of them so a large explosion erupted. "At least for me."

"I am going to kill Maya," Selin seethed determinedly, glaring into his eyes without an ounce of fear.

The ground rumbled beneath his feet. "And I'm going to kill you."

Entry #1906

They've tried far too many times. They've depleted the stock. The morons weren't doing it correctly. Death is a story, and an epic climax requires a practiced hand. The supply could have been far greater had they not killed off the lot.

But the ancient had too many ambitious, greedy, power-hungry.

Today, it is only me.

But today, the dust is dirt. It's nothing to those of a millennium ago. The morons of past depleted my stock. Today, there's only one who continues to hold the ancient dust, and I will get it from her. There are too many stories of the successful transfers of the dust for so many of the morons to have gotten it wrong.

But I must thank them.

Because of them, the world is as weak as today. The world will not be able to disobey me. I will rule them.

14

Maya was left at Warren's side, sitting on the ground and resting on his shoulder to control her emotions. Kai wasn't entirely certain how long she would be able to hold herself together, but he'd grown to learn of her strength and knew she would do as much as she could in order to protect the baby she was carrying.

And that meant calming down so the babe wasn't under so much duress.

Kai also knew that at that very moment, Warren was the only one who would be able to help her. His blood relation to Hunter, the brotherhood rather than Augustine's parenthood, was the closest Maya would get to her mate, and she needed that to remain stable. It was the reason he'd insisted, softly and quietly so as not to disturb Maya's slow breaths, that everyone else leave so she wasn't surrounded. She needed only Hunter, and at the moment, Warren's breaths and heartbeat would be the closest she would get.

They'd been begrudging but had listened. Kai was the Demon Warlock for a reason—he was very aware and knew when to use his knowledge to his advantage.

Plus, Kai had insisted he knew of a way to find Hunter, and

Augustine had immediately been keen to the idea since the demon mate had taken his precautions and made himself untraceable.

Basically untraceable.

Kai knew a way.

The Delvaux patriarch was obviously affected by the events more than any of them would have expected, though Kai wasn't naive enough to think it was for Hunter's case.

It was all for Maya.

And that baby.

"We need to get to a faerie. Their dust is nothing compared to the era of Selin, but their saliva holds magic in it too. We need some for the spell," Kai said after he'd insisted with the group that black magic was required.

It was the second time he'd insisted on using dark magic.

And the second time he'd had hardly a fight before everyone agreed.

"Kellan," Camilla said quickly, her beautiful hazel eyes still wide from finding out her new brother was gone to protect her sister and niece or nephew.

Before she could elaborate, Kai seethed, "Who?"

Why did she know a male faerie so closely that he popped into her mind within a second's thought?

"Kellan," she insisted. "He's Juliette and Felix's friend, in the Ragtag House. He'll help, no questions! And if we need anything from the other species, we could find them at the House."

Kai wanted to argue that he wasn't going to get any help from this Kellan man, but knew he was being ridiculous, especially given he was good friends with her ex-boyfriend.

And the fact that they needed this done quickly and he knew the Ragtag House had already offered any and all help.

They were all ported and shadowed out to the location Juliette had given to Loretta the last time they'd met and were quickly met with a light shield, one Kai knew was meant to notify the residents to visitors. Especially when a moment later, the door opened to…

A human?

What was a human doing in there?

A witch walked out after her, and Kai could tell they were reading the seriousness of the situation on the entire group's faces.

"What's happened?" the human asked.

Vera turned to them. "Celine, Cora, this is Kai, Augustine, and my parents, Bishop and Loretta. Juliette and Felix told you about Maya and Hunter's position?"

Cora, the witch's, eyes hardened, and she turned back to the house. "Let's go."

They were stopped in what Kai assumed must be the living room, even though there wasn't much furniture within, and were met with another group of people.

"You're here?" Juliette questioned in a worried manner.

"What do you need?" a faerie asked, and something instinctive inside Kai told him *this* was Kellan.

Something instinctive also told him to throw the man through the closest window.

"We need saliva, faerie," Augustine said roughly. "And a pixie's hair and the feces of a wolf."

The last bit was part of the dark magic aspect. Not to mention some other ingredients that Augustine would be able to grab from his stores. Kai was sure Augustine could conjure up the other ingredients from his stores too, but the fresher, the better was always a motto in dark magic.

Celine was out of the room and back in moments with a small vial in hand and a couple of girls behind her. She moved instantly to Kellan and held up the vial as her hand landed on his chest.

He spit into it immediately, his gaze soft on the human the entire time.

Kai's heart settled as he watched him, his eyes narrowing on the two. This house was primarily for couples in mixed relationships, so it wouldn't be a shock for this Kellan to have a missus.

When the faerie leaned into the human for a kiss, Kai finally let out the final breath he hadn't realized he was holding.

Celine had the vial corked and handed to Augustine a moment later.

"I will take care of the wolf part," Felix said with a grimace as he turned to leave.

Everyone's attention dropped to the two new girls. Pixies.

The slightly taller of the two smiled and stepped forward. "I'm Lillabell, here with a faerie as well. This is my sister, Aster."

Aster smiled shyly, and her eyes shined a bit as they landed on Kai.

"Who're you here with, Aster?" Loretta asked politely even though they all simply wanted to get their ingredients and leave.

Aster blushed and looked down before meeting Kai's gaze again. "Only my sister. I am not paired."

Kai froze as a soft touch slid down his arm while Loretta smiled kindly at the girls and Bishop explained to them what was needed. Kai smelled Camilla's heavenly scent before he turned his head to find her pressed to his side, her hand falling into his, and her gaze latched onto the pixie's.

When Kai turned, Aster's face was bright with embarrassment as she tried not to watch Kai any longer.

He forced himself to hold in the pleased smirk as his fingers intertwined with Camilla's. She was laying her claim, even if she would never admit to it, so that Aster didn't get any ideas. He shouldn't be feeling so happy given their current situation, but his heart was running with giddiness.

"We can both give some hair if you'd like? Do you need it from one person or is a variety better?" Lillabell asked, bringing Kai back to the situation at hand.

"Both will be nice," Kai answered, his hand tightening in

Camilla's simply because it could. "Only a few inches from the ends is truly needed."

Both girls turned as Celine moved to them with scissors and expertly cut their hair, making it look like it was professionally done as she retrieved two inches from the bottom off both girls.

By the time it was placed in a baggie and handed to them, Felix was back with a small black box that he grimaced at while he handed it over. Augustine didn't wait around as he shadowed out, off to his stores in the basement of the Theology building at Camilla's school to pick up the rest of the ingredients.

"That can't be all you need," Kellan fought before anything else could be said. "There must be more we could do."

"For now, this is everything, Kellan," Camilla said softly, and that part of Kai that had thought him a potential suitor stood to attention, and he held her tighter, pulled her closer into his side.

"We will reach out if and when we need more," Harry reassured. "This was perfect."

***

Warren hated that all he could do was hold Maya into his side as they sat leaned back into the wall. Her hand lay on his chest as she followed his heart beating and slowly breathed in and out.

Her other hand was cradled against her stomach, and Warren had no doubt she was trying to think of Hunter and their baby in the future rather than the possibilities of what could happen.

He needed to keep his mind busy so he didn't fall into the hole of emotions. At the moment, everyone needed to show a strong front for Maya, so Warren would do that for her.

He thought back to the beginning of his acquaintance with the Whittles and how different life was now. Not only because now they also knew they were supernaturals, but because

Warren wasn't trying to do things to be accepted by his family. Now, he did things because he wanted to.

Now, he cared for his family in a way he never had before. Before, he'd wanted their acceptance but equally hated them for being so different. So demon.

Now, he saw them for what they were, the way Maya saw Hunter, and accepted them for it. It was the real reason his fondness for his brother had grown so immensely. Partly because Hunter had been forced to calm down with a witch as a mate, but also because Warren could see the complete puddle of love his brother turned into in his wife's presence. Hunter would never be good, but he was a better man because of Maya.

Augustine too.

And all of it had made the three of them closer. They weren't so affectionate with one another as to speak on it—or even acknowledge it—but in the few months that they'd been intertwined with the Whittles—especially Hunter and Maya's relationship—his family had become a real family.

And he was not going to lose that now. Not when Hunter was about to become a father. Not when Warren now had a sister whom he loved and who loved him back. Not when he had a niece or nephew that would need its parents.

So Warren wracked his brain.

Could anything from Jenkins' lectures help them with Selin?

He doubted it. The man was a narcissist. Warren doubted he would want to spend time on Selin when more focus could be on power and himself.

Maya shuddered into his side, and more tears slipped down her cheeks, but she remained breathing calmly. Warren pulled her in tight and kissed the top of her head as he thought back to all the lectures, PowerPoints, and notes from the first half of the class with that monster.

Warren had already gone over every aspect, separating them between what he believed to be based on Jenkins and what was based on stories.

Selin's background was based on the story *Grandmama Told Me*. Warren thought back to the specifics of that story, remembering aspects that he may be able to tie to the course. A family murdered? A scattering of bodies? A climb up or down a mountain? The closest he could think of was all the talk of faerie dust. Many of Jenkins' notes from that final reading, his journal, were around faerie dust. Warren knew the man needed it, and that was the only reason he had attempted to help Selin at all.

So he focused there. Faerie dust. Ancient faerie dust. The ones of current day hardly held an ounce of the power they used to.

There were journal entries speaking of coming by the faerie dust—sections relating back to the way Selin's husband had done it, by stealing. There were entries regarding what the dust could do for spells or potions. And least mentioned but still there, entries regarding the effect of the dust when in the body. Though dangerous to complete—Selin's life an anomaly—this was the most powerful use of the dust.

Entries about the dust within the body were few, but Warren remembered the mention of acquiring it. Killing someone with the dust had always been the easiest way of transfer, though it had to be done correctly in order for the dust to properly transfer. Simply any form of murder would not have worked. That had been learned when faerie after faerie had been killed for the dust, but none had transferred. Warren wondered how Jenkins had planned to get the transfer to work. He wouldn't have risked losing his only chance at ancient faerie dust. He was too smart for that.

Warren also wondered if that was all the faerie dust did. It was ancient, back when the supernatural were more than the humans and didn't need to hide. Back when the powers of the supernatural were far greater than the modern ones. He knew it made a person stronger, heightening their abilities to new depths—something Selin had proven—but he couldn't help but know there was more to it. Did it affect any other part of a person? Of a mated person, considering Jenkins wanted Hunter's body, and no matter what, Hunter's body was mated to Maya's. Their souls, hearts, and bodies were forever intertwined.

Warren promised himself to do some more research regarding the faerie dust as he pulled Maya in closer and held her. His sister.

## 15

He allowed her to push away from him as the ground's rumbling ebbed away. Allowed her to get to the end of the small clearing they stood in before she turned frantic eyes on him.

He respected that the fear washed away rather quickly and amusement entered. From his history reading body language and picking up the scent of those around him, Hunter knew she wasn't faking it either.

Yet demons were deemed the conceited ones.

Her gaze shot around, and Hunter knew it was to look for a way to hurt him. "I must thank you for this opportunity. Nothing would've made me happier than taking Adramalech from Miradora. Now I get to do it."

"If Adramalech was a ruler and Miradora was able to create the magic required to open Hell's Gate, do you truly believe you would've been able to hurt them at all?"

Hunter had wanted that moment to watch her fear when he let her push away from him. But now that it was gone, he slowly moved toward her, picking up the subtle hints of fear in her scent. It was nowhere near what he normally enjoyed while on the hunt in these woods, but it still fueled him.

Selin growled. "I don't care how powerful they thought they were. How powerful you believe to be." Her eyes widened with her hysteria. "I *will* get retribution for my family!"

Hunter was only a few feet away as he laughed, not out of amusement but because he knew it would infuriate her more. "And I will protect my family."

Selin moved for him, but Hunter was stronger and faster, so he moved out of the way and had the old woman in a head-lock without breaking a sweat. He laughed cruelly in her ear as he turned his hands, knowing he would get nothing about Jenkins out of her and ready to be done already.

But instead of hearing that snap that he loved and knew meant a neck was broken, a white shine spiked his hands and forced him to release her.

Selin's eyes were frantic, like she didn't know that would happen, before they turned cocky.

Hunter growled, knowing he now had to deal with the faerie dust that had created Selin, helped her remain long enough for her retribution, and now aided in keeping her alive.

He'd figured the faerie dust might be a problem. It was the reason he had to write that letter to his wife, but he had hoped against it. Normally, he would have loved the challenge, but not when his family was on the line.

Selin's eyes glimmered as her mouth twisted into a disturbing grin and her hands shined in that dust that spiked Hunter before. It was the same magic that had knocked him out when he'd allowed the halfies to capture him weeks ago, but something about the way it was being used—the way it was protecting—was different now.

"I will get my vengeance, boy." Her voice turned hard, the type demons had in human movies.

Then her hands shot out with that dusted shine the way he normally shot out flames, and Hunter just barely shadowed out of the way, shooting flames from his arms the second he was landed several feet away.

He growled when the flames bumped off an invisible shield that he knew the dust was creating for her, and just barely shadowed out of the way as another spike came his way.

The woman was moving quickly, and Hunter wasn't sure if she was in control at all or completely crazed with the power she'd just garnered.

The white shine came at him from every angle, and as quickly as he shadowed, he was barely making it out of the way. He felt the grazes as he just missed the magic, and instantly felt the tingling burn, so unlike his fire, shoot through his body. Any and all magic he attempted to throw her way disappeared within a foot of her body.

Hunter grabbed for a spiked branch and threw it, attempting a non-magical approach, and watched as the branch grazed the edge of Selin's calf. She barely processed the pain, so lost in the magic as she was, but it gave Hunter the in he needed.

He shadowed high onto a branch where she could not so easily track him and watched from above as she shot her gaze around, frantically looking for him.

"Come back out, coward!" she roared in a tone Hunter knew would've scared most creatures.

He ignored it and kept his attention on her as he searched for a strong, spiked piece of branch he could use as his own weapon. He couldn't lie, as much as he enjoyed killing with his magic, Hunter had always preferred a more personal method. It was part of the reason he loved snapping necks—it was personal, with nothing but his hands.

Hunter edged from tree to tree as Selin shot her gaze around, unable to locate his well hidden form in the forest, as he searched for the perfect weapon. Each movement hurt him as his body reacted to every strike that had grazed him.

His right arm, left ribs, right thigh, and both ankles had gotten it. And each time, the pain had spiked there before spreading throughout his body. Now, he felt the ache everywhere, but nowhere compared to the exact spots he'd been hit.

He knew the only reason he could continue moving at all at the moment was the adrenaline pumping through him to keep his family safe. It was almost an unbearable pain, even for all the tortures he'd been through as a demon.

Then, finally, he found it. A hard piece of branch that was just bigger than a baseball bat and fit into his large palm perfectly. The weight of the thing made Hunter positive it would take the old woman out, so he ignored the pain of picking it up with his right hand. Though he'd always trained both sides of his body and was easily ambidextrous, Hunter knew his right side was slightly stronger, and he would not risk anything for this moment.

Hunter wasted no time in shadowing down from the branches and landing a few feet beside Selin. He had just enough time to hit her side before another spike moved for him.

He ducked out of the way and felt the graze off his left shoulder. It burned so badly, he wanted to roar with the pain.

But he had gotten her. Selin was distracted from the hit, and all he needed was another hit, straight through the chest this time, before she was no longer a problem.

As Hunter moved for the final strike, a tingling shot through him like his flames were calling his attention. He'd never felt it before, and he only allowed himself the second to turn in the direction his flames begged him to.

And froze.

His face drained.

His mate was there.

16

Maya was pregnant.

Camilla still couldn't believe it. She was going to be an aunt.

Her big sister, who had watched over her when their mother had been 'dead' was going to be a mom herself.

She would be the most perfect of mothers.

And as much as Camilla hated to admit it—because though they were good now, he still wasn't a good guy—she knew Hunter would be the most devoted father. Though she liked him now, even while he continued to irritate her regularly, the thought of praising him sounded too far-fetched to Camilla.

But it was a fact she would not deny in her own mind—Hunter Delvaux would make a perfect father. He would love and dote on Maya and their child to an unbearable, overbearing extent, and Camilla could not imagine anything more deserving for her sister.

Camilla took the letter from the table they'd placed it on before leaving while the others prepared around a desk that had been pulled forward. The entire group, apart from her sister, stood around it to watch as the Delvaux men—namely Augustine—prepared the potion for the spell that would find them Hunter while Kai instructed.

Instead of joining them, Camilla reread the words her new brother had written for her sister.

*I will protect you and come home to our family.* He'd said it before, 'our family,' but every time, Camilla had considered it in regard to only Maya. She knew now that he had looked at his wife—his mate—every time and seen the life she was bringing into this world.

*Show the world what horrors we'd bring to this earth. Show the world what beauty we'd bring to this earth.* Those were the lines that got to Camilla the most of all and the reason she'd had to set aside the letter before she allowed herself to cry in front of Maya. They needed to be a united, strong front for her sister.

Maya was seated on the ground against the wall, her head tipped back and her breaths coming in and out evenly. Her hands were lit aflame as they sat on her crisscrossed knees and she simply breathed.

Camilla wondered if she was using her supernatural gift to figure out a way to her mate or if she was merely trying to calm herself down because this much stress wouldn't be good for the baby.

When Maya's flames spiked and more tears strolled from her closed eyes, Camilla concluded it was the latter. As much as it pained her, Maya was trying to meditate, to clear her mind of what may be happening to her mate and focus on the baby she was carrying. Their baby.

Maya would be the best of mothers.

While she sat by the wall and tried to bring peace to herself —which Camilla knew wasn't working—the others continued preparing the magic and whispering so silently Camilla couldn't hear it from her side of the room.

She knew above all else, they were simply worried. Every few seconds, a different person would glance in Maya's direction to make sure she was all right. With all the time that had passed since she last felt Hunter's presence through the rings, Camilla knew no amount of meditation or magic would help Maya. She needed her mate.

Camilla watched Augustine and Warren work. As demons, they had no qualms about practicing dark magic, and it was fascinating to see how calm even Warren was in the face of things. She knew he was more opposed to the type of magic than his family, but would do anything for his family, for Maya.

And in instances like these, even Camilla didn't mind the use. Anything for her own family, which now included Hunter and the baby he'd created with her sister.

Camilla moved toward the table and stopped at Kai's back so she could look around his arm, but not so much as to witness whatever grotesqueness was needed for the spell. Hearing the need of Felix's feces was plenty enough for Camilla.

Kai didn't turn to her, but his hand reached back to take hers and intertwined their fingers. The simple act almost broke Camilla to tears as she closed her eyes and laid her head to rest on his back.

He stiffened, then relaxed as his hold tightened on her hand. Like he needed her to know he was hers and he was there for her. It was the same feeling she'd gotten when she slipped her hand in his earlier and he'd intertwined their fingers.

She knew it was stupid to play this with him, but she needed the comfort. And she needed it from him.

Camilla breathed him in and fought the tears that tried to build up. She'd always been protective of her sister, and this was too much for her to handle alone.

When everyone gasped around her, Camilla's head shot up to pitch blackness. The flames coming off her sister's arms illuminated her spot in the room as they all turned to watch her. Eyes still closed, breaths still attempting to come in and out slowly.

Only a couple of seconds later, the room returned to the dimly lit it had been, but the suddenness before showed just how painful this was for Maya. Camilla hated herself for not being able to do anything to take it away.

When Camilla turned away from her sister, her eyes were watering as they clashed with Kai's. He watched her with determination as his hand squeezed hers again.

He turned back to the table, and Camilla missed the reassurance that came from those hazel eyes.

She sighed and didn't fight herself as she rose to the tips of her toes and softly kissed the back of his neck. He froze under her lips as she kissed him again, a thank you without the use of words.

He squeezed her hand in his and lifted it to his lips so she was basically hugging him from behind. The softest of kisses met her knuckles before his lips remained skimming her hand.

Camilla didn't pay any more attention to how their magic worked as she leaned into Kai's back once again, but it wasn't long before they had what was needed to locate Hunter.

Augustine's sharp gaze landed on Maya. "Let's go, darling," he called, and her eyes snapped open. "Let's go get your husband for you, darling daughter."

Maya was on her feet in an instant, her hands still rimmed with flames that Camilla wasn't sure she could control in her moment of distress. Everyone was paired off in their couples as per usual, and no one took time to think before moving.

Kai's clasp on her hand didn't break for even a moment as they all prepared their pairings to port or shadow off. Camilla was glad when Warren took Maya's hand even though her sister could easily shadow herself.

Camilla turned to meet Kai's stare and didn't break from it as the other occupants of the room slowly disappeared.

Kai took their moment alone to cradle her face with his free hand, then leaned in to kiss her forehead softer than she'd kissed him only a few minutes prior. His lips hovered over her skin for another moment, like he wanted to do it again, do it harder, go lower and kiss her lips. Then he pulled away and ported them after her family.

## 17

*H*is mate was there. She couldn't be there.

Hunter's moment of distraction seeing Maya only thirty yards from them cost him everything he'd been leading to.

He hadn't seen or felt Selin pick it up, but one moment he was holding the stake-like branch, and the next it was in her hand.

He'd trained himself not to fall victim to Maya's distractions while in battle, but he'd always known that nothing could prepare him for a true moment his mate would be in danger. For this moment where his magic pulled his attention to her on its own accord.

As he prepared to shadow out of the way, towards his mate to get her away from the woman who wanted her dead, then back to those around her to kill them for allowing Maya to come in the first place, the stake pierced through his chest.

Hunter fell to his knees as the stake ripped straight through his chest, so close to his heart he felt the graze of the wood against his most vital organ.

He didn't need the rings to feel Maya's dread.

Or fear her screams.

Know she was running for him.

Feel the ground rumbling hard beneath his knees.

See the skies disappear and a blackness so dark fill the air before it was enflamed with blue and white flames and the edges of a cage.

Hunter growled through the pain of the stake and forced a shield up to stop Maya from getting any closer to Selin. He didn't know how it worked since they were in a part of Hell's Gate Hunter knew instinctually was the deepest depths.

Magic went extinct in Hell's Gate.

He didn't know how the shield formed, but thankfully it kept his mate and the old woman away from one another. Though using that much power, added with the stake through his chest, could kill him, Hunter would not—could not—allow Maya to get near Selin.

Blood dripped out of his mouth as he met Maya's beautiful browns, the tears freely falling down her cheeks as she banged against the shield. Though he knew she did it in order to break his hold and get through, he didn't think she understood how strong his will was. He would hold that shield up to his death if he had to because he cared far more for Maya and their child than his own pain.

Their family behind him looked frantic, but thankfully, none of them attempted to break through the shield. Hunter wasn't sure how long he would be able to hold it up with all of them beating against it.

"Awe, you're stuck behind the shield?" Selin mocked, and all eyes shot to her. There was fear there that went along with being so far below, but it was outshined by her closeness to her end goal. "Do not worry, child, he will be dead soon, and you may have your way with me."

"I'm going to kill you," Maya seethed, gaze finally shooting off of Hunter and to the woman who caused this entire mess.

"No, you won't." Selin laughed. "You will run to your mate

because that is what mates do—they put their partner above all else, above themselves."

Maya's gaze shot to Hunter in the darkening spot he'd been left, the flames lighting the single spot Selin stood, before her gaze shot back to the old woman. "No. I'll kill you for what you've done. I still need to live, if only for a while longer."

A while longer. Just enough time to bring their babe into this world. Because Hunter knew his mate. Once the babe was here and in the care of their families, she would join him in death.

Selin laughed. "Whatever for, darling?"

Hunter slowly wobbled up to his feet while everyone watched the two women in the center.

The pain of all the strikes he'd taken clouded his vision, and he almost fell back to his knees. The stake bled through his chest and mouth, and he knew he only had so much longer before even the adrenaline wouldn't be enough to protect his family.

When Maya didn't answer, tears streaming down her cheeks as she watched Selin, the old woman continued, "You would not be able to endure it. You will want death as I do. Because, trust you me, once I kill you, I will welcome death peacefully."

A burn seared through Hunter's chest, but he didn't pull the thing out as he silently forced his steps toward the woman who threatened his entire reason for being.

Maya pushed against the shield, and Hunter had to swallow back the desire to cry out at the pain her push on his magic had when added to the stake in his chest and the earlier strikes from the faerie dust.

"Think." Selin smiled deeply. "I am doing you a service as well as myself. You will be with your mate in death as I will be with my family."

Hunter used his final remaining strength to push his hand into the back of the old woman's chest—an act so violent he'd only ever done it once before—while his other hand stabilized her by the shoulder. "No." His fingers sunk into her chest as she tried to wiggle out of his grasp. "You will meet your family in death having not completed your retribution." His fingers circled around the beating organ that kept her alive. "You will never know peace, *Grandmama*."

He yanked her heart out of her back and allowed her body to fall to the ground before him as he held out the heart in his hand.

Maya no longer banged into the shield as she stared wide eyed at him. Their family mirrored her expression as they huddled around his mate.

Now, with nothing more left to lose, Hunter grabbed for the stake in the middle of his chest and yanked it out. The shield he'd barely managed crumpled away with it as he lifted the stake with a shaky hand and ran it through Selin's heart.

He held out the heart on a stake as an offering as he wobbled two final steps then fell to his knees.

The act knocked his mate out of her shock, and she rushed for him, falling to her knees before him as she held up his face so their gazes met. "Baby, baby please…"

A final chuckle left Hunter as his free hand shook its way to her stomach. "Yes, baby. Our baby."

More blood trickled out of his mouth.

Maya's hands shook as they held his face up. "Dad," she yelled. "Dad, please! Please!" Her head began to shake as she pressed her forehead to his and begged, "Please, please, please…"

Hunter dropped the stake and brought his bloodied hands to her face, knowing magic wouldn't work down below. "Take care of our baby, Maya."

"No," she begged as a heat hit his back. "No, Hunt, you'll take care of it with me!"

He brought her lips to his as the heat filled the rest of his body.

What he thought would be his final kiss with his most beloved of bleeding hearts felt revitalizing.

That's when he realized the heat encompassing his body was that of a warlock healing. That's when he realized, as he kissed his mate, his wife, the mother of his child, his body healed. When he realized, somehow, the warlock's magic was working down below. When he realized, Maya's control went beyond opening portals, and she was allowing for the healing to take root.

When he realized his kiss grew stronger as he held her face in his bloodied hands.

When he finally pulled away to look her in those perfect eyes he hoped their child inherited, he watched her exhale in unbridled relief, then fall into his chest as she clutched him, fists gripping at the shirt over his wounded chest.

The embrace gave Hunter a moment to look around and see that it hadn't only been Bishop healing him, but all three warlocks. They'd all put their power together to make sure nothing happened to him.

Hunter kissed the crown of his mate, knowing all three men had done it for her benefit and having no problem with that fact. He wanted everyone to do everything for her, wanted to give her everything her heart desired.

A small chuckle left him before he fought to conceal it and tried to look more serious to hide it.

"What?" Maya shot her head up to look at him, her brows furrowed with worry.

He tried to control the grin, but it was a losing battle. "I'm just thinking. Now that this is over, I think you should take me home, clean me up, and…" He wiggled his eyebrows.

She giggled into the nook of his shoulder, kissing his neck softly, before looking back up at him with a wide smile. "And give you a nice, long fuck?"

He winked. "That's my girl."

18

———

Tamire and Lila didn't come over as often since finding out about Selin's attempts against Maya. Not because they didn't want to, but because Maya had asked them to leave. To keep Aurelia safe.

But that hadn't stopped the calls every few days—because weekly left too much space for things to happen in their hectic lives.

When they found out Maya was pregnant, and Hunter had a close meeting with death, they instantly ported into Whittle House with little Aurelia jumping for Hunter's arms.

Bishop watched the way Hunter rolled his eyes at the babe, making it clear he wanted to take his wife home and fuck her instead of spend any time with the family. But he took the little girl without argument, knowing Maya would've made him anyway.

It was all entirely too amusing to Bishop.

And though he made it abundantly clear he didn't like Aurelia, Bishop saw quite the opposite. He also saw how doting of a father the demon would make.

Bishop stopped at Tamire's side, the oldest man in the room beside himself, as they watched the group in the house.

The girls were concentrated around Maya as they tried to learn more about her pregnancy through spells they found in the Book. Warren and Kai stood off to the corner laughing about whatever crap those kids came up with. Harry was back in the kitchen cooking what smelled like a roast. Augustine didn't dine anyone with his presence, merely standing back and watching Maya with a glint in his eyes. It made Bishop especially happy to see the man's attention on his middle daughter. It meant the demon patriarch would protect her. Protect their grandchild.

The only missing person was Hunter, who Bishop hadn't realized was gone until he glanced around for Aurelia.

"Your daughter is missing," he said to Tamire, who was watching Lila interact with Maya adoringly.

His gaze shot around the room. "Should I trust that Hunter wouldn't have hurt her?"

Bishop fought back a laugh. "After what they just went through, Maya may give him some leeway if he did anything to upset her."

Tamire grumbled and pushed Bishop so the two of them could move for the hallway, in search of the demon and his daughter.

Bishop was ready to lead him up to the rooms when he heard a soft sound coming from Loretta's old office, the space Maya had made her own.

The door was left ajar, and they could see them perfectly through the glass as Hunter jumped Aurelia on his lap, her chubby feet kicking with excitement. He sat on one of the chairs left for guests and watched the little girl with a spark in his eye.

"I'm going to have one of you in a few months, then Maya won't bother me about taking you because I'll have my own child," Hunter spoke to Aurelia, and the little girl giggled back.

"I hadn't thought of that. Aurelia quite literally may kill us if Hunter has another babe in his arms. The girl will be so jealous," Tamire whispered as they watched.

Bishop laughed because of the pure accuracy of the statement.

"I sure do hope we have a daughter, Aurelia," Hunter continued. "One that looks just like her mother. But if she does take from me, I hope she at least gets her mother's beautiful eyes."

Aurelia jumped in his hands, a grumble leaving her like she knew he was talking about another little girl and didn't like it. A lightness Bishop had only ever felt during the birth of his daughters came to him at the sight of his now son's desire for his own family.

"Don't worry, you ugly little thing," Hunter spoke with a grin that fooled the babe into more giggles. "My mate wants a boy that looks like me. And my mate tends to get what she wants."

"I could definitely live without him calling my daughter an *ugly little thing* though," Tamire whispered.

Bishop laughed again, unable to chase away this glee he felt watching the demon and the babe.

"I don't know, rascal, does it make me sound too human to say that all that truly matters is that my mate and babe are healthy?"

Again, Bishop thought back to having his daughters and feeling the exact same thing—wanting only for Loretta to be safe and healthy. And in turn, for their child to be healthy.

It was that small bit into Hunter's mind that he would never share with their group that told Bishop that the man was going to make a devoted father to his grandchild.

But it also worried him. Because like himself when Loretta was pregnant, Hunter was only thinking of his family and not himself. He wasn't thinking about his own safety, his own health. Maya was going to need him healthy as much as he needed her healthy.

Bishop couldn't look away as a whisper left him. "Do you remember when Jenkins mentioned the faerie dust? His need for it?"

Tamire nodded but didn't peel his gaze away from his daughter.

"Selin is gone now. But I have an unsettling feeling the dust didn't go with her," Bishop finished as he remembered the recounted story Hunter had given them of the events that had transpired before they'd gotten to him, of the faerie dust that spiked into him.

An unsettling feeling that Hunter would not remain healthy, if for nothing else than because he wasn't safe from Jenkins. And if he also somehow carried the faerie dust, he would be far more desirable to the lunatic. It would be a step that Jenkins wouldn't need to deal with.

Finally, Tamire faced him. "What are you trying to say?"

Bishop nodded toward Hunter. "He was the one to kill her. Literally pierce her heart out. That's how Jenkin's planned on getting the dust—killing her."

Neither one spoke as they watched through the glass window and listened to Hunter through the cracked door.

"In any case," Hunter jumped the girl on his lap again, "hopefully they're almost done hogging my mate's time so I can take her home and fuck her." Aurelia laughed. "But you don't understand anything I'm saying, do you?" He spoke with a giddy laugh about his tone. "No, you wouldn't. You're only a disgusting little thing, aren't you?"

---

Maya's back slammed against the wall as Hunter leaned over her. "You did such a good fucking job cleaning me earlier, love."

He bit her neck.

Hard.

Enough to leave a mark and show everyone who she belonged to. She loved when he did that.

"Now, I think you've made me wait long enough for the best

part—let's see how good a girl you are as you fuck me."

She tsked as her teeth skimmed his jaw. "I think you need to fuck me, baby. I want you to bruise me, Hunt. Claim me."

"As you wish, my witch," he growled against her lips before beginning with her mouth with a bruising kiss.

"You know, love." He kissed down her jaw. "I can't be as rough as you'd like." Nibbled at her ear. "I'll have to be more careful by your stomach." Licked down her throat. "For the baby." He bit the dip of her neck.

He'd had to be more careful for weeks now since he realized she was pregnant. Hunter assumed she thought the fact that they weren't merely fuck buddies anymore was the reason why, but it certainly wasn't. He couldn't wait to be a little too rough with her again.

"Babies," she said breathlessly.

Hunter froze and lifted his head away to look at her. "What?"

"Two. Twins." She pulled him in for another kiss that lasted only a few seconds before she continued, "The spells they were trying on me earlier. There're two."

Though he'd had weeks over her few hours to come to terms with their pregnancy, Hunter was still shocked that this extra news wasn't freaking her out. He was just as shocked to find that it didn't frighten him as his heart raced with excitement.

A laugh passed through his lips as a scoff. "Maybe now we'll each get one we want. A girl that looks like you and a boy that looks like me."

Maya's brows furrowed, her breathing growing more accelerated as she yearned for his mouth to be back on her. "I want two boys now. Just like you."

He growled and slammed her arms above her head. "You just want to torture me, don't you?"

"I think you're torturing me, baby." Her tongue brushed his lips. "Now take your clothes off. Take mine off. Fuck, baby, just get inside me."

Hunter laughed as he released her and tugged his own shirt

off, reaching for his trousers when her hand stopped him with a delicate touch to his chest. "Baby…"

He looked down to find a scar about the size of her little finger beside his left pectoral. Some scars, if deep enough, wouldn't disappear on the supernatural even with the healing powers of a warlock.

This one was in the exact spot the stake had gone through his chest. A forever reminder that the threat to his mate was gone. Now his favorite scar.

Hunter shrugged. "If I'm not completely covered by the time old ages kills us, I haven't made a good mate."

"Hunter." Her gaze was soft as she eyed him, her fingers softly tracing the white, raised skin.

She leaned over and kissed the scar, right above his heart, and he felt that blasted organ speed up with something other than need. Something he didn't understand.

Maya met his gaze again. "Thank you." She kissed the scar a final time. "For loving me and our family this much."

Hunter didn't know what to say as she leaned back against the wall, but he did feel his brows furrow. That word kept following him around, and now she was using it for him.

So, like always, he didn't hover on it. Instead, he leaned in and cradled her face. "I'll always protect my family, my wife. Maya, you three *are* my world."

Her eyes watered as she leaned in for the kiss.

Hunter led her off the wall and over to their bed as he kissed her tenderly. He would fuck her, but first, he'd take things slow.

Hunter stripped them both of their clothes in record time and loved the sound of Maya's laughter as he did so.

He tried to fight his own as he growled at her to get on the bed, then hovered over her. He gave her one final gentle kiss before demanding, "Hold on to the bed posts. If you let go, I stop."

Her eyes widened as her arms listened of their own accord,

but Hunter knew by the way she bit down on her bottom lip how excited those words made her.

He kissed her lips, her nose, her forehead—with a whisper of how thankful he was for the life she'd given him—then down her cheek, across her throat, down her chest. Kissed the valley between her breasts, then each breast individually. Then down still.

When he reached her stomach, which was so slightly rounded with proof of their future, he kissed it lovingly. "Turn away, little ones. Daddy's got some dirty things he'd like to do now."

Maya arched her back into him as her grip tightened on the posts above her head. "Stop it, Hunter. I'm not supposed to like that."

He rose until his face was in the crook of her neck as he chuckled. "What, love? Calling me daddy? That's what I'll be."

She moaned again but argued, "I've never liked it before. I *don't* like it."

His fingers caressed her face. "Convincing me or yourself, Witch?"

She growled at him, but it was more sexy than it was scary.

His grin traced her jaw. "You're right, love. I don't like it either." He caught her gaze with a mischievous glint. *"You're* supposed to call me Daddy."

She shook her head and breathed against his mouth, "No."

His fingers traced down her form until they reached her cunt, spreading her lips and playing with the wetness there. "If you'd like to come, love, you'll do as I say."

"No," she breathed, defiance strong in her chocolate browns.

He laughed as his finger drew circles around her most sensitive spot. "Do you truly believe yourself in control here, Witch?"

"You'd do anything I say." She smirked as her eyes hooded with desire.

"Mm." He laughed against her jaw as his fingers dipped inside her, and he relished in the sound of her gasping and her chest hitting him. "Except," he pulled his fingers out, "I'm having so much fun now."

He skimmed those two fingers up her body and circled a nipple.

"Hunter!" Her body writhed beneath him to get his touch back down. "Hunter, please!

He tsked. "That's not my name."

"Hunt," she begged. "Hunt, I need to come. Hunt, please."

His fingers dipped back inside her as his thumb took root at her clit. "Maya…" His fingers moved until he could feel her clenching around him. "You know what you need to do."

When she didn't, he pulled his fingers out again.

"Please," she screamed. "Fuck, Daddy, please."

"That's a good girl," he whispered into her ear as his fingers dipped back inside her and his thumb played with her little nub.

"Yes, Daddy," she screamed as he felt her tighten around his fingers.

"That's a good fucking girl," he teased, licking and biting at her neck, until she was crying out and coming around those two digits inside her.

He brought his hand to his mouth to lick clean as she came down from her high and glared at him. "I hate you."

"Oh no," he teased. "Daddy'll make you change your mind."

She moaned, and her body arched into him at the words.

He laughed. "You're loving it, aren't you, Witch?"

"No," she bit out, determined.

He laughed again. "Daddy wants you to turn around now. Stick that beautiful ass in the air for me."

She leaned up to kiss him, and their tongues fought for control before she bit down on his bottom lip a little too hard to be playful, then did as instructed and turned on all fours. And like the good girl she was, she never let go of the bed posts.

Hunter's hands caressed her pristine skin as he took in the pleasure of seeing her face down, ass up. "You wanted to bruise, love?" His hand slowed on her cheek. "You'll get as you wished for." He smacked her ass hard enough he already saw the red mark of his handprint.

She moaned as she cried out, "Make it even, baby."

Hunter chuckled deeply as he spit down and watched it trickle between her cheeks. His hand slipped into her cunt again, fucking her roughly with two fingers before collecting more of her arousal and spreading the moisture around that hole he still hadn't gotten the pleasure of exploring. He spit down again, soaking her hole as he smacked her other cheek.

His breathing came in hard as he looked down at his handiwork.

He slowly slipped the tip of his finger into her ass and watched her back arch as she cried out. He pulled back softly, then moved again, fucking her ass slowly with his finger until he could fit the whole digit.

Then his cock slipped into her cunt, and he moved slowly as both cock and finger fucked her, stretching her out before deepening until both entered to the hilt.

Maya screamed so loud as she came her voice cracked, and Hunter couldn't wait to continue this adventure of her ass with his cock at a future date.

His free hand slipped into her hair and pulled at the scalp until she was forced to release the bed posts, and her back came flush to his chest. "How does that feel, Witch?"

"Amazi…" she huffed. "So goo…Hun…I'm gonna c…"

Hunter growled into her ear as he hooked his finger in her ass and she came around his cock again. He bit down on her shoulder to keep himself from coming as both his finger and his cock continued to fuck her.

He lapped at her and enjoyed the view of her breasts peaked and heaving. "Fuck, love, those girls are going to get so much fucking bigger. You'll have to make me come extra hard to cover them."

She cried out again as Hunter let her fall back to the bed, her cunt pulsing around him with another orgasm he wasn't sure she was even aware was coming, and he finally allowed his own to follow her. He buried deep inside her and let his every drop fill her, his finger never stopping its attention to her ass.

When he finally slipped completely out of her, Maya whimpered with the loss of contact, but Hunter hovered over her raised ass and delighted in the sight of his handprints on each cheek and his cum slipping down her thighs.

19

Harry had the Book open where he stood in front of the podium in the attic. It'd been a while since he'd gotten the tomb to himself in this room, but he wasn't exactly expecting to find anything new.

At least, not on his own.

The Book would have to lead him to a page he hadn't previously come by, like it had for Camilla, for this to even be a worthwhile approach.

But Harry quite literally had nothing to lose and everything to gain by trying. After Hunter's near death, Harry wanted to do more for his family. He wanted to learn something that would protect them and rid them of Jenkins, that could possibly help in the future with Maya's portal control. Because being thrown down to a depth of Hell's Gate even they hadn't been to before had been terrifying. In all the years Harry had been alive, he'd never lived through something as skin-crawlingly chilling as those minutes down below had been.

Or as powerful as Maya's magic as she took them down there, allowed for magic to be used so he and the other warlocks could heal Hunter, then returned them all back up top.

It was a frightening power, but Maya had joined the right

135

family for it. The Delvauxs would teach her how to wield such power and protect her if anything ever felt like it was too much.

Until then, Harry needed to find something in this tomb. He needed to do this for his family, but also to help distract himself. It had only been four days since Vera had gone 'missing' at the school gym, and Harry still hadn't been able to get her to talk to him.

When she got back from the school with her father, she'd showered and gone right to bed. She'd hardly even looked at him. The only thing Harry had been glad for was that she still allowed him to hold her as they slept.

Then she constantly put herself around her family so they didn't have the time alone to speak, keeping herself busy baking so they couldn't talk about this. What the bloody hell was going on in that beautiful head of hers?

Harry had been at his breaking point when Maya had come out frantic about her mate and they'd all ported to Delvaux Manor to find out Hunter had gone to Selin.

It was now the day after, and he felt Vera crawl out from his hold in bed that morning and leave silently. She hardly ever woke before him, and when she did, she *always* kissed him awake. Harry needed to know what was going on with her, but she was obviously hell bent on avoiding him, so there he stood.

Hopefully this book could give him something about the Jenkins predicament because his woman was doing quite the opposite.

"C'mon," he spoke to the Book. "Give me something."

"What would you like?"

Vera's soft voice made his head snap to the door of the attic.

Harry sucked in a breath at her beauty, but also at the fact that she had finally come to him again. He wanted to storm to her, take her beautiful face in his hands, and kiss the life out of her.

But instead, he gave a fake smile. "I'm hoping for any kind of help in the current Hunter situation."

Harry was looking down at the Book, so when Vera wrapped her arms around his waist from behind and laid her cheek to rest on his back, he was pleasantly surprised.

Then she said, "At least he took care of Selin, so we don't have to worry about that anymore."

"Yes," Harry sighed. "But I would like to be of more help to them. This is our family, and I need to aid in protecting them." *I need to know what's going on in that head of yours.*

The nods of her head against his back sent shivers down his spine. "I know what you mean." She pulled away and stopped beside him. "You're trying to speak to the Book the way Camilla had?"

"It's not working, but I have hope."

Vera said nothing else, so Harry moved her until she stood before him. She stared up into his eyes as he wrapped his hands around her hips and leaned in to kiss her temple. "Talk to me, sweetheart." *Please.*

She sighed, then met his gaze once more. "I...it's hard for me to accept...this love. I think I was so excited to finally have you and to finally feel love that the fear didn't really hit until now, until those covens. I knew people would judge our relationship, but I couldn't get out of my mind that maybe we'd be better off if we weren't..."

"Together?"

She swallowed and nodded slowly.

Harry brushed a curl behind her ear and held her jaw softly. "If you would like to end our relationship, do so. Do not hide from me. But whether you do so or not, I am yours. I will be dying alongside you, whether that means you have another male at your side or not. I will be at your beck and call, and I will suffer through anything—even watching you love anyone else— if that is what would make you happy."

The thought made him sick, but Harry knew he would do it. If she wanted another, he would let her go and watch from the sidelines.

Tears lined her eyes until one finally fell. She clutched at his shirt as she said, "I don't want anyone else, Harry. I could never. I love you, and I know I could never feel this for anyone else. That's what I've been thinking about, testing, for the past few days. I've thought about actually letting you go. Would that truly be better for us, past what our hearts say? I've kept my distance to see how it felt." She reached for his face and held him close. "It felt wrong, Harry. So wrong I couldn't even fully complete it and sleep away from you. I cannot live this life without you, and maybe mating isn't a thing with us, but you're my mate, Harry. I thought Maya was able to more easily handle the hate because Hunter was her mate, but it's just that she's that in love with him. The way I am with you. I can't, won't, leave you, Harry."

Tears now lined Harry's hazel eyes too, but none fell as he leaned down to kiss her tenderly. "I love you, Vera. And the next time you feel insecure, you come to me, okay?"

She nodded. "It'll happen again. It'll take some time for me to get used to the stares and judges."

He kissed her forehead. "I know, sweetheart. Just use me as your anchor. Don't run from me."

"Deal." She kissed his chin.

They stood like that for long minutes before Vera turned in his arms to look at the Book, and his arms wrapped around her waist to hold her to his chest. "I keep trying with the Book too. Maybe that's why we're together. We both keep trying and trying and keep getting the same results. Isn't there a word for that?"

Her eyes twinkled as she looked up at him over her shoulder, and Harry kissed her softly. "As long as we're insane together, I have no problem with it."

"C'mon, Book," Vera tried this time, "give us anything."

The Book sat at the random page Harry had it opened to and didn't move. Harry huffed and tried himself, creating a pattern where he would ask, then Vera, then him again.

They were ten minutes into their game when Vera sighed

and fell back into his chest, her fingers intertwining with the hands he had around her waist. He held her close and kissed the side of her neck. He couldn't get enough of her, especially after the fear of possibly losing her.

Harry nibbled at her neck when she brought their intertwined hands to her lips for soft kisses. "I love you, Vera."

She met his gaze from over her shoulder. "I love you too, Harry."

Harry didn't want to break his gaze, but finally, they turned back to the Book, and together, without planning to, begged, "Give us anything, Book."

Harry held his breath as the Book's pages suddenly began moving before them. Camilla had told them all about what it was like when she spoke to the Book, but it felt surreal to experience it listening.

It flipped and flipped, paused at a page, and before they could look at it, began flipping backwards.

Then, finally, the Book stopped at a set of pages with small potions on them. Each one looked to do something a little different, but put together looked like something to hold off a variety of animal demons. Harry didn't know why this was the page the Book gave them, but he wouldn't question it.

Harry didn't want to look away lest the pages disappear, but he peeled his gaze to meet Vera's equally astonished one.

They both smiled to one another, then turned back to the Book, looking over the potions and ingredients that would be needed. They'd need to go shopping for some of it, but at least they had somewhere to start, no matter that he didn't understand why they would need such potions. It looked ridiculously complicated, and it wasn't like they didn't already have a ton of potions against animal demons. But again, this was a gift from the Book, and Harry would follow it.

Vera turned in his arms, and her arms reached up to wrap around his neck as she stared up at him. She smiled, warm and content, as her fingers played with the hairs at the nape of his neck.

Her deep brown eyes, so perfectly unlike anything in the world, shined, and he knew she was thinking the same thing as him—finally, they could do something.

"We're going to end this with our family. Then, sweetheart, I'm going to take you to see the world. You'll play on the nicest pianos in all the world."

"Let's start with France. And not Paris, either. I want to go to those villages around the country."

"Anything, sweetheart. I'll introduce you to every square foot of this world."

She rose to her tip toes so they were more eye-to-eye and beamed. "Well, now I want to finish this sooner so I get you and this world all to myself for a few months."

"Only a few months?"

"Well, we have to be here for the babies' births."

Harry pecked her softly. "I'll take you somewhere every weekday and be here for the babies during the weekends."

She laughed. "Deal."

"Mm," he murmured against her lips. "But first I'll have to make an honest woman out of you."

She growled in such an endearing way, it was difficult not to ravage her immediately as she said, "I'll kill Jenkins with my bare hands tonight to make that happen sooner."

Harry's heart stuttered as he kissed her.

20

Hunter shadowed into the living room of his manor with his brother and father in tow. Maya had insisted he finally show them where his manor was, and given this was now their manor, he would do as his mate asked.

Now more than ever, Hunter trusted the two men would keep it private. That they would not use his place of residence as a spot for when things went south and they wanted revenge.

Because Maya would be there.

Because their children would be there.

And if there was one thing Hunter had become aware of in the last few weeks, it was how fondly both his father and brother viewed his mate. From Warren it was expected because of his human half, but Augustine's affection towards Maya had been a shock. Especially knowing it wasn't all for the power Maya would bring to their family. There was true affection there.

Maya was lounged back on the dark couch with her feet propped on the coffee table and her shirt raised to showcase her stomach. Her index drew soft shapes around her navel, and she whispered so low Hunter couldn't hear what she was saying to their children.

But he enjoyed the view.

So much so, he wanted to send Warren and Augustine away so they could have this moment to themselves.

Warren threw his arm around Hunter's shoulders and teased his easy grin. "I think the big, bad demon is getting a heart."

Maya's head snapped up, and her warm smile grew as she saw the three of them standing at the end of the room. "Hey."

Hunter pushed Warren's arm off and moved for his mate's side, dropping to give her a kiss. His hand landed on her stomach as he asked, "How's my wife?" He knew how much she enjoyed that term.

Her hand landed over his, and for a few seconds, they were a family. Just him, his wife, and their children in her stomach.

"Much better now that you're here."

Hunter leaned in for another kiss as Warren dropped to the spot on Maya's other side. Hunter grumbled as his brother's hand landed over the ones he and Maya had on her stomach. "Get your hands off my mate, Brother."

"Aw." Maya laughed as she cupped Warren's cheek. "Be nice to Uncle Warren."

Warren's brows furrowed as his eyes shined. "Yeah, be nice to Uncle Warren." He pouted to get extra points from Maya. "I only want to say hi to my little nieces or nephews."

Hunter pulled Maya's shirt down as she sat up and pulled her into his side. "Fuck off."

Warren laughed as he pulled the book he'd placed on the table and handed it to Maya. "I also wanted to give my sister this storybook. You were wondering about Adramalech and Miradora. I found a children's storybook for it. I'm sure there're others, but that's the one I have."

Maya's smile was enchanting as she leaned over and gave Warren a kiss on the cheek. "Thank you."

Hunter growled and pulled Maya onto his lap. "Keep it up and I'll send him away and clear his memory of this manor, Witch."

Maya's laugh was exhilarating as she turned in his lap and softly caressed his cheek. "Don't be mean, baby."

When he didn't back down, she leaned in for a kiss. It moved from the innocent light kisses they normally shared in the presence of their families to a heated clashing of tongues. And Hunter forgot all about the company they had.

Until a throat cleared from the opposite couch and Augustine said, "We *are* still here, you know."

"Then leave," Hunter growled as his mouth searched again for hers.

Maya laughed against his lips and pulled away. "Sorry. This emotional thing also has me super horny."

Hunter kissed the back of her neck as both his brother and father scoffed and Warren said, "Please. You've been this horny for him since the beginning."

Maya winked at him as Hunter sat back on the couch and pulled Maya closer as she opened the new storybook. She flipped through the pages. "Whoa." She threw a quirked brow at Warren. "I thought you said this was a children's book?"

"It is," Warren argued, a furrow entering his brows. "Why?"

"Warren, there's full on sex in these drawings." She turned the book around so they could see the girl on top, leaning back so her breasts were in full view and the spot the two connected plainly visible.

Hunter laughed and pulled her in. "It's a demon's children's book, love. We're not shy about what happens between a man and a woman."

The man's thumb was even on the woman's clit. Demons weren't just not shy about these topics, they made sure to teach them young too.

Maya turned dark eyes on Hunter. "We're not showing our kids this stuff."

"They're educational," Hunter argued.

Her brows narrowed. "Hunter."

He laughed and took her face between his hands. "Anything you say, love."

Hunter leaned in for another soft kiss as Warren made the sound of a whip. Hunter didn't have time to react before Maya turned on their brother and smacked him with the book. "Behave, Little Brother," she teased.

Hunter laughed as he caressed her hair. "You make me a proud mate, Maya."

There was a shine in her eyes as she turned to look at him that made Hunter's heart settle. These small moments when she showed how proud she was to be his affected him more than any other part of their relationship.

"Anyway," Warren interrupted, garnering Maya's attention. "The story basically reads of a demon from the underworld—what humans know as Hell now—mated to a witch on Earth, and it was that connection that brought them together. It was that connection that made Miradora do whatever she needed—along with coming up with the power to open the portal to Hell's Gate—in order to be with her mate, even when said mate was causing havoc on Earth. It's basically what Selin had said. The only part not explicitly in the story is how Miradora acquired the powers."

"What does the book say?" Maya asked as she flipped the pages.

Hunter knew she'd read it herself later, as he would, but this condensed version helped to begin to think about their situation.

"It says she persuaded the others to give up some power in order to help her get back to her mate," Warren answered.

"Demons may not fully understand love, but we do matings," Augustine added. "This is a demon's storybook, so it speaks of the mating more than the love, but if a witch's version exists, I'm sure the mating and love would both be there, but the love would take precedent."

"Okay. Now the big money question—what does this have to do with my family?" Maya asked.

Augustine watched her closely. "From what I understand of Bishop's past, darling, before mixing with the African tribe, your ancestors came from Greece."

"And all stories, all myths, everything, comes from something real," Warren finished.

Hunter knew something about the story had sounded familiar, and as he caught his mate's gaze, he knew she'd picked it up too.

She watched him for long moments as she visibly tried to compartmentalize her thoughts in the most adorable way Hunter had ever seen. Then Maya turned back to Warren. "You think Adramalech and Miradora are the inspiration to Hades and Persephone?"

Warren shrugged. "A lot's different considering Adramalech was stuck in prison and needed Miradora to free him. And the fact that Miradora's mother wasn't involved, and she didn't need to split her time, but I think Hades and Persephone would've been the witch's story. Make Hades the demon who stole the good witch away and used dark magic to make her fall in love with him, make her stay with him. Plenty of dark magic includes eating things."

Hunter understood where his family was going with this and kissed his mate's shoulder as he thought over the consequences of such events.

Maya then turned to Augustine. "And what does this have to do with Jenkins? Does it have anything?"

Augustine watched her for a moment, then his gaze snapped to Hunter and remained there. Hunter read in his father's eyes that they were on the same page.

So, he answered his mate, "It's a fact I never doubted, that what Selin said was the truth. And considering so, then I do not doubt that she would've told Jenkins everything in the crux of their deal.

If Jenkins knows that this is your ancestry, he'll wonder if something about me is also similar to Adramalech. If he had my body and all the stolen powers he'd like to add to it, he'll have a powerful being on Earth. But if I am somehow like Adramalech—or Hades —then he would also have control of Hell—the underworld."

Maya just breathed as she stared at him before she finally muttered, "Are you fucking kidding me?"

***

Maya had wanted nothing more than to hot glue herself to Hunter after finding out that Jenkins may have yet another reason to want her husband. At least that way, he'd keep himself out of harm's way in order to keep her safe.

But since she couldn't reasonably do that, Maya resorted to snuggling in closer to him when he tried to get out of bed in the morning.

Then, when even she wanted to get up, she argued that breathing in his scent quelled her stomach of the morning sickness. Maya learned quickly that Hunter always tried to ease any of her pregnancy symptoms, so it was a little white lie she didn't mind telling, especially considering it was sort of true. His scent always eased her. It wasn't her fault she hadn't been hit with morning sickness as badly as most. Or at all, really.

He knew her lies though. Knew her inside and out. But he let her run with them.

So when he decided to shadow them to the trail she used to run when she lived in Whittle House, Maya was confused.

"What're we doing here?"

His hand settled at the small of her back. "You need fresh air if the sickness is still bothering you. We can walk to your parents' house."

Maya bit down on her bottom lip, taking in her mate's stare that told her he knew she was fibbing. But she couldn't admit to it. "You're right. Fresh air has always been my friend."

Hunter kissed her temple as he led her down the path, his fingers at her back distracting her from their problems. She loved when it was just them in their little bubble. It was moments like these that Maya wanted to take Hunter up on his offer to lock the two of them in their manor and let the world figure out Jenkins on their own.

She smiled to herself, ready to turn and ask him for a quickie in the forest—because she hadn't been lying to Warren and she genuinely always felt horny now—when she noticed a spark flying towards them from the left. It was a light dusting of sparkles and flowed gently through the air in no particular direction.

She didn't know how, but Maya knew it was magically related.

And the only times she'd dealt with magic in these trails was when animal demons—the nasty monsters humans thought of when they heard the word demon—were after her sisters for their powers at the beginning of finding out about being witches, and when Colette, her sister-in-law, had sent a child after her.

It was in the moments that the sparks grazed the air around them and shimmered, but boomeranged in a different direction, that Maya realized Hunter was holding a shield around them.

He had her pushed behind him, his hand on her stomach, as his gaze darkened and a growl left him.

She loved when he did that—protected their children. He'd started doing it when he'd found out she was pregnant—even though she'd still been clueless—and it made her love him more every time he did it.

"Hunt?" She knew he'd know what her question would be about even though she definitely should be more focused on whether there was a threat in the forest with them.

He merely shrugged but didn't meet her gaze as he searched the forest for the meaning behind the spark, leading them toward the direction it had come. "I have a family to protect."

His hand on her stomach hardened, and as Maya followed his line of sight, she knew why.

Standing ten yards before them was Jenkins over the body of a werewolf, blood dripping down his mouth like this was some vampire movie.

He looked up to them with a twinkle in his eyes as the sparks she knew Hunter had sent his way fell off another shield. That's when Maya realized the witch whose eyes were glazed over standing behind him. The poor girl wasn't in control, and knowing her mate, he wouldn't care. She'd be collateral damage.

Maya didn't need a lifetime of being in the supernatural world to recognize the dark lines down the witch's arms—the same as those around Jenkins'—as dark magic.

She also knew that the Delvauxs had been feeding her antibodies to said magic and didn't need anything but the security in her relationship to know that Hunter had also been slipping those antibodies into the food of her family to make sure they remained immune as well.

But most witches didn't possess the antibodies. Because performing a smaller act of dark magic was required for the act, and witches were too *good* for that.

Jenkins' grin was disturbing as he said, "Come now, *Hunt-er*, do right by your witch. Give yourself up, and this one"—he nodded to the witch beside him—"will be released."

Maya growled at his use of Hunt's name. She now understood why Hunter didn't like it when some people used her name. "Fuck off."

Apparently she was okay with some collateral damage as well.

The witch's arms, wrapped in those black veins, lifted, and another spark filled the air, this one more controlled and electric.

Hunter's growl reverberated as the spark came for them and blasted off of Hunter's shield.

More sparks came at them in quick succession, and Maya

could visibly see the witch wearing down with the use of so much magic, but Jenkins' crazed gaze said he didn't care.

Jenkins' eyes glowed, which only made Hunter push Maya behind him by another inch. Not enough to hide behind him, but enough to show Jenkins that he'd be a dead man if he tried anything.

It was a fact Maya knew the man understood.

"Come now," Jenkins teased, giving the witch the barest of breaks as he addressed Maya. "You're the witch. Would you truly allow your fellow to die?"

"I'd burn her and every other person on this planet for my mate." Maya didn't tell the man anything he didn't already know.

"Yes, yes, I've heard mates were like that."

The witch wilted against the bark of a tree as more sparks moved for them, Hunter's power too strong to allow even a slightest of breaks through their shield.

Finally, Jenkins gave the witch a break so that the attention was on him as he spoke. His eyes shined happily. "You killed my companion, *Hunt-er*."

Maya ground her jaw, wanting to rip the man limb from limb for the way he said her mate's name. And she could tell through the rings how irritated Hunter was growing with not being able to get through Jenkins' own shield. Whatever black magic he had that witch under, it was strong enough to attack them and hold up that shield.

"Oh fuck off. You cared as much for Selin as we do you," Maya bit out to control her urge to run to him and rip his heart out, a fact she knew wouldn't be easy since Hunter had yet to do it.

"Maybe." Jenkins's grin grew. "But I cared for her faerie dust as much as you two care for one another."

Maya almost believed that, but didn't understand what…

Her gaze snapped up to Hunter. "Impossible."

Jenkins laughed out with glee. "He did kill her. And now I

see, eliminated the part I wasn't yet a hundred percent clear on —how to get the faerie dust to the body required."

The faerie dust hadn't been what kept Selin immortal—that was a magic even current demons didn't know of. But it had kept her vital, strong, powerful, old as she was. If this was true and Hunter truly had the faerie dust, Maya could finally breathe a small sigh of relief.

Though this made him even more desirable to Jenkins, it also made him stronger. And if she guessed correctly, would make his powers stronger too. She really hoped for that part.

There were flames on the grounds, lingering at the edge of an invisible shield that Hunter was no doubt still trying to break through. Maybe it was his way of distracting the psycho in front of them or maybe he was just curious, because while he tried to push his fire through, Hunter barked, "What are you doing with the wolf? Trying to make vampires real? Be one of them now?"

"How else do you expect this magic to give me such beautiful control of Elly here? Though I was hoping Maya dearest would come on this run alone."

Maya's stomach recoiled at the thought of him drinking a wolf's blood simply for the control of a witch. She wasn't sure if it was pure disgust or whether the disgust was mixing with her pregnancy because she felt two seconds from throwing up.

Jenkins gave them a final smile. "Well, I truly am glad we had this conversation." He turned to his witch and watched as she threw down one of those marbles the halfies used to use. "I will see you two later then."

The shield broke as they stepped through the portal, and Hunter's flames chased after them, and Maya was positive she heard the curse of Jenkins getting burned. It brought her great delight.

When an entire minute passed from his departure, Hunter finally turned to her and held her face softly in his hands. "Love."

"I'm all right, baby," she soothed him even though they both knew nothing had happened. "Is the shield still up?"

"Yes," he whispered.

"Is it always up?"

"Whenever we're not at the manor. Or our parents' houses."

"Since when?" She felt like she should be mad, but she wasn't. She understood.

She also knew he was never going to let her off alone so long as Jenkins was still around.

"Since I thought I lost you in that warehouse." He closed his eyes to breathe her in before opening them again. "Are you not angry?"

She shook her head. "I told you before, Hunt. I love you. And I love how much you love our family. I would never fault you for protecting us."

She kissed him tenderly, and now her heart ached to simply hold him. She wanted more than anything to shadow back to the manor and cuddle into him all day.

His smirk was teasing when they broke away. "I'm so-so on the kids. But you, Maya, you're my everything."

She laughed into another kiss. "Asshole."

## 21

"Stop following me, Kai," Camilla ground out as she stomped through the wet grass of these beautiful Scottish hills he'd brought her to. Albeit she needed him to port her back home, she'd asked to be left alone for an hour or two.

One moment he was behind her, and the next, she felt him press against her side as he smirked. "There's a lunatic after your sister's family. Don't you think getting to you would be an easy way to her? I'm protecting you, princess."

He knew she hated when anyone referenced Kai as her protector. Just because she had non-active powers didn't make her useless and defenseless.

When she threw a dirty look his way while continuing to stomp away, she grew more frustrated by how pleased he looked. "Jenkins isn't going to find me in the middle-of-nowhere Scotland, Kai."

"I love when you say my name, princess. It makes me hard and gives me the perfect sound to remember while I touch my coc—"

"Kai!" She turned on him. "Go. Away!"

His smirk grew. "No, princess."

She huffed and turned to continue on her trek.

"So why are we here, princess?" When she ignored him, he only continued, seemingly unfazed by how much she didn't want him there. "Is this to visit Nico? Because we're in the wrong part of the country. You know, Nico would've loved you for not taking my shit, and he would've flirted with you only because he'd know how much it would piss me off. Especially because he was a better man than me, and you would've liked him. But you wouldn't have touched him. You would've flirted because you like torturing me like that, but we both know you only get wet for me anymore, the same way my cock is leaking for you every time I'm around—"

"KAI!"

He chuckled. "Mm, is that how you scream my name when you come touching yourself thinking of me? Fuck, princess, you're really going to get me hard like this and ignore me?"

She turned on him. "What is your problem!"

He smirked, pleased at getting a reaction, but his eyes were clouded with darkness. Camilla's eyes widened at seeing it as she realized he probably hadn't been jok—

Her gaze dipped down to his trousers, and her eyes widened again at seeing the dent there. He was hard.

And from the looks of things, large.

She didn't realize she was staring, or that her breathing had changed and her tongue had dipped out to lick her lips, until he growled. "Don't look at me like that, princess. I'll fuck you right here, right now." When she snapped her head up to meet his gaze for a moment before looking away with a blush on her cheeks, he took her by the back of the neck and forced her to look at him. "Do you want that, Camilla? You want my cock in that perfect little pussy right now?"

"Kai," she breathed, their lips so close it would take nothing to be kissing him as her fingers dug into the shirt at his chest. "Stop it. Sto—"

He dipped his head into the crook of her neck and breathed in her scent. "You're wet for me, aren't you, princess?"

She was soaking to depths she'd be mortified would stain her jeans if she weren't wearing a long coat that covered, but she would never tell him that. "Never," she forced out.

He nipped at her neck, and she dug her fingers into his shirt and had to force the moan not to come out. "Kai…" She was breathing too hard to form words.

He pulled back to look into her eyes, which she had no doubt showed the same desire his did. "You're my own brand of torture, Camilla. But rest assured," his hands dipped to her hips and held her so tight it hurt, "this pussy is mine, and I will play with and please it for the rest of my life." Before she could form words, he moved one hand to one of hers still clutched at his shirt and detangled her fingers before dipping her hand down. When her hand touched the stiffness between his legs, her eyes widened, but he didn't let her pull away. "And this cock, princess, it's all yours. You can touch it, lick it, fuck it." He squeezed her fingers around the dent in his trousers and moaned as he stared at her. "This cock only gets hard for you, princess, and it's going to please you for the rest of your life."

"Kai…" She didn't want to let go, but if she got any more wet, it'd slip down her jeans, and he'd surely see that.

"Fight us all you want, princess, but we're inevitable."

She was breathing hard as she finally got a coherent sentence out. "I just want to sit by the cliffs and think about the beauty."

His gaze was still hard on her, but he wasn't teasing any longer. "I'm not leaving you."

She swallowed. "Then just stop talking."

He moved his hand to hers still clutched at his shirt and brought that palm up to kiss as his other hand squeezed hers around his cock. It made her want nothing more than to drop to her knees at that very moment. "Deal, princess."

That incessant need Maya had been having to be glued to his side when she found out Jenkins may want him even more for his possible similarity to Adramalech, Hunter now understood. After running into the maniac on Maya's trail, Hunter could hardly focus. He needed to keep her safe. It was eating away at his sanity that she could've gone on that run alone like she always had before.

Thankfully, Maya didn't argue with him every time he pressed her body closer to him and kissed any inch of her skin. She didn't complain about the shield he constantly had up or his ridiculous need to reach for her stomach to check on the babies, as if he would be able to feel them this early on. She didn't roll her eyes or huff in frustration at any bit of clinginess Hunter might've been showing, and for the billionth time, Hunter was thankful for his mate in particular.

Now, as they moved for the door to Zathrian's shop's cottage, Hunter held onto the belt loops of Maya's jeans as he followed her in. As Adramalech the bird cawed to let the two behind the counter currently sucking at each other's faces know they had visitors, Hunter leaned into his mate. It was obvious Zathrian, being the demon he was, didn't care that he had visitors and wanted nothing more than to continue kissing his mate. If it hadn't been for Acacia, Hunter would have to send a flying ball of flames at the man to get him to break.

Acacia smiled wide as she turned to see them, her belly so much bigger than the last time. "Maya! Hunter! Hi!"

Maya smirked. "Pregnancy hormones have you extra horny?"

Acacia blushed but nodded anyway.

"Me too."

Both Zathrian and Acacia's heads snapped toward them as the female said, "What?"

Maya leaned back into Hunter's chest, her smile cheeky as she responded, "I thought I was horny before, but I swear this pregnancy is making it tenfold. Either that or I really am obsessed with my mate."

Acacia shrieked. "You're pregnant!"

"Twins," Maya giggled and pulled away from Hunter as Acacia ran for an embrace.

Hunter could die a happy man watching that smile on his mate's face as she spoke to the other witch about her pregnancy, and just finding out, and how her ass of a mate had known this entire time.

Then Zathrian was at his side. "Jealous my mate was pregnant and yours wasn't? You had to one up me?"

Hunter turned his gaze on the demon and winked.

They both laughed as Zathrian brought him in for a bear hug. "Congratulations, friend."

"Thank you." Hunter pulled away and glanced at the girls before turning back to his friend. "I've never been jealous of you, Zath, you know that. But right now, I'm jealous your mate is safe."

Zathrian's eyes hardened. "We'll figure this out, Hunt."

"I know."

Zathrian's gaze narrowed on Hunter's pinched lips. "Did something happen?"

"Jenkins was waiting for Maya on her running trail she normally goes on alone this morning. I was lucky to be there with her this time."

Zathrian stood up straighter, dark eyes harder, as he moved to pull his mate from Hunter's. "You two can celebrate when there isn't a danger lurking over the Delvauxs head." He pulled his mate with him to the workstation, and it was obvious she was only there to keep him calm. "I've been working on the daggers. I have these two perfected and another two in the middle of the process. I'll get started on more tonight."

"Great," Maya started as Hunter took his spot at her back again, his hands settling over her tiny bump. "We'll give those to my sisters."

Hunter stiffened, ready to argue when Maya's hand settled over his and she tipped her head back to look at him. "I can shadow away, Hunt. They can't. I need to know they'll be protected from any dark magic coming at them."

Hunter ground his jaw, but he knew this wouldn't be an argument he would win. She was already being lenient on his clinginess and his constant shield. He knew he couldn't push his luck. Plus, considering he insisted on always being at her side—or having his brother or father there—he didn't necessarily need to worry about her getting out of the way fast enough since they would do it for her. He would never trust her to shadow away without her sisters, but his family would do it for her, even if it led to a fight.

"Fine," he huffed out as he leaned into her hair and let his lips settle there.

One glance in Zathrian's direction showed a glint in his eyes. "What?"

Zathrian's smirk came up now. "It's just amusing, you see. The great Hunter Delvaux being told what to do by a newbie witch."

Hunter scowled at the man. "You get told what to do by your witch all the time, Zath."

Zathrian glanced over to his mate. "Yes, and you used to tease me for it incessantly. Retribution is quite the bitch, Brother."

Hunter rolled his eyes. "Whatever, Zath. Just help keep my family safe, and you can tease me all you'd like."

Zathrian's teasing nature vanished with those words, and a lightness entered his eyes as he gave Hunter a small, genuine grin. "I'd never tease you for protecting your family, Hunt." He placed his hand over Acacia's stomach. "I'd do anything for mine as well."

Maya tipped her head back to look into Hunter's eyes as the other couple had their own private moment, and smiled. "I love you, Hunt."

Hunter leaned down so their lips brushed together. "You're my world, Maya."

"You mean we're your world."

He smirked against those delicious, soft lips. "Didn't I tell you before? I'm so-so on the kids, but you're my everything."

She laughed against his lips. "I hate you."

"Good, love." He kissed her tenderly. "Good."

## 22

*V*era had the prickling feeling that she was being watched.

Not in the way of intrigue or fascination. Or in lust or envy. Not in the way people watched beautiful things. Nothing that made her feel even remotely comfortable or desired.

She felt the stares on her like she was being judged. Like everyone around them was ridiculing her. Like everyone was laughing at her.

She'd known her relationship with Harry would bring some problems, but up until meeting with those other covens, she hadn't really felt it. But now, as she and Harry moved through the supernatural market to load up on some ingredients, she felt the judgement spiral like a snowball, getting bigger now that it had started. The covens' stares were a lot, but that had only been a few people. In this market, Vera felt the stares all around her, though she had no idea how anyone knew Harry was her family's warlock.

She knew Harry could tell she was becoming uncomfortable by the way he tightened his hold on her hand and ran his thumb along the top of it. It probably frightened Harry now too to be judged because he knew how sensitive Vera was to the matter.

159

Vera hated herself for putting any of that on her warlock, but he didn't show it as he kept her close to his side, and as they walked through the market, brought their conjoined hands up for a kiss.

Though she still felt weird having all those eyes on her, that kiss sent a tingling feeling through her, and she swore she felt herself levitate a few centimeters off the ground.

They were restocking herbs, but also specifically trying to find a way to help her sister and her family—though it was still weird to think of Maya as having her own family. She'd only recently become Vera's family.

But they needed to protect them. Especially now that Maya was carrying two of her nieces or nephews.

And since they'd had that run-in with Jenkins on Maya's usual running trail and found not only him waiting to capture Maya in order to get Hunter to give himself up, but the types of black magic Jenkins had fallen into, this was a more adamant search than before. The man was long gone, and they needed to figure out a way to end him for good.

Harry already had a woven bag filled with vials of all sorts, herbs and oils and mini hearts galore, but they needed a couple more things before heading home. Especially if they wanted to create those potions from the Book to ward away animal demons. Vera still wasn't sure why the Book had shown them those pages in particular, but she didn't question it. She trusted that the potions would come in handy.

Harry stopped them at an old wooden table and spoke in that English accent that still sent shivers down Vera's spine. "Two sharks' tongues, laced by an ore's saliva."

Vera couldn't imagine ever doing this on her own. Some of these ingredients were just…ugh.

The salesman's gaze snapped between the two of them as he slowly moved for a large, oddly shaped vial to hold the purchases. Vera noticed the way the guy turned to look at his friends, the way he quirked his brow to the people behind them, the way he judged her for standing there. The way he eyed her hand in Harry's.

Vera instinctively pulled her hand free and brought it together with her free one as her fingers began to fidget together. She had no idea how Maya took this judgement *all of the time* from *everyone*. Because it was mostly other witches that judged relationships like Vera's, but *everyone* judged relationships like Maya's. *She* had judged Maya.

She still hated herself for that, for putting her sister through even a fraction of this feeling.

Harry turned a worried gaze on her, then his hazel eyes moved to the salesman slowly wrapping up the first tongue and preparing for the second. Harry's gaze met hers again before he dropped the bag he was holding and pulled her by the hand until they were completely away from prying eyes.

He had her pulled into an alcove so small, they genuinely had to be pressed together to both fit, then slowly took her face in his hands and dropped his forehead to hers. "Are you all right, sweetheart?"

She nodded without thinking. "Fine."

"Vera," he said slowly. "Don't lie to me."

She swallowed and met those beautiful hazel eyes. "How do they know you're my family warlock? What gives away that you're my family's warlock? Those other covens, I understand, but these people are strangers. We could be from any coven!"

He breathed out slowly, and his eyes closed like he was preparing the answer.

Vera's heart jumped. "That bad?"

An airy chuckle left him as his eyes opened and met hers. "No, sweetheart, not so bad."

He kissed her softly and almost distracted Vera from wanting to know the answer.

But before she could pull away and ask again, he did. "Everyone knows of your family, love. It was a coven most only knew by name because of the power within it and their interference with demons, meaning no other coven had to deal with the species, but recently, it's been more than that. With Maya allowing her relationship with Hunter to be so public, word got around. But now that everyone knows they're mates—and since warlocks have always known of demon matings—it's less shocking than other species but still insane. But they're also now really starting to believe the demon mating thing. It was difficult to do so before when they've never personally seen evidence to it, but now? It's really brought attention to your family." He kissed her nose softly. "Not to mention both your parents coming back from the dead. All the covens have paid attention, and they know that the Whittle family warlock fell in love with his charge."

Vera held his gaze. "Do they know that his charge fell in love first?"

Another chuckle that sent shivers down to very inappropriate areas. "Impossible."

He kissed her, and every stare from the market left Vera's mind because this was the most important thing in her life —Harry.

And his lips on hers.

When he finally pulled away and rested his forehead on hers, he whispered, "It's also gotten around that I have stopped my immortality. That's taken very seriously. They're both judging us our relationship, Vera, but also fascinated. Because I've fallen so deeply for you that I *need* to grow old with you. Die with you. It's something even I didn't understand. Something I was fascinated with when your father, when Rupert, any warlock went and stopped his immortality. But it's even more intriguing to them because I'm your family's warlock. It's forbidden. Taboo."

Vera's heart beat unsteadily. "I don't think I'll ever tire of hearing you say those words."

"I'll never tire of saying them, sweetheart."

This time, she kissed him. Filled it with the passion she felt for him, for the need to get him home and rip his clothes off.

She'd also never grow tired of this feeling she hoped never wore off.

"We need to leave. Now," she whispered breathlessly against his lips.

He brought her in for a deeper kiss, and with their bodies flush together, Vera felt how very affected he was by this kiss. "Tongues should be wrapped by now. We're porting to our bed right after."

Vera laughed against his lips. "Or you could port us somewhere else. Maybe an unused room at the university…*Professor*."

Harry growled low as his eyes turned from that beautiful hazel color to a deep black. He held her forearm roughly as he led them back to the stand with their ingredients and grumbled to the man who watched them with more intrigue now as he paid, and ported them out.

Vera laughed when they landed in a room that was very much in use, considering the door was open and it looked like a professor was headed for it.

Harry shut the door and cast a spell before it, so they wouldn't be allowed in and silenced the room.

Then his gaze landed on her, sharp and ready to play. "Ready to please me, Ms. Whittle?"

Vera fell over the desk and spread her legs. "Yes, Professor."

---

Augustine did a good job holding his head high, but Maya could tell he was nervous. It brought her a little too much joy being the one to make him so.

She could tell Hunter and Warren also enjoyed their father's discomfort with being the target to her practicing her powers.

But they were all in agreement that she needed to test these powers, and Augustine was almost certain that if Maya could imagine Hunter in enough danger, her instincts would cause her to attack.

She wasn't as sure but wanted to believe she could conjure the power on her own. Needed to know if there was a way for that power to show itself without the need of a life-or-death situation.

"Are you ready, love?" Hunter brushed his hand down her hair and stopped to massage her neck.

Maya nodded as she tried to fight how nervous she felt. "As I can be with this stupid power."

"That sexy power," Hunter corrected her as he kissed her temple, then moved to stand at Warren's side.

Maya took a deep breath and turned her attention onto her new father, meeting the dark eyes of the man who had been nothing but perfect to her. This would be a lot harder than any of them imagined because though Warren and Hunter had some bitter feelings toward their father, Maya didn't. Not even a little bit.

She let her imagination take route, almost like when she was freestyling her drawings when she didn't have client work.

An image of Augustine holding Hunter down and beating on him. The blood splattering as it flew from Hunter's mouth. Augustine's joyous laughs as Hunter's skin turned from the beautiful caramel to black and blue.

The thought made her sick, and her blood boiled, but nothing more happened.

She tried again with an image of Hunter with his hands tied behind his back and on his knees as Augustine stabbed him through the chest. Over and over and over again.

Again, more blood splattered, and again, Maya could hear Augustine's laughs. But again, nothing more than her blood boiling over, the flames begging to come out.

She took another deep breath and tried to conjure up the portal like when she needed to control her fire or darkness, but to no avail. Not that she hadn't tried a million times before.

This time, she imagined Augustine hurting her. Hurting their children. All while Hunter was tied back and unable to get out, get to them, protect them. Imagined Hunter's cries, his voice breaking as he screamed for them, his limbs hissing with the pain of pulling on his restraints. His plea to end his own life to protect them.

All throughout, Augustine laughed and laughed.

The room dipped into darkness, and her flames lined her arms, but again, nothing more took place.

Through the few tears that had fallen without her knowledge, Maya huffed, "This isn't working."

Hunter moved to her immediately, wiping at the tears that lined her cheeks and kissing her softly. Maya held onto his wrists and pulled herself up for a deeper, longer kiss.

When she finally pulled away from him, she saw the anguish in his eyes at causing her any of this hurt before she turned to Augustine and Warren, who were both watching them closely.

Augustine kept his gaze on her a few moments longer, then breathed like he was afraid to suggest the next bit. "It's because it's all an imagination. Your instincts know it's not real."

"Well then how am I supposed to practice?" Maya let out an annoyed breath.

Augustine swallowed as his gaze jumped from Maya to Hunter and back again before he looked to settle on his plan. "We'll need to make it real."

"What?" Warren asked before Maya could.

"Hunter needs to be near death himself. The hope was to see if you could conjure the portal without life-or-death, but that may not be possible. So, life-or-death it is. We need to see if you have any sort of control. And if I'm to be the target, I'll be the one to do it," Augustine finished.

"Are you insane?" Maya and Warren exclaimed at the same time.

"That's not going to work anyway. I'll know that you're not actually going to hurt him," Maya argued, her heart speeding up at any thought of Hunter getting hurt.

"Except I will," Augustine said with finality. "I don't necessarily need him. I have another heir. And you'll be bringing me two more."

Maya turned incredulous eyes on Hunter, which widened when she saw him considering it. "Are *you* insane? I'm not letting this happen."

"Love," he said softly as he took her face in his hand once more. "We need to test your power. If you can open the portal and control it, we'll be making progress. If he gets sent down and you can bring him back up, we'll have even more control."

"And if you can't," Augustine interrupted, "your family still holds the key. You can simply bring me out with it."

Maya didn't turn from Hunter's gaze as her head shook softly. "No, Hunt. No, no, n—"

His forehead fell to hers. "You'll protect me, my wife."

Her head still shook, but she knew this would be happening. Somehow, she found the strength to mutter out, "I hate you."

His lips quirked up. "Good."

He kissed her softly, then moved toward his father as he said to Warren, "Throw a shield up and hold it. Keep yourself on our side so she can't stop you either."

Of course Hunter would know that Maya would try to darken the room, burn her way through, before the portal power would make itself known.

Augustine watched as Hunter pulled chains down from the ceiling. "I'm going to instinctively fight back. We need to make sure I can't."

The chains ended with the power repellent cuffs, and as Warren and Augustine tied Hunter's arms up, Maya was brought back to finding Hunter chained up when he'd been caught by Selin the first time.

She already felt sick with what was about to happen, and she knew a large part of that wasn't because of the pregnancy. "Do we really want to do this? This much stress can't be good for the babies."

"Love," Hunter called to her from his spot chained up. "We

need to make sure you're safe. The babies will be fine. We'll have every concoction made to be sure of it."

She knew that. Knew that if there was any real danger to the babies, Hunter wouldn't risk this. Even if it was to keep her safe. Because his decisions weren't just made to keep her safe any longer, they were made to keep their family safe.

Maya watched as Warren walked away from his brother and back toward his original position.

He faced Maya. "Ready?"

Maya's gaze snapped to Hunter before she closed her eyes and breathed evenly as she nodded.

When she opened her eyes again, there was a shield before her, separating her from the three men. But where Warren stood off to the side, Augustine stood beside Hunter and let a blade slip down his hand.

Augustine wouldn't be able to use his power since it was only a variation of a heat power, and since Hunter had a fire power, he essentially was the heat power.

There were his other powers, like his ability to make it feel like something was crawling on the skin, and his stolen powers, like freezing bodies in order to snap limbs around without a fight.

But none of those would be useful against what they needed from Maya. They needed a visual representation of Hunter getting hurt in order for Maya to know it wasn't faked and her instincts to call on the portal.

Augustine didn't start slow. In a matter of a second, he whipped around and jabbed the knife through his son's chest. And after what Maya had witnessed with Selin, she was ready to throw up as Augustine pulled the knife out and went for another in a matter of seconds.

"Stop!" The plead tore out of her without her permission as the room flickered in and out of darkness, and she slammed against the shield, her flames licking at it to try to get through. "Stop! STOP!"

Augustine turned to face her. "You know, it is all right that the children grow without a father." His knife went into his son's back, and Hunter arched as he growled out. "Demons tend to be raised by a single parent." Another pierced through his back. "Ask my boys. They don't know their mothers." He didn't allow Hunter to rest as he moved around him and stabbed him in the thigh. "And my only child to know her mother turned out an abomination."

Maya banged at the shield, her flames at her feet begging for entrance. "Stop, please. Augustine, stop! Please!"

He laughed. "It brings a father great joy, you know, to finally put the child he's supposed to care for in his place." Augustine stabbed him through the chest again.

Maya began to see red, her flames taking over her reality. A flash of darkness passed her eyes that almost reminded her of the depths of Hell's Gate past the cage.

"So maybe it's a good thing he won't be around for your children." Stab.

Like the insinuation that Hunter would be a bad father broke her, Maya felt the ground rumble beneath her, but all she could focus on was her husband, her mate.

And the image she'd created earlier of Augustine hurting her and their children in order to hurt Hunter. Because that's the type of father Hunter would be—one who wasn't entirely comfortable saying he loved them, but showed it in every way possible.

The flames flickered around her irises and cast Hunter in a halo before her gaze shot to Augustine as he picked up his dagger once more.

The ground trembled until she felt an opening coming up. It was one that encompassed the entirety of this room, and Maya wanted to allow it to eat up the whole of the space, take both Augustine and Warren down so she could be safe with her mate.

But she wouldn't do that.

Because only one man was to blame here. And he would reap the consequences.

Her gaze narrowed on Augustine, and she didn't know how, but the portal moved before opening and sucking Augustine down. But not before the Delvaux patriarch watched her with deep rooted fear in his eyes.

Her gaze shifted to Warren.

Hunter's weak call for her was the only thing that broke her from sending the younger Delvaux down as well, even though she knew he wasn't hurting anyone. Her instincts simply needed Hunter away from *anyone* who may hurt him.

She pulled the darkness back, and the flames subsided as Warren pulled on the chains and Hunter fell to his knees.

"Harry," Maya screamed as the shield dropped and she ran for Hunter.

She heard him pop up behind her right before he exclaimed, "What happened?"

"Practice," Warren answered as Harry moved behind Hunter and began healing him.

Hunter ignored them as his breath brushed her lips and he held her tear-stained face in his hands. "You need to bring him back now, love."

Her head shook violently. "No, no, no, I can't. You…"

"I'm fine, love." He brought her gaze to meet his. "And you did so fucking perfectly. You controlled that so exquisitely. But I need you to do this too, love. Keep your eyes on me and bring him back."

"What?" she whispered as her hands skimmed up and down the arms that held her face.

His lips turned into a grin. "The last time, we were dropped to Hell's Gate when you were angry with me. But we were brought out when you were good on me again. I have a feeling that had your sisters not found the key the first time we were down there, we would've come out then too, when your hand fell into mine. Because we both know you would've reached out for me eventually, whether there was a rumble or not. The problem is you were always focused on the others over me. Them hurting me. Now focus only on me. Look at me, love. See that I am here and yours and bring him back."

Maya did as he said, put all her trust in him.

She stared into those black depths that she found herself lost in constantly. The most reassuring eyes to exist and her favorite place to settle her gaze. The blackness that held that special spark just for her. The ones she hoped their kids inherited, even though he wanted them to have her eyes.

And she felt herself calm, her heart settle like those times they'd lain together in Hell's Gate and she'd been content with him.

Then she pictured Augustine in one of the Hell's Gate cages and told the magic to bring him out.

She didn't break her gaze from Hunter as the ground rumbled around them.

Didn't break it as gasps filled the room around her.

Didn't break it as she heard Augustine whisper, "Incredible."

Hunter held her gaze as his grin grew. "You are. Incredible, my wife, my mate."

Maya's heart settled completely. "You know, I'm getting real tired of you getting hurt for me."

His grin was small, but there. "It's what happens when you're mated, Witch. Remember what I told you—I expect to have scars marring my entire body by the time we're dead of old age or else I wasn't a good mate."

She closed her eyes as the tears strolled down her cheeks, ones Hunter stopped as he cradled her face, and she fell into him. Calmed to the feel of him kissing the top of her head with a million kisses.

A million small, indescribably perfect kisses.

23

"He is an old friend," Adela said as she led them through the crumbled building towards a man who sat at an old table.

Loretta was barely able to hold her shock in as she got a glimpse of the man. He had to be over a hundred years old. And unlike her husband, he very much looked it.

"This is Krok. He lives in nature and does not like to be within doors for long periods of time," Adela explained as she took her seat beside the man. "But he has agreed to be here to tell us about Bishop's past."

"How would he know anything?" Bishop asked.

Anna answered from her spot behind them, "Krok spends most of his time in Czech's natures, but he was a nomad before. He is part of the reason your family trusted our coven, why you would later be sent back here."

"So he used to sleep with someone in Bishop's family," Loretta dumbed down.

Adela's smirk said she hoped that irked Bishop a bit. "Precisely."

Bishop met Loretta's stare with an annoyed eye role before

171

turning to the man who would hopefully help them. "Krok, thank you for coming."

"Yes, Byron." Krok's voice was raspy and filled with age.

Loretta moved to correct the man when Jakub said, "Byron was the husband of the woman he was sleeping with. Bish may look like him. Just go with it."

"Right, um…" Loretta was still stuck on the fact that this nomad would travel around and sleep with married women. "Well, we were hoping on getting some information about Bis… Byron's family's past. Maybe all the way back to the Greeks."

Krok laughed and wiggled a finger at her. "Witches are the real evil ones."

His laughter continued as Loretta looked to her mother. She knew her thoughts were plainly written on her face—was this man even sane enough to give them any information of use?

Adela turned to her companion and calmed him. "Krok, Krok, enough."

Krok looked to her with a wide grin. "I am Krok."

"Yes," Adela answered. "And you will tell us of Byron's Greek past. Why are witches the evil ones?"

"Witches never liked demons, you know. Always angry." Krok's gaze began to wander around the room.

"What were they angry about, Krok?" Anna took the man's other side.

"Witches got the Power first. No other supernatural. Then demons got it, and witches were very *angry*."

"How, exactly, does he know all this?" Bishop asked, and Loretta knew it was to make sure they weren't wasting their time.

"Krok's not magically inclined at all, but in his thirties, he slept with a seer, and when she was ready to die, she transferred her ability and knowledge to Krok," Adela answered.

"Why were witches angry, Krok?" Jakub asked to get a deeper understanding.

"They had to share the Powers. They wanted to say the

demons stole it, but the Powers are not something to be stolen. No one that is not a Power may be one."

Loretta believed that from the mere fact that Jenkins needed Hunter's Power body to get to his end result. And she knew if there was anyone who would find an alternative to a universal fact, it was Jenkins.

"So what does this have to do with my background?" Bishop asked calmly, patiently.

"Demons became everyone's enemy because of you." Krok pointed that old finger again, his withered, raspy voice making the statement chilling.

Yet, still, his little laughs made all of it sound false.

"What does that mean, Krok?" Anna asked just as softly.

Krok looked to her, then a smile came upon his face. "I had a demon lover years ago. I think she was my favorite. I love demons, they…"

"Krok, Krok," Adela brought him back.

"I am Krok."

Adela looked like she was dealing with a child as she said, "Yes. Now, what about Byron's family made demons the enemy?"

"Not Byron's family," Krok laughed. "Byron's family loved demons. They *are* demons."

"So how did demons become the enemy?" Jakub asked, finally taking his seat beside Anna.

That finger shook again. "Miradora was only getting to her mate. She didn't want to do all the things, but she needed her mate." The finger shook a little harder. "Witches did not like that it was their side, so they made the story that she was abducted, fed dark magic to remain by Adramalech. The only reason the entire story isn't completely against the man is because Miradora threatened the witches that wished to do so."

"But I have found an old storybook of Adramalech and Miradora. It says nothing of Miradora doing anything against her will," Adela said.

Loretta looked to her mother, already needing to get a look at that book. She wondered if the Delvauxs had a copy in one of those massive mansion libraries?

Krok laughed again, that sound beginning to irritate Loretta when her daughter's future clung to the facts of this past. "That is only the demon's book. The demons have the true story of the mates. But everyone knows the witches' story."

"What is the witches' story?" Anna asked.

Krok smirked toward Bishop, which was disturbing on his wrinkled face. "You are Greek. Miradora was taken to the underworld."

Loretta met her mother's gaze as she clung to her husband. "This still does not tell us much to help them."

"It does show Miradora's situation with the Maya from your other lives," Bishop said, which snapped Adela's eyes to Loretta. "They may not have wanted to, but they did what was needed for their mates. Selin may truly not have been at fault back then."

"Ah, Selin!" Krok said. "Lovely old woman. Afraid of everyone because of her husband. Made them stay away. Poor Selin, no more family." He huffed as he rested his chin onto his hand.

Loretta met the eyes of her husband, then the others around her. If Krok said this, then Selin must've truly been the victim. Then her family truly had been killed ruthlessly.

It still didn't excuse her what she did to innocents a millennium later, and didn't garner Loretta's sympathy considering she tried to kill her daughter, but it made her understand more clearly.

"Selin, yes. She is dead now. My son killed her," Bishop said.

"Yes. Selin." Krok smiled as his eyes glazed over and that finger came back up. "She is the only one left up that knows."

"What, Krok? What does she know?" Anna asked.

"When Miradora…" He coughed so aggressively Loretta was afraid for him. But then he looked back up like he hadn't almost died in the middle of that speech. "When Miradora met with her Adramalech, they mated." His wrinkled brows tried to dance on his face.

Jakub tried to bite back his laugh as Adela and Anna gave Krok an annoyed look. Loretta saw that, like herself, Bishop also tried to hold back his laughter.

"They had sex, Krok," Adela said. "That is not something *you* should be shy to speak of."

Krok gave Adela a flirty smirk, which looked just as odd on his old age as imagined. "But they are mates. When mates *mate,* and lose control, they open their powers."

Loretta leaned in closer because this was something that most definitely applied to her daughter. "Meaning?"

Krok leaned in as well as if he were going to tell her a secret as that finger came back up. "That is how a mate transfers powers."

They all gasped as Anna muttered, "That's impossible."

Krok chuckled as he fell back in his seat. "Witches made demons the enemy. Everyone forgot that they could mate. But more importantly, even demons themselves forgot how powerful their own matings are."

"So, what? They completely transfer their powers?" Jakub asked.

"No, no. *That* is impossible," Krok said as his head began to move from side to side. "They only share powers. If you get a mated demon pair, you can see it. Especially if he is with a witch. That's both sides of the Powers. For some time, he can have her power and she can have his. They must continue lost control while mating to keep it up, but we all know mates cannot keep their hands off each other."

Loretta gasped as she met her husband's gaze. "That will give Hunter access to the portal."

Bishop searched her eyes for long moments before he asked, "And Selin knew all this?"

Krok's brows furrowed as he nodded, those eyes beginning to glaze over.

"Why does that matter now?" Adela asked.

"Because if Selin knew, there's a very high probability Jenkins knows too," Loretta answered. "And there's no way we can allow Jenkins to learn of Maya's most demonic power."

"Backtrack, Krok," Jakub interrupted. "You said Selin is the only one left up? What does that mean?"

"She is the only one alive and up here with us," Krok's head swung softly from side to side like he was a toddler.

"But Selin's dead, Krok. Our son killed her," Bishop reiterated.

"Oh, what a shame, what a shame." Krok's small grin told them enough about how much attention he was currently giving to their conversation.

"The others who knew? They're all dead?" Loretta asked.

Krok tsked three times, his fingers falling from side to side with each one. "Krazen is in Hell's Gate. He's the one that told Selin."

"Krazen?" Bishop clarified. "And no one else."

"No one alive." Krok's eyes closed as he swayed in his seat, then shot open. "Oh, me, I forgot me!"

Loretta knew they were losing him to his own mind, but she didn't care anymore. They'd gotten plenty of information, and from the sounds of it, they might need to find a way to speak with this Krazen.

Without their daughter and her mate finding out.

One look Bishop's way made clear they were of one mind on the matter.

Camilla was shocked when she turned the corner to the formal dining room in *her* house and found her ex-boyfriend and his new bestie. "You two just hanging out in my house without me?"

"Ah, princess," Kai teased and threw his arm over the chair she was moving towards. "Jealous?"

Camilla moved for the other empty seat, but Kai's legs beat her to it. "Really?"

"What, princess? My legs are tired." He nodded for the seat beside him. "Anyway, there's a spot right here for you."

Camilla turned to Warren for help.

And instead of doing so, Warren only gave a cheeky grin. "We're going over the readings. Would you care to join us, Cam?" He pointed for the seat beside Kai.

"You guys are so annoying," she grumbled as she plopped beside the Demon Warlock, trying not to look at him as the memory of touching him came to the forefront of her mind.

Kai's arm fell from the chair to her shoulders and brought her in close. "And yet you still slept with him and are now dreaming of sleeping with me."

Camilla's elbow hit his gut before she could control it—not that she would've stopped herself, but she would've put more force into it. "I don't dream of you."

"But I dream of you." His whisper at her ear was loud enough for Warren to hear, but low enough to send shivers down her spine.

Her nipples peaked, especially with the memory of the other day, and Camilla had to wrap her arms over her chest as she threw an annoyed glare at Kai before meeting Warren's beautiful hazel eyes. "Can you please fill me in before I kill him?"

Warren did a terrible job of hiding his amusement. "We're thinking the class is a backstory for himself. All those stories he had us read are what made up how he came to be. Like the prologue of his own story."

"Why?"

"The last reading, you can only buy it from the school library, who got it from a 'private institution.' By Eli Timothy. He just switched his names around. I think it's his journal. That's what it felt like while I was reading it, at least," Warren answered.

"We were discussing my skipping the other books and getting right to that one," Kai added. "Then I'll go backwards."

Camilla nodded. "All right. I'll jump to that one too then."

"Okay, well, spoilers then," Warren started. "It basically ends with how this whole mess has begun. He needed a load of bodies, like hundreds. Not to take their powers, but to even make himself a viable contestant to become this all-powerful Zeus guy. Hunt told me how they bumped into him the other day while he was drinking wolf blood. It's some messed up shit like that. This lunatic has done some gross shit. I'm assuming that part's mostly done now though because he's pretty much at the end here, just needs to find a way to acquire Hunt's body."

"So where are all these bodies? Humans?" Camilla asked, knowing that couldn't be it. If Jenkins had been doing to those bodies what he did to the most recent wolf, he would need supernatural beings.

Warren shook his head. "Need to be magical. From what I read, even better if they're Powers, so witches and demons only. I'm guessing he did Powers as much as he could and did the other magical beings for whenever he needed them, or they were easier to find."

"So where are these bodies?" Kai asked.

Camilla sighed and fell back into her chair, which she didn't realize until it was too late brought her right into Kai's side. She knew she should pull away but had so much on her mind she didn't care.

She didn't even care when his arm around her shoulders brought her in a little closer.

"That's the million-dollar question," Warren answered. "And how Jenkins would've convinced anyone to help him get the bodies of all these Powers. Or possibly what dark magic he used to get to the bodies."

Camilla looked up and analyzed Kai's face—which looked entirely focused—for a couple of minutes before asking, "What're you thinking, Mr. Smartypants?"

A barely there chuckle left his lips before he met her gaze, bringing their faces closer, and said, "I need time to think about it, princess."

Camilla nodded numbly, then turned around to distract her gaze from hovering to his lips only inches from hers. When she turned to find Warren's amused smirk on them, she knew her cheeks burned a little too brightly.

*Shut up,* Camilla sent the thought to her ex-boyfriend.

His lips tipped into a wider smirk. *I didn't say anything.*

*You're thinking too loudly.*

He laughed because they both knew she couldn't hear his thoughts, but his gaze on the two of them gave away exactly what he was thinking.

24

$\mathcal{V}$era would feel completely disheartened by her potioning skills if Harry wasn't also failing miserably. In the two days since they'd returned from the market of judgers with their final ingredients, Vera had yet to get past the second step of making these potions. Harry had gotten all the way up to step four before the thing would bubble over and completely ruin their progress.

It was bad enough that they couldn't get all the way through one of these potions, but they needed to make six of them before they could be mixed together, each one a little more different than the ones before it. Maybe that's what made these pages of the Book so special—on first glance, they seemed like simple potions against animal demons, but on closer inspection, they were advanced methods. Vera hoped that meant they'd have advanced outcomes when the time was needed for this concoction.

"We're running out of half of these ingredients, Harry." Unsurprisingly, considering they'd run through these potions at least a dozen times each.

Vera had hoped it was the fluke of trying with the most difficult of the six potions first, but as it turned out, they were all as difficult as the one before. She could only wonder what the final outcome would be like.

"I know, sweetheart," he muttered as he picked up the baggy of squirrel dung with only a few pieces left. "Let's finish using what we have, and we can head back to the market. I'm thinking we can each try once more."

Vera only nodded, a large part of her wanting to call the demons to come figure this out, but she knew they were busy, so she'd figure this out on her own. It gave the perfect excuse to practice up on her potion making too—a fact she'd been ignoring more than embracing since finding out she was a witch.

"Okay," Vera spoke to herself and began reaching for everything needed. "Clean little cauldron over a small fire that makes me feel like I'm in one of those witchy movies. Start with a single drop of a lion's tears, add in the tooth of a three-days dead shark—making sure the dead tooth is covered in the salt water of natural deaths and not poachers—then pour in a half cup of watered-down bear's blood. Then mix, mix, mix. Mix for two minutes, mix, mix, mix. Then add in the spokaan berries, elven berries, and sherban leaves. Mix, mix, add in a quarter cup of vinegar; mix, mix, add in a half cup of sea salt, mix mix; add in three pomegranate seeds. Stop mixing and let bubble up."

This part was where she always messed up—the after bubbling part. While Vera waited for the bubbles to form, she looked up and caught Harry staring at her with a glint shimmering in his eyes and a small smirk.

"What?" she whispered.

"You're so beautiful when you're focused like that. And when you speak to yourself like that. I could watch you all day and never grow tired."

Vera's skin flushed, but she gave him a small smile as looked back down to her cauldron. She had a couple more minutes to wait as she readied the next part—mortar and pestle at the ready.

Into the mortar, she threw in two cloves of garlic and a drop of that squirrel's dung, then she began to break it down with her pestle. Without consciously realizing it, she was back to speaking to herself. "Mix, mix, add in a drop of water and mix, mix. Then some leaves that I can't pronounce but are from the New York forest for supernatural beings, and mix, mix. A drop of milk, and done."

When she turned to her cauldron, the mix was bubbling, and she nervously picked up the mortar. This was the part she kept messing up because she never got the timing right, but as she stared at the bubbles, she forced herself to calm down and be patient. The goal was to have the bubbles covering the entirety of the surface of the mixture, but not so much that it over-flowed. It only really gave a couple of seconds to get this next part down.

When the final bubble covered, Vera dropped her mixture into the cauldron and held her breath as she mixed the two parts together. After a minute, she released that breath, realizing she'd finally made it past part two. Now, part three.

"First make sure the two parts are well intwined together," she whispered to herself. "Then leave it be for one minute exactly as you grab a cup of powdered sunflowers." Timing was the hardest part of most of this potion as it worked in exacts. "Fifty-eight, fifty-nine, sixty, and pour and mix at the same time, baker. Now, hold your breath and hope it doesn't bubble over ruined..."

As she continued to stir the contents of the cauldron, she looked up to meet Harry's gaze again.

Her blush felt bright. "I can't help it. Talking is keeping me concentrated, and I'm about to be on part four!"

He laughed. "Don't help it. It's keeping me concentrated too. Maybe we'll both make it past part four this time."

"Okay." She looked back down. "Now for the slices of shark's tongue covered in ore's saliva that I still cannot believe I've touched so many times. One slice, never stop stirring, Vera. And ten seconds, nine, eight, seven, six, five, four, three, two, add in another slice of the tongue cut so thin it could pass for sandwich meat and completely takes away my appetite for anything, making me happy I'm a baker and not a chef." Vera followed her internal count down, and on one again, she dropped another slice. "Ooo, now stir, stir, stir. Mix it all together. And for the finale of part four, add a crushed quarter cup of sage and let sit."

She looked up to find Harry smiling at her wide with the fire turned off under his cauldron.

"One out of six, done. Your voice is so soothing, love. I need you to keep talking so I can get through some more."

They weren't making the same potions, so it wasn't her instructions that had helped him, but her actual voice. That made Vera smile too bright and laugh at herself at ever questioning whether she should remain with Harry.

"Glad I could help. Now back to mine." There was only one more part to her potion and that was turning the fire off at the right moment. This was all about timing, and Vera was far too nervous to be controlling anything at the moment, better yet a fire.

She needed to turn the fire off when the potion was heated, but before the first bubble popped up. It's the reason Harry had failed when he'd tried this potion.

She stared at the potion so hard Vera swore she started seeing double when she got the sense a bubble was about to pop up and turned the fire off. She stared at it for long minutes, waiting for the failed result, when nothing happened.

Her smile was wide as she met Harry's beautiful hazel eyes. "Two out of six!"

Only four more potions, then the most nerve-wracking—putting it all together.

In the two weeks since their first training session, Hunter had gotten Vincent better already. At least, that's what he said. Maya was never there for their trainings, but she had to be there today.

Because Bella was there, and no matter what they'd done, she'd insisted that if he was getting better, she should be able to see it. Eventually, she'd won Vincent out with a cute little pout and puppy dog eyes. Hunter had rolled his eyes at the move, but it had simply made Maya laugh.

Now, she sat at the edge of the room with Bella as Hunter brought out another demon from the dungeons to stand in the middle. Normally, he wouldn't have any shields up so it could be more of a real-life experience, but Maya knew he wouldn't risk her safety around these demons who'd already seen them together, who knew of Hunter's attachment towards her.

Surprisingly, Bella hardly reacted to watching Hunter force the demon's mouth open to swallow back a vial. It shouldn't have been too big a surprise though. If she was, in fact, Vincent's mate, nothing would deter her from being with him, and certainly not something like dealing with this lowlife demon.

Then they were looking into the body of the demon as Hunter instructed Vincent around him. Maya leaned down as they saw blood trickle within the body of the demon. "How are the mermaids? Anything against them we should know about?"

Bella didn't take her eyes off Vincent, not bothering to deign anyone else in the room her attention. "No. I would tell you if we needed help."

"Would you?" *Or would you keep it to yourself thinking you don't want to bother us with more problems when we already have so many of our own?*

She sighed but didn't turn to meet Maya's eyes as she said, "I wouldn't want to. Especially because of your babies. But I would. At least to keep you in the know."

Maya smiled and brought her little friend closer to her side as they watched Vincent focus on the one demon as Hunter brought another out. "Good."

Hunter forced a vial down this second one's body as well, then tossed him into the circle that held Vincent and the now two prisoners. "Good job, kid. Now deal with two of them."

Then he was gone, not bothering to stick around and see if Vincent could do it. Maya would be annoyed, and even angry, with her mate if she didn't already know they'd been training whenever they could for two weeks, and Hunter knew Vincent could handle himself.

But Bella didn't know that and stiffened into Maya's side, body already moving toward her demon.

Maya forced her arm down on the mermaid's shoulders to keep her still. "He'll be fine. This is training, Bella. Remember that. If Hunter hasn't allowed him to get hurt in all this time, he certainly won't start with me around."

Bella ground her teeth but sat back down.

Then, to distract herself as she followed Vincent's every move as he continued to make the two demons bleed, then hold back like he was playing an instrument with their insides, she said, "The faeries are okay too. My parents are friends with Finlan. They were talking the other day about being glad their species weren't affected by your problem." She ground down as she muttered the final part beneath her breath, "Though if Jenkins comes to power, they will be affected, but apparently I'm too young to have an opinion."

Then Hunter was back with another, who had already drunk his vial from the looks of his transparent body, and traded him out for the first prisoner who had been in there with Vincent.

"He's tiring Vincent out." Bella leaned forward.

Maya knew she wasn't going to bolt but held her anyway. "In war, he'd need to be ready to keep going, even tired. He's training him, Bells."

When a minute later, Hunter traded in the second prisoner

for two others, then came back to watch, Maya asked him, "How's he doing?"

"He could do more than this. Faster than this," Hunter answered without taking his eyes off the middle of the room. "But he's distracted by Bella's presence, so this actually works out. The same way I needed to train myself to your scent, and your basic being around, he needs to train with the fish. Plus, he thinks I dropped the shield, so he's extra worried the demons will get to you two, and he knows I'd take you and leave the fish in a heartbeat. He has a lot of distractions, so he needs to take on less to train his powers up, but he's doing well."

Maya smiled down to her little friend. "See, Bells. He'll protect you like Hunt protects me. He's a lot stronger than you're imagining."

Bella huffed. "Was it not shocking for you?"

"Well, no." She met her mate's gaze for a moment, smirks lining both of their faces. "But then again, we met while he was pulling a staff from a priest's chest, so I assumed from the very beginning he was powerful and could take care of me."

Bella was about to answer when Vincent turned a second's gaze toward her and the three demons within the shielded middle got on him. Bella was out of her seat and running before Maya could stop her, and the fear was plain in Vincent's eyes as he roared, "No!" and raised his arms to keep them away.

He seemed to calm when she crashed into the shield he didn't know was protecting them, but the three prisoners were far worse for wear than Hunter liked going during trainings. He never let any of them be killed because they were being kept for a reason, and these three looked close to Death's doorsteps.

But Hunter didn't look upset.

Instead, he narrowed his eyes on the kid and gave a satisfied grin as he moved the prisoners back to their cells, dropping the shield as he did so.

Bella was in Vincent's arms immediately, muttering what, Maya couldn't hear but figured was a lot of chastisement for getting distracted. Vincent, like Hunter with her, looked to enjoy the spark in his girl's eyes as she got mad at him.

"You two are free to go," Hunter interrupted them. "We can pick back up later."

Vincent nodded and kept his hold on Bella's waist as he walked them up the stairs of the dungeon since shadowing wasn't viable within the Delvaux dungeons.

"I've given you a good ally, huh, babe?"

Hunter's smirk was teasing as he moved for her, hand up to ask for hers. "You've given me a great ally, love."

She took his hand and moved with him to the middle of the training grounds.

He placed his free hand on her stomach and stared into her eyes. "When you tested the portal on my father, staring into my eyes worked to bring him out. Being with me helped to bring us out that time we were fucking in Hell's Gate and when we'd dropped below with Selin. I have a feeling being with me would've brought us out the first time too."

"Your point, my mate?" Her free hand played with his stubble.

"You can bring back when you're with me, but can only send when it's life-or-death? I don't think so, love. I think you have the power to open that portal just by staring at me and knowing I'm here with you."

"We've tried, Hunt..." She wanted to please him, but they'd done this before to conclusively negative results.

He only gave her a small smile, still staring into her eyes. "So don't try. Open the portal, Maya."

Maya stared up into those eyes. Those black, depthless eyes that were her source of comfort and her favorite things to look at in this world. The eyes she hoped with all her might their kids inherited even though everyone else thought her brown ones or the family's hazel—because both her side and his had hazel, albeit Warren's eyes came from his mother—were better.

She thought about the way he always looked at her with such

adoration, remembered the pride he held in his eyes at every dark thing she'd done, from the first time she'd open the portal to the time she'd stolen a power. She couldn't help but smile at the thought of the way he watched her every time she ate, like he loved that she kept grabbing for more.

Then she was back to that first time again.

When she thought he was dead from the icicle slicing through his chest.

The way he'd stared at her on one knee. If she were honest with herself, she'd known in that moment that she loved him. She remembered wanting to run into his arms in that moment and kiss him in front of their siblings but having to refrain from doing so.

But while everyone else had been scared, he'd been in awe.

The ground began to rumble under their feet, but all Maya could focus on was Hunter's hand in hers, his other hand over her little bump, and his eyes, still filled with that awe, on her.

The rumbling underfoot continued, and neither of them broke their gazes to look over to it, but Maya knew a tiny portal opened, felt it.

Then it was gone, and she was simply staring up at her mate, wide smiles on both of their faces and pride shining all around him.

"Good job, Momma Maya."

Her grin grew wide enough to eat up her face. "Thank you, Daddy Delvaux."

Entry #3673

It is only blood, yet it makes me so powerful. Only blood.

I have tried with human blood. Human blood is weak, powerless, disgusting.

Supernatural blood is filled with the taste of magic, so unlike the iron taste of drinking from humans. It's addicting.

It's powerful.

It gives me the magic to control.

Fools are afraid to drink the blood because they think it wrong. Fools will never rule this world. Fools will be my peasants.

I am all powerful because I am not afraid.

I will control this world, live longer than the vampires folklored into drinking blood.

I am God.

Entry #3874

Humans fear serial killers because they fear

189

death. They fear eating their peers because they think it gross. Cannibalism, they call it.

What they don't realize is it is sustenance. Especially from a supernatural.

It is not cannibalism. I am not one of the supernatural, but their meat gives me power almost as great as drinking their blood. An elve's meat gives me more power than a wolf's, but a wolf's blood is strong. It gives me the power to control a Power.

I have learned my consumption amounts.

Too much will cause problems to my frail human body. I need a Power body, but for now I will need to stick to one slice of meat a day.

It is good because I can last a body a long time.

It gives me much power, much control of these species. It gives me the black magic needed to bring her back to life. I need her faerie dust. She must come back to life.

I will use my magic from the meats and blood of these supernatural to control halfies—the beautiful mix of the species—and bring her back.

Grandmama will give me my final Power.

## 25

*H*arry landed them right in the middle of savagery. The scene depicted what Vera imagined blood-baths to look like in long ago stories.

Except this was the wolves against…zombies?

She didn't know, but the dead within the bloodbath weren't the wolves. They were the ashen bodies of all sorts of creatures.

Her parents had gotten the call from the wolves about a minute before Harry ported them over, and her parents followed close behind.

Whatever this was, Linc, Hayes's second, believed it to be involved with Jenkins and his twisted ways—especially after they'd learned that he'd killed one of their own for some blood drinking.

Luckily for them, the wolves were heavily on the winning side. Vera couldn't tell exactly, but she didn't think any wolves had died. Injured, surely, but no deaths.

They were there to stop this sooner and hope no wolves were killed or too seriously injured along the way.

Then they could figure out what the hell this was about, which Vera guessed could possibly have something to do with the fact that the wolves were their greatest—and only, really—ally within the supernatural species.

Vera's attention snapped the moment they landed to a hoard of white ashen bodies moving like they had no care for their lives—which the dead look in their eyes indicated they probably didn't—and her hands moved on instinct, throwing them all back so fast she heard some of the crunches of their spines hitting trees.

She needed to give her mother time to pick out who she needed frozen so Loretta didn't inadvertently freeze the wolves along with the bodies attacking.

Vera threw another three bodies back and watched as a wolf flew through the air and caught one between its sharp canines, ripping it apart before moving to another.

Then all froze over, and the wolves were given a reprieve.

Or so she thought.

A dark caramel colored wolf transformed in front of them, and Vera was face-to-face with their leader, Hayes.

"They need to be ripped apart. The one's we've killed without tearing apart keep getting back up. I don't know what black magic is within them, but they need to be ripped..."

Before he could finish, a hoard of those zombies were moving again, fighting her mother's freeze and too much for Vera to focus her attention on all at once. They were attacking, and Vera was horrified to see one land on Hayes's human back and bite into his shoulder.

Hayes roared and plucked the body off his back and ripped her apart with his bare hands. Blood oozed out of him as he transformed back into wolf form and joined his tribe in the fight.

Vera stood in the middle with her mother, trying to throw as many back as she could while her mother focused on freezing as many as she could focus on. All while Harry and Bishop blocked them, blades at the ready to kill. Now they knew the bodies wouldn't die with the wounds, but it would push them away from the girls long enough for the wolves to do their damage. Plus, it gave Harry a moment to test the magical dagger Maya's friends had made for them.

Vera felt sick with the amount of gore around.

With the blood splattered, guts flying, and the random limb or head rolling around the grounds.

She tried with all her might not to focus on any of it, to keep her focus high so she didn't get distracted and throw up the entire contents of her body.

But focusing high wasn't easy.

This way, she saw the wolves actually ripping the bodies apart.

This way, she saw what the bodies did to the wolves. The injuries that looked to ooze, and Vera knew they would need to port home for some remedies to make sure the wolves were fine in the long run. Thankful now more than ever that Maya still enjoyed over-making potions for fun and practice.

She was also thankful for Hunter's constantly pushing her to train as hard as she could with expending her powers because a few months ago, Vera would've already been too tired to continue fighting the bodies back.

But she continued.

Continued throwing them back, sometimes lucky enough that their backs cracking against the trees made them immobile for a few minutes.

Continued moving bodies in the direction the wolves needed them in order to get an easier purchase to kill them.

Continued to push wolves out of the way when it looked like they weren't going to make it out without a serious injury— meaning too many bodies were on them to get around to ripping them all apart.

Continued as her periphery caught onto Harry's use of the dagger and the fact that any who were killed with that magical dagger stayed dead. Whatever that friend had put into those daggers—equal shares dark magic, no doubt—Vera was glad for it.

Those long minutes dwindled, and finally, *finally*, the bodies were scattered in pieces around the field and Vera was able to take a large breath—which she regretted immediately—and threw up over the arm and head of different bodies.

When she looked up, Harry's hand on her back to ease the sick, she spotted the wolves in their human forms. Some okay with only a few scratches, others weak with their injuries, and others leaning against barks of trees or their fellow wolves for support because of the seriousness of their injuries.

"Go." Vera weakly pushed at Harry. "Go help them. I'm okay."

She knew he wanted to remain by her side because of the effect this entire event was having on her, but it was far more important to help the wolves.

Her father was already healing some of the more injured ones when Harry joined him, and her mother's hand took his spot in comforting her.

"There's our tight-knit family!" Kai called out as he followed Camilla into the living room.

The wolves who were too injured to leave with the tribe were in the back family room, resting as they healed from the final uses of the potions to heal them.

Their family had done all they could to help the wolves in the hours since their attack, but some of those wolves would need more rest time. Ironically, it was the macho wolves, the ones who insisted they get back to protecting their tribe, who were the worst injured. Along with them, their leader, Hayes.

"We're not your family," Camilla grumbled as she dropped to the edge of the couch. "And stop following me."

He fell beside her, so close her crisscrossed leg fell over his thigh. "If I stop following you, how will I have the pleasure of hearing you moan my name as you touch yourself?"

Camilla's cheeks burned as her gaze met her father's. "I do not..." She turned on Kai. "I do not do that."

"Touch yourself?" His eyes roamed her body. "I find that hard to believe. Though it would be a shame if it were true."

Camilla growled low so her father didn't hear, "Moan your name."

Kai met her eyes and smirked. "So you do touch yourself?"

"That's none of your business," Camilla whisper-seethed.

"I think it's plenty of my business if thoughts of me are what're getting you wet and horny," he said in his normal tone, not a single attempt made to conceal his words from the others. From her parents. "By all means, bite that little lip to keep from screaming my name, but we both know you think of me when you come, like I think of you."

Camilla shot out of her seat and moved to stand at the other end of the room.

She hated herself for it, but her body was reacting a little too much to his words, especially with the memory of the other day in Scotland still *very* fresh in her thoughts. She could feel every cell in her body get excited and hated that one glance at Hunter told her he could smell how affected she was by the warlock's words.

"We're here to talk about Jenkins," Camilla muttered to get the attention off of her.

Augustine rolled his eyes from his spot on the opposite couch. "Don't be insufferable, girl. Just fuck him already. We all know you want to."

"Fuck off," Camilla grit and wanted badly to say he wasn't family either, but Maya's marriage-mating made that false.

"Camilla," Loretta scolded, and Camilla felt herself fold into herself at being chastised by her mother like she had been as a child.

"Sorry," she muttered as her father got everyone's attention.

"Warren had mentioned you guys had found something else," Bishop said. "What is it?"

"The class he was teaching, the final book indicated an excess of bodies needed, preferably Power bodies, but not necessarily, as we can see by those bodies the wolves were fighting," Warren explained.

The bodies against the wolves had turned out to be those of humans and the lower magical of the supernatural, all fed black magic to act on Jenkins' behalf. His undead army.

Camilla had no doubt Jenkins had killed them for more of his sick purposes and figured he could get more use out of their bodies. Though the carnage to kill them had been brutal, the poor souls were finally free.

"We've been thinking about where Power bodies could come from, and I think Kai figured it out this morning," Warren finished.

Camilla's head snapped to the man who wouldn't leave her alone. "You plan on not telling me again?"

"I was looking for you when War showed up, princess."

"What is it?" Augustine asked, obviously annoyed by all the other conversations.

"The Bridgers coven," Warren answered. "They killed hundreds, if not thousands, of Powers. We thought it was for nothing, and a lot of it probably was, but what if this new leader had a reason, something other than her prejudices?"

"You think Melusine and Jenkins were working together?" Camilla asked.

"Come back and sit, princess." Kai ignored her question, then smirked. "I won't bite. Least not until I get you alone."

"Behave, warlock," Bishop called, but Kai ignored him.

"Come here, princess," Kai repeated.

And Camilla listened. Not because he told her to or because she wanted to, but only to get everyone's attention off of her.

When she was settled beside him, Kai finally turned to the others. "I read that journal of his, then I got to thinking about mass bodies of Powers. It's almost impossible to find times with so much Power loss. Then I remembered my little search into the Whittle family and the more recent of problems you had in the supernatural world—the Bridgers. I had looked into that coven months ago, and from what I could find, they've always had Power bodies, but it was an unbelievable amount these past few years. It's the only mass loss to the Powers even remotely close to a time Jenkins would need it. As for the other supernatural, I've found reports of groups missing, but nothing so large as the Powers at the Bridgers covens. Jenkins has been working on this a long time. It wouldn't be shocking that he's been amassing his numbers through the years."

"But what could Melusine have needed from Jenkins?" Vera asked.

"And how are we supposed to find that out now without the Bridgers coven? Mr. Mate over there killed them all," Camilla said, not to be derogatory, but because it was a fact. She was glad Hunter protected her sister so much because Camilla had no doubts Hunter had made sure to rid of the entire coven when he heard Maya was the one they wanted.

Even before they'd officially mated.

Before they'd slept together.

Before they'd been anything but enemies with a similar cause.

Hunter didn't argue her statement, though he looked lost in thought as he held Maya in his lap.

But Augustine did answer. "You have friends from that coven, no?"

Vera shook her head. "They left when Harry killed Lila's mother. That was before Maya was born."

"Well then, we'll check the coven grounds," Bishop said.

Hunter tsked. "That won't be necessary." He met Kai's gaze. "We'll find out from the source herself."

26

Maya wasn't sure what Hunter meant by the source herself, but he wasted no time in showing them.

His hold never dropped from her hand as they rose off the couches, and everyone followed as he shadowed them to the original Delvaux Manor.

Then followed as Hunter led them through the manor and down to a space Maya was quite familiar with at this point—the dungeons.

As they passed the cages, Maya ignored the snarls and vulgar insults thrown her way. It was done on purpose to get Hunter's reaction since her hand tight in his was a clear indication they were emotionally involved, but he didn't allow any of it to affect him.

Instead, Hunter continued down the corridor to the end. A spot Maya hadn't gone back to.

"Where're we going?"

Hunter looked like he was going to answer when one of the prisoners heard her and did so instead, "To a whole new world once I stick my cock in you, sugar."

Maya didn't even have time to react before Hunter's flamed

hand was shooting at the man. She only realized afterward that Warren and Augustine's hands had been up too. Melting and heat. The man would be scorched with Hunter's flames and burned from the inside out by the others.

She snuggled in closer to Hunter's arm and smiled against his bicep as the prisoner sputtered but remained alive, albeit crisped.

"Something amusing, love?" He spoke so only she could hear.

She smiled up at him. "I like that your brother and father are just as protective of me."

He didn't miss a step as he leaned down to kiss her, his lips snarling in jealousy as he said, "Me too."

Though he didn't sound it, she knew he meant it when he said that. It meant two other powerful demons would protect her and their babies if need be.

Then they were finally turning the corner to a section Maya hadn't even known existed. It was darker, but not by so much. Just enough to tell the difference.

"Hunt, why are we here?"

He stopped before a caged cell. "You needed to speak to the source."

Maya turned to look through the caged pillars of the cell and gasped as she came face-to-face with a woman she didn't think she'd ever see again.

But there she sat.

Melusine.

"I thought you killed her!" Maya exclaimed, spinning back to her mate.

"I planned to. Eventually. But I figured she could come in useful at some point in the next decade or two. Until then, she could rot for wanting to hurt you."

Maya smiled up to her mate. "We weren't even fucking then, Hunt."

He took her face in his hands. "I knew you'd be my future the moment I heard your name, love."

"Ugh." Camilla pushed them. "You two need to stop with the lovey dovey. It doesn't suit you, demon."

Hunter grinned and pulled Maya away without breaking his soft hold on her face. "You lot have your fun talking to her. I'd like to speak with my wife."

Maya laughed as she pushed him away. "Everyone knows what you mean by that, baby."

"Then they'll be smart enough not to disrupt us."

Maya laughed harder. "Baby, stop it. After! I wanna hear this too."

Hunter exaggerated a roll of his eyes as they moved back to the group. "Fine."

As they settled before the cell, Maya felt her parents' stare on them and turned to see their lips slightly downturned. They were turned back to Melusine quickly, but it still caught Maya off guard. They hadn't looked at them that way since they believed her to be a threat again when they'd 'come back from the dead.'

Melusine was dirty, and the bravado of being in charge was gone from her features, but she still looked at them with disdain. And as she eyed Maya, a bit of fear.

"You're married now? That was soon, no?" she spoke as if she wasn't the prisoner.

Maya smirked. "When you're mates, no, it's not too soon."

Her head tilted. "Demon mates. I believed that to be a folktale."

"Very real," Camilla answered, her tone defensive of the relationship she used to be most opposed to.

A grin rose on Maya's lips as Hunter held her from behind, his hands settling at her stomach, which was slightly rounded, but not yet enough to look like anything other than gaining weight.

And still somehow, Melusine noticed.

Her eyes sparkled as they landed on Hunter's hands. "And you're pregnant too? Mates work fast then."

"They are none of your concern," Bishop ground out as Hunter growled, that mating instinct to protect her at all costs acting up even against a defenseless witch behind bars.

Maya soothed his arm as she glanced toward her father, who stood before her mother at the other end of the room. Then she turned back to the cell and answered the prisoner, "Quite. But we're not here to speak of my family. We're here to speak of yours."

Melusine's brows shot up. "Mine?"

"Your coven and its involvement with the human Jenkins," Harry answered.

"You know of Jenkins?" Melusine looked genuinely surprised.

"Should we not? He came to us," Bishop answered.

Melusine shrugged. "I suppose I see how he would've failed coming to you. If demon matings are true, he definitely entered unprepared."

"He seemed very aware of our mating," Hunter said, his tone darker than normal.

And too sexy for the moment. These pregnancy hormones were really doing something to her.

"And still unprepared? I must know less of this mating than I believed."

"Interesting," Harry said, bored. "But we're not here to speak of my sister's mating. What was your business with Jenkins?"

Melusine shrugged. "If you know I was involved, then you know he needed Power bodies."

"And what did you need?" Vera asked.

Another shrug. "The excuse for more bodies."

"Tell us something we'll believe, Witch," Augustine said in an unamused tone.

She signed. "It always was more difficult to fool a demon."

"Don't waste our time," Warren ground out, then nodded toward Maya. "My sister here has since learned to control that little power of hers."

Any fight left in Melusine fell away as her gaze shot to Maya, then back to the others as she backed up in her cell until she hit the wall. "Deal was I got immortality and the freedom to do as I wished after he got control."

"Why would you allow him the control?" Loretta asked.

"He had everything worked out. Obsessed. I knew I wouldn't be able to beat him out for it, so I figured I'd get the best that I could. Something I would actually care enough about. I didn't care for his plans the way he did."

"So the deal was your immortality and free reign for Power bodies?" Kai asked. "How many?"

"Yes. He needed three hundred and thirty-three. Split evenly between the two Powers."

"How did you split an odd number into the two Powers?" Kai asked even though they could all guess the answer.

"A halfie."

"When was your part finished?" Harry asked.

"About a month before your visit."

Maya scoffed. "And still there were about a hundred bodies in that basement."

"We'd gotten good. Perfected our skills in working with Jenkins. Things escalated faster then. Why quit when we were doing so exceptionally?"

"And now your coven's gone." Augustine smirked.

Melusine looked like she wanted to hurt Augustine for those words, but she remained pressed against the far wall of her cell, her gaze jumping from Maya to the others constantly.

Then Loretta asked the most important of questions. "What does Jenkins need with the Power bodies? Or the other supernatural?"

Melusine looked around, then finally landed back on her. "You don't know?" Her lips tipped up slightly, and her eyes shined. "Well, at least he's still got some leeway on you."

"What is it, Melusine?" Vera growled.

Her brow quirked. "*I* don't know. I got to kill those abominations and got my end of the deal. When he didn't answer after I asked questions, I gave it up."

Hunter's arms tightened around Maya's stomach, and she knew he despised remaining in the dark regarding Jenkins.

---

Harry's hand tightened in Vera's, telling her there was a disturbance he was picking up. They were back home, and her demon sensing wasn't tingling up her arm, so she hoped it wasn't anything bad.

"What?" she whispered and followed his line of sight to the living room window.

"Lore," Harry called out. "You expecting anyone?"

Loretta came out with Bishop and Kai on her tail. "Why?"

Harry nodded to the front without a word.

Vera didn't know what to feel as her mother's eyes widened after looking out the window. Vera saw the people out front but didn't recognize them.

As her mother went to the door, Vera turned to Harry. "What is it?"

That thumb ran soothing circles on her hand as the other reached for her cheek. "Nothing to worry about, sweetheart. Hopefully."

"Harry!"

He chuckled and leaned in for a chaste kiss. "It's family."

Vera's eyes widened as the others moved to the living room, asking their own questions, before Loretta walked back in with the three people who had been standing outside.

The man looked around Harry's age, the woman about her parents' age, and with them stood an older woman. And as the older woman's gaze landed on Vera, her breath left her.

Vera stepped closer to her warlock as a whisper left her, "Harry." *Not another judgmental witch. Please, not another one.*

"It is big news, you know, that our Harry has fallen in love with my eldest granddaughter," the woman said.

Gasps filled the room, and Vera was sure the loudest came from her and her sisters. Or maybe just her. She'd gone from only having her father to no one to this—a whole family with a grandmother and relatives.

It was astonishing. Especially the grandmother part. They'd never necessarily been told they didn't have grandparents, but Vera had always assumed so.

But as she looked to her mother now, she realized that had never been the case.

Loretta stepped up, looking more nervous than Vera had seen her mother look in their short acquaintance. "Girls, this is my mother, Adela, and the leader of the European coven, Anna, and their head warlock, Jakub. Momma, this is Vera," she turned to the others, "Maya, and Camilla, your granddaughters."

Adela stepped forward and motioned for the three of them to come to her. Camilla moved almost instantly as Vera hesitated a moment before Harry's reassuring push told her all would be okay. After all, he'd been their warlock before coming to America, so he would know whether to trust them or not, would know whether they would hate on her relationship with him. Maya was the last to move from her husband's arms, but eventually, they all stood before their grandmother.

That still sounded odd to Vera. Almost like when she'd learned she had sisters for the first time. It was all surreal. Six months ago, she had no more family left. Now, she had sisters and parents and a grandmother.

They stood oldest to youngest a foot before their grandmother before Adela's hands raised and she softly caressed Vera and Camilla's cheeks, bubbling them into their own circle. She looked from one to the other slowly before her eyes dropped to Maya's stomach.

Her old hands moved from their cheeks to her stomach, and Vera saw from her periphery Kai and Bishop needing to hold

Hunter back from getting involved. She couldn't fault his protective instincts, especially now with everyone after them specifically.

"I hear you will make me a great grandmother of twins," Adela said in a loving nature.

One that made Vera's heart crumble for the pain the old woman must feel not having known her grandkids for almost three decades.

Maya's hands settled over Adela's wrinkled ones on her stomach. "With hopes they'll look just like their father."

Vera had a feeling her sister could pick up the hurt behind the old woman's words too. They could all see the prickle of tears at the edges of her eyes which refused to fall.

An airy laugh left Adela as she met Maya's eyes before her gaze moved beyond their shoulders to Hunter. "He is quite handsome. I could not fault you the desire."

A genuine smile entered Maya's features, and Vera knew it was because her relationship was being instantly accepted, so unlike how they, or most everyone, reacted.

"But he wishes they'll look like their mother," Camilla countered.

Adela laughed as a hand moved from Maya's stomach to cradle Camilla's face. "I must say, while he is quite handsome, my girls, you three are beautiful." Her hand fell to hold Camilla's as she turned to Maya. "I must agree with him here."

Hunter finally fought off the men and moved to stand behind his wife, his hands circling her waist as Adela's hand moved from Maya's stomach to hold Vera's hand. "I'm glad to have another on my side. But I must warn you, in our world"— his arms tightened around his wife lovingly—"Maya always gets what she wants."

The most grandmotherly of smiles formed on Adela's face. "And I must thank you for giving them to her."

Now Vera was grinning widely as Harry's hands moved around her waist. She froze, fearing the reactions, but after a moment, fell into him as she noticed the way all three new family members looked on adoringly. Vera glanced over to her parents snuggled together, tears freely falling down Loretta's cheeks, and wondered how it must've been, how much it must've hurt her mother, to keep her children away from their grandmother.

The tears told Vera it had been more painful than Loretta would ever let on.

Adela turned to them. "And now you, Harry? You've been away from us for six months and you've gone and fallen in love with my eldest."

"As will you as you get to know her," Harry answered proudly.

Adela smiled warmly at them before finally turning to her youngest grandchild. "And you, my child? Do you not have a love?"

Camilla blushed as her body turned instinctively before she forced it to stop. Vera knew—they all knew—she wanted to turn to Kai. But she refrained, lodged the desire deep down.

"No," she stuttered before putting power into her words. "No, I'm single."

Vera could tell instantly that her grandmother was no fool as Adela's gaze moved beyond Camilla's shoulder to the spot her body had been turning toward. Kai stood there wearing an unconvincing grin, but Vera could tell he wanted to step up and take her into his arms the way Harry and Hunter had done.

"The Demon Warlock?" Adela asked with a trace of amusement as she turned back to Camilla. "An amalgamation of your sisters' men?"

Camilla's blush brightened as she stuttered, "No, we, no…"

"No," Maya teased. "Camilla doesn't like demons."

On Camilla's lighter skin, the blush burned. "We're not… there's nothing…"

Adela laughed. "I'm only teasing, darling. You're young. Take your time choosing your partner."

"But not too long. Poor man shouldn't wait forever," Warren muttered from the corner, which got a death glare from his ex and laughter from the others.

As the laughter died down, Vera explained. "Warren, Hunter's little brother, Camilla's ex."

Adela's brow quirked. "So she must like demons a bit, no?"

Camilla growled as she softly pulled away from her grandmother and stormed for the kitchen while Adela turned to Kai. "It does not bother you? Her ex here?"

Kai's smirk was unconvincing. "As she said, we aren't together."

Warren's arm fell over Kai's shoulders. "But no, it doesn't. Cam and I were never in love. I'm rooting for the two of them more than anyone else."

"The Demon Warlock has been known to favor the demon's friendship," Anna teased from the end of the room.

Kai's arm fell over Warren's shoulders too as he grinned. "What can I say? They're better people."

Adela turned to her companions, then back to the family. "Now, for the truest reason for our visit—I've a family to protect."

27

---

$S$he had more family.

Though Harry had told her about the Wittlieff coven since he'd been warlocking there before her family had needed him, Vera had never put two and two together. She'd never considered the Adela he told her about was her grandmother.

But she was, and she accepted their relationship. It made Vera giddy, and when she was that happy, Vera wanted nothing more than to simply please Harry.

"Port us somewhere private, Harry," she whispered seductively into his ear as they entered their room in Whittle House —with her distant relatives now here as well, the last thing Vera was going to do was have sex in it.

He made a slow turn of his head, and those beautiful hazel eyes dropped from her eyes to her lips and back again before he gave her a teasing grin. His arms wrapped around her waist as he whispered back, a low groan about his British accent, "I think I'm going to buy us a little cottage in the countryside of France, sweetheart. Make it our little hideaway."

Vera smiled against his lips. "I love that."

He kissed her and ported.

Into a cottage in a cute little town in France.

"Is this the one?"

"Not technically. But if you like it, it most certainly will be." He pulled her around the small table in front of bay windows towards the couches that made the living room. It looked very cozy.

"I'll check it out, but I already think I'm going to love it." She pushed him so he fell, legs wide open, onto the couch. "But we'll have time for that later."

His eyes widened with anticipation as she dropped to her knees. "Hungry, sweetheart?"

Vera's tongue darted out, licking at her lips as her hands greedily unclasped Harry's trousers and began pulling them off so his cock was free. Her gaze latched on as she continued to push the clothing down, wanting it out of the way so she could touch all of him.

Her hands glided slowly up his legs, watching him twitch with sensitivity as she slowly licked the inside of his thigh, stopping right before his twitching cock laying on his stomach.

Her hands moved to his vest and shirt and pulled fast, listening to the buttons clash around the cottage as she took in the sight of his bare chest, speckled with a dusting of dark hair. "Mm, yummy."

"Vera, sweetheart?"

She caught his gaze from beneath her lashes, knowing he was enjoying the way she watched him, the way her tongue licked her lips with anticipation.

"Please, sweetheart." When she didn't move, his hips kicked off the couch, his cock twitching to get closer to her mouth. "Please."

Her hand slowly moved to take hold of his cock, holding it still as she softly kissed the tip. "I like when you beg, Harry. It makes me feel powerful."

"Please," he roared. "Let me fuck your mouth, Vera. Please! I'm begging you. Please!"

She kissed the tip again, licking it once, before going back to watching him. "Harry?"

"Vera, please," he growled, his hips thrusting up for her mouth.

She giggled. "I love pleasing you, Harry."

"Then, I beg of you, please me, love!"

She didn't tease him this time. Instead, she took him into her mouth and sucked at the tip, delighting it the way his head rolled back. Her fingertips moved up and down the sides of his cock, knowing how sensitive to the touch he was and loving when he twitched in her mouth.

She sucked at the tip, swirling her tongue around it, then caught his eyes before she pushed him deep, gagging on his cock but loving every moment of it. Especially when his head rolled back and he became incomprehensible.

His hands fisted into her curls and his thrusts raised, fucking her mouth the way he'd wanted to before while she continued to suck on his cock. She drooled around his cock, saliva dripping onto his thighs as she took him as far back as she could.

Vera's cunt clenched with need, and she sent a hand down to play with her clit as Harry fucked her mouth.

Her moans as she brought herself close to orgasm sent vibrations through his cock, and Harry came into her mouth, grunting and growling as his cum filled her mouth.

She came as she swallowed his seed, needing to be filled with him desperately.

Harry's head rolled to the side, a grin rounding his pleased, and not-fully-back-from-the-stars, face.

Then he pushed off the couch, pulled the shirt off so he was completely naked in front of her, and clutched at the front of her shirt so she followed him as he pushed her over to the small table before the bay windows.

Harry turned her around and made her look out at the flowers, making this space her little cottagecore dream.

"Later," he whispered into her ear as he began tugging at the bottom of her shirt, "I'm going to take a blanket out there and fuck you in the flowers, Vera." Her arms lifted as he pulled the shirt off completely and began working on her bra. "I think I want to stare into your eyes while I take you in the flowers. It would be the most beautiful of experiences." The bra fell to the floor beside her shirt, and Harry palmed her breasts. "But I think first I want you on all fours, sweetheart. I need you to look out at the miles of fields around us while I pound into you. I want to hear your screams and my pounding echoing through those fields."

Vera leaned back into his touch. "Why later?"

His hands dropped from where they were pleasuring her breasts, causing a whimper of complaint from Vera's lips, and continued down to her trousers. He had them, and her panties, pulled down in too slow a motion, one of the things Harry liked to do when he wanted to tease Vera to the brink before allowing her to fall over.

When, at last, he got the last article of clothing down her legs and she could shove them off, Harry moved slowly up her body, his fingertips and lips grazing her softly. Too softly. It made Vera desperate to have him inside her as her arousal pooled at her center and she felt a bit of it slide down her thighs.

He laughed when she whimpered his name, reaching her ear again as his hands tweaked her nipples. "Because right now, I'm going to bend you over this table. I'll listen to the echoes the house has to offer before taking you out there."

He pushed her back, and she fell over the table instantly, arms barely catching her in time.

"Look out into the fields, Vera. Let me know if this is the house you want."

"I already know." There was no way she would allow anyone else to have this house. It would be theirs, almost like the piano room. Except this would solely be theirs.

His chuckle sent shivers down Vera's spine as he palmed her cheeks apart and let his cock slide up and down her ass, coating himself with her arousal from her cunt before continuing to tease her.

"Harry, I know! I know, I already know!" she cried out. "It's this cottage, the piano room, every place we'll port to! It's you, Harry! I know!"

His cock slammed into her so hard, Vera had to take a sharp breath and remind herself to continue breathing.

He pulled out slowly and slammed into her again. "I know too, sweetheart." Again. "I know that I intend on marrying you when this mess is over." Again. "I know this cottage will not be the only one I get for you." Again. "I know that I intend to charm that piano room in your parents' house so only the two of us are allowed in there." Again. "I know that your brother may have known what he was doing when he got Maya pregnant." Again. "I know that your body is mine." Again. "Like mine is yours."

Tears strolled down Vera's cheeks from the possibilities of everything he spoke of, from loving him this much.

"I know that every one of your orgasms are mine," he continued as he slammed, and an involuntary orgasm crashed through her. He laughed as she screamed, her arms giving out beneath her as she fell over the table, still staring out at the fields.

"I know I need nothing more in this life that to feel your cunt clenching my cock, sweetheart," he ground out, pounding into her harder, less controlled.

"Pl-plea-please." Tears still strolled down Vera's cheeks, but now they were from how desperately she wanted him to finish inside her.

"I know"—he pounded hard, unrelenting, pushing her and the table into the windows—"that your pussy is mine. Your ass is mine. Yours breasts are mine. Those long legs, sweetheart, belong to me. These hips"—he gripped her tightly and moved with more vigor—"mine. That lovely curly hair, those beautiful brown eyes, those ears that stick out just a little more than normal, those lips that wrap around my cock perfectly. They're all mine, Vera. I own you."

He groaned as he came, taking Vera with him as she cried out. This orgasm felt more powerful than any she'd had before, and a part of her had to wonder if it was the longing to be owned by him—fully—that made it so.

He was still coming when Vera calmed down, filling her too much to hold as more and more of his cum fell down her legs. She didn't care though, as she rested on top of the table, because she was his, and he could do whatever he wished with her. She wanted to please him.

When he pulled his cock out, more of his cum slipped down her legs, and it made Vera's cunt clench to have him in her again.

Then his hand slipped down her leg, up the inside, collecting his cum along the way, then to her cunt where he pushed his seed back inside her. "This belongs right here." He continued to do so with all the cum that had dripped down her legs and all the cum that continued to fall out of her pussy, fingering her to fill her, until she came again, crying out his name.

## 28

The fact that Hunter had truly let Maya out without him was quite the impressive accomplishment to Warren. How Maya had convinced him, Warren couldn't be sure.

But having him around was definitely a big selling point, he was sure.

"He's making you hold a shield up, isn't he?" Maya laughed as she held onto his arm.

Warren laughed too, glad she found humor in his brother's protectiveness. "He's normally an insufferable man, but I'd have to agree with him here."

She shrugged and cuddled into his arm. "I do too. It doesn't bother me."

Warren kissed her crown. "How did that asshole get so lucky with you?"

Maya smiled up at him. "He asks himself that every day."

Warren led her through the market filled to the brim with humans. "You know what would bother *him*, though?" He looked down at her with a seductive smirk. "The way you're clinging to me."

Maya laughed and snuggled in tighter. "I've always wanted a brother."

"And I've always wanted a sister I liked. Still waiting."

Maya smacked it. "Stop it or I'll tell your brother you came onto me."

Warren laughed. "Then he'll kill me, and you won't have a brother anymore."

"Still have Harry…"

Warren pulled his arm away and threw in over her shoulders "But you won't have a little brother, and we're so much better."

"Then listen to your big sister." Maya wrapped her arm around his waist and snuggled in.

"Hey, I brought you to this market, didn't I? Hunt hates human things like this."

Maya laughed. "I know. That's why he let you bring me. Got him out of it."

Warren rolled his eyes, which only got Maya to laugh harder. He loved making her laugh. Loved bringing joy to her world. Loved that she was going to be the mother of his nieces or nephews.

And he especially loved those nieces or nephews. He'd always wondered about the instinctual protectiveness people got about their siblings' children, always wondered whether he would get the same way with his siblings since he hadn't loved his siblings like humans tended to. Now, he loved Hunter in his own way.

But Maya? He loved Maya like a true sister.

"How about you stay here like a good boy, and I'll go get us some frozen yogurt?" Maya pulled away from him and motioned to the stand selling the dessert.

"You know the shield's following you, not me. Walk away as far as you'd like, I'm keeping that shield around you," he warned.

Maya rose to her tip toes and kissed his cheek. "I know. And I'm thankful to have you as a brother. I'm thankful Hunt has you as a brother."

Warren scoffed. "I'm thankful he has you as a mate. Otherwise I'd have no reason to like him."

She grabbed his hand and brought it to her stomach. "Well, now you have two more reasons to like him."

Warren winked. "Strawberry, please."

Maya handed him the small, glass vase she'd bought from an artisan and walked away, but Warren could still feel her through the shield's magic. Even out of sight, Warren would be able to hold the shield for a few minutes. It was more of an energy burner, but when it came to Maya's safety—the twins' safety—neither he nor his father or brother cared. They were all ready to protect until the end.

It was something Warren hadn't expected from his father, but ever since he'd seen Augustine with Maya, he'd known the man would protect her. Warren knew it was the biggest thing that Hunter was thankful for, past his annoyance at how close the two of them were with his mate.

Because of his height, the crowd wasn't too much of a bother as he watched Maya smile politely at the man serving the frozen yogurt. As he watched her, he understood his brother's view more and more—a daughter that looked like her would wrap both Hunter and himself around her little finger. Probably their father too. She'd have too much control.

And she'd be perfect.

Warren was smiling when a shoulder bumped into him, and his gaze dropped to a woman probably his age, maybe Cam's. Her black hair fell in waves just past her shoulders, and her eyes beckoned for him as they met his. They were a green that mesmerized.

Warren's breath caught as they stared at one another, the heat in him bubbling until he felt the need to melt something.

Then his cock was awake, and all he wanted was to lean down and get a taste of...

The moment broke when he felt a dewiness on his hands,

and they both looked down to the red smeared off the glass and down his hand.

When his gaze fell to her arm, to the gash bleeding out, Warren paled. Not only was this beautiful woman hurt because of this fucking vase, but she was bleeding out.

She covered the wound quickly with a rag she had hanging in her back pocket, ignoring Warren's attempts to cover the wound.

Then that stunning face met his gaze again, a light blush lining her cheeks, and she mumbled so low he barely heard it, "I'm so sorry."

She turned to continue on with her friend too quickly for Warren to say anything to her, and he stood dumbstruck watching her walk away. He wanted to apologize himself, take the pain away from her, heal that wound.

But he wouldn't.

He didn't know the girl, and he was sure she wouldn't want to be chased.

But he needed to know her name.

Her name—

Her name—

Her…

"She's cute." Maya's voice brought him back, and he realized he hadn't been paying attention to the shield.

It was still up, thankfully.

A blush filled his cheeks as he shrugged. "Yeah."

Maya quirked her brow. "You and my sister broke up. You weren't right for each other. And we all know she's gonna get with Kai. No one's stopping you, War. Go talk to her."

Warren searched her chocolate browns for a moment, loving her more and more as the seconds passed, then searched the crowd for the girl.

He needed to know her name. Needed to hear it. Taste it.

But she was no longer there.

He knew he wasn't missing her in the group. She was gone.

Impressively vanished quickly in this large crowd. He scoffed as he looked back down to the broken vase in his hand, filled lightly with her blood.

Maya followed his gaze down and gasped. "What happened?"

He shrugged, his gaze darkening as he stared at the vase, and ground his jaw. "She bumped into me, cut her arm." Warren met Maya's gaze. "Sorry about the vase."

She shook her head vehemently. "I'll get another one. Was she okay?"

He shrugged. "I think so." *I hope so.* "She ran off before I could see much else."

Maya sighed. "You can throw that out next trash we see. I'll get another."

Warren nodded, but knew he wasn't going to be throwing this vase out. Instead, he moved for a booth and asked for a bag small enough to hold it and make sure it didn't move around too much.

Back to his sister, Warren took his frozen yogurt from Maya as she said with downturned lips, "Next time, talk to the girl. Chase after her if she runs. At least let her know you want her. Though I doubt anyone else will make your eyes shine like that."

Warren rolled said eyes as he shoved her to continue walking. "Fuck off."

Maya laughed, then changed the subject to the booth she'd wanted to stop by—one that made homemade clothing. She wanted to see if they had any baby things. Warren couldn't lie, buying the babies clothes did sound kinda fun.

Then they'd return to the booth for another small artisan vase.

Yet the entire time, he found himself distracted with the need to find her. That black hair and those beautiful green eyes.

Hunter had the sheets freshly changed by the time Maya got out of the bath. After the mess they'd made, she was glad to be able to snuggle up into the warm sheets now.

She was naked as she laid back against the propped pillow and spread her legs for Hunter to join, but it didn't feel seductive. It felt intimate, a moment between an expecting set of parents.

It made her feel almost entirely human.

Hunter crawled up the bed, equally as naked, and laid between her legs so his face rested at her stomach. He kissed her navel softly as his fingertips caressed her sides.

"Warren was a great protector today," she opened in a macho tone.

"Make fun all you want, love, doesn't bother me." Hunter kissed her stomach a multitude of times without glancing up.

Maya giggled. "I'm being serious, baby. I love your family. I'm glad the mating gave me War and Augustine too."

Now he quirked his brow at her. "Augustine?"

"He's a great man!"

Hunter scoffed and looked down to her belly. "I think Momma's tired, little ones."

"I'm serious, baby." She pulled at his hair to force him to meet her eyes. "He raised you, didn't he? And you're the greatest person in my life."

A genuine softness entered his eyes as his lips tipped to a small smirk. "Am I?"

"I wouldn't give my love to just anyone, Hunt. Mating or not."

He ground his jaw, and Maya knew it was because of that word again—love. She knew he didn't understand. That he wanted to.

It made her wonder if it was because of the importance everyone put on the emotion because he had no problem with any other emotion. He never lied to her, so Maya knew he was taking the use of this word seriously. He wouldn't use it until he understood it.

He looked down to her stomach and followed his fingertips as they traced nothings around her belly. "I'm sorry, Maya."

"For what, baby?" She played with his hair, loving the softness of it between her fingers.

"Not saying it back. I know caring creatures like to hear it."

He wouldn't look up at her which made Maya's heart pang a little bit harder, made her fall a little bit deeper.

She pulled at his hair until their gazes met. "I don't want you to say it, Hunt. Even if you don't know it, I know that you love me. That's far more important to me."

"What if I never say it?"

She shrugged. "I'd rather never hear it and know you feel it than hear it and know it's not true."

He scoffed and started following his fingers again. "You say that now. We haven't even been together six months. But what about twenty years from now?"

An airy laugh left her. "If you still treat me the same in twenty years—which something in my gut tells me you will— then I'll be okay, baby. All I care about is us. I don't need to follow what the rest of world desires."

He sighed and dropped to kiss her navel again before remaining glued to her stomach. "I've known the longest and still, it's only now beginning to feel real with this little bump."

Maya laughed now. "It's barely there, Hunt. It still doesn't feel all that real to me."

He looked at her through his lashes and smirked wickedly. "I know your body, love. Have every inch of it memorized. And I can tell when even the slightest of changes have happened."

"Oh no," Maya pouted. "So you'll really notice when I turn into a whale. Or after when my body's not the same as the one you have memorized."

He kissed her stomach, then lifted himself to kiss her lips. "I don't think you can understand how obsessed I'm going to be with your body afterwards. I'm going to see the mother of my children. I'll truly see my mate then. It's what I've been looking forward to since I began making the rings."

She pushed him away so weakly he didn't budge. "Hunt, if you like my body more after, I'll never not be pregnant."

That smirk grew as he leaned in for another kiss. "We can only hope."

The kiss was deeper, intimate, and promising Maya the life she'd been dreaming of since she began constantly spending her nights at the manor.

He pulled away after a few moments and stared into her eyes. "Thank you for choosing to come to my manor that night."

She held his face between her hands and softly kissed his lips. "Thank you for promising to never let me fall off those trees."

He chuckled, then fell back down so his lips rested on her stomach. He hugged her waist and closed those beautiful eyes of his. "I'm going to sleep here tonight."

Maya's smile was warm as she stared down at her family. "Okay."

She moved down so she was more lying than sitting, then watched as Hunter snuggled into her stomach. She barely heard it, but she could feel his lips move across her stomach, telling her he was talking to the babies.

She smiled to herself as her hands fell into his hair. He may not know it, but every fiber of her being felt how much he loved her. It made her feel almost selfish to hold so much of his love all to herself.

But she didn't mind being selfish. Not when it came to her mate.

Her husband.

Her family.

# 29

The last thing Camilla wanted to do was be at this meeting with the other covens. Those pretentious assholes had sticks shoved up their asses regarding her family.

Not to mention the way they had tried to bring up Kai's past. There were many things about Kai that grated on her nerves, but his past would never be one of them. She knew she was only hearing one side, but she trusted Kai that his account was truly what had taken place. And if she'd been in that position with one of her sisters, Camilla would've killed the entire coven as well.

But this meeting was an important one to discuss how other covens may help her family and keep her sister safe, and whatever they discussed, they would need the knowledge of the Demon Warlock around whether they liked it or not. And there was no way Camilla was going to send Kai to them on his own. She knew he would keep his composure when they inevitably said something, but she wanted to be there to stop it from happening altogether.

Because she might not like him, but she would never say what those assholes so easily threw in his face. It was cruel and unusual punishment for a man who didn't deserve any of it.

"You already look angry, and they haven't even arrived, princess," Kai whispered in her ear from where they stood in the corner of the room.

They were in an empty room in a house that was going for sale somewhere in the middle of Minnesota. It wasn't exactly the center of the country, but it was middle ground enough for the many covens to port to.

Camilla stood with her arms crossed over her chest, Kai at her back, as they watched the rest of those in her family who had showed up. Even though this was regarding Hunter and Maya, some of the covens had insisted they not show up.

Correction, they had insisted Hunter, or any other demon, not show up. And there was no way Hunter was allowing Maya to show up without him or someone of his family to watch over her.

But at least their other family was there—the Wittlieffs. The relatives Camilla hadn't known of before, but a quick conversation with Kai told her he had. She wasn't angry with him for not telling her. She hadn't asked. She truly hadn't ever thought to question whether they had any other family.

"We've already met some of them, Kai. I know they're assholes."

She felt his smirk at her ear but didn't turn to it.

"I like when you say my name, princess," he whispered, and it sounded so sincere. Too sincere. There was no teasing behind his words.

Camilla swallowed but refused to turn to him.

Then slowly, one by one, the covens began showing up. There was a total of six covens meeting with them, bringing more representatives from each group. The first to show were the Lennox coven. Of course the first to show would be the group with the witch who had tried to bring up Kai's past.

Camilla stiffened and felt Kai's hand at the small of her back, rubbing small circles to ease her. She hated that it worked, but at least he wasn't commenting on the fact.

At least, not yet.

Then two more of the covens they'd already met showed up —the Riddler and Loman groups—before a new group named Lopez, then the Wremon group, before finishing off with a final newbie set, the Barkins.

There were a lot of people now and too many names to remember. Too many names of people Camilla already hated to waste the energy remembering their names. She wouldn't bother.

But they were the more powerful of the covens within the North American witch community, so they would be the ones bringing in the allyship of other covens if needed. But they doubted it would come to that unless Jenkins actually killed Hunter—meaning killing Maya's soul in the process—and won.

Most of the beginning of the meeting was greetings, introductions, and catching everyone up, with only a few insults thrown at their family, which Camilla surprisingly held herself from sniping back. She had a feeling Kai's hand on her back had something to do with her control.

Another thing she would not be telling him.

"We have an old nomad seer we talked to," Loretta came to the end of their story and a part Camilla hadn't heard before. "He told us of Krazen. He was apparently sent to Hell's Gate around the time of Selin's actual life. A little before her family's death."

"What of this man do you need?" a Lopez warlock asked.

Camilla wasn't too upset with the Lopez group so far. They didn't look at her family like they were filth the way the other covens did. They didn't side eye where she stood pressed against the Demon Warlock. They didn't speak with any derogatory spark.

It wasn't enough for her to set aside the energy to learn their names, but she didn't hate them the way she did the others.

Bishop and Loretta looked to one another, nervous, before looking to the Wittlieffs, then back again to the other covens.

Then Loretta answered, "Krok, the seer, told us he may know more information about the connection that Hunter and Maya share. One that may be more connected to Adramalech and Miradora than we thought, that may make them more powerful than we thought."

"And we believe he may have more information about Jenkins," Anna, the witch from her family's European coven, added. "Even though Jenkins is from our time, this Krazen man may have insights of what Jenkins may have up his sleeve. Information that Jenkins could've found to use against us that we may not have. The man, for all his faults, is very good with finding whatever it is he requires."

Hanna, the bitch whose name was ingrained in Camilla's mind, turned toward her corner. "So send the Demon Warlock. He wants to be a demon so bad, let him travel down below to where they all belong. Then if something were to happen…oh well."

Hell and Hell's Gate were two completely different places. Hell was where demons originated and did no harm to them. It was merely a location, nothing like the human version. Hell's Gate was a prison with supernatural abilities.

"You can shove your 'oh well' up your—"

"Princess," Kai interrupted with a reprimand before her parents could. "Behave, love."

Camilla grit her teeth and fell a little into him, her gaze hardening on the covens before her. On that bitch who looked at her with disgust.

"I do not say this out of spite," the Lopez warlock started, "but I agree that the Demon Warlock would make the most sense. He's lived his life as a demon but is still a warlock through and through. He will have a better understanding of the two groups than anyone else."

Camilla was going to argue when Harry said, "I agree."

Her head snapped, and the argument was on the tip of her tongue when Kai's voice snapped her to turn around. "Me too."

"What?" she exclaimed.

"He is the most qualified to go, sweetheart," her mother called out, and when Camilla turned, she could see her entire family agreed. "And we have the key to pull him out." *And your sister*, she didn't say aloud.

"No!" she growled at them, her gaze snapping to the triumphant look of that Lennox witch. "No!" She turned to him. "No, Kai! You're not going down to talk to some lunatic. Who knows how crazed he's gotten in a *millennium*? He won't be sane!"

Kai's finger swept a hair behind her ear softly. "I know, princess. But someone needs to do this."

"No." She gave her final decision. "Someone doesn't have to do it, and you most certainly don't."

He gave a low chuckle, and his eyes glowed down at her. "You're right, princess. I don't have to."

Camilla sighed out and turned back to the group, relaxing now that Kai's hand was on the small of her back again. Most of the others around the filled room looked annoyed or disgusted, others looked like they were lost in thought. Her family looked defeated.

Camilla didn't care. Kai wasn't going down to that lunatic.

Hanna watched them with revulsion. "Why don't you just get on your knees and suck him. It'd be less revolting than the way you stick up for that worthless—"

"Just because I don't have active powers doesn't mean I won't kill you with my bare hands," Camilla growled.

Kai's laughter at her ear calmed her as both of his hands grabbed for her waist and pressed her to his front.

Her father was the one to finally get the attention off of them. "We also need to discuss what each of your covens have and your willingness if this comes down to a fight. We have the surety of the North American wolves on our side, along with some individuals from other species. Your being here means you are willing to help, but we don't want to ask for more than you're willing to give."

It probably would've been less trouble to deal with the other covens' bullshit and join the meeting because getting a call from Hayes and being the only one left in her family to assist hadn't been on Maya's agenda for the day.

And it most certainly hadn't been on Hunter's agenda.

The only real way she was able to convince him to help the wolves was by telling him she would be shadowing over with or without him. She would've done it if he called her bluff too, only because she knew he would follow along.

But he hadn't. He knew to take her seriously on dangerous matters. He grumbled about her bleeding heart as they shadowed over after quickly calling Augustine and Warren for backup.

Maya especially loved having all three Delvauxs wrapped around her little finger.

Then they landed, and Maya felt Hunter's anger radiate off of him. Met his angry stare as his arms burst into flames and a shield reverberated around them as someone fell, her arm swinging in the air.

Hayes hadn't been kidding about needing their help. This was insane.

And the second time Jenkins had gone after the wolves. Maya knew it was him because she saw the black veins in the witches' arms—they were hypnotized.

Hunter wasted no time, reverting back to his pre-Maya days and getting to revel in his savagery.

He didn't leave her side, but Maya saw the fury put into his flames, and some water from his stolen power, as he attacked the hypnotized witches. She felt for those witches, knowing it wasn't their fault they were attacking and being killed by the wolves, but also knowing her mate would stop at nothing to protect her against the threat. And though they were merely a threat to the wolves at the moment, none of them were fool enough to think Jenkins wouldn't turn them on the Whittles next.

There were wolves in their true forms everywhere, growling and biting with their incredibly sharp canines.

And every single one of them was injured.

Every.

Single.

One.

Unsurprisingly, considering they were going against Powers. But they held their own. Wolves were known to do that. Especially if their mates were in the vicinity.

Maya snapped herself out of watching the witches attack, their powers and spells unaimed and careless. The goal was undoubtedly to take out as many as possible even if it meant hurting their own.

Then she noticed a wolf get hit with a power and slump with a whimper, and Maya lost all control of herself. The wolves were her friends. And this attack in particular was at least partly done to make them useless allies to her family.

Her arms whipped around with flames, then she and her husband were throwing bursts of fire toward the witches, watching as they burned enough to stop their assaults—or die—before quickly moving on to another.

But there were so many.

Even with her new father and brother by her sides, there were too many. She knew their powers were being put to use when bodies crumpled with no attack since both of their powers worked internally.

But Maya was too focused on the fight. On the wolves ripping into the torsos of the witches and tearing them apart. On the blood splattering everywhere. On the burnt smell of the bodies and the burnt smell of the injuries on the coats of the wolves. On the limps and whimpers some of the wolves let out because of the struggle to continue fighting Powers, especially considering Maya didn't know how long they had been fighting. But she knew they'd held down their tribe, protected who was theirs.

Hunter growled with unmatched fury as body after body reverberated off his shield, all falling to their deaths rather than trying to attack them. She knew he wanted to send her away, have her shadow home while he dealt with this. But she wouldn't leave him or the wolves.

Then she saw it.

As they continued forward through the mess of bodies, Maya finally saw him. Jenkins.

Standing on a small hill in these forests, his hands were held up to his sides and he wore a smug grin, black veins flowing over his body. He looked deranged. No longer Camilla's hot professor, but a complete lunatic.

Hunter growled especially loud when Jenkins noticed them and turned witches in their direction. So many wolves were injured, Maya was sort of glad for the fact.

But she was also angry. Angry that Jenkins had hurt the wolves, and especially angry that he was trying to hurt her family, her mate.

Maya growled as the seven witches moved for them and fell off of a shield a little farther back than the one Hunter had up. She smiled inwardly, knowing Augustine or Warren—or more likely both—had put up their own shields.

She wanted nothing more than to open portals beneath each one and send them away, but she wouldn't give away her power to Jenkins, on the theory he didn't already know about it.

As their attacks continued, one replacing another when she or Hunter burned them alive—or Augustine or Warren burned their insides—Jenkins laughed. "They are good little pets, no?"

"What are you doing?" Maya ground out.

He tilted his head and kept the grin in place, mirth easy in his eyes. "I needed wolf blood, I got wolf blood."

"Good for you," Hunter lilted. "Now take your puppets and leave."

Jenkins laughed in his own little protected shield that meant Maya wouldn't be able to open a portal beneath him. "But why would I do that when I have you here now?"

They needed to rid of those few witches surrounding him, holding up his own shield. Hunter wouldn't be able to get to him, and Maya knew it irritated him more than was imaginable, but she also didn't like the idea of letting him know about her portal.

Or sending innocent witches down below because they were hypnotized by a lunatic. Even though the alternative was them being killed. She didn't know what to think.

More witches attacked against their shields, and Maya knew it was only so long before they got through and Hunter shadowed them out. Even as powerful as the Delvauxs were, this was an immense number of Powers, hypnotized so they didn't care for their own lives, all at once.

That's when the grumbling underfoot began, and Maya wondered if she was causing it. It felt eerily like when she opened her portals, but as angry as she was, she didn't think she was so much so that she'd lose control. Her control was still not strong on the portal, but she knew that much.

The ground rumbled as the fury radiated off her mate.

And Jenkins' smile grew past his eyes as his gaze jumped between the two of them. "You're mating." His hands clapped together, then moved before his chest. "Oh, how wonderful."

They're mated. He knew that.

And Maya didn't care for his stupid remarks.

More flames blew through their shield toward the witches attacking, the stench of crisp bodies filling the area.

Maybe Maya had to give up hiding her power and just send him below already, starting with the witches holding his shield up. From the crazed look in his eyes and how much Selin knew about her, it was already so likely he knew about her portal control.

Jenkins eyed them a final time before he stepped back to five witches, the black veins all over them. "Well, I believe it is time for me to go. Happy mating!"

Then a portal opened like one the halfies had been using—one her family were still trying to learn the spell to create on their own—and he was gone before any portals could be opened.

Then one by one, all of the hypnotized witches followed by throwing up their own portals.

Gone in the blink of an eye, before any of them could jump through to follow them to the next location.

The following quiet rang in Maya's ears as she turned to look at the carnage, the injured wolves slumped on the ground or against trees, but all of their animal eyes looking at them with thanks.

When she met her husband's gaze, Maya only saw fury.

*Entry #4673*

  I controlled my first Power today. She was a witch. Witches are so much easier to control than demons or halfies.

  It is because they are pure good. Only another example as to why goodness is sickness. If they were darker, like their counterparts, then they'd better be able to resist my control. But this makes them easy toys for me.

  They look better with my black veins on them too. It makes it so much sexier when I fuck them.

  Momma used to tell me to only make love to the woman I loved. It is disgusting, the thought of 'making love.' It is fucking, and I do it to any of the Powers I can get my hands on, especially if they are veined black with my dark magic.

  I wonder how thrilling it would be to be with a demon, to control a demon.

  I will need to begin with halfies since they still have that half other side and that other side—that caring side—is always so much easier to control.

  Once I have my fill with this witch, I will take on more. I am smart.

I am patient. I will wait for the time to control a demon as well. I will learn the worth.

I am smart. If the control of a demon is too much more taxation on this magic of mine, I will use the witches and only play with the demons.

All that is important is to know that I will be victorious.

I am God.

Hunter wanted to bend his mate over a table, a couch, a bed, anything, and fuck the ever-living shit out of her. He was so angry, he wanted to pound into her, hear her cries of pleasure, to help soothe himself.

But he wouldn't get that release.

The moment they landed back in Whittle House—because that's where Maya insisted on going after helping some of the wolves—she was moving toward her family.

The house was full now, and they all looked shocked to see the sweaty, albeit unhurt, states his family were in. Maya quickly recapped the events before all four warlocks—Harry, Bishop, Kai, and Jakub—ported to the wolves' tribe, ready to deplete themselves healing the animals.

Before leaving, as she'd told the story, Maya's parents looked toward one another with worry. Looked toward those of their European coven who were at the house with worry. Their gazes continued to snap between him and Maya, then one another, like they knew something they weren't sharing. Hunter was already so pissed at his mate for putting herself in the situation they'd been in, he truly did not have the patience for whatever it was they were hiding.

Hunter wanted to get it out of them no matter what he had to do, but his mate wouldn't appreciate his methods, and as angry as he was with her, he lived his life to please her.

So he leaned back against a wall and flexed his hands at his sides to control himself. Knowing his bleeding heart, she was too worried about the wolves and the hypnotized witches to care that he was angry with her at the moment.

With the warlocks gone, Vera turned back to the hypnotized witch part of the story. "If they're hypnotized, we can help them. Don't hypnotists have power over whatever spells? If we can get one, then maybe she can…"

"I'll have a call to the covens," Loretta interrupted. "See if they have anyone. Hypnotists aren't as rare of powers, but we would need a strong hypnotist to block dark magic, and especially that much of it. Just anyone wouldn't be able to do that."

"We'll call around too," Warren added. "See if any demons can be of use."

Augustine grumbled about helping those witches but moved to make his calls anyway. His contacts would be far greater than Warren's, so it would be important.

Hunter didn't move to join them. For the most part, he and his father had the same contacts. And he knew none of them were hypnotists. Illusionists? Memory readers? Hell, even amnesiasts? Yes. But no hypnotists.

Maya moved to him in the half hour they waited for the calls to be made and wrapped her arms around his waist. Hunter looked down at her, making sure the anger was still clear on his features, and didn't return the embrace.

"C'mon, baby, they needed our help. You'll now be owed a favor by the wolves. Shouldn't you be happy about that?"

He quirked a brow, trying to figure out if she was seriously asking whether he was happy about his wife and children being anywhere near that lunatic.

"Okay, not happy, but you're a demon, and you now have an

advantage. You have a stake over their heads. You love things like this."

His brow remained quirked, now trying to figure out how much of this crap she was going to spew. They both knew his greed wasn't anywhere near comparable to what he felt for his family. For her.

She sighed and hugged him tighter, resting her cheek against his chest. "I love you, Hunter. I'm not going anywhere without you. You protected me. You always protect me."

Hunter was still angry, but he knew instinctually she wanted him to return her embrace, so his arms moved on their own, wrapping around her and pulling her close. His lips moved on their own too, kissing the top of her head softly. Her wish, whether said aloud or not, would always be his command.

They stood like that until the group reconvened, the others having gone to call other contacts, or simply to give them their privacy. He knew they could tell his agitation and wanted Maya to calm him before returning to his presence.

It had worked. Slightly.

When they returned, they didn't look so happy with their findings. Most people knew hypnotists, but modern hypnotists weren't as strong as old ones. Most of the modern powers weren't as strong. That's another reason his family was at the top, they were all powerful. Even his father and brother's medium-level powers were stronger than most high level since the degree was based on how much damage could be made rather than actual strength of the power.

It was Vera who said, "I actually called Celine, the human with the faerie in the Ragtag House. She said they may be able to help us."

"May?" Hunter didn't have time for games. Though he was agitated, he also knew Maya wanted these witches protected, or at least an attempt to do so, and whatever Maya wanted, she got. So he would stow away his annoyance at these caring creatures.

Vera shrugged. "Apparently a very powerful hypnotist witch."

"What's the problem then?" Augustine asked with the same agitation Hunter felt.

"Apparently she's the sister of one of the members of the house. And doesn't approve of cross relationships."

"Well, then let's hope she cares for the supernatural's existence," Hunter barked. "Or at least those of her own."

***

Hunter was still angry, and an angry Hunter might not help them with a reluctant witch. Vera was nervous about that, but there was no way for him not to come. They needed Maya for a firsthand account, and Hunter wouldn't allow her to go without him, not that Maya necessarily wanted to.

Vera had hoped that the time in Maya's company as they'd called contacts would calm him—and though it did, it wasn't enough.

The demons shadowed them since the warlocks were still with the wolves, draining their energy to heal the tribe. Vera had called Harry to let him know what was happening, but this would have to go on without them.

When they landed at the house, Celine and Kellan were already outside with another couple. Understandably, the males wouldn't want their women going off on their own, especially to a witch who didn't accept them. Though the halfies weren't much of a problem anymore, those in cross-relationships had learned to protect their relationships.

And especially for Kellan's sake, since Celine was human and had no magical abilities about her.

The witch gave them a weak smile, eyeing the demons with nerves. "I'm Alla. This is Robert." She pointed to the gargoyle next to her. "My sister, Ama, is a powerful hypnotist."

"I'm surprised she hasn't changed your mind about your relationship if she's so powerful," Augustine remarked, and it made Vera wonder.

Alla gasped. "She doesn't approve of what we do, but she's a good witch. She would never use her power to manipulate."

"And how else, exactly, would one use such a power?" Hunter asked with a tone that suggested she were stupid.

"She helps survivors. She's good. She uses her magic to help, and if what you're saying is true, then she'll do so now as well." Alla was affronted. Her sister didn't approve of where she was and with whom, but she still stuck up for her.

Vera stepped up before either Delvaux said something else to offend the girl who was merely trying to help them. At least Warren was still caring. "Have you spoken with her? Can we see her now?"

Alla shook her head, a sadness filling her eyes. "She won't speak with me. Refuses to associate with *my kind*. We will need to go uninvited."

The look in her eyes sent Vera back to that year without her father and before finding her sisters and Harry. Though she'd always felt lonely, her father had always made her feel so loved, she'd never paid much attention to it. But that time without him had been awful. She could not imagine meeting her sisters and being refused. Could not imagine refusing her own sister when she hadn't approved of her relationship with Hunter. It had never even crossed Vera's mind.

"Then let's go," Augustine said, obviously annoyed this was taking so long.

Alla looked hesitantly toward the three men. "It would probably be best if…"

"No," Hunter barked. "Wherever my mate goes, I go."

Alla looked to Celine and probably saw that there was nothing that could be done about it. Her own male, Robert, squeezed her hips as if telling her that he understood the reaction. That he hadn't even wanted her to take this meeting without him. It was a dangerous time, and there was too much to lose when separating from your love.

Vera understood it greatly. Even knowing Harry would be fine, only depleting his energy with the wolves, she worried. She wanted nothing more than to be with him, for him to be with her. Wanted to call his name, knowing he would port over in the blink of an eye and remain by her side if she asked. It was selfish and she would never do it, but she wanted to.

And they weren't even in a cross relationship. Supernaturals weren't disgusted with their relationship, only the witch species. And even then, not to a degree to hurt, just to shame.

"Let's go," Camilla called.

Alla gave them the coven, and the demons shadowed them out quickly. Vera had to wonder how much energy they were expending shadowing so many people. She knew that warlocks were always able to transport more than even the more powerful of demons.

Alla moved before the rest of the group, heading up to the manor that her sister lived in with the rest of their coven in the outskirts of the state of Georgia. The rest of their group stayed back, but Vera could still hear them when someone opened the door, asking Alla what she was doing there.

After asking for her sister, for something important, Alla moved off the porch, and she and Robert waited as the witch reluctantly went to get Ama.

Only a couple of minutes later, Ama showed up. She was beautiful with her dark skin and resembled her sister greatly, though she looked older than Alla by close to a decade, which made Vera almost positive she had been like a mother and sister to Alla. It probably made the rejection sting worse.

Ama crossed her arms from her position on the porch as she looked them all over before settling on her sister and Robert. She sneered at how close the two were standing, Robert's hand around Alla's waist. "What?"

"Ama," Alla said softly. "We need your help."

Ama rolled her eyes and turned to go back inside.

"It's for innocent witches!" Alla called quickly, and her sister froze with her back to them. "They're hypnotized by dark magic. You're the only one strong enough that any of us know who could help break them out of it. They're dying in hoards, Ama."

Ama turned slowly. "What's happened?"

Alla sighed a breath of relief before looking over to their group. Finally, the rest of them stepped forward so they all stood beside Alla and Robert before the stairs that lead to the porch.

Ama grimaced as her eyes settled on the hold Hunter had on Maya. "More crosses. It bothers none of you that those two are joining? That it could lead to *mixing*?"

Anna, the Wittlieff head witch, and her mother looked to one another like they had a secret before watching Maya and Hunter again. It made Vera's brows furrow, but she tried not to pay much attention to it. She was sure it was only the worry for their lives.

"She's already pregnant," Camilla said with a snarky smirk.

Ama grimaced. "What happened?"

Maya soothed Hunter's arms around her waist, then began with the story she had told them.

Again, Vera wished Harry were at her side. She wasn't being attacked, but she wanted him.

31

The warlocks spent the entire day and night healing wolves, resting, then continuing to help. After speaking with Ama, the rest of them had returned home, planning on calling her again whenever she was needed. She insisted she would be ready on standby when they found the hypnotized witches again. It proved that she really was a *good* witch.

Maya had been glad for the night's rest, but she worried the entire time for their four warlocks and the wolves.

That morning, the wolves who were too injured to merely heal and leave behind were resting in the back family room, their mates at their side—all but Hayes, who still didn't have a mate—as the rest of the family met up in the kitchen. Maya especially hated how hurt Hayes had been, nearly on the brink of death, but knew as their leader, he'd done everything to protect his tribe.

But they were all fine now, and Maya had other things to deal with anyway. She knew Hunter had noticed the way her parents and the Wittlieff coven members had been acting even if he didn't mention it to her. She wondered if the others had, but she certainly had. And it was irritating.

"Okay, what have you not been telling us?" Maya asked as she moved to stop by the counter, Hunter following at her back.

When they stopped, he held her to his chest and stared at her parents with a deadly quirked brow. He was one protective motherfucker when it came to her.

"What do you mean?" Vera asked with furrowed brows as she helped Harry with breakfast.

"Mom and Dad. Anna, Jakub, Grandma." It felt weird to refer to Adela as Grandma, but she did so out of respect and because she knew both her mother and grandmother liked it. "They've been hiding something. What is it?"

"What makes you think we're hiding something?" Bishop asked, his body a little stiffer than before.

"I see the way you look at me and Hunt." Maya crossed her arms before her chest. "What is it?"

Loretta blew out a defeated breath and met Maya's stare. "We've found something out that we presume Jenkins knows. And if he does, it'll make his need to get Hunt deeper."

Maya froze, then ground out, "What?"

"Maya," Bishop tried to calm her.

"Do *not* keep something about my mate away from me." The ground rumbled ever so lightly, and Maya only had the forethought to control her reaction when she felt Hunter's hands run soothingly up and down her stomach.

Loretta sighed. "We are more worried about your mate's reaction."

Now Hunter froze because if they were more worried about his reaction then it had to do with Maya.

"What?" Hunter ground out this time.

"Momma has an old friend who knows more of the backstories," Loretta explained, meeting the gazes of the three Wittlieffs before continuing. "He also knows things about matings that have been lost through the centuries, especially regarding demon matings."

Maya's heart raced. "What?"

"We believed it impossible to share powers," Adela said. "Apparently, between a mated demon pairing, it is not."

Hunter's arms tightened around her waist. "Meaning?"

"Meaning, all the powers that you have can get transferred to Maya—like sharing because you'll still have them too—for a period of time when you lose control together," Bishop explained then grimaced as he added, "in bed." Then he met Hunter's eyes. "And vice versa."

Augustine stepped up through the silence. "You're telling me my son has the ability to open a portal?"

"All we know for sure is that when they lose control in bed, not only do their powers act up, but their magic opens up. It allows for their mate to take use of some of that power for some time," Anna answered.

"Think about it," Loretta added, "it's why the ground rumbled when we thought Maya would be gone with the warehouse. It wasn't her power trying to get her out like we thought, it was Hunter. Ready to crumble the world for her, the same way she'd do for him. Has done for him."

"This little friend of yours," Hunter ground out, not sounding happy about the matter, "said I have Maya's powers now too?"

Jakub shook his head. "He said you can share powers. But for the ability to continue, you would need to continue *losing control* together."

"Which we all know you two do often enough," Loretta mumbled under her breath.

"You're telling me," Hunter bit out, "that it wasn't enough that that psychopath wanted my body for my ability to hold powers, but now he can have Maya's too?"

"It's what we've come to understand," Loretta answered.

Harry stepped forward. "Why don't we check? I'd presume you two have lost control together recently."

"This morning," Maya answered as she soothed her hands up and down Hunter's arms around her waist to calm him.

Bishop grimaced as Harry said, "All right then, Hunter, darken the room."

Maya looked back into her favorite black orbs and waited. He'd been stealing powers, working with foreign powers, for almost two decades, so she didn't need to explain anything to him.

Only a few seconds passed before the room dipped into pitch black.

"It's just as strong as if it were mine to begin with," Hunter muttered.

The room slowly came back to its brighter hues as Bishop said, "So it's true then. Maya, you try it now, with his stolen powers. Let's see how far it goes."

Maya stood motionless for a few moments, thinking about the ramifications of this—knowing Jenkins would continue to need her if he ever took over Hunter's body—before she lifted her hand to the sink and watched as the water sprouted out the way flames would. She had to put more thought into it than if it were her own flames, but it came just as easily as a stolen power would come to Hunter.

"It feels like a stolen power," Maya whispered. "Like it's not mine, so I have to think about it, but still just as simple as if I were in Hunter's body."

Loretta looked like there was a final part that she dreaded most.

"What?" Hunter bit out, the coldness telling Maya he was fighting himself to keep calm.

"He said Selin knew of this. Which we presume would mean Jenkins would too," she answered. "Our only saving grace is that no one else knows of Maya's portal power."

A deep breath flew out of Hunter's lungs as he hugged her closer still and his head fell to her shoulder, a whisper so low she barely heard it coming out, "I can't lose you, love."

"You won't," she whispered back, caressing his arm to keep him calm. "You won't."

But all she could think was that she couldn't lose him. Jenkins couldn't know that Hunter had all that power and now, because of her, possessed the power to open the portal to Hell's Gate too.

She met her sisters' gazes and saw them both pick up exactly what she was feeling—she couldn't lose her mate, her family.

The determination in both their eyes calmed Maya slightly.

Camilla had Warren meet her without the others because he was the only other one the coven was going to trust. The two of them had saved a matriarch from the Salem coven months ago, so she knew they'd feel comfortable and safe around the both of them.

And she needed someone to take her, so going alone hadn't been an option.

Her options were any of the warlocks or Warren's shadowing.

Warren's shadowing meant he'd be with her too, and as much as she knew they weren't right for each other, she still felt safe with him. Still wanted his company.

"Remind me again why we're here." Warren stared out at the array of cottage style houses in the fields outside of Salem, Massachusetts where the Salem coven settled.

"I've kept in contact with Genevieve, the one that had been coherent enough to communicate when we got to the Bridgers coven last November. She's told me about her coven. They're a small one, with weaker powers, and can't afford to lose any in joining a fight, but they're probably the best potion makers on the planet, definitely in the American territories."

Warren whistled. "Maya's gonna be angry you kept that from her. You know how many vials of potions she could have made by now."

Camilla laughed. "I'll bring her here after this is over. Maybe after the babies, when I want to steal them for myself. I'm sure Hunter would be intrigued to learn more too." Because for all his faults, Hunter was always wanting to know more, always curious. Of course he was, that's how he remained so powerful.

"Damn," he cursed. "Now I need to think of a way to steal the babies for myself." As Camilla laughed, Warren merely shrugged. "I'll just tell them I could keep the babies while they fuck. They're both horny bastards. They'll give in immediately."

Camilla gasped. "That's cheating! We could all do that!"

Warren shrugged and slowly began the trek up the field toward the houses. "Too bad. I called it."

Camilla slammed her shoulder into his as they walked, his strides smaller to keep up with her.

"You're hoping they can help with some type of potion?" Warren asked seriously after a bout of silence.

Camilla shrugged. "I know they can. There's *something* they can help with, and I will do anything to protect my sister." The desperation in Maya's eyes had been enough to push Camilla to the tip of these protective heights. "Especially now that we have the transferring. I know they won't be able to stop it, but anything that could help. Or any potions that could help the rest of the family, the injured. Even if it's not directly for Maya or Hunter, it'll take a lot of stress off of them if the rest of us are more protected and they'll be able to focus more on themselves."

Hunter was solely focused on them. But Camilla knew that a bit of his concentration veered toward the family for Maya's sake. It would be nice for them not to have to worry about that any longer.

Warren nodded but didn't say anything as they came up to the front door of what looked to be the main residence. Camilla had no idea which one Genevieve lived in, but it didn't matter. Once she was requested, Genevieve would come to her.

As she knocked, Camilla's gaze jumped around, shocked to find that there were no protective shields around the coven grounds. Though, she realized, being that they weren't a powerful family, they didn't have the same worries as her family, both North American and European.

A blonde woman who looked to be in her early forties opened the door and gasped. "Camilla?"

Camilla's brows furrowed. "Yes? How did you…"

The woman was already pulling her and Warren in. "Come in, come in, child. Oh, you've brought your demon too! Oh, how wonderful it is to meet you."

Camilla let her guide them to the living room, then turned to face her once again. "How did you know who I was?"

"Oh, dear, Genevieve is an artist. She's drawn you multiple times. Both of you. The whole coven knows you."

Camilla's mouth hung in the shape of an O, but she didn't know what to say to that. One glance in Warren's direction said he was flabbergasted as well. Even though most of the coven may recognize him from all the drops he made of the witches they'd saved from the Bridgers coven, neither one of them had expected this.

"Sit, sit," the woman insisted excitedly. "I'll call for Gen and the heads of the coven."

They sat silently and waited only a few minutes before the same woman came back with a tray of tea and biscuits followed by two witches, a warlock, and Genevieve.

Genevieve's smile was light and warm, her eyes shining like she was glad to see them. "My children, you're here."

Genevieve sat on the couch across from them, next to the woman who'd ushered them inside, then one of the other two witches took her seat beside them. The other witch stood a little too close to the warlock to be mistaken as anything but a relationship like Vera and Harry's.

"Alain, you've already met." Genevieve pointed to the woman beside her, then to the one at the end of their couch. "Evelyn is the head of the coven." Then toward the other two. "Anthony, our head warlock, and Rose, a top witch here."

Genevieve's glint said she didn't have to speak about their relationship considering how obvious they made it. The wary way Rose watched them told Camilla she'd been criticized for her relationship one too many times, meaning theirs was exactly like Harry and Vera's rather than her parents—she was his ward.

Camilla nodded softly. "I'm Camilla, this is Warren."

"Yes, and what a beautiful couple you make," Genevieve said fondly.

Both she and Warren stiffened. Last time they'd seen one another, they had been together. And their breakup hadn't exactly been something she felt the need to inform Genevieve of before.

"We're no longer together," Warren answered.

"No?" Alain's eyes drooped.

Warren's smile was beautiful and reassuring. "No. We found we love one another as friends and nothing more."

"That's very mature of you," Evelyn replied, glancing between the two of them. "I wager this isn't a mere visit?"

"Unfortunately, no," Camilla said. "I've spoken with Genevieve these past months, and I know you hold the best potion masters in the species and wanted to speak with you about helping my family."

"After what you've done for us?" Evelyn said with a small smile. "What is it?"

Camilla turned to meet Warren's gaze, his warm hazel eyes transporting her back to the beginning of their relationship when she'd get lost in those eyes. They still had that power, so intriguing and beautiful and hypnotizing. She didn't want to look away, like back when they'd been together.

But finally, she snapped herself out of it and saw the reassurance in his gaze that they could tell this coven what was needed to help. He trusted them, and she did too.

Camilla turned back to the five before them. "It all starts with a witch and a demon mating..."

# 32

*amilla was on her hands and knees, and a whimper left her mouth as a kiss dropped to her spine. Soft and promising more.*

*Another hovered a little lower down and teased her with the need for the touches to dip all the way south.*

*"Please," Camilla whispered, then felt his hands caress her sides. Another cruel tease.*

*She looked up to distract herself from the lips and hands of the unknown man and found herself on the astronomy tower basking in the glows of twilight. It was beautiful, a sight she knew they could cuddle up to watch afterward.*

*But first, she needed her release, needed this man to stop playing with her.*

*"Plea..." she whimpered as his lips pressed against one ass cheek, then the other. Softly, slowly making his way down.*

*Camilla wanted to turn, to see the man whose light kisses gave her more pleasure than she'd ever felt before. But something was stopping her, immobilizing her from turning.*

*And somehow, that didn't frighten Camilla. She simply held herself on all fours and let him taste her. Especially as close to her cunt as he was.*

*He didn't tease her too much as those hands caressed her ass, then held the cheeks apart to open her cunt up to him. His tongue slipped straight through, and Camilla cried out in ecstasy.*

*"You taste delicious." His voice was low, guttural. And impossible to make out through the haze of pleasure in Camilla's brain.*

*Camilla dipped to her forearms to give him more room as his tongue lashed out on her folds, licking through and fucking her opening. She held on to the blanket they were on to ground herself in reality, but nothing could've prepared her for the insanity the feeling of his mouth around her clit would bring.*

*She screamed so loud, the sound echoed in the night sky around her, and the man only chuckled, redoubling his efforts until Camilla was incoherent.*

*"I'm...com...co..." she could barely mutter before his mouth left her cunt.*

*Her cry of frustration as only air touched her almost made her tear up.*

*"You're going to come around my cock," he said as his teeth skimmed up her spine, "before you come into my mouth." He bit her right shoulder blade hard.*

*"Then please." Camilla lifted herself for more leverage to throw her ass back into him. "Please fuck me. Make me come around your cock."*

*She needed to turn around, to look at him. Needed it.*

*But still, something forced her not to.*

*His chuckle made her wetter as he kissed her shoulder blade. It was inviting and sexy and mysterious.*

*"As you wish." He lined himself to her center, then roughly took her hair into his hand as his lips touched her ear. "Camilla."*

*She cried out at the use of her name and the rough way he slammed into her; his breath at her ear, down her neck, over her shoulder; his hand tugging at her scalp, causing that delicious form of pain and pleasure.*

*He released her head as he sat back to slam into her, that hand skimming down her spine as he pushed her down to her forearms, this new angle making Camilla scream louder. It was all so much and so very good.*

*Those fingertips skimmed her back and ass, teasing her with the delicate touches as his free hand moved around her form and began to play with her sensitive nub.*

*There was so much happening she needed a distraction, so she reached through and played with his balls. The growl he released at the contact made Camilla clench as release came to her.*

*Which only went away when that hand on her clit stopped its play to move her hand from his balls. "This is all about you. Trust me, this is as much pleasure for me as it is for you. But right now, let me touch you."*

*She was thankful to yoga for preparing her for this puppy pose as he slammed deeper into her, that hand finding its way back to her clit as the other played with her ass, caressed her sides, down her spine. All of it tingling until she felt that intenseness that came with losing control of powers.*

*But so much more than before.*

*She not only felt the elevated desire, like she was feeling this for both herself and him, but she also felt the sensitive prickling of a release coming. And that's when she realized, the touch part of her primary power wasn't sending through messages, it was sending through feelings. Far more than ever before. Because she'd never felt this before. This, this...*

*She screamed, and her hands glowed, but she couldn't think of what that meant as his hand crawled up her back and back into her hair. He scratched her scalp and growled as his own body shivered, and that's when Camilla knew what had happened—they were losing complete control of their powers, possibly transferring. Impossible.*

*But his fingers rubbing circles on her clit as his cock pounded into her were too distracting to think of that.*

*He pulled at her hair until she was off her arms and flush on her knees, back to his chest. The light prickles of his chest hair hit her back and sent another round of shivers down her spine.*

*Her hands instantly moved behind to fall into his soft hair, slicked with sweat, and she pulled in order to keep herself sane. That bit of contact made the power sharing more thorough, and they both cried out with the pleasure.*

*His voice by her ear was too much, and as he licked from her shoulder to her ear, then suckled on the sensitive spot behind it, she clenched around his cock, no longer able to hold back.*

*As she cried, he whispered into her ear, "Come for me, princess."*

*She didn't know who this was, but only one name came to mind. A name she couldn't voice. Couldn't want.*

*Camilla turned her head and found herself eye-to-eye with that man, and the climax hit harder than she could've expected.*

*"Kai."*

Camilla woke with a start, her voice breaking with his name, and a sheen of sweat glistening off her body.

Her thighs pressed together, and she whimpered at how sensitive she was. How very wet she was. She felt it soak onto her bed.

That was the first dream she'd had about him. And as she la there thinking about it, she remembered the way her hands had glowed like he'd lost control of his power too, shared it. It was impossible for his healing to go to her, but she could imagine the light losing control and filling the space around them, bathing her in the glow. Maybe not with all warlocks, but Camilla could imagine losing control with Kai would lead to that.

A tear slipped down her cheeks. Not because of the dream, but because she needed his tongue on her now. Needed it like she needed breath.

And her stubborn pride would never allow for it.

---

S oft brown hair. Beautiful hazel eyes. Stubborn furrow between the brows. And that elbow that always seemed to make its way into his gut. Those were Kai's thoughts as he fell through the ground into Hell's Gate.

Hopefully Maya's control on her magic would allow her to push him into the correct cage and hold on to know when he needed to be pulled out. This was all a gamble.

Especially so for him because he could already imagine Camilla's anger when she found out he'd come down even though she had told him she didn't want him to. The silver lining that it proved how deeply she cared for him was truly the only thing pushing him.

And the need to get back to her.

When the blackness finally ended and Kai landed, his entire body reverberated with the impact, and he lost his breath for a moment. He definitely hadn't expected such a hard fall. It would've been a nice thing to be warned of by the two people who had been down to these cages before. Because as Kai lay on his back catching breath, he knew this wasn't the same as the one they'd all fallen into when Selin was killing Hunter. That had been a far more terrifying depth of Hell's Gate.

As he slowly picked himself up, Kai's gaze landed on the other end of the cage, and something instinctual told him he was in the correct cage. The crazed smile on the man didn't exactly help his nerves, but Kai was down there for a reason, and he intended on executing.

"Am I to believe this?" Krazen, name perfectly matching his crazed look, spoke. "Hell's Gate is giving me a treat?"

He palmed his junk, and Kai had to swallow back his bile as he rose to his feet. "Unfortunately, Hell's Gate isn't so kind."

"Then to what else do I owe a partner in my cage?"

"A witch with control who sent me down to speak with you."

"A witch?" He still looked crazed, but there was a spark in his eyes. "You are friends with Miradora?"

What year did he think it was?

Though Hell's Gate time worked differently, he probably

thought he'd been down there for a millennium but it had only been a couple of years on Earth.

Oh, how very wrong he was.

Kai didn't answer but kept his stare on the man, trying with all his might not to let his gaze waver, especially with the way his hand continued to move over his dick. It was making Kai sick.

Krazen laughed wickedly. "What could Miradora need from me?" His gaze turned sinister. "Adramalech not pleasing her thoroughly?"

Kai could only imagine what Adramalech would've done to him had he heard Krazen wanted to defile his mate. It'd be the most vicious thing Kai would see in all his years, he was sure.

"There's conversation about transferring powers between a mated pair." In his time, demon matings were well known and not completely forgotten about as they were now. Speaking of one wouldn't be a shock.

A wicked quirk of his brow made Kai swallow back his discomfort. "Adramalech would want the whore's power. Control of this prison would make him unimaginable."

Kai had no doubt the two had transferred powers and Adramalech had had the same control of Hell's Gate as his mate—which was nowhere near Maya's control. Kai also knew that he never abused the power, that he loved seeing it on his mate. The same way Hunter did.

It was the demon in them loving only one person. It really evidenced to Kai why he preferred the species.

He also had no doubt calling Adramalech's mate a whore would get Krazen dropped to the depths Maya had taken them when Selin was killing her mate.

"Simple mating between the pair transfers the powers then?" Kai asked and got a blank stare in return, the quirked brow telling Kai he was waiting for a different word. Of course the pervert would want more graphic terminology for sex. It made

Kai sure he was down in Hell's Gate for vicious sexual acts. "Simple fucking between the mated pair transfers powers?"

He laughed mockingly, knowing he was making Kai uncomfortable and obviously enjoying it. Sick bastard. "Of course not."

"Then what?" Kai ground out.

Krazen didn't answer. Instead, he began moving forward, his hand in his pants now.

Kai moved around the cage. "Don't think about it, Krazen."

The man didn't listen for a moment as he pranced for Kai, knocking them both to the ground as he tried to reach into his pants for his dick again. Kai kicked at him and jumped back to his feet.

He circled the cage, waiting for the next attack. "Krazen, don't…"

Krazen pranced again, his fist moving for a punch that Kai moved out from. He threw his own punch and barely skimmed the man's jaw before a blow hit his gut. Too bad for the man, his gut was used to the abuse because of his princess.

The pervert's hand was in his pants again, so Kai did the most probable thing—kicked with all his force for the one area no man ever wanted to be kicked. If Kai could, he would've ripped the man's dick off and fed it to him. The fucking pervert.

Krazen doubled over but tried to reach for Kai again. Before he could, Kai moved out of the way and kicked the man's back so he fell to his knees. Kai grabbed a fistful of the man's hair and shoved him down into the dirt, wanting to choke him in it even knowing he wouldn't die because they were in Hell's Gate and the prison made sure deaths weren't possible. It made the prisoners suffer indefinitely.

Kai held the man down, his knee digging into Krazen's back and hoping to break a few ribs, even in this prison. "Answer me."

Krazen still gave that evil laugh when his face was pulled away from the dirt. "A mated pair transfers powers with the dust. Everyone knows so. You know that's not why you're here. If you wanted it rough, you could've said so."

The man lifted his hips as if he was offering his ass, and Kai pushed his knee down harder.

"Dust?" Kai ground out, needing to get out already.

"Faerie dust. Of course. It is well known, boy. Adramalech and Miradora have already fucked with the dust. They already have a transfer. Why don't we get to why you're truly here? Make it enjoyable for both of us."

Faerie dust? He'd been in Hell's Gate a millennium so to him it wouldn't be ancient faerie dust. He still believed modern faerie dust was just as powerful. He still believed modern day was ancient day.

*Had they told Krok about Selin's death before or after he'd mentioned the transferring? Or had he simply not known that detail, or guessed the pair had faerie dust? How had the old seer known, if he had at all.*

"That's it? Faerie dust and a mated pair?" Kai pushed into the man harder so he couldn't wiggle away.

"And fucking, of course. Fucking, fucking, fucking." He wiggled his hips again. "So why don't we get to it?"

Kai spit down at the man and wondered if there was a way he could reach out to Maya to get himself out already. He didn't want to spend another moment with this monster.

Then the ground rumbled like Maya had heard his request, and he felt himself move off of Krazen and the flabbergasted look as he was removed from the cage. The crazed need to catch onto Kai so that Krazen could get out too.

## 33

*He's okay.* Camilla's brows furrowed at the text, unsure what to make of it.

Then another came. *Just another concussion. The wounds are all already healing, should be good as new in a few.*

*What the hell are you talking about?* Camilla texted back to her sisters' group chat.

*Kai went to Hell's Gate.*

Camilla's heart stopped. What did they mean he went to Hell's Gate? They'd talked about it and agreed it'd be too dangerous.

But of course he would've done it anyway. The Demon *fucking* Warlock.

Camilla jumped from the vanity in her room and made her way down the stairs and through the house to the room she heard her family in.

She barged in with a growl, "Kai Georgette Sinclair."

Kai froze as different voices filled the room. "Georgette?" and "You gave him a last name?" and "Isn't Georgette your middle name?"

Camilla didn't remove her gaze as she answered only one of those questions. "I didn't give him anything."

"Cam," Vera said softly. "He doesn't have a coven, so he can't have a last name."

"But he has a brother, so he has a last name," Camilla argued, the anger bubbling up in her.

There was a sense of awe in Kai's eyes as he numbly walked up to her, his hands moving slowly as they took her face between them. "I'm going to marry you, princess."

"No," she bit back. "You're not."

The softness in his eyes almost melted Camilla as he chuckled and leaned in close so only she could hear him. "Camilla Georgette Sinclair. It sounds perfect."

Camilla didn't make a sound because it did sound perfect.

And it reminded her of that dream and how badly she still wanted that *perfect* tongue of his on her. Reminded her of the way she'd touched him in Scotland, and how badly she wanted to do so again, with no clothes this time.

"Ohhhh shit." Hunter's voice brought her out of her thoughts, and Camilla remembered that new brother of hers could smell how affected she was by the warlock before her.

So she tried to push away, but Kai held her still and brushed his thumb down her cheek and softly over her lips before asking, "Now, why are you angry with me this time?"

Camilla looked up into his hazel eyes, so different from any she'd ever seen, then forced herself to look away and pull back from him.

Her gaze snapped to Hunter. *Not a word.*

He smirked as his hand caressed Maya's thigh as she sat on the counter beside him. *Whatever could you mean, Little Sister?*

*I'm serious, Hunter.*

*Your sister is very aware of your feelings for the warlock, Little Sister.*

*You and I both know I've never reacted like this.*

Hunter looked like he was preparing to respond when Kai's breath hit her ear. "I'd appreciate it if you had your secret conversations with me rather than with your brother."

Camilla jumped, unaware her cold stare had been so focused on Hunter. She sent a final one. *Please just don't mention it.*

Hunter winked before Kai blocked her view of him. "Princess."

She grimaced as she looked him over. "What?"

"Why are you angry with me?"

Camilla eyed him, hyperaware of the fact that the wounds, whatever they may have been, were healed now. But as she met his gaze again, she wondered how long the concussion would need.

"What did you find in Hell's Gate?" There was no reason for him to think she cared. He'd already gone off and done the trip.

Kai's gaze narrowed on her like he knew why she was angry, knew it before she'd come downstairs and needed her to say it.

They narrowed deeper when she crossed her arms before her chest and stubbornly stared back at him.

A low growl, so very similar to that of her dream, left him, and before she could think, she sent another thought to Hunter. *I'm sorry, I can't control it.*

*Well, try. We need to stick around to hear this, and the last thing I want is to smell how badly the two of you want to fuck.*

Kai finally turned around, and his angry stare met Hunter. Camilla could tell by the way the men stared at one another— Kai with jealous rage and Hunter with stubborn indifference— that Kai could tell why she and Hunter had been communicating. Hated that it meant everyone else probably figured it out too.

"I was just telling your family," Kai said as he moved back to the table to take a seat, "about what I'd learned regarding transferring between a mated pair."

Camilla swallowed and moved to stand in front of the fridge, taking a nectarine in hand to keep from fidgeting. "What?"

"He obviously thought it was still his time," Kai began. "Thought I was there on Miradora's behalf. But he wasn't convinced. Apparently, back then, this was common knowledge, and Miradora and Adramalech had already been transferring powers. I would wager Adramalech simply didn't use it because it wasn't as strong as Maya's is now and…"

"And he enjoyed watching only her use it," Hunter finished matter-of-factly.

Maya held in a chuckle and met her mate's gaze, her own shining. "You did say that to me our first time."

"I still mean it, love." He stepped in between her legs and kissed her softly, then whispered to Maya, though Camilla still caught it. "I enjoy it every time, and I loved watching you just now, love. The way you controlled Kai's descend and ascend was hypnotizing."

Kai coughed to get them to break apart. "Well, apparently, it only happens between mated pairs who are having sex…"

"We already knew that," Camilla interrupted, her anger at him throwing himself in a dangerous situation for that useless information rising.

"*And* faeries' dust," Kai said snarkily, his gaze sharp on her, still angry at her. "Ancient faerie dust, that is. Krazen didn't exactly say that, but he thought we were in ancient times, and today's faerie dust is weak."

"So they can transfer powers because Hunter has the dust in him from killing Selin?" Vera asked, bewildered.

As Kai went to nod, Harry argued, "But that's impossible. If that rumbling underfoot at the warehouse was Hunter, he'd had the ability before he'd killed Selin."

Warren shrugged from his spot sitting on the other side of the table, Maya's usual spot. "It isn't said anywhere that a death must occur. Only that at least one person must have the dust. Hunter could've gotten some in past meetings with Selin. It could've come from when she'd knocked him out and he had that shine. It could've lingered on his skin. The difference being now, it's permanently in him."

"Very true," Kai agreed. "I'm assuming you got that from the entries?" When Warren nodded, Kai turned back to the group.

"I've looked into a lot about ancient dust in my years, but especially recently. Jenkins' journal he was going to have his class read talks about the ancient people killing off faeries to get their dust and it not working, for the most part."

Warren nodded as Camilla remembered back to the journal. She needed to begin taking the entries literally and not as part of a literature course because obviously Jenkins was on a mission and he knew what he was talking about.

"There're methods," Warren added. "It's not mentioned what those methods are, but whatever they were, they worked to give Hunt some dust when he was captured and all of it when he killed her."

"So there's really nothing that can be done?" Adela asked, her grandmotherly worry shining in her words.

Maya glowered at her husband, and it caught Camilla off guard for a second. "Oh, something is being done."

Camilla didn't know what that meant, but as she met Kai's own glowering eyes, she realized that maybe that trip below was informative. She still hated that he'd gone, without her knowledge, and somehow gotten hurt. She couldn't—wouldn't—admit it to him, but she was mature enough to admit it to herself.

And she needed to know exactly what had happened while he was down there. She just didn't know how to ask for said information without making it sound like she was worried for him in some extra way.

When Kai's eyes narrowed on her, Camilla's anger rose again. What was he angry about? She should still be the angry one.

<hr>

Maya almost seemed as angry with him as they landed back at the manor as Camilla had been with Kai.

She'd been especially edgy these past few days, and Hunter

had to wonder if it was because of the emotional effects of the pregnancy or something else. Or a combination.

He watched as she stripped out of her clothes and had to fight the urge to follow her into the shower as she rinsed off the day. His cock was awake and begging to be inside her, but he ignored it as he watched the loofa dance over Maya's skin.

And when she was finally out and dried, Hunter barely fought the urge to bend her over the counter and take her there.

But almost like she'd read his thoughts, she bent herself over, those legs spread apart and giving him a delicious view of her cunt.

"Offering up dessert?" Hunter stepped up and teased at her ear as his hands began to skim her body.

"No, I'm not offering dessert!" Maya turned and pushed him. "Fuck, Hunter, all you've done is have *dessert*. I want you to fuck me!"

Hunter tried to remain calm, her anger turning him on even more than before. He wanted to fuck her as much as she wanted him to.

He took her face between his hands. "Love, you know why we can't."

"No." She pushed him away. "I know why you won't!"

"Maya…"

"Baby, we don't lose control every time! It's not like it happens *every time*!"

"Maya, love, please," Hunter begged, both of them knowing losing control wasn't the only guaranteed way to transfer powers. And both of them knowing they had no control of *when* they lost control of their powers, so they wouldn't be able to stop it if they needed to. He needed to keep to his decision. "Once Jenkins is gone, I will fuck you until you forget how to walk. But I can't risk Jenkins finding out about your portal. If he were to get to me, I need to know he couldn't get to you to try to get the transfer to continue."

He was convinced that would be impossible since he knew

Maya wouldn't even be able to be with anyone else, even with his body as the physical being she was with. But a part of Hunter feared Jenkins would be able to figure out a way if he really wanted to.

And that was one determined man Hunter would not call a bluff to.

"Hunter, if something happened to you, it would happen to me too. I'm not living this life without you." Tears strolled down her cheeks, and Hunter knew they were both out of sexual frustration and the thought of losing him.

"But you will live it for our kids," he argued. "At the very least, you'll stick around to have them. I won't risk Jenkins hurting any of you, figuring out a way to force you to stay when you want to go. I can't risk our family, Maya. I…"

After long seconds of silence, she asked, "You what?"

"I don't know," he answered, frustrated. "All I know is that you're my mate and I will protect you. And if that means having you angry with me because I'm refusing sex, then so be it."

Maya sighed. "Hunter, I love your fingers and your tongue, but I need the release only your cock can give me."

Hunter hardened his gaze. "And I wish I could give it to you."

He could tell she was trying to fight the tears as her jaw ground, but that was all he saw before she pushed past him and into their bedroom. She was in bed, her back to him, and he hated himself as he watched the small movements of her body trying to hide the tears rolling down her face.

He climbed in after her, wrapped his arm around her waist, and brought her flush to his front. They both needed the release of being inside her, but he needed to hold her more.

And luckily, she didn't fight away from him as his face fell into the crook of her shoulder and the tears silently fell down her cheeks.

"I'm sorry, love," he whispered. "I'm sorry, so sorry, sorry…"

## 34

"We do remember the part of my becoming a witch where demons were after me, right?"

Harry's lips twitched into an infinitesimally small smile as he said, "We are here on business, Vera. And no demon is dumb enough to try to attack your family now that the Delvauxs are part of it."

"Still." Vera felt antsy in her spot standing behind him. "I don't like this."

"I don't either, but without something to hold that final potion in, all the work we put into making all of those potions will be for naught. The point of the potion is to make the person able to block animal demons from entering this realm, so we need a demon with experience with animal demons to help us hold it."

"And how do we know he'll actually help?"

"We're paying."

Vera quirked a brow.

Harry gave her an incredulous look over his shoulder. "You know, not all demons are out for harm."

"Oh, yes. And I should've guessed that one known for his work with animal demons would be moral."

"Don't forget, sweetheart." He dipped his head so their noses brushed. "Your brother is also a Delvaux. Problems with you mean problems with him."

Vera narrowed her eyes. "And you don't forget that he's not here right now."

Harry gave a small, soft laugh and turned back to face the grand space of the coffee shop. They'd chosen this place because of how public it was. With this many humans around, the demon would be less likely to play games with them.

Vera and Harry were up against the far side wall so the man couldn't try to come up behind them, and though Vera was nervous about this meeting, her gaze continued to hover to the baked goods on display. She couldn't help it. The baker in her needed to taste all of them.

Harry had promised to grab a box of them on their way out. She wouldn't forget to try one of their specialty drinks while they were at it.

They were having this meeting for one simple thing that was apparently not so simple to come by—a vial to hold the potion the Book had made them make against animal demons. Not only was the potion too powerful for any simple vial, but it was important that any random person not be able to get into it as they only had this one and no time for attempts at another.

Since this demon worked with animal demons, he was the go-to expert for all things animal demon related. Usually, his services were used to bring animal demons out, not hold them in, but apparently, as long as he got paid, he didn't care which services they needed.

Vera's demon sensing tingled, and she knew without looking over to the doorway that he was there. Her hand involuntarily squeezed Harry's, which she had been holding in case he needed to get them out of their quickly.

Harry met the demon's gaze with a hard one of his own, but the demon looked relaxed the entire way.

He didn't move directly for them. Instead, he cut the line for a coffee, which was made okay by the teenage girls swooning over his good looks. When he finally got his coffee, he deemed their meeting important enough to come to.

It was the same type of stunt Hunter would pull. It made her wonder if it was a tactic to make them uneasy before the meeting, or if they simply did it because it was in their personality?

"Ah, my witch and warlock couple." He shook a teasing finger at them. "Naughty, naughty. You're supposed to fuck someone *not* in your coven from what I hear."

"You have the vial?" Harry didn't beat around the bush. He hadn't been happy about making this deal so it made sense that he would try to finish it as quickly as possible.

"Of course I have the vial, friend. But why jump to business so soon?" He eyed Vera. "Why don't we sit, talk, get to know one another a little?"

"How much?" Harry ground his jaw.

The demon laughed as he met Vera's eyes. "He's no fun, is he?"

Vera swallowed but remained strong as she questioned, "How much?"

"Money? Oh, money is a pretty thing." He gave them a sweet smile that said 'run as far as you can.' "But you now have a demon in the family. You should know favors are worth more than money."

Vera's gaze narrowed. "He works for money."

The demon laughed. "He tells you he works for money. And maybe sometimes he does, but the man has more money than it's worth. He works for favors. The Delvauxs have so many favors owed to them, it would be impossible to go against them. You didn't truly think they were this powerful family simply based on their powers, did you, sweetheart?"

Harry gave a slight growl, and moved his body to cover more of Vera. "What favor?"

The demon's cocky grin made Vera want to punch that bag at Camilla's school gym. "Any."

"No," Harry answered swiftly. "It's not worth that much."

Harry's hand tugged on Vera's to walk away, but Vera forced him to stop. They needed this.

She faced the man. "What favor?"

He quirked an amused brow. "From you?" He eyed her body like a Michelin star meal. "Oh, the favors I could ask of you."

Harry's quick response in grabbing the man and bringing him nose-to-nose got some unwanted attention from the humans, but most of them brushed it aside as an asshole saying something to a man's girlfriend. Nothing humans don't go through on a daily basis.

"How about I kill you and just take whatever I want?"

The demon rolled his eyes as he grinned. "A favor. You port me from point A to point B when I tell you to, no questions or arguments."

"A one time thing?"

"A one time thing."

"Deal." Harry threw the man away from him, and stuck out his hand. "The vial."

At least the demon handed it over without argument.

He walked away after that. As simple as that.

Before Vera could do anything more, Harry pushed her back so they were less in sight of prying eyes.

"What are you doing?" she argued, ready as she had been to go buy pastries and a drink.

"What am I doing? You nearly caused a much bigger problem between us."

"How?" she exclaimed.

"Vera"—he breathed hard—"I was not pulling you away for some fun games. The demon wouldn't have given up a chance at a favor from a warlock. He was going to stop us."

So Harry had been bluffing. He couldn't exactly be angry with her for not realizing. Harry never bluffed.

"Well, we still got—"

"No, Vera! Now I owe him a porting favor."

"Why is that such a big de—"

"Because it came with the condition that I cannot question what is happening. If he decides he wants to blow up a school, then be ported away, I cannot argue with him. I cannot stop to save the kids. Nothing. All I can do is port him away. These favors aren't petty human promises. They're very real."

He stormed off before she could say anything.

How was she supposed to know any of that? They'd been so bombarded since the moment they got their powers that they hadn't had too much down time to learn any of these basics.

Harry didn't look at her as he stood by the counter to order the box of pastries to go. He didn't know she wanted a drink as well.

Vera didn't want to go to him with that because all she could think of was what kind of favor would that demon ask for in the future?

35

Maya shrugged out of her mate's arms the moment they landed in Canada. A pang of hurt traveled through her ring—which made her realize just how badly this situation pained Hunter—but she didn't care at the moment.

Though a bit of guilt did ride up her throat.

Zathrian and Acacia's shop had the closed sign up, but Maya ignored it as she walked in, moving for the back before either one of them had the chance to greet her in the front. Hunter followed close behind her, and she knew he was fighting himself from reaching out and touching her. And though she loved his touches and desired them constantly, at the moment, they angered her more.

Adramalech, Zathrian's pet crow who bore the same name as her ancestor, cawed to let the couple in back know it was friendly visitors. Maya wondered if that caw somehow let Zath know exactly who it was because he didn't seem shocked in the slightest to see her walk into the room in the back.

They both moved for an embrace, Acacia's belly larger than before, and Maya smiled as she hugged them. Her smile widened when Zath bent over to her belly and whispered, "Hey, you two. How are you treatin' Mama?"

Maya laughed as Hunter brushed past them for the couch. He was trying to act like they weren't in a fight—for her sake since she knew if it were up to him, he'd let everyone know he was angry or annoyed.

Because that was his outward appearance.

On the inside, she could feel through the rings how hurt he was. And she would wager it was because she'd laughed, smiled, acknowledged in a friendly manner—all of the above—with Zathrian and had been giving him the cold shoulder for days.

That guilt grew a bit bigger inside her as their friends moved for their own couch and Maya was left to choose a spot to sit. One look in Hunter's direction said he wouldn't be surprised if she chose to sit anywhere but near him. He sat with both hands interlocked in his lap, smaller than his usual take-up-all-the-space stance.

That broke her.

She was angry with him, but not that angry. She didn't want to hurt him like that. Fuck, she loved him, for crying out loud.

Maya moved in his direction and realized as she was going to sit, how desperately she needed his touch. When she settled by his side—basically on top of him—both of them were shocked. But Hunter only wrapped his arm around her waist and pulled her closer as if there was any more space between them. His free hand landed on her stomach, and his face dropped to breathe her in.

Such a large wave of relief washed through her, and the guilt tried to choke her for putting him through any of that pain. Especially because what he was doing—denying her sex—was done to protect her and their children.

They sat talking for an hour, enjoying the distraction this gave them from the rest of the world, the problems that were plaguing her family, before the crow flew into the room and settled on the couch head by Zathrian.

Maya's gaze settled on it as the others continued on their

conversation. Little Adramalech, the same name as Miradora's Adramalech.

"Why'd you name him Adramalech?" Maya interrupted whatever they'd been speaking of, her gaze not wavering from the bird.

Zathrian smiled warmly as he looked over to his bird. "I didn't. That's his name."

Maya quirked a brow, and Hunter answered her unasked question. "Familiar-like animals come with names, their own histories, everything."

Her brows shot up as she watched Adramalech before turning to Zath. "So what's his?"

"Even as my bird, I don't know it all," he answered. "I've been learning slowly through the years, but I don't know his origins or his name—"

Caw. Caw. Caw.

Zathrian turned shocked eyes on the bird before turning back to them. "Apparently, he'd like us to know now."

Maya couldn't help but smirk. "You speak bird?"

Acacia giggled into her husband's side as Zath rolled his eyes. "Do you want to know?"

Maya motioned for him to continue, falling into Hunter and feeling his body shake in amusement as well. She looked up to meet his gaze and was lost in those beautiful black orbs. "I love you," she whispered, then turned back to their friends.

His smile fell into her hair before he kissed her long and hard and pulled her closer so she fell into his lap, his hand on her belly growing like he wanted to hold all three of them already.

Zathrian's own hand was on Acacia's belly as the crow cawed, and he translated, shock lingering in his voice. "Adramalech, named after the grandfather of the family he was born into. His family of birds weren't shewed away from this home's land, and they were each named because of the family's liking to them. Them being magically inclined probably brought both families—birds and Powers—together."

"So he was named after Miradora's Adramalech?" Maya gasped.

Caw, caw.

"Apparently they both had that brooding, annoyed look whenever they were around people they didn't want to be around," Zath laughed and met Hunter's gaze. "Maybe you should be named Adramalech."

"Fuck off," her mate growled.

Maya laughed. "What else?"

The bird cawed and looked at her like it knew exactly what she was asking—*anything about Miradora and Adramalech?*

"After coming out of Hell's Gate," Zath continued to translate for the bird, "Miradora and Adramalech were feared. Everyone knew Adramalech had been sent below and the High Priests were the only holders of the keys. He shouldn't have been out, but there they were, hand-in-hand. Mates. Everyone was shocked *and* scared. Especially when it became known that even though going into Hell's Gate was difficult, but not impossible, for them, going to Hell was as easy as shadowing below."

That wasn't how Hell worked. Demons had to be banished to the underworld in order to be there, and Maya couldn't remember hearing about a witch going below.

"Why was Adramalech sent below anyway?"

More caws before Zath answered, "You must remember that though this is a love story, he wasn't a good man." He said it for the girls' case because neither he nor Hunter would care about any of Adramalech's indiscretions. "He'd burned down entire villages for fun. It was partly greed, but mostly for fun."

Maya gasped, wondering how Miradora looked past that.

Then she remembered that Hunter had a gym full of children ready to burn to death, and she'd been turned on in his presence rather than disgusted. Miradora had likely been in Maya's shoes—angry with him, but wanting him nonetheless.

"The gilded cane that was used to send you the first time, that was the main way to send anyone below. The High Priests had enough at a certain point and trapped Adramalech in a candled circle, then sent him below," Zath continued, his own awe at hearing this story that no one knew shining in the way he spoke. "The problem was, he'd already met Miradora, and she hated him, but she wouldn't let him go."

"How?" Acacia asked, looking at her mate with glowing eyes like this was the best bedtime story she'd ever heard.

"He didn't just walk past and burn a village. He did so slowly to breathe in the fear of the villagers. Most of them would end up dying in the fires, but he had fun with it." Zathrian watched the bird with fascination as it cawed. "Sometimes, he would put up a shield around the town and mess with them slowly so they couldn't leave even if they wanted to before the entire place burned down. One of the last places he burned down, it was his second day there when he came across an angry long, dark-haired beauty. He didn't know what the feeling was, but he grew curious about her when she got in his face, yelling at him. He'd smirked, wanting to know her name, when she smacked him across the face."

All four of them laughed. At least Miradora had a backbone on her. One glance in Hunter's direction said he knew if he'd actually done anything to those kids, she would've smacked him, and he would've welcomed it.

Maya rolled her eyes and turned back to the story.

"Because of Miradora, Adramalech worked that village slower because he wanted to be near her. It was a foreign feeling, but he followed it. The next time they met, he'd sought her out. They ended up in her tent—they were small bedroom-sized tents that many alone villagers lived in—and she argued with him. Apparently, she ended up beneath him so to say, but he pushed away before they could unite. He didn't want to force anything. He wanted her to crawl to him. For his witch to come to *him*."

Meeting Hunter's gaze, Maya remembered their first time—*I won't let you use the excuse that I seduced you into this. If you want it, take it.*

Turning back to the couple across from them, Maya could tell they'd had the same experience. It was probably what happened when a demon mated with a witch. She would be too good, and he would want her to come to him, to want it, to admit she wanted him.

"It wasn't long before she went to him, and through the carnage of the village, they got together. She hated herself for it, but she loved him," Zath finished for the bird.

"And he still burned the village?" Acacia asked.

Zath nodded. "Then one more after that before the priests got involved. They were now nearing Selin's village. When Adramalech was sent below—without lack of fighting, of course. Miradora couldn't handle it. She needed him, loved him, knew him in a way no one else did—his story, his heart, his soul. She loved him."

"So she went after him," Maya finished. They all knew how—killing Selin's entire family being the biggest part of it, so she didn't need to voice that.

And a simple glance in Acacia's direction said she would do the same for her mate. Maya knew she would.

"When he came back, with Miradora at his side," Zath reverted back, "they were shocked, scared. But there was a sense of respect from the demons for both of them—for the witch as well. Demons envied them their magic and control, but every single one of them respected the couple."

"Unlike the witches, I suppose," Acacia commented, and they all chuckled.

It was the truth. Witches ended up making the story one of the demon kidnapping the witch and forcing her to remain with him in the underworld rather than the truth—she'd done horrendous things on her own to get to him. She'd chosen him above all else.

"They became the rulers of Hell," Zath finished the bird's story of the couple she and Hunter were the most like. "Meaning they had the one control that no one else did—it wasn't something that could be born with or acquired with greed and power, no matter how much it was desired. It was a control that was honored upon them by Hell itself, and one Adramalech wielded better than his mate."

"Which is?" Acacia breathed, in her own awe of the story.

The bird cawed, and Zath answered, "Control of all animal demons. Every. Last. One."

*Entry #5211*

Demons have counterparts to look after them. These animals are weak, yet they bring so much power to the demons.

Witches need these counterparts.

I have found a cat who is attached to a demon. I thought if I could control the cat, the demon would come running. I was wrong. The cat did not go without a fight and now I can hardly walk without wincing.

The cat showed me that my human body is much weaker than I am.

The demon's animals will make my job more difficult. Witches need an animal familiar to protect them. They are the weaker ones.

When I am ruling over the world, I will make the demons with animals my security and they will all obey me.

I am God.

36

ontrol of animal demons?

Warren didn't know what to do with that information. He was with his family—Augustine, Hunter, and Maya—in his father's study discussing what Hunter and Maya had found out from their visit to their mated couple friends.

The couple sat together in Hunter's green leather chair, their father across from them, and Warren stood off beside the bookshelves. He felt too antsy to sit.

"I don't think that's a power my mate acquired, Father. Wipe that greed out of your eyes," Hunter barked.

Augustine laughed. "They got control of animal demons, and you have an unlimited access to Hell's Gate. Seems fair."

"Not unlimited," Maya corrected.

Augustine rolled his eyes. "So you need to think about your mate for the power to work. I'm sure with time, through the years, we'll be able to tweak that ability."

Hunter rolled his eyes, but it was obvious he agreed. Part of Warren did too. He knew Maya was strong and she would be able to wield her emotions to work for her whenever need be.

"Plus, my son now holds your powers as well. So we can

277

experiment on him before doing anything more to you," Augustine added, his grin a little too pleased. "Hunt has two decades' experience against your six months. He'll be able to compartmentalize and utilize the power."

"Not to mention, he's not caring, so he wouldn't be bothered with hurting innocents," Maya added what they all knew sarcastically.

Augustine chuckled. "Be glad it's not you, darling."

Maya rolled her eyes and turned to mumble something against Hunter's neck. The man tried to suppress his amusement, but the sparkle in his black eyes failed him as he pulled her tighter into his chest, mumbling back against her ear.

Warren turned away, staring into the flames in the fireplace his family sat around. His thoughts wavered to the glass of the bloodied vase he hadn't thrown out.

Warren sighed and turned to the bookshelves, allowing his fingers to skim the spines as he thought of the story of Miradora and Adramalech. It was such a fascinating one, he'd have to go to Canada and meet these friends of theirs. Ask Zathrian, who he assumed would need to ask the crow, if Warren could transcribe the story. Have a full story of Miradora and Adramalech before she'd gone into Hell's Gate. One from the demon's side. The truthful side.

Currently, most of the demons' stories spoke of when the two were already together and their time together in Hell's Gate. But nothing about how they'd met and fallen in love. Warren wanted nothing more than to turn that story into its own book.

One where the witch wasn't a victim, but the villain herself. One where two villains fell in love. One where demonic matings were revered and special. One where the story of the ounce of Hell's Gate power was traded in for the control of animal demons, albeit without choice.

Warren gasped, staring at the spines as he spoke. "You have the Hell's Gate portal power." He turned around and met Maya's gaze. "But that doesn't mean you won't have some of the animal demon control. Miradora had some portal control and an abundant amount of demon control. You may have the opposite."

Maya gasped, and Hunter's gaze narrowed.

Augustine's smirk widened as his gaze jumped to each of them. "As I've been thinking."

Hunter growled, and those black eyes of his turned deathly as they turned on their father.

"Don't worry, Son. In the story, Adramalech—the demon—wields the power more, whether that's because he is stronger or because he cares less, I'm uncertain and do not care much. In that case, you should have better reign when the power comes in, then we can use those decades behind you to bring it back. At least partially."

"You're one greedy fucker," Maya teased.

Augustine stared into her eyes proudly. "I'm a patriarch. Ruling this family and finding our best advantages is my job."

Warren had to suppress an eye roll as he leaned over the desk in front of the bookshelves and crossed his arms. "What exactly are you doing, Mr. Patriarch? All that's happened is your son and his mate keep getting more powerful. You haven't done a thing."

"My job is not to get them to power, War. My job is to use that power when they have it."

This time Warren didn't stop the eye roll. Maya threw a bigger one at the man.

"I'll kill you before you use Maya," Hunter said calmly, not needing to growl or bark the comment for everyone to hear the threat behind it.

Augustine merely smirked. "That's why I have you and the transferred abilities."

W orking with the other covens was far more annoying than Vera could've fathomed. She hadn't imagined they'd be quite so snobbish.

Though she knew not all witch covens were like this, working with these lot—the more powerful in the North American territories—wasn't setting a positive precedent. Or helping the witch image.

Vera could only imagine the demons, and Kai as the Demon Warlock, were far more annoyed by the lot by the simple way the groups continued snickering at them.

They were in another huge mansion for sale in the middle of Nebraska this time. The land had acres on it, so they wouldn't need to worry about unwarranted guests arriving for a showing or randoms walking by and overhearing them. Which was a good thing because arguments were easy to break out between the pretentious and the uncaring.

The Whittles and Wittlieffs, for the most part, remained out of the arguments, peacekeepers. The 'for the most part' came in because Camilla wasn't even trying to be friendly with the others. She stood in front of Kai with her arms crossed over her chest and glared at the covens. Kai seemed completely unfazed by the groups, but rather looked to enjoy every time they insulted him. That, no doubt, had to do with Camilla sticking up for him each time. It was nice to see Camilla so passionate about a relationship, especially considering they weren't even together yet. It showed exactly how much she loved him even if she wasn't ready to admit to it yet.

Maya's love for her mate came differently. She didn't argue back with the covens which coincidently seemed to anger them more. That, and the constant touches and kisses she and Hunter continued to give one another.

Her sisters and the Delvauxs made Vera and Harry's relationship look like a Heaven-send to these witches. Even while looking down at the fact that Vera had been his ward, the others made them look like a normal, accepted couple. It was selfish to enjoy it, but Vera couldn't help herself.

The arguments only seemed to get worse anytime one from the Ragtag House, Hayes or his seconds, or the Bridgers couple —who held an adorable baby Aurelia in their arms, thankfully not screaming for Vera's demon brother—tried to interject. The Wremons and Lennoxs especially didn't make witches look like pleasant people the way they regarded the other species. There was a reason most species tried not to hang around the Powers. It wasn't out of fear; it was out of disgust.

"You're trying to give *that* demon more power?" one of the Wremon warlocks spit. Vera couldn't remember his name. There were so many of these new groups and too much going on in her life for her to put the effort in. "Control over animal demons will give him power over every creature. Witches won't be able to be the natural barrier for long."

It was obvious the man didn't like admitting that his species would be defeated, but it was unreasonable to believe any coven could go against a hoard of animal demons. From what Vera understood, most of them remained in Hell and hardly ever were used in groups. Hunter, old Hunter at least, would've had fun bringing them all up.

"That's not what we're saying," Maya said with some condescension.

"Not to mention, it is Maya with Adramalech's blood, not Hunter," Loretta added, her voice calm as she attempted to be peacekeeper.

"But they're transferring powers," the Lopez warlock, the only group who wasn't as bad as the others, asked without snide but simple curiosity.

"Well, if they stop having sex..." Bishop started but cut himself off slowly because they all knew Mr. and Mrs. Sucking Each Other's Faces Off weren't going to stop having sex.

"That's not true actually," Warren cut in from where he leaned under an arched doorway.

"What do you mean?" Juliette, their banshee friend and the unofficial leader of the Ragtag House asked. Her wolf mate, Felix, eyed Hunter and Maya all the while with teasing eyes and wiggling brows. They were some of the first to support the couple, and he obviously found it amusing that they may not have sex.

"I've been looking into the dust's mixing with matings, which wasn't very easy because of the lack of studies or written work about demon matings."

Vera looked around the room as Warren began speaking, following Aurelia's line of sight as she stared off into the corner of the large room.

The corner. Where Hunter currently had Maya pulled into him and his tongue shoved down her throat. Vera scrunched her nose when she saw their tongues fighting and had to turn back around, surprised the baby wasn't screaming for Maya to get her hands off Aurelia's love.

Vera laughed to herself as her gaze fell onto a couple of the witches standing across from her, and a frown immediately dropped her lips. The two looked disturbed, and it was obvious it wasn't because of the excessive PDA, but because of who was in the middle of the tongue fight.

Fucking assholes.

Then Vera calmed her breath. There'd been a point when she didn't like Hunter. Though, to be fair, that had been because all her experiences with him had been negative, not because he was a demon.

"But I've found," Warren continued, "that it doesn't matter whether sex is taking place as long as it had happened at least once while the dust was within one or both of them. Meaning, once the dust was fully Hunter's and not just a lingering of Selin's power, then sex didn't have to be continuous."

"So before Hunt killed Selin..." Harry left the question unasked.

But more than anything, Vera couldn't pull away from his use of the name—Hunt. Only Hunter's family called him that, and Vera decided in that moment that she would start too. She knew Harry had done so subconsciously, but Hunter was family, and it was time she allowed more people into her life. Being afraid because of the fear of returning to that loneliness if she were to lose them couldn't continue stopping her.

"Before he killed Selin, the faerie dust was residual, which means they would need to continue having sex for the transfers to continue, basically until there was no more dust on his skin. Now that it's fully within Hunt, they don't need to. They would've had to do so once, *lose control* once, to allow the full transfer—and I'd bet my entire family's fortunes they've done it far more than that in only the couple of days after Selin's death —but that's it. It's taken place, and it's permanent now."

"How, exactly, did you figure that out?" Hunter asked, talk of his mating finally pulling him from sucking her sister's face off.

Warren shrugged. "Kai and I went to your friend and had a talk with his bird. I had some more questions rather than merely listening to the story of Miradora and Adramalech. They permanently shared powers, as you two do now. And if you continue stealing powers and having sex, Hunt, then Maya will continue to hold all the same magic."

Vera couldn't believe this new information, but one look in her sister's direction had her blushing. The way Hunter and Maya stared at one another now—like they were hungrier for one another than ever before—looked more intimate and sexual than the way they'd been shoving their tongues down each other's throats.

"I think it's time this meeting ended," Hunter growled in an obvious attempt to control himself from ripping Maya's clothes off at that very moment.

Vera wondered what it was about finding out that information that made the two so feral for one another, but they were gone—shadowed—before the question could be voiced.

She stared at the others in the silence of the room and read the same confusion there.

37

He didn't need to continue denying sex. No matter what happened, their transfers were permanent, and Hunter couldn't use the denial of sex to keep her safer from Jenkins any longer.

So he would be ravishing her. Making up for the last couple of weeks. For all those lost encounters. He had about a hundred orgasms he'd like his cock to give his mate. They might have to remain locked in their manor for the next month or three.

Maya ripped at his shirt as she pushed him back into the ottoman at the foot of their bed. "You could've been fucking me this entire time! You held off for no," she scratched at his chest, "fucking" she gripped his hair and snapped his neck back, "reason!"

She kissed him roughly as he ripped her clothes off her body. He understood her frustration more than she'd ever know, but Hunter wouldn't change any of it for a second. The simple fact that it could have helped would have him doing so again for his mate, even if said mate grew feral with him.

When she was standing naked between his legs, she pushed away from his lips as she pulled at his trousers, ungraceful and savage as she tried to get him naked.

Her desperation would make Hunter laugh if he didn't feel it too.

He pushed his clothes off and hardly had time to think as Maya took her spot on his lap, straddling him, and lowered hard onto his cock.

They both groaned, and all around them the lights flashed into darkness as flames burst out, and a light rumble shook the grounds, pillows flying off the bed and the faucets turning on in the bathroom as some of his stolen powers lost control too.

Hunter had her ass in either palm, fingers grazing her puckered hole, as he helped bounce her over his cock. They moaned, groaned, and filled the air with their cries as they both came in the matter of minutes.

It was fast and intense, but it was needed. Now they'd be able to focus better, last longer.

Back from the high, Maya pulled at his hair to get him to look back into her eyes and gave a soft smile. "Finally."

He chuckled against those soft lips. "I'm not even a fraction of the way done with you, love. We needed to do that because it's been too long since I've come inside you, but I plan on doing so at least a dozen more times before I let you out of here."

He rose to his feet with Maya still impaled onto his cock and moved for the ensuite. Hunter finally pulled her off his cock and settled her to the ground as he turned her to look into the mirror.

Standing behind her, Hunter turned them softly so that they could see her side, the bump of her belly that indicated the twins inside. His hands were large compared to her body, so when he moved them over her belly, he was able to cover most of it. "I'm holding my three, Maya. I'll always hold my three." He moved his hands to her hips so they could see her bump in the mirror again, the swell of her breasts above it inviting. "I'll always protect my three. If not being inside you gave any possibility that I could keep you three safe from Jenkins, I'd do it over and over again."

Maya smiled at him through the mirror, then found his hands at her hips and moved them back to her stomach as hers rested over them. "I love you, Hunt. I know you'll always protect us. Even when I'm frustrated by it, I love you even more for it."

He kissed the side of her neck softly, still staring into her eyes through the mirror. "It's easier now, love. You're carrying them, so protecting all three of you simply means protecting you. When you give birth, I'll have three individuals to protect." *Whether I'm here to do so or I need to leave my father and brother to do so.* "I need to make sure Jenkins is taken care of before that happens."

Maya didn't say anything, but there was understanding and determination in her eyes. She knew he had suicide missions planned out to protect them, and he also knew she was fiercer than anyone else on this planet, and if there was ever a hero, she would be it.

Hunter turned them again so they were facing the mirror and softly pushed at her back so she'd bend over, forearms resting on the counter so her belly had free range to hang. He'd have to be calmer than he'd like—because he'd like to fuck her until her body was banging against every surface—but that didn't mean he couldn't leave some bruises. Some hand and finger marks, at least.

"Look at me, love," he commanded low.

Her gaze shot up to the mirror and met his, and there was a smirk about her lips. She loved moments like these, when he controlled her.

Hunter kept his gaze locked on hers as his fingers dipped into her cunt and soaked up to the knuckles. He individually fingered her with each one of his fingers so his entire hand was soaked, then returned his thumb back to really cover it.

Then he replaced his hand with his cock and slowly rocked into her as his thumb moved to that puckered hole left for him to play with. He inserted only the tip and needed to hold her hip tight with his free hand when she gasped. He needed to be slower with this movement to ease her into it, but those sounds always had the opposite effect on him.

"How does that feel, love?" It wasn't the first time he'd put his finger in her butt, but it'd been a while, so he needed to hear her words.

"Full, but so good," she moaned.

He chuckled. "You want more, love?"

"I always want more of you."

He leaned in to bite her back, leaving his teeth marks by those of his fingers, then pushed harder into her. His thumb moved, easing its way inside, until it was fully inside her, and Hunter reveled in the sounds she made with it.

He held her hip hard as he rocked thumb and cock into her, hard and steady once he found the movement that had her screaming every time.

"More, more," she huffed. "I'm so full, but I want more of you, baby!"

"You want all three holes full of me, love?" he growled, eyes feral as he held her gaze through the mirror.

She gave desperate nods as her cunt clenched around his cock, making her ass hold onto his thumb even more.

He leaned over her. "You're so close, my girl." He moved his free hand up her body, tweaking at her nipples along the way, until he collared her throat. "The second you come, I won't be able to control myself. I already need to fill you so fucking badly."

"Please, baby, yes!" She slammed her hips backed into his, and Hunter had to groan back the need to release at that moment.

Instead, he held her jaw roughly as he slipped two of his fingers into her mouth and commanded, "Suck."

She did so feverishly, cheeks hollowing in as she licked and sucked at his fingers, gaze never leaving his in the mirror.

That look made the animal in him come out, and he no

longer cared to be slow as he slammed his cock into her as his thumb fucked her ass with equal vigor, fingers finding their way to the back of her throat to gag her.

Tears shined in her eyes, but they were so full of mirth, he knew she was loving every moment of it. As if to prove it, her moans filled the room around his fingers and had him biting into her shoulder to keep from coming just yet.

Her juices were sliding down both of their legs with how wet she was, but he couldn't allow himself to finish yet. A form of torture Hunter had never known, yet wanted to relive for the rest of his life.

He fucked all three holes roughly and growled low into her ear, "Come, Maya. I swear to the lords...fuck, Maya, milk me."

Her body clenched so tightly with his words Hunter could no longer hold it, and he growled loud, mixing with Maya's cries as they both came. His load continued to shoot into her as her aftershocks rocked his cock still inside her.

When they both finally calmed, Hunter softly kissed her shoulder and removed his fingers from her mouth. "You don't truly think we're done, do you?"

"I would kill you if we were." She smirked through the mirror.

Hunter traced his wet fingers down her spine, then slowly removed his thumb from her ass as he palmed both cheeks.

Without warning, he smacked both of them to leave his hand marks. They blossomed red almost immediately. He did so again a few more times, reveling in her moans, to make sure they truly marked her, and when he was finally satisfied, Hunter met her gaze in the mirror again.

He finally slipped his cock free of her warm cunt and moved to take a fistful of her hair and spin her around to face him again, come dripping down both of their legs and over his cock.

Hunter kissed her savagely, collaring her to keep her in place as he shoved his tongue inside her. He kissed her every single day even without the sex, yet he still needed to do this as if he hadn't done so in weeks.

When he finally pulled away, she bit at his lower lip hard until she drew blood and smirked when he gave a light wince.

He met that evil glint. "You're bringing out the animal, love."

"Mm, yum." She licked his lips, swallowing back his blood.

Hunter leaned into her neck and bit down hard. "If you were hungry, love, you should've just said so." Before she could respond, he pushed her to her knees and pulled on her hair so she met his gaze as her lips grazed his still semi-hard cock. "Enjoy, my mate."

Some may classify her look as crazed, but Hunter loved it as she held his gaze and licked his cock, collecting the mixture of their come off his shaft.

"How do we taste, love?"

She had his cock shoved to the back of her throat, so her answer was a mix of moans that vibrated around his cock.

Although he loved the view, Hunter pulled her hair back so his cock popped out. As she went to argue, he forced her jaw open with the other hand and spit into her mouth, then closed her mouth. "Swallow."

She did so instantly, then fought against his hand to open again. "More."

Hunter did so without hesitation and almost came again at the sight of her taking his spit and licking more of them off his cock before swallowing.

"We taste that good, Witch?"

She nodded slowly as her tongue lazily licked at his tip.

He smirked. "Come up here and show me."

She gave him a wicked smile as she rose to her feet and held onto his shoulders as he hefted her into his arms and those delicious legs wrapped around his waist.

When she kissed him, it was slow and sensual, but he got the taste of their mixed come off of her tongue and growled with it.

He kept the pace of the kiss intimate as he walked them to the bed and dropped her to her back as he hovered over her. When he finally pulled away, he smiled. "We taste fucking amazing, love."

## 38

"*I*f you touch him again, I'll kill you!" the little mermaid hissed at his father. The chick had more nerve than most demons.

"How exactly would you kill a Power, little girl?" Augustine grimaced at her, conceited mirth in his eyes.

"Just because the other species aren't as magically inclined as the Powers doesn't mean we don't have our own tricks, *old man*," Bella ground out, Vincent having to hold her back from jumping the Delvaux patriarch.

"What the hell is going on in here?" Maya asked as she entered the room, giving Warren a stern look for the amusement he was finding in the moment.

"Your little friend is feisty, My," Warren answered. "She's protective too."

Vincent pulled on little Bella until they were farther away from the patriarch. "Augustine was training me while we waited for you guys. Bella didn't like his methods."

Hunter laughed behind Maya. "So she threatened him?" He met Bella's storming eyes. "I'm liking you more and more, Fish."

"Don't call her that!" Vincent barked and finally released Bella behind him.

She just moved back out to stand beside him while giving Augustine a dirty look. The little ten-year-old had more balls than grown ass fucking men.

Maya huffed out and met her mate's father's eyes, knowing whatever his answer was would bother her too. "What did you do?"

"Nothing I haven't done to my own boys."

"That's not helping your case, Augustine. What did you do?"

He smirked and lounged back in a chair at the end of the room. "I simply tied him up to help him train getting out of the holds."

"Then he began punching at Vincent!" Bella barked, jumping forward only to get held back by her little demon.

Maya gave Augustine a stern look that looked so motherly that Warren was transported to five years from now when Maya looked at her own children like that when they inevitably got in trouble with Grandpa Augustine.

"Did you at least teach him how to get out before tying him up?" Maya questioned.

"Yes," he answered at the same time Bella gritted, "He told him what to do as if hearing it once would make him a master!"

At Maya's next look, Augustine smirked. "Come, Daughter, if he were captured and tied up, it's far more likely he be hit than not. He needs to get used to getting hit so it doesn't bother him. How do you think your mate is able to take any type of beating with a smile on his face? Vincent knows this is for his own good. He was okay with it. It's his little mate who's the problem."

Both Bella and Vincent froze at his words, which caught Warren's attention more than anything else. It was obvious they were mates, and he was sure they knew it, but he also couldn't imagine what it felt like to find a mate so early on. They weren't yet at the stage where the physical aspects of being mates were active—thankfully, considering how young they were—but the emotions were running wild, and they were so young, it was probably all confusing. Especially with being in different species and having to hide any time they were together or how they felt from the rest of the world.

Warren felt for them, especially because he didn't know the specifics to their relationship, so he didn't really know what scared them about acknowledging they were mates, but he was envious too. His entire family knew he wanted his mate. He didn't have to voice it for the desire to be obvious.

He pushed the thoughts aside as he refocused on the room and Maya chastising his father about doing so in front of the mermaid while trying to explain to Bella that the way demons trained was so far off from what caring creatures did. The mermaid didn't look happy or convinced, but at least she wasn't trying to jump at his father any longer—for her safety, not Augustine's.

"Yes, darling daughter, whatever you say," Augustine gave her a smile that they all knew was a little too sweet for him. "In any case, I'm here to see that animal control."

"We already told you, we're not sure we have it, Father," Hunter responded before turning to Vincent. "If my father already got to you, you need to rest. We'll continue later, and I'll begin incorporating more fighting." He winked, telling the kid they would also have more of the trainings with his father.

It was obvious Vincent wasn't going to ask for it in front of Bella even if he wanted it. At the end of the day, even while Warren had resented his father growing up, he couldn't lie that those trainings made him a great fighter, able to endure whatever he needed to. A demon with a mate would especially want that.

Vincent would especially want that.

Hunter hadn't known he would mate. Warren himself hadn't known much about matings and how much he would want one. They'd simply been training to be able to protect themselves. Vincent was fighting for so much more already.

"I know you're not certain, but I am. That's why we're going to test it," Augustine replied. "The difficult part will be knowing how to call upon them. Once we figure that part out, the rest will follow like basic power trainings."

Hunter rolled his eyes. "Aye, aye."

Augustine motioned for his son. "You know how magic works."

Warren smirked as he leaned back against a far wall. "You really think *your* son hasn't already tried summoning them like calling to our magic?"

Augustine returned the gesture. "You're my son as well. Would you have tried it?"

Warren shrugged. "I probably would've been curious. Also probably wouldn't tell you."

"Greedy prick," Bella muttered at Augustine's pleased look, which only made them laugh.

"In any case, we've tried," Maya brought the conversation back to trainings. "I've tried wanting them to come, Hunt's tried. We've tried calling to them like a spell, imagining them coming, literally calling to them. Nothing's worked. There's definitely a method behind it that Adramalech would've known."

"Come, darling, we're smart. We can figure this out." Augustine smiled at her, the only person who got his genuine grins.

Maya rolled her eyes. "I don't think this has to do with smarts. I think it's just a simple knowing what to do or not. It's probably more basic and common sense than we think, but we're overlooking it because the magic is lost to us."

"Which is why I revert back," Hunter started, "to not being certain. Even if we had the ability, the knowledge of how to use it is lost to a millennium of drifting powers. I can only imagine how much more powerful all the species were back then."

"You think it has to do with the dust?" Warren asked.

Hunter shrugged. "Probably. Which means I would have the ability and pass it onto Maya through the transfer. But I don't know how to wield the dust. Selin didn't really either, and she was made of it. She was just as shocked as I was when it began to protect her."

"We'll figure it out," Augustine insisted.

"Maybe," Hunter responded. "But not now. Right now, I need to rid of Jenkins for my family."

Maya rolled her eyes. "Positive news. I can pretty much open the portal now."

"Pretty much?" Warren questioned as Augustine's eyes sparked and both Vincent and Bella stepped forward to hear more, both knowing not to speak of the events of this meeting around others.

"Basically anything Hunter related, even him not getting hurt, gets me. It's more instinctive when he's getting hurt, but when I'm calm, I'm better able to control it. The 'pretty much' comes in because I could get through most shields, but Hunt tried it with one of his more powerful shields and I couldn't get through."

"Which means she won't be able to get through dark magic shields either," Hunter added.

"But we're making progress," Augustine smiled.

Warren caught Maya's gaze. "You're such a fucking badass, Sister."

She gave Warren a bright smile as Hunter hugged her from behind. "You truly are, wife."

Maya shrugged him off. "Is that why you keep putting yourself in danger? So I can save you?"

Hunter smirked. "What can I say? It's sexy."

Warren laughed as Augustine turned to Vincent. "Is this how you'll be with yours too? You want her to *save* you?"

Vincent didn't say anything, but his gaze hardened as he watched Augustine while Bella blushed against his side.

They weren't comfortable with being mates yet, and apparently Augustine enjoyed pointing it out because of that. He really was a fucking jackass.

39

With all the craziness of their lives, it was difficult to get a moment with her mother like when she'd been younger. But it was one Camilla had wanted more and more recently, so when Loretta walked into the back family room to find her alone, it brought a smile to Camilla's lips.

"Hiding away?" Loretta asked as she moved to sit pressed to Camilla's side.

"Never." Camilla furrowed her brows in that way she did as a child when her mother used to say she was being childish.

"Well, I believe a certain someone was looking for you."

Camilla knew exactly who she meant. "Whoever that certain someone is should have no problems finding me because I'm not hiding."

Loretta smiled warmly at her. "You've always been quite stubborn, you know. I used to call your father crying when we'd get into arguments because you got *his* personality."

Camilla laughed. "Really? I always thought it was your personality. From what I remember, you were quite as stubborn."

Her mother tsked. "Maya and Vera? Vera, especially? That's all me. Calm."

Camilla smirked. "Really?"

"Really." Loretta winked as she tugged Camilla into her side.

"Just because it doesn't suit you doesn't make it his personality, Mother."

"Of course it does. Always the way of the world, Daughter. When something of your child annoys you, blame it on your spouse. Maya will be doing so soon."

Camilla shrugged. "At least I gave you the excuse to hear his voice."

Loretta nodded, her eyes glazing over like she was lost in thought. "I heard his voice no matter what. We spoke every single day, no matter the circumstances. Those times, I would just call more than once. Or the one time I did call, I'd be crying."

"Awe." Camilla cuddled into her mother's side. "I'm sorry, Mama."

Loretta laughed. "That was a long time ago."

"Yeah." Camilla's voice was far off. "Lots changed since."

"But you're still a stubborn, beautiful girl."

Camilla pushed away, mock afront about her. "What did I do now?"

"The boy loves you, Camilla."

It didn't happen often, but at times, Loretta sounded wise far, far beyond her years. Camilla used to think she'd lived a dozen lifetimes the way she spoke. And it was never because of what she said, but how she said it.

Now, she knew her mother had lived quite a few lives, even if they were each only for a few months.

"You're being ridiculous." Camilla turned away from her mother, back to staring at the wall.

Loretta's arm around her shoulders tightened and brought her in closer as she chuckled. "My stubborn child, give him a chance. He's crude and anger-inducing and annoying sometimes, but that boy has done everything since the moment he arrived to this house to show his interest."

Camilla rolled her eyes but refused to look up to her mother. "He hated me. Still hates me."

"He hated you, past tense, maybe. But he definitely doesn't still, hasn't for some time, Camilla. And you know that as well as I do."

Camilla pushed away from her mother and began pacing the room. "He's…he's…"

"The Demon Warlock?" Loretta asked calmly.

"Exactly!" Camilla blanched, then continued her pacing. "He's basically a demon and does and acts the way Hunter would, and it's taken me long enough to like *him*. And even that's only because of the way he treats Maya. Kai is…he's… he's…"

Loretta gave her that knowing grin. "*Can* you say anything negative about him, Camilla?"

"Absolutely!"

"Then go ahead. What is it about him that just makes him *ugh*?"

Camilla grit her teeth. "The way he sexualizes everything regarding me in front of Dad."

Loretta laughed. "Oh, now you're just being picky, baby."

"I'm allowed to not like him!" she exasperated.

"That's true. If it were a fact." Loretta patted the seat beside her. "But we know it's not."

Camilla huffed and flopped down beside her mother, letting Loretta play with her hair.

"It's okay to like him, Cami. It's okay to want him. It's okay if you're falling for him. If you've already fallen for him." She had a knowing look about her.

Camilla only shook her head, staring straight ahead, the picture of Kai in Scotland clouding her vision.

"It's okay to want to kiss him every time you see him. To want to hold his hand constantly, the way you did when Hunter went to Selin and we were searching for him. It's okay to take and want comfort from him, my love. It's okay if he's the first person you want to see in the morning and the last at night. It's okay to be aroused by him…"

Camilla blanched and pulled away, but Loretta laughed as she brought her in close again.

"It's okay to want him sexually, emotionally, to want to talk to him every day. It's all okay." Loretta pushed her hair back. "It's also okay to take your time. I just need you to know that all your feelings are okay, baby, so don't torture him, and don't torture yourself fighting it."

"You know how you used to call Dad when I annoyed you?"

"Mhm," she hummed as she played with Camilla's hair.

"I used to close my door and scream into my pillow."

Loretta laughed. "Then run off to your room, sweetheart. Get a good scream out, then…talk to him."

---

Hunter didn't know how the man had orchestrated it, but Jenkins had gotten word out to him for a private meeting. He didn't know what exactly the man may have to talk to him about, but the correspondence had spoken of keeping Maya out of harm's way, and that was a sure-fire way for anyone to get his attention. His weakness.

Hunter made sure he could not be touched, wrapped in three layers of shields that even the darkest of magics would require at least a few minutes to break through. Far longer than the second he would need to shadow away.

Jenkins stood before a pile of logs out in the middle of a forest. On the logs were what smelled like celery seeds, dandelions, cumin seeds, and valerian. All used for power and protection. This was the start of dark magic.

He looked up as he was dropping a vial into the loaded wood. There looked to be a few already within. Jenkins was here for a deal.

Off to the sides were two women, one demon, one witch.

They were holding protection shields against Hunter so he couldn't hurt their master. It wasn't surprising for Jenkins to have thought of it all.

"What could you possibly have for me to make a deal?" Hunter opened.

Jenkins laughed. "I like demons. They never try to talk to the enemy. They simply get to the point."

"We talk to the enemy."

"When you're trying to ease them into a sense of security. That only works on the dimwitted. I appreciate a demon's work ethic."

"Fabulous." Hunter felt about three seconds away from shadowing off. He didn't have time for petty conversations.

"And I understand deals are made every day for demons so I have one for you. One I believe will interest you more than any have before."

Hunter didn't speak. Normally when someone wanted to offer him a deal he didn't speak. That way they could ramble on and end up offering more than they had originally planned. Jenkins didn't seem the type to do so, but Hunter was so used to his ways that he couldn't stop now.

"You're a mated male, thus your family will come before all else. Even before the selfishness you carry as a demon."

"That is common knowledge."

"This will be a bloody war. We both know no matter what, that is what it will lead to if I don't get your body. Your family won't only be in danger because of the war, but they are your weakness. The simplest way for me to get you would be to get your mate, who has your children so that will make capturing the family much easier."

The thought of his hands on Maya made Hunter see red.

"We both know that is the route that will be taken if I take her."

"What do you offer?"

"A dark magic deal. You give yourself to me and I will not

touch them. Your mate and children will be safe from me and any I rule for the rest of their lives. They will be powerful as others will go to them for help, and no matter what, whether they try to go against me or not, I will not harm them in any way. I will not even be allowed to imprison them."

His family was his weakness. It was a well-known fact. And he was idiot enough to take a deal like this. "In turn?"

"You offer yourself to me the way I have been wanting this whole time. The deal will keep them safe from me and me safe from them."

*Me safe from them...*

Hunter sighed. He couldn't make a deal on their behalf, but if that's what Jenkins wanted to believe, who was he to stop him?

Jenkins stuck out his hand, the flames close but never touching, as he gave a grin. "What do you say?"

Shaking his hand over that fire would be a lock of dark magic, as strong as shaking hands with blood. Except this deal wasn't about him, it was about his family, so a blood seal would do him no justice.

Jenkins left his hand in the air, silently waiting.

He'd told Maya he found it sexy when she saved him. He'd only partly been joking. It was sexy, and it was powerful. She was a goddess every time she charged into a room and got him out of harm's way.

He didn't want to put her in that position because of the possibility of her or the babies getting hurt, but as Hunter stood there staring into the gone eyes of a man whose greed far outweighed anything he'd ever met, Hunter knew that was what would happen. This wasn't about sacrificing himself to protect his family, some suicide mission. This was finally accepting the power of his mate—she would be the sole protector of their family. It wouldn't be him and all his years of trainings; it would be her bleeding heart that finally saved his family, his life.

He remembered the first time he'd truly held her, in order to comfort rather than pleasure, and what he'd said to her—*don't get used to it, my bleeding heart.*

He internally scoffed at himself now. He hadn't followed his own words and was far too used to holding onto his mate. It was time to let go and allow her to show the world how instrumental she'd be to this life.

She was his wife, his mate, his goddess.

And she would bring Jenkins to his knees.

"Deal."

40

Hayes and Felix were at the door, and they both watched Maya with intent concern. She let them into Whittle House, unaware as to why they watched her, and not anyone else, with those looks.

"What's happened?" Vera asked before Maya could.

Both swallowed, looking uncomfortable to be the ones speaking, but eventually Hayes, being the leader he was, spoke up. "It's time. Jenkins has put his plans to action."

Maya's heart stopped, the thought that these actions could lead to Hunter's getting caught and hurt immobilizing her. "How do you know?"

"It's taken weeks," Hayes answered, "but my wolves finally found the bodies. The ones Jenkins had gotten from the Bridgers coven before your lot had infiltrated them."

Everyone's eyes widened. "And?"

"He had three witches guarding," Felix continued. "We called Ama, she got them out of their states, and we got what we needed to know."

Maya stood taller, needing to know everything in order to figure out how best to protect her mate. "Why did he need the bodies?"

"Apparently, back when faerie dust was more extraordinary, the Powers especially wanted it. Witches and demons were vile in their gatherings. Most of it dispersed into blood so weakly that the people hadn't known they had any. But get a specific number of Powers together and you could build the exact power needed in order to give yourself a warlock's life—near immortality."

"Jenkins has one chance to use the bodies," Hayes continued. "He had his best shield witches guarding the bodies."

"But that's okay, right?" Kai asked, his brows furrowed in that way that said his mind was running a thousand miles a minute trying to figure out the next course. "We got the witches, we got the bodies."

Both wolves sighed before the leader answered, "Jenkins is a smart man. He had the bodies stacked tight with three more witches with them in case they needed to get the bodies out. My wolves couldn't precisely smell the number of alive witches past the hundreds of bodies. When they were found, the three within took the bodies. Wherever they went, Jenkins won't wait longer. The ones Ama got out of hypnotization said they'd been given only enough to live off of for a few more days rather than the two weeks he normally gave—something Jenkins had to do so they never ran out of energy to hold their shields. They were stuck under the black magic, but inside they knew they were as good as dead. At that point they wanted it over living the way they were."

"So what's next?" Camilla sounded more worried than normal. "How do we figure out where he is and how to get to him, how to stop him?"

Felix met Maya's gaze. "We suspect if Jenkins is no longer waiting, he will have already gone for his final—and most prized—piece of the game."

An unlimited amount of power storage *and* the ancient faerie dust. *Hunter.*

Maya's gaze jumped from one wolf to the other when Hayes

stepped forward, his hand tightening as he held her arm and spoke softly. "Maya." His gaze dropped to her stomach. "Maya, love, calmly. We have everyone here, have already called the House, and your family will be calling the other covens. Just remain calm for the babies and reach out in that ring, love."

Her eyes were wide as her head shook, refusing to believe this could be possible. Refusing to believe that Hunter could be in danger with Jenkins at that very moment. But knowing if hers or their children's lives were on the line, he would've easily given himself up.

The same way she would've.

The same way they promised one another they would the last time they were in Hell's Gate.

"Darling." Augustine's voice at her back made the breath leave her as she turned to look into the eyes of the man her mate had inherited from. "Find him."

Maya closed her eyes as she reached through the rings, which hadn't gone up with strong emotions to alert her of anything wrong, which scared her even more now. If he was with Jenkins and his emotions were calm, he was okay with his decision. He wasn't in pain or crying out for her, but content with his protection of their family.

She reached through the rings and felt him, out in the fields of a Montana empty land. He felt calm, and Maya knew now that he could feel her anxiety skyrocketing within her because she felt the inkling of guilt come from him before it was washed out with that calmness again.

She wanted to shadow to him, to be impulsive and go to him. To know that if he was dying, she was dying.

But she couldn't.

Not for a few more months at least. Like him, she had a family to protect.

Maya opened her eyes and met Augustine's. "I have him."

His gaze searched hers like he was trying to figure out why she wasn't shadowing already, why he didn't need to hold her down from leaving on her own. Maya wondered if his uncaring heart would understand that she needed to protect her children at least.

Finally, Maya turned away from him and toward the others in the room. "Gather everyone. Let's stop him already." There was no real conviction to her tone. She was simply tired, a matter she knew partially had to do with the pregnancy that was now obvious and partly to do with wanting her mate safe and back with her without the worry of a psychopath after him.

***

"This is exactly what it's all been leading to, Harry!" Vera exclaimed quietly into his ear even though he was still angry with her.

They'd all just landed on the top of a hill overlooking Jenkins's army. This would definitely be bloody and the most difficult fight Harry had been in, but he had no hesitations about going into it. Not only for Maya's sake, but especially to keep Vera safe.

There was an invisibility shield held around them by one of the witches in the Wremon coven as the entire group of them prepared to go down. But as they stood there, Harry finally *heard* what Vera had been saying. This was what it was leading to—not the fight with Jenkins, but the use of animal demons. This was the reason the Book had given them the potion.

Harry met her eyes and hoped she knew how much he loved her.

Then he took her hand and got everyone's attention, pulling out the vial he'd been carrying of the potion. "A couple of weeks ago, Vera and I were talking to our coven Book, trying to see if it could give us anything to help, and it came up with this potion that combines six to make one. It was really complicated and took us a while to get, but we have it completed. We weren't sure why, as there are individual spells for animal demons, but this must be it. This potion, if drank, can help fend off a hoard of animal demons."

"What makes you think there'll be animal demons?" a Lopez witch asked. "Aren't the demons normally the ones to send those?"

Maya sighed. "Part of my ancestry is control of animal demons. We haven't figured out how to use it, so we've continued on the assumption that we don't have it."

Vera turned for Jenkins' mass, catching Hunter in the middle. "But that doesn't mean Jenkins won't know how to get it out of Hunter and use it to his advantage."

"Fucking great," multiple people, and not just those from the asshole covens, mumbled.

"Give it to me," Adela ordered.

Loretta stepped forward before Harry could refuse. "Mother, no!"

"Don't 'mother no' me!" Adela chastised. "This is my granddaughter and her mate. This is the future of the supernatural world. I will protect us. I am not as helpless as you seem to think of me." She turned hard eyes on Harry. "Now give me the potion."

Harry wanted to argue, but one look in Anna and Jakub's eyes said it would be foolish to do so. Plus, he remembered living with her at the Wittlieff coven. Harry didn't necessarily want to get on Adela's bad side.

When he handed it over, Vera squeezed his hand, making him turn to her, so when she whispered, their lips brushed. "I'm sorry for every worry I put in you and for whatever worry I will probably put in you during this fight, but I promise afterward, it's gonna be about us, Harry. I'm gonna get better at us."

He grinned against those lips. "I know, sweetheart. And we're going to start by my taking you out in public every chance I get in every part of this world. You'll be so used to people seeing us together that you'll begin to think it odd when witches judge us."

She laughed softly and kissed him as Camilla stepped up. "I also have a few potions. There's a potion's master in the Salem coven who made this potion for us. We have enough vials for most pretty much everyone to get one."

Harry turned on her. "You knew a potion's master and we had to spend weeks failing at making that demon one!"

Camilla smirked. "Good practice, Mr. Mentor Man."

Harry's jaw ground, but he ignored the comment because at least it got a small smile from Maya who had come up with that insufferable name to begin with.

Harry turned back for a kiss from Vera and caught her equal amusement. He whispered low so only she'd hear, "You think that's funny?"

"Never," she teased.

He growled against her lips. "When we get out of this, I'm taking you back to that cottage. I think we have a few lessons you need to learn before I can take you out in public."

She giggled, and for a moment, Harry forgot they were in the middle of fighting off a psychopath.

## 41

arren played with the ring on his finger, his nerves jittering his entire body. This was what they'd been waiting for—to finally end Jenkins. He was excited to be over with it, excited to kill him, but more than anything, that stupid caring heart of his—that human piece of him—was worried for his big brother. Whatever the reason behind Hunter's being with Jenkins, it was to protect Maya and the babies, so Warren worried less for them. He suspected Jenkins would've made a dark promise, one that could not be broken, to keep them out of harm's way to get Hunter's cooperation.

But Hunter wouldn't be safe. If it kept Maya and the babies safe, he'd easily give away his safety. It was the mating that made his uncaring heart pound for only his mate. It was what had made Hunter a better man, if still the bad guy who killed for fun. It was what had made him a brother Warren loved, one he needed to protect.

As much as he wanted to get to his brother, Warren knew the only one who would be able to get to him, if at all possible, was his mate. So Warren would remain at the top of the hill overlooking the battle. He would protect Ama whilst the witch tried to unhypnotize as many of her people as possible. He would protect Vincent and Bella as the demon used his rare biokinesis on those below, and Adela as she tried to keep Jenkins from unleashing animal demons unto them.

Until then, the wolves of Hayes' tribe, the six other covens, and those within the Ragtag House with the addition of the Bridgers couple whose baby was with a trusted grandmother in the Salem coven, helped. It was the greatest togetherness of the species that Warren had seen in his lifetime.

And in this instance, it would be especially needed.

Looking out at the field Maya had directed them to, Warren was shocked at the uniformity and savagery he witnessed at the bottom of the small hill they were standing on. Warren didn't know how much dark magic Jenkins had poisoned himself with, or how much it had all cost him, but the man had amassed his own army. There were the hypnotized witches that did most of the magic he needed—from fighting to shields to overall protection—but there were also different species mixed within the lot, humans included, who all looked ready to fight to the death. They weren't hypnotized, but Warren would wager they were worse off—or better, since their souls were as good as dead if Jenkins had done as Warren suspected and completely taken over the different members, turning them into zombies.

The three hundred and thirty-three dead Power bodies Jenkins had gotten from Melusine were precisely positioned in three rows in a circle around the middle with Jenkins standing there, a head-dropped Hunter on his knees before him.

Surrounding the bodies were the hypnotized witches, hands raised to their sides and heads held high as if they were in the middle of spells at that very moment. They very well could be.

Surrounding them was the first defense—and the first set of deaths Jenkins did not care for—the other species who'd turned into Jenkins' personal zombies.

As Warren turned to their group, large but nowhere near the size of Jenkins'—though probably twice or three times as strong —his gaze hovered over Maya's face as she stared without emotion down at Hunter. She hadn't broken down at the thought of him with Jenkins, and she hadn't broken down at seeing him now. It almost scared Warren more than any other reaction—this coolness.

Ama stopped beside where he stood with Vincent to his side. "How is this to work, demon?"

Warren knew she wasn't speaking to him, so he remained quiet until Vincent answered, "I'll be able to feel your magic fill them at the same time as mine. If I feel you there, I'll pull away. I'll try to slow them down enough for you to get to them, but if I need to, they're dead."

A quick glance in Ama's direction showed that she wasn't very happy with the answer. As a witch, she would want to save all of her own kind. Vincent's full-blooded demoness didn't hold that same regard. He was as uncaring for others as Hunter was, so the only reason he would want to save any of them at all was because Bella would want that. And with the girl at his side, he would do anything in his power to make her happy.

Warren sighed as he twisted the ring on his finger some more and looked back down to Jenkins' lot. Ama and Vincent would have the best vantage points from up here, and because it was the one spot Warren would be with a protected shield, Adela would use it too.

He didn't expect much of a problem up there, but he couldn't be certain, and they had been the ones to ask for Ama and Vincent's help. He wouldn't allow anything to happen to them because they graciously said yes.

"Ready, Witch?" he called back to her before finally turning to meet her stare.

Her jaw ground, but she gave a small nod. "Ready."

Warren turned to Adela and quirked a brow.

The older woman gave a small nod too, but hers was laced with kindness. "Ready."

Then he met the eyes of the warlock who had just shadowed

in beside Adela and gave a nod of acknowledgement for his presence.

Finally, Warren turned to the children of his little group and hated that they had to be part of this. A simple look into Vincent's eyes though told him everything—the boy would do anything to keep the world Bella lived in safe.

Warren turned back to watch the battle and stepped into the middle of the others with Adela at his back, Ama at his right, and Vincent at his left, then slowly breathed out and pushed out their shield. Their allies now stood outside of their bubble as they waited.

Ama stepped forward, raised both of her hands to her sides, and twisted her fingers as if indicating to everyone behind them to head down. Her focus was trained, and Warren knew as he watched the others make their way down that the witch was in her element.

While he waited to see if anyone would come up and try to stop Ama, Warren focused his power. Melting was a severely painful method, and thankfully one that did not require touch for Warren's case—though it always worked best with touch. While Vincent, the biokinetic, bled people from the inside out, Warren would melt their internal organs or the weapons any of them held. It would take more concentration and effort from this distance and with no touch, but he couldn't stand around waiting, watching as everyone he loved went into the fight, watching as his brother knelt there without a fight.

If it weren't for the feeling of mating, Warren would be repulsed by his brother's actions—giving up. But Warren knew, as he twisted that ring on his finger, that Hunter wasn't giving up. He was giving his all, every bit of himself for their protection.

So as Ama, Adela, and Vincent worked, Warren held up his shield around them to alert him if anyone came by while he used only a small bit of his melting to help the others.

Then his attention was on the massacre below.

42

era was a sight to behold with her arms thrown up and bodies flying around them as she controlled the species-zombie-like creatures. Harry had half a mind to stand there awe-struck by her beauty.

It was only the push of her parents at his side that really grounded him. He needed to protect her.

Harry had a dagger out in one hand, one of the ones that Hunter and Maya had gotten from their friends in Canada, while Bishop pulled out one of his own on Vera's other side. Vera moved with strategy, throwing around smaller quantities that would allow her to last longer in battle rather than expending herself all at once. With her mother at her back freezing as many attackers as her body could handle at once, Harry and Bishop were able to protect both women as they truly took on the show. They were both spitfires in battle, and Harry knew Bishop was as delighted as he was to see them as so.

Thankfully, he knew Kai's love for Camilla would keep her protected, and Augustine wouldn't leave Maya's side. It was a small bit of peace on Harry's end, but it made all the difference. It meant he could protect these two women—his old best friend, and his forever best friend—while these dark, magically powered zombies and witches came at them.

The dagger he had was unlike any he'd ever handled before. Zathrian had made it specifically to cut through the dark magic in any of these bodies, so they wouldn't have to deal with bodies coming back up, but it was extraordinary how well they worked.

Harry slashed through the neck of a faerie and slid the blade down the torso of a mermaid and was already on a gargoyle jumping for Vera when he realized that these kill blows were actually killing. With dark magic running through their systems, Harry had feared they'd need to rip the heads off of each 'zombie,' and as powerful as he and Bishop were, ripping that many heads off while making sure their women weren't touched was more difficult that he cared to think about.

Harry slashed through the body of a pixie as he caught sight of a witch behind her. The black veins around the witch were fading, and she looked to be blinking in the carnage around her. Ama was doing her job. Even if she only got through a few of these hypnotized witches, it would be lives saved.

"Go, Harry." Vera pushed at him. "Go!"

As much as he hated to do this, Vera still had her magic working at its highest capacity, so Harry ported to the awakened witch, took hold of her, and had her ported to Ama's side in seconds. He knew he wouldn't be able to see every single witch who was unhypnotized, but if he was able to save one, it was still worth it.

He ported back just as he saw Bishop port toward the witches as well, his hands on two whose veins were fading.

By the time Harry had a dagger through two more zombies, Bishop was before his wife again.

There were bodies flying back all around him, hitting other zombies coming at them like a bowling ball to pins. It was exceptionally attractive to know his woman was responsible for all of it.

"Harry." He heard her whisper like she was calling to him to port to her.

He moved backwards so his back was basically pressed to her front. "What is it, sweetheart?"

"We're done."

Done. Meaning she and her mother had conserved as much as their powers of they could, but they were running out of fuel.

As powerful as they were, anyone using this much magic without a single moment's break would crash sooner than they wished. Considering each witch was holding off dozens, and especially considering Vera was a new witch, they'd lasted longer than most. Harry knew that was the powerful Whittle—Wittlieff—blood in them, and in Vera's case, knew it was Hunter's trainings that truly made her this capable.

"Drink up, sweetheart. I won't let them touch you."

They were depleted, meaning it was time to use the potions Camilla had had made by a master of potions in the Salem coven. They were advised to only take the potions when required, so they'd had to wait until they were completely exhausted from magical use, but Harry knew that was for their overall safety. The last thing they needed was their bodies overutilizing their own magic and making mistakes they were trying to avoid.

Harry took note from his periphery as each woman took a vial out of their front pockets and shot back the potions while he and Bishop stood before their back-to-back women and fought off the onslaught.

Without Vera's power throwing them through the air and far away from them, or Loretta's power freezing them so only a few ran up at a time, Harry felt his own energy begin to deplete faster.

They needed five minutes for their potions to set in, so that was five minutes Harry would fight past his exhaustion. For his future. For Vera.

He needed to protect her. He still had a cottage in France he intended on buying her. He still had the town he was born in to show her. He still had to take her to the Czech Republic so she could see where he was before coming to her.

He still had to marry her.

The magical dagger in his hand swiped through the air, taking species after species of affected zombies down before he realized he had a black-veined witch before him. One of the ones who had been guarding the bodies laid out had moved for him.

Before he could swipe his dagger from the throat of an affected wolf to her, a force he was unable to fight shook his hand until the dagger flew past the carnage and landed blade down into the dirt in the middle of the field of bodies.

"Fuck," he muttered as he pulled another dagger from the back of his trousers, this one not magically inclined, and fought off three more zombies.

Each slice made its impact and distracted them, but none killed. He would need to rip some heads off. Starting with that witch. He couldn't have her taking any more away from him than she already had.

He moved quickly, porting behind the witch and leaving Vera uncovered, and he wrapped his hands around the witch's head to twist with all his might. Thankfully, Vera had a dagger in hand and was able to fight off the couple of zombies that got too close, but he needed to get back to her.

The snap of the witch's neck made his stomach roil, but he ignored it as he ported back before Vera and slashed through two more necks.

This would be nearly impossible if he couldn't get them dismembered.

Then he heard it.

Caw. Caw. Caw.

From above, he saw it. The black crow. One that he'd thought himself crazy to recognize at Bishop's grave, but now knew was the familiar to Zathrian. The bird Adramalech was swooping through the air right for them.

Then his claws were deep in the hair of a gargoyle Harry had just slit the throat of and he was swooping back up.

The zombie's head snapped right off his body with no effort, the blood splattering everywhere and catching in Harry's half-open mouth.

He gagged and spit the blood out, then caught the eye of the bird as he moved for the other whose neck Harry had just slit. Harry got the message loud and clear—he would slice, the bird would snap off.

They had another three taken care of, with too many coming for him, when he saw bodies begin to fly through the air. His five minutes were up—Vera was back in the game.

And right on time too.

The animal demons had joined the fight.

43

Hunter's gaze was glued to his mate.

And she stared back. Enchanting as she burned her way through the massacre, all the while keeping those beautiful browns locked on him.

Kneeling on the ground, waiting for her to save him. Jenkins wasn't going to know what hit him. The man underestimated his mate, and that would be the grave mistake in all his well thought out plans.

Jenkins stood behind him, his hands clutched to Hunter's shoulders where he bled from multiple of Jenkins's cuts. The man wasn't in his Power body yet, so he'd found a loop around to still control Hunter's magic. And it was incredible listening to the man whisper out the spell that brought the animal demons out.

How did he know it? How did this one puny human know so much about how to get through every step of his plan?

It didn't matter to Hunter. Once his mate saved him from this—because he had no doubts about her strengths—he would now know the way to bring up the animal demons. His father was going to be extra excited he'd made it out alive.

Jenkins's hands burned his back as they pressed into the

bleeding out wounds, aiding in his repetition of those words that brought the animal demons out.

Hunter wasn't sure if Jenkins simply wasn't doing the spell correctly or if his family had some way of stopping them, but there were far fewer animal demons than it felt like he was calling on. Which taught him also that his body could tell how many demons it had called upon. It made sense, given control of that many animals would require some way of knowing and controlling.

Finally, after repeating the spell six times, Jenkins released him and spread his arms out, his hands bloodstained with Hunter's power as he whispered, "Anima mea requirit existentiam. Anima mea est Timotheus Eli Jenkins. Anima mea vivet in aeternum."

He continued to refer to his soul rather than himself. He'd thought it all out. With Hunter's blood on his hands and the black magic coursing through his body, he had power. But if he wasn't specific, his body would inherit the immortality rather than his soul, and his soul was the one being transferred into Hunter's body, not the other way around.

He repeated the words, and out around them, the bodies littering the grounds glowed grey before settling back down. Hunter had heard of this magic. Immortality was impossible, but it was possible to gain a thousand years with some of the deepest black magics. Each body gave three years. Three hundred and thirty-three bodies would give him the thousand.

Jenkins clutched Hunter's battered back as the magic worked to keep himself standing, and it clouded Hunter's vision with the amount of pain that seared through his body. It was an odd feeling, given all the torture and beatings he'd been through in his life, but it burned more than he could've ever fathomed.

His mate's family made a bloody mess of the place with how well they fought. Hunter was proud of them. He was proud of the others who had come to aid in taking down Jenkins, and especially proud of Vincent, who stood at the top of the hill next to his brother and worked on taking witch after witch down. He was newly trained and definitely not strong enough for a battle like this, yet there he stood, showing up to aid his allies. Hunter would reward him properly when the time was right.

As the others fought, Hunter wanted nothing more than to get up and kill Jenkins, finally finish this problem. But he wouldn't break his promise to the man. That would be a death sentence on the both of them. But seeing one of those witches almost get to his mate had him straining against his own control to remain kneeling in the middle of this circle.

"It is all coming together now," Jenkins laughed joyfully as he watched the scene before him—covens against zombies, wolves against witches, species against animal demons—like it were the epic fight scene to a movie.

Hunter sneered, then felt it—the blade seared into his neck, and he knew it wasn't a regular dagger. Whatever was done to that dagger was what had made the cuts around his shoulders burn so deeply, and now his neck burned too. He wanted to thrash out of Jenkins's hold and roar with the pain, but Hunter glued his eyes onto his mate and remained still.

Then he felt the reason behind the cut. It felt like stealing a power when Jenkins dropped a vial of shimmering light into him. This was one of the powers Jenkins wanted in his body. The man had thousands, and Hunter doubted he was going to insert all of them into his body before taking over, so why do any at all? He had a feeling these few he decided on first were his most treasured of magics, and if he had to guess, they would be the strongest forms of keeping himself safe—the power from one of the strongest shield masters, from one of the strongest witches because strength was a power within the Powers, from one of the best sensors so his eyes, ears, and scent would work as well as a wolf's. There was at least a dozen of these powers that would make the most sense to begin with in order to make sure he wasn't so clueless when stepping into Hunter's body.

Hunter preferred stealing them himself. This way of

inserting the magic through the veins in his neck burned. He didn't know if it was because of the dagger that had cut him or because they were being manually inserted rather than taken with magic, but it all burned so badly, he wasn't sure how much of this his heart was going to be able to continue beating for before he passed out.

So Hunter kept his gaze on Maya and took whatever power Jenkins gave him. If Maya wasn't able to save him, these powers would be lost to the world as his body died because rest assured, Maya wouldn't allow Jenkins to live if anything happened to him.

But if he was saved by his powerful wife, then these powers would be his, once he learned which powers they were and how well they were wired in their non-primary body.

Until then, Maya, Maya, Maya…

"Maya," he groaned lowly to himself to help get through this. "Maya."

## 44

Camilla didn't have active powers. She was a scary kicker, and her arms had more strength than her petite body indicated—as Kai was very aware from his constantly bruised ribs—but she didn't have active powers.

She had one of the magically enhanced daggers that Kai hadn't gotten around to teaching her how to use yet and her unadulterated fury for all the lives that were being hurt. But she didn't have active powers. She wouldn't be able to freeze anyone like her mother or throw anyone back like her sister or burn anyone like her other sister. She wouldn't be able to port out of the way, and no matter how strong she was, she wouldn't be able to rip a neck off of the zombie's heads.

Yet somehow, she was the most inspiring person on the battlefield.

Kai didn't know if it was because he was more distracted with keeping an eye on her than the tasks at hand, but her pile of bodies—which thankfully stayed dead because of the magical dagger—was bigger than his.

That awe only stuck in him for so long before he noticed the animal demons coming for them around the edges. Warren at the top of the hill had a shield that he had to really concentrate to keep up with the few that went for him, but the rest were coming for them.

"Take my dagger, princess." He moved to stand behind her after throwing the nearest zombies back.

"Are you insane!" She tried to hand the weapon back, but Kai wouldn't take it.

"Do not argue with me right now, Camilla. Take it and wield both. I need to hold a shield over us for the animal demons. They have powers that these zombie creatures don't, and we can't fight both right now!"

Camilla didn't fight him after that as a zombie's hand landed on her shoulder, and Kai had to grit back his instinct to port her out of there. Instead, he watched as the shield against animal demons came up as Camilla turned and uppercut the pixie up the nose with the dagger, blood splattering everywhere.

Between them, her parents, her siblings and their partners, the Wittlieffs, the other covens, the wolves, and the Ragtag House, the zombie-like creatures were dwindling down quickly. It was obvious they weren't meant to be the actual competition. Just the first hand, so by the time they broke through to the witches, they were already exhausted.

Though as Kai concentrated on holding up his shield, he found the others around them. Cora and Rory, the Ragtag House's resident witches, were holding up the same shields he and Warren had up against the animal demons as the remaining warlocks ported the unhypnotized witches out of the battle. At least Ama's power was working.

Kai didn't necessarily care about saving those witches—that was the 'demon' part of his Demon Warlock title—but he cared that it made the number of magically hypnotized witches less to deal with.

There were a few more zombie-like creatures, but no more around them as Camilla ran into his chest. She clutched to get in close, though she ended up speaking to him through his mind rather than aloud. *I just spoke to Vera. They took their heightening potions already. I need you to take one too.*

*I don't need—*

*If you're going to keep holding up this shield, yes you do.* She uncorked a vial and tipped it to his mouth.

The potion tasted very sugary sweet and almost made him want to gag, but he was too distracted with the need to keep Camilla safe and the way she was clutched to him at the moment.

They had five minutes before it kicked in.

In theory, he would easily be able to hold a shield for another five minutes without growing tired, but in actuality, now that the first defense was taken care of, the second—and third, if animal demons counted as another line of defense—were before them.

And these were the truly powerful of the lot.

Though most witches weren't as powerful as the Whittles, this many witches juiced with dark magic were a nightmare.

The bird that had swooped down earlier—who Kai assumed was Adramalech, Zathrian's familiar—flew over the witches, clawing their skin to distract them any way he could.

At the same time, a few of them began to bleed through every hole in their body, blood seeping through their mouths, nostrils, ears, and through their pants. That's when Kai knew Vincent's powers were taking affect. At twelve years old, he was likely one of the scariest demons Kai had ever met.

And he was the sweetest kid for his Bella.

Then they were moving. He and Camilla were making their way forward through the bodies littering the grounds to get closer to the witches since Camilla's non-active powers meant she couldn't fight from far away. Kai's shield followed them every centimeter of the way.

That's when he noticed her limp on her right leg.

"What happened, Camilla!" he roared louder than he'd intended as he took her arm to face him.

"Now's not the time, Kai!" She pushed his hand off and continued to move.

Kai ground his jaw together to keep from starting a fight. This wasn't the time, and she obviously wasn't hurt enough for it to affect her fight.

Then Kai felt a knock against his shield so hard he almost tripped over.

He turned in time to see the animal demons that had joined the fight.

To think Vera and Harry's findings were keeping off most of the animal demons, Kai knew these were the more cunning or powerful of the lot that got through.

And three of them were banging against his shield.

He was thankful for Camilla even more now. Had she not forced that potion down his throat, he wouldn't have stood a chance at keeping the shield against all three of them.

One made of a slime that looked to be falling off of him in chunks, but still, more filled its spot.

One that looked like a large teddy bear with the eyes of the scariest sea creatures around.

One that looked like a large mirror where Kai could see himself covered in blood and gore. This one was the worst, as the mirrored skin seemed to reflect off his body and pierce into their eyes.

Camilla threw one of her magical daggers at the mirrored demon. The blade went straight through the middle of the thing, and it broke into a million little pieces, hitting Kai's shield and just barely missing from piercing through both him and Camilla as he covered her body and ducked.

Thankfully, the witches holding the other shields covered those closest to the glass-made demon.

Kai stepped over broken glass underfoot as he fought the power of the animal demons to keep his shield up. Even with the potion's help, these were the animal demons who had gotten past their first defense of Vera and Harry's findings—the most powerful.

And it meant each of their bangs against his shield felt like getting punched in the stomach.

Until finally, like they were working together now, they took turns in quick succession banging against his shield before giving their final blows together and completely knocking the wind out of Kai.

He fell over the shards of glass, fighting for breath so he could put that shield back up, so he could protect his princess. Fighting to stand and move for her. Fighting to die for her.

But he couldn't move.

He knew it was because his body needed a moment to bring air back into it so his healing powers could work their magic, but he didn't have that time. He needed to be healed and by her side already.

Then a splattering of light filled the night sky around him, making him need to close his eyes to fight off the shine, and Kai grunted as a heaviness fell over his body, his chest pounding with the need to get it off.

Then it was gone, hovering rather than on him.

Even in this wreckage, it had the faint scents of chamomile and clementines.

"Camilla." His voice was hoarse as he whispered into the air.

A relieved sigh hit his cheek as a wave of magic passed overhead and she mumbled, "You're okay, Kai. I promise, you're okay. You're going to be perfect."

He could already feel his healing powers working in his body, but with the amount of pain he was in, he figured it would take a bit of time before he was truly mobile.

Kai rolled his head over, glass shattering around his scalp, so he could stare up into her eyes, a small smirk forming on his lips—an action that hurt too much, but he needed to do for his girl. There was hardly an inch of distance between their lips as her body pressed above his, and he whispered, "I knew you liked me, princess."

Tears fell down her cheeks and onto his. "Never."

A crippled laugh pushed out of his lips as the ground shook again, and his body rumbled with it, too much for his frail body to take. "Liar."

45

Warren knew that explosion had come from one of the potions the Salem coven had given Camilla.

And as he watched her jump over Kai's body to protect him, he knew she'd thrown it in order to keep the animal demons off of the Demon Warlock. That girl truly loved him.

It made Warren happy to see them both finally get who they deserved, but he was too focused on protecting those around him to allow the joy to spread.

Adela, Loretta's mother and a Wittlieff elder witch, still stood to the back of his shield, back facing the fight as she continued swiping that potion on her wrists and reciting the spell that kept the majority of the animal demons away. There was only so much they could do against the more powerful of the lot. Even his family's reputation would mean nothing to a calling by someone who controlled them. Hunter had that control.

Which meant at the moment, Jenkins had that control.

Behind Warren was Luka, a Wittlieff warlock who was healing the unhypnotizted witches while also attempting to port into battle and collect any Harry or Bishop couldn't get to in time. All of his energy was going into healing these witches.

To his right was Ama. She stood with her arms open at her sides and her gaze focused down below. She looked almost scary in her concentration.

But she was working her magic. Bringing witches back to them, giving these witches a second chance as Jenkins had attempted to use them with his black magic.

To Warren's left was Vincent—the scariest of the lot.

Hunter had been training Vincent, and he was a great ally to have, but still, his ability to bleed people from the inside out freaked Warren out. Even though his entire family's abilities included heat and could easily sear a person from the inside out.

Bella by his side didn't do anything. As a mermaid, she would have no power out in the open as they were. They weren't near the oceans for her to use any control of the waters against those in battle, so she merely remained by Vincent's side.

His tight grip of her hand solidified to Warren that they were mates. It made him twitch for the ring around his finger, twisting at it, before focusing back at the battle.

Vincent was slowly dropping witches, an obvious ploy to allow Ama time to bring them back, but not so much so that they'd have the opportunity to kill any of their own.

The Salem potion was ringing through him, making him more powerful, and Warren knew it was Bella's hold on him that was keeping him from killing all of the infected witches below.

Then the ground began to rumble. Slow at first, then so much so that Warren had to use every strength in his core to keep himself stable and hold his shield up.

Not that it truly mattered.

Every single one of the animal demons attacking his shield rolled off, unable to keep standing, then were gone. Like the magic that had brought them here was now taking them away.

Warren zeroed in on Maya in the battlefield with his father following behind her.

She'd been fighting her way through, burning bodies and letting Augustine deliver the killing blows with the magical dagger as she single-handedly moved for her mate.

Warren wondered if she knew her magic was rumbling the ground and sending these animal demons back, or if she was so worried about getting to Hunter that her magic was working on instinct?

By the look on Jenkins' face as she neared the shield he had up around him, he was shocked to see her take over the control of the animal demons. Maybe he'd truly expected since she was stronger with the Hell's Gate portal—indicative of Miradora—then Hunter would be stronger with the animal demon power—indicative of Adramalech.

But he didn't falter.

Jenkins still stared ahead as he cut through Hunter's skin again, pouring another vial over him, like he knew he was indestructible. In theory, he'd planned so meticulously, he *was* indestructible.

But he hadn't planned for the type of love a mated couple shared for one another. No one, especially not anyone as greedy and power-hungry as Jenkins, would ever be able to account for that. Because without knowing the feeling—or even an ounce of that feeling—they wouldn't realize how deep it went.

Jenkins would see it now.

It would be the final thing he witnessed. That scary sister of Warren's would show him. She'd burn this world down before letting anything happen to Hunter.

Entry #6662

Momma told me once about love.

She tried to convince me it was more powerful than anything else in the world.

Momma was stupid like that.

She didn't know that the most powerful thing in the world would be me. She didn't realize that I would do anything to be the ruler of them all —their God.

Momma is dead now. I had to show her what true power was.

She's dead now, but I proved to her love wasn't the most powerful thing of all. I proved that every time she told me she loved me didn't mean anything.

Because love doesn't mean anything.

It's all about Power.

I AM GOD.

## 46

Her entire family was here. Her friends and the covens that had come to help. They were all here, but Maya didn't care.

She hated herself for it, but she would rather they all died than Hunter.

Maya hardly paid attention, her flames blasting around her and the stench of burnt bodies filling the night air as she moved through the carnage to the middle of the field where Hunter and Jenkins were.

There was a shield around them, hot with what she assumed to be dark magic, that stopped her from getting too close.

As the others fought, Maya narrowed her gaze on Jenkins. "Release him or I'll kill you. I don't care how powerful you believe yourself to be."

Jenkins laughed. "You will not hurt me, and I will not touch you or your children."

"What makes you think that?" Maya already knew Hunter had something to do with why the man would even believe that much.

"A deal is a deal, sweetheart. A dark magic deal, especially."

"I didn't make a deal with you."

"But your mate did."

Maya gave a sardonic smirk. "He may own me, but he cannot make deals on my behalf. Your dark magic is very aware of that."

Maya's fire trickled around her, hitting the shield that surrounded her mate and the psycho, and paused, looking for a way to get through. The ground rumbled around her but didn't make it through the shield.

Jenkins laughed at her attempts. "The darkest of magics, sweet Maya. Even your evil powers will not break through."

Maya snorted. "Isn't that the pot calling the kettle black?"

Jenkins winked as the flames wrapped around his shield and the ground rumbled some more, none of it penetrating the shield. "Take your mate's deal."

"Kill yourself." Maya's eyes, everything around the two men she was focused in on, turned red to orange to hints of blue as her body raged with flames.

Jenkins held onto the shirt at Hunter's shoulder within the blaze shield now, almost like he was nervous. It pleased Maya to cause that within him, but all she could truly focus on now was Hunter on his knees, staring at her with dry eyes. The streaks of long-gone tears fueled Maya's rage deeper.

"Sweetheart." Jenkins smiled to her. "Take your mate's deal. This will be best for you, your children. Think like a parent now, *Maya*, not a lover. Think of your family."

To think she could ever think of anything but her family. It was all she ever thought about. What she thought of as she stared at them in that very moment.

It was what she thought of as she reached the shield that kept her away from her mate. As she banged on it, calling to him.

Hunter only gave her a weak smile as his gaze dropped to her stomach before coming back to meet her eyes. Those black orbs that calmed her held everything he'd never said, everything he'd always said. *Everything.*

"I love you, Maya."

Her entire world stopped.

"No!" She dropped to her knees as she banged on the shield. "No, Hunter! No! Please, no!"

"I'm growing quite bored of this," Jenkins huffed in the background, but Maya could hardly focus on him.

"Had mating not been a thing, I would've still fallen in love with you. *Maya*," he tasted the name like their first meeting. "I love you."

She shook her head. "I hate you."

Jenkins's hands stopped on either side of her mate's face as Hunter gave her his signature, perfect, cocky smirk. "Good."

*Good. Good, good, good...good. Good.*

She's always hated him, and he's always loved it.

*Good*. It broke her.

Maya could only stare at her mate as the ground rumbled everywhere but within the shield.

Jenkins laughed. "Sweetheart, I have made sure I cannot be hurt so. We know this."

*Maya, Maya, Maya,* he'd tasted on his tongue.

The ground shuddered, and flames burst out around them, amplified the ones with the shield.

*You. I'm always thinking about you,* he'd whispered late at night.

The flames grew around her, and she could tell the others were backing away as Jenkins gave her a cocky grin.

*You're it, love. All it for me,* he'd moaned against her lips.

The ground rumbled against the shield but couldn't break it.

*You hear that, Mini Maya? Mommy doesn't want me to jinx it,* he'd murmured against her stomach.

Jinxing it had been the best thing that had ever happened to them.

The ground split within the shield, and Jenkins's eyes widened as the cracks continued all around the shield, slowly moving in.

*Don't get used to it, my bleeding heart.* He'd held her.

A pit broke out within the shield, and only the spot which held Hunter and Jenkins remained intact.

Jenkins stared at her with plain fear as his shaky hand brought a dagger to Hunter's throat. "Stop it or he'll be a dead man."

The flames broke out in blue, burning a heat even Hell's Gate didn't hold.

The pit within filled with the blue fire, but all Maya could do was focus on her mate.

Hunter stared at her with the same awe he had the first time she'd opened a portal at the Bridgers coven.

And pride.

He always stared at her with pride.

*I make you this bond that we are in every decision together up until the very basis of your safety, because, love, I don't care how much you hate me for it, if your safety is on the line, I will not hesitate to kill myself to save you,* he'd promised her.

And she'd made the same promise back.

Maya rose to her feet and felt the blue flames engulf her as her gaze moved from her mate to the man responsible for this. "I always think about my family."

White noise filled Maya's ears as the flames grew, and her focus zeroed in on Jenkins. The ground rumbled and thrummed in her bloodstream.

Then, like a firework show, it all exploded with flames so tall and bright she couldn't see anything but the two within the shield. Everyone else was gone.

Her hands rose at her sides, and she breathed out her last restraint and watched without mercy as Jenkins cried out, trying to cling to Hunter in order to remain unhurt.

But what he didn't account for was that Maya would never hurt her mate. The flames would do nothing as they touched Hunter's still kneeling form.

But as they grazed Jenkins, he screamed.

Maya made sure he would not burn. He had forever to spend

within the depths of Hell's Gate, where the flames burst blue and suffrage was far worse than anything most people knew of for the prison down below.

*I love you, Maya,* he'd said without restriction or hesitation.

The ground opened up and swallowed Jenkins, refusing to take Hunter along as the former man clung to him.

When Maya was content with the sounds of Jenkins long gone, the ground closed once more, and slowly, it stopped rumbling.

The flames around her calmed but never settled. She could see everyone else beyond, but could only focus on her husband, her mate.

"Hunter," she whispered into the air.

Hunter slowly rose to his feet and moved for her. She could tell he was weak, but he didn't allow it to stop him.

When he stopped a foot from her, her flames settled a bit more.

When he dropped to his knees, a little more.

When he lifted her shirt to kiss her stomach, the world calmed around her.

And when he whispered her name like a prayer, she was entirely back to him.

## 47

*H*er family was okay. Vera found herself in that selfish thought first. The Whittles and Delvauxs—because they'd now cemented themselves as part of the family—were okay.

Her next worry went to her distant family, the Wittlieffs. There were scuffs about them as with her own family, but they were alive.

Vera followed Harry around as he moved from one injured person to the next, healing them. She needed to be in his presence, but she wouldn't be as selfish as to keep him from healing the people that had come to this fight partly for the protection of those she loved most. But she needed to remain by his side. She wanted nothing more than to settle into his arms and breathe in his scent. The way he brought her in for a hug and quick kiss after each person he healed told Vera he felt the same way.

And it gave him a moment's rest that his body needed as much as anyone else there. That selfish part of Vera also wanted to steal him away so he could heal himself before worrying about the others.

Most of their lot—the other covens, the wolves, the Ragtag House, and the few others—were injured but alive.

Guilt rode up Vera's throat every time her gaze landed on those who hadn't made it—three from the Ragtag House, two wolves from the tribe, and six from the five covens. Overall, their loss of eleven was a speck compared to all the other dead around them, but they hurt Vera more. These were allies. People who had come into this fight at her side, and though she hadn't known any of them really, they mattered to Vera.

When all were as healed as they were going to get, the heads of each group met together with her family at the edge of the hill. Vera remained huddled within Harry's arms as the coven leaders were the first to speak, announcing they would be leaving with their covens. They did not offer help with taking care of the bodies of the other side or helping find the covens for each of the hypnotized witches Ama had been able to help.

Vera wouldn't blame them for that. Though they were basically strangers to her family, those covens were greater friends with one another, so a loss to one was a loss to all. And they'd had six to the zero of the Whittles.

As they walked off, Vera turned to those standing around them.

Tamire held Lila close to his side, the way Harry held Vera, and kissed the side of her neck while whispering low to her. It was especially relieving for those two to be all right as they had a daughter to get back to.

To their right stood Alloy and Brynn, the gargoyle and North American mermaid heir. They hugged one another as they stared off at the others within the circle. When her gaze met Brynn's momentarily, the mermaid sent her a small, close-lipped smile.

They were good friends with Maya, and Vera was glad her sister had them. And she was especially glad her sister had the other mermaid heir standing next to Brynn.

Bella stood with Vincent, her demon, at her side, their hands clutched as they waited. They were strong and fearless, but they were still children, and it made Vera smile that they did not act as if they knew everything. Instead, they waited for guidance. To think, his faith in her strength was what saved them from Jenkins after all.

Beside them, Hunter and Maya stood wrapped in one another's arms. Now that Maya was completely calmed, she looked far less scary. Hunter had one arm tight around her waist as he held her into his chest while the other hand touched her stomach between their bodies. The man was a monster, but the way he touched and kissed Maya and her belly would've fooled Vera every time.

Beside them, Augustine watched his *darling daughter* and feral son with something akin to love. Or as close to love as his demonic, uncaring heart could come up with.

Warren at his side watched the couple too, except his love was easily readable on his features. His fingers twitched where they played before his stomach, and on closer inspection, Vera noticed a ring on his finger she'd never seen him wear before.

Vera and Harry stood beside them, and to their other side were Camilla and Kai. He was pressed into her back, his hands gentle on her hips. Almost like he wanted to pull her into him and hold on tight, but he was afraid of her rejection. Camilla's stubbornness insisted that now that they weren't in trouble of dying, she would need to resist him still. Vera could imagine how infuriating it was for Kai.

Beside them was Adela, their grandmother from the Wittlieff coven who had stopped the majority of animal demons from attacking with the use of the potions Vera and Harry had found, looking on fondly to her and her sisters. Then those soft eyes turned to her parents, and back again. She was a beautiful old woman, and Vera was glad to have finally gotten the chance to meet her.

Her parents stood to Adela's side, whispering to one another with what Vera guessed was the realization that they were now free to live their lives wholly for themselves, for their own love.

Beside them were Anna and Jakub, the head witch and warlock of the Wittlieff coven. They were a fearsome duo to behold, with a friendship like that of Loretta and Harry's. Strong, unconditional, and ever lasting without the chance of romance.

Luka, the other Wittlieff warlock who had helped them, stood beside Jakub, quietly looking on

At his side were Cora and Rory, the main witches from the Ragtag House. They were never very powerful witches, but they'd always been there for those in their found family and did everything they could for the House. They were the truest of friends and incredible allies on the battlefield.

To their side stood Kellan, alone. Celine hadn't come with him since she was a human and even she understood the ramifications of her being in a battle against all supernaturals. It would get her killed, and Kellan would be so distracted with her, she'd get him killed as well. She'd remained at the House to keep down the fort, and it was obvious all Kellan wanted to do was head back to her. He'd already been on a call with her to let her know he was alive. They'd talked the entire time the warlocks had healed, and he'd only hung up for this final meeting.

To his other side were the heads of the Ragtag House and some of Hunter and Maya's first friends in the supernatural world—Juliette and Felix, the banshee and werewolf duo who were similar to her sister and her demon in many ways. They held one another almost like Hunter and Maya too.

Beside Felix were the other wolves, Hayes and his two seconds, Linc and Lo. While both seconds were fine, Hayes had come away with a gash along his torso, peaking against his neck, that the warlocks hadn't been able to heal since he'd insisted everyone else get attention first, and by the time one had gone to him, the wound was too settled. It had been cleaned up and the pain taken, but he would scar. The gash was nasty, but Vera suspected that was what happened when his wolf form was almost ripped apart.

And finally, flying in circles around them, was the black bird that had flown down in battle and helped Harry rip heads off of those zombie-like creatures when his magical dagger had been lost. Adramalech, Zathrian's familiar bird, was still with them, wrapping up before he flew back to his demon and pregnant mated witch.

The mumblings of the group faded as Bishop cleared his throat. "I'd like to thank all of you for your help here tonight."

Before he continued, Brynn interrupted, "Why thank us? Even if we didn't do it for Hunter and Maya's protection, we would've done it. This affected the whole of the supernatural world. It will be written about and talked about for centuries to come. Maybe stop the next Jenkins from attempting the same thing."

Bishop gave her a cheeky grin. "In any case, I thank you for helping protect my family. We are in your debt, every one of you." His gaze met Hayes' for an extra-long second before continuing on with the group.

"We will help you clean up…" Lila started.

"No," Loretta stopped her. "You need to get back to your daughter." She turned to Kellan. "And you, to your mate." Then Cora and Rory. "And he needs to be taken."

They all laughed as Kellan gave her a thankful look and Cora mumbled, "Yes, ma'am."

When they moved for the few others from the Ragtag House waiting for them, Loretta turned to the wolves. "And you need to get your tribe home. *You* need to rest."

Given they weren't too far from home and wolves were fast runners in their animal states, their injured and tired states shouldn't be too big of a problem. Thankfully, Hayes didn't argue with her and only nodded with respect before turning with his seconds and moving for the other wolves waiting for them.

She turned a final look on Brynn. "Take your sister home. The four of you need to be together right now. Let them go back to being children."

She spoke of Vincent as part of their small family, and it was obvious it made the young demon proud.

Being the demon of the group, he would be shadowing them, one at a time since he was still too young to have the energy to do them all at once, not to mention the amount of energy he exerted during the battle.

He started with Alloy to make sure protection was ready if need be at home. Then Brynn. Then, finally, he wrapped Bella into a tight embrace, and they were gone.

"The rest of you"—she didn't even bother to shoo Juliette and Felix, knowing they wouldn't leave—"let's clean this and get home."

Something about the way she said it brought a lightness to the group, and everyone was laughing while mumbling, "Yes, ma'am."

There was something about her mother, that authority, that made her a little scary.

As Vera turned with Harry at her side, her gaze settled a final time on Hunter and Maya and the bump that indicated to her nieces or nephews, and smiled.

48

There was a protectiveness that came about in the presence of Maya that Warren thought would've happened with Colette had she not tortured him the first chance she'd gotten.

Watching Maya lounge back on the couch in Whittle House with the others around her, he knew though she was far scarier than any of them in that room, he'd do anything to protect her.

She was talking with her family, the Wittlieffs included, who were leaving the next morning with promises from both ends to visit one another often, about the names she and Hunter were thinking about for the babies. Listening to the conversation only made Warren more protective—because in a few months, she wouldn't just be his sister, but she would also be the mother to his nieces or nephews. He would *have* nieces or nephews.

"Just one girl, Esther," Maya said to no one in particular. "I still want it, and Hunt said he loved it. Two girls is when it gets tricky. I like Amethyst, Holland, and Khaleesi, but Hunt doesn't love them. And I refuse to call my child Torianna, so we're still thinking."

Hunter smirked at her. "It means 'to conquer.' We're named

Hunt and War. My daughter will have us as protectors, thus she will conquer those before her."

Maya rolled her eyes. "You don't care about the meanings to any of the other names."

He laughed as Loretta asked, "You don't like any of her names? They were beautiful.

Hunter gave Maya a teasing look. "I could be persuaded on Khaleesi."

Vera grinned as she leaned back into Harry. "And if they're boys?"

"Boys are a tougher one," Maya said, glancing Hunter's way as he leaned against the frame leading to the hallway. "We can't seem to agree, and Hunt's getting on my nerves with naming with an M since they'll be boys, so he should get something out of it."

Loretta laughed. "Well, if he doesn't get his daughter, at least let him name the children with your initial."

It was sort of backwards. One would think Maya would want her own initial, but it was Hunter who was pushing for it. He was that obsessed with her.

"Thank you," Hunter snarked and got a cheeky grin from his mate.

"I do like one of the names he suggested. And it matches well with Nicolai, which is another at the top of my list. We could…"

"You can't have Nicolai," Camilla interrupted, the humor gone from her features as she tried to pass the comment off as nothing serious.

Warren narrowed his gaze on the girl as Maya simply said, "Well, looks like my sister's called dibs, so no for that M name too."

Warren shot his gaze to Kai, who stood on edge off in the corner of the room. The two hadn't spoken much past clipped answers since they'd been back, and Warren was surprised the warlock wasn't doing more after what had happened.

After Camilla had jumped over him.

After she'd been ready to go with him.

He wondered what they were waiting for at this point.

But Kai watched Camilla with a hard glare. The man looked like he needed something from her, and Warren didn't have to think hard to know the two just needed their time alone.

He was shocked though, when he turned to find Camilla staring at the warlock before leaving the room altogether. Even more so when Kai didn't immediately follow.

Warren moved for the couch to sit with his new sister and took her hand in his as the conversations moved away from the babies and the room filled with too many to keep track of.

"Miss me already, Little Brother?" Maya's head fell to his shoulder.

He gave a humorless chuckle as he let his head fall over hers. "Can I ask you something?"

"Always," she said in what he could tell was a smile. "That's what big sisters are for."

"I wouldn't know," he muttered as another image of Colette came to mind.

Maya gave an airy laugh as she asked, "What is it, War?"

"What was your initial response to meeting Hunt? Like that first time?"

She was quiet for a few moments before answering, "A bit scared. I *had* walked in on him stabbing a priest through the chest and looking unfazed, even excited about it. But realistically, I was really turned on. It was…weird. I'd never been so affected so instantly by looking at anyone, but I *had* to push my thighs together. It was…" she shook her head, "crazy."

"What happened afterwards? That's when you met in the forest, right?"

"Afterwards, we came home and talked about what had happened, and the idea came about to lure him out to the forest to find out who he was. I was volunteered because of our similar powers, but I was secretly so excited. I was annoyed with myself for it, but I wanted to see him. Then I practiced my power by thinking about him in order to try to control myself a bit. It's odd, now that I think back, how vividly I could bring up his picture and how instantly my body would react."

A flash of green eyes shot past his memories as Warren looked down to his and Maya's intertwined hands.

"Then I went out and *knew* he would be the one to find me. *Knew* he wouldn't let anyone else near me. And when I say I knew, I mean in a primal way. I genuinely knew I was his, even if I would've never admitted it back then. And for that same reason, I wasn't really scared. I was more nervous because obviously big, bad demon, but not scared. And again, very horny."

A flash of stroking himself to the picture of cropped black hair and green eyes. Over and over and over because it was never enough.

"He came up behind me, and I knew he wouldn't hurt me. The entire time we were together there, I knew I should be more scared, but I just wanted him so badly, and I *knew* he wouldn't hurt me. Then again, afterwards, I should've been terrified as a new witch having angered a seasoned demon. I mean, we'd knocked him over the head and ported out." She laughed. "But when I saw him in that gym with all those kids, I was disgusted at what he'd done, but again…"

"Turned on," Warren finished with her, and they both laughed.

"He just looked so sexy lounging back on that chair, and he had a dagger he was flipping between his fingers. It was fucking sexy, War. Then, I don't know, I was just never worried about him hurting me. It got to a point where I started to understand my power over him without us ever having to talk about it. I mean, especially since we didn't really talk down below. I just knew where we stood."

"So you started to boss him around?" he teased.

She grinned. "We teamed up."

And they had. From agreeing to take down the Bridgers coven to working together to set those witches to flames to allowing Hunter to take all the powers he'd like to protecting one another against Melusine. They'd always been a team.

"When did you realize he was it for you then? I guess your equivalent to realizing the mating?"

She shrugged. "It happened so naturally. I don't think I ever actually realized it. But I guess…I started to realize something really different between us when we shadowed down from the trees at the Bridgers coven and he said something to me…*I could've been across the field, and had you fallen, I would've caught you.* And then, after that first night with him, we woke up that morning…"

"In his manor which he never allowed anyone to!" Warren interrupted.

Maya laughed. "Yes, in that blasted manor!" They both laughed. "I woke up, and we were both lying on our sides, facing each other, and he was still asleep, and I was just watching him, and it felt so…right. I don't think I was ready to admit it to myself yet because of my family, but I think I knew then that I would spend the rest of my life by his side and—"

Hunter came out of nowhere and pulled Maya away from Warren's side.

Warren blanched. "We were having a conversation!"

Hunter took the spot Maya had just been sitting in and growled. "You were touching my mate. Far too much."

"Oh, grow up." Warren pushed at his brother as Maya took her seat in Hunter's lap.

"As I was saying," she snuggled into Hunter as she faced Warren, "afterwards, it kind of naturally progressed. Especially after everyone knew, it just naturally became us, I guess. I just knew I was in love with him, and this was it for me. It honestly felt human."

"What did, love?" Hunter closed his eyes as he skimmed his nose down Maya's jaw.

"My side of the mating."

"I was asking my beautiful sister, whom you hardly deserve," Warren cut in, and Hunter smirked his way, "what your initial meetings felt like and when she realized her side of the mating."

"Ah," Hunter cooed against her cheek.

"Tell your side too." Maya didn't ask.

"No," Hunter barked.

"Baby," Maya said in a soft, almost begging tone.

"He didn't ask, love."

"But I like hearing you talk about it." She pouted her lip, and Warren could tell how transfixed his brother was with that small act.

So he added to it. "And now I wanna know."

Hunter rolled his eyes at his brother, but now Warren truly wanted to know. Because as half human, he might react like Maya. But as half demon, he was more likely to react like his brother.

And he'd always been curious about how the matings came about. Not that his brother had ever been willing to speak on it. Having Maya on his side was really turning things around for him.

Hunter huffed. "What do you want?"

"Initial reaction. Church and forest."

"Church. Nothing really at first, too distracted with being a demon and having witches before me. Thought it'd be fun to scare them. Then she shot flames at me, and I was intrigued."

"So nothing...dirty?" Warren asked, eyeing Maya with a quirked, teasing brow.

Hunter chuckled in a way that told Warren he knew exactly why that question came about. "No. Intrigued. And all I knew was I was going to be the only person to get to her, so I guess the mating was speaking out a bit. But that's it. Forest. I started to really feel the consequences of being near her. I was hard as a fucking rock between my legs. Then she said her name..." His head fell back with obvious bliss as he lost himself in memory.

Warren froze. *Then she said her name.*

Her name.

Warren needed to know her name. Taste it.

He tried to calm his reaction. He was taking things far out of proportion. He just wanted a mate and saw a hot chick and was making far too much out of the situation.

"How'd you know to make the rings?" The one question he'd always wondered about his brother.

"Colette came around."

It was answer enough, and one Warren understood best out of everyone there.

"I couldn't risk anything happening, but it wasn't just for her safety, just for feeling her emotions or location through the rings. It was primal—I needed to make her mine." He shook his head. "I don't think I'll ever be able to explain it to someone who hasn't experienced it. That day I got the call that Colette was here, that entire life that I hadn't even realized I'd already pictured with Maya came crumbling down because if Colette was around, there was a high probably Maya could get hurt. When I got here and saw Maya was all right, heard her say she wasn't touched at all...staring into her eyes, I knew she was my mate. It was an instant decision—I would deal with our sister, then begin on the rings."

Warren nodded his acknowledgement but said nothing more.

When Hunter realized so, he turned Maya to him and began whispering to her. Warren smiled to himself watching the two of them laugh and whisper to one another as one of Hunter's hands remained glued to her stomach while the other pulled her in closer by the hips. It was wholesome in a way Warren never expected from his brother.

As he turned to the rest of the room, a warmth settled within him for this group, one he'd never expected to be lucky enough to find himself a part of.

And as he turned to his newest friend, Warren watched as the Demon Warlock finally huffed, and was glad for the distraction from his own thoughts as he watched the warlock leave the room, no doubt after the little Whittle.

# 49

$\mathcal{H}$arry softly tugged her hand to follow him to the piano room. *Their room.*

Vera was glad for it. Though she enjoyed spending time with her family, especially with all that had happened since finding out about being part of the supernatural world, Vera wanted this time alone with Harry. She was especially thankful for a more peaceful life with him now. One where they didn't have to be on the search for psychopaths trying to kill their family. They'd just be going back to a life with the occasional attack from animal demons, though even that Vera doubted with Hunter and Maya's control over them now.

In any case, time alone with her warlock was a small piece of Heaven brought down to her. Especially in their room.

Harry allowed her to walk in, then whispered at the door.

Vera narrowed her gaze. "I thought the silencing charms were permanently placed in every room already."

Harry turned to her with a smirk. "But locking charms aren't. I don't need anyone interrupting us, sweetheart."

Vera flushed and involuntarily stepped back, the backs of her knees hitting the piano bench. "Why would we need to lock the door?"

Harry's smirk was wicked now. "I want you to play for me. And only me."

It took a moment for Vera to catch up with what he was saying because of the distracting burn of her body. "W-What?"

He chuckled, sexy and delightful. "Play me my songs, Vera. All of the ones you've written for me. In order. I want to listen to your feelings for me from the beginning."

Her body was still distracted with being in a silenced, locked room, and the memory of being pressed against that glass wall or bent over as she clung to the window or piano.

Vera breathed heavily to bring herself entirely back to the present, and smiled at Harry, something genuine and warm on her features. "Let's sit then."

Harry took his usual spot at her side, and his gaze fell immediately to her hands, the same way they had since the very beginning. The same way they still did most of the time if he wasn't watching her face for the passion he said was always there.

Vera turned to him for a moment, reaching to hold his face with one hand as she leaned in for a delicate kiss. "I love you, Harry."

"And I you, sweetheart." He kissed her once more.

Turning back to the piano, Vera's hands danced over the keys before she settled on the first song she had written for Harry. It had been about wanting him and not being able to have him because he was her family warlock. About believing she was stuck in this hopeless, unrequited love.

That night he'd told her about finding out about her parents had showed to Vera that he cared for her, and she'd wanted nothing more than to run to her room and cry with how desperately she wanted to be pulled into his arms and held by him.

When he'd pulled her into his arms a moment later and kissed her, Vera's entire world had exploded. Shattered into pieces she could hardly believe possible.

Since that kiss months ago, Vera had written a few songs for him. And though it was the most painful one, her favorite was still this first one.

When she finished this first melody, Vera's fingers paused on the keys. "I think that will always be my favorite song."

"Mine too."

Her head snapped to look at him. "Really? But the others speak more of my love for you."

His head shook softly. "This one speaks of your love for me when you thought it hopeless. You didn't love me because I loved you, but simply because that is how you felt. It is the same way I did—I didn't care if you didn't reciprocate it. I loved you, and that was that, Vera."

Unshed tears came to her waterline, but Vera only smiled as she turned back to the piano and began with the second song she'd written for him—this one when she already had him.

---

The astronomy tower was officially their tower, and though Camilla wanted a break from him, she needed to be there. It was *theirs*.

What she really wanted was to be in his arms.

She scoffed at herself as she stood by the edge and stared out at all the stars shining down at her, knowing one of them was Nico, and he was berating her for hurting his brother.

"I know," she whispered to the stars. "I don't want to, but...I can't get myself to stop."

The breeze was soft around her, and Camilla swore it spoke to her as if someone was whispering, *He's difficult, but he's the best person around.*

A close-lipped sad smile lifted on Camilla's face as she thought back to the conversation she was ready to have with him after screaming into her pillow as her mother had suggested, and how that opportunity had been ripped away when they'd had to go after Jenkins. When she thought about the fact that she hadn't been able to tell him how she felt before going into a possible life-or-death battle.

Then she looked down at the folded paper she'd been fiddling with the entire time she'd walked to and been at the tower.

Her gaze finally jumped back up to the stars, to Nico. "I want to tell him that I'm in…"

"Hiding from me?" Kai's voice broke her as she turned with a jump. "We don't have this little problem keeping me around any longer. Hide away long enough and you won't even have to deal with me, is that it?"

She knew she should be more understanding of his pain, but the annoyance still rang from her. "If I was trying to hide from you, why would I go to the one spot we share?"

"I don't know, *princess*," he almost spit the word out. "Why do you do a lot of the things you do?"

Camilla flashed back to covering him in the fight, knew he was thinking of the same moment. Their lips had been so close, and she'd wanted nothing more than to kiss him.

But she hadn't allowed herself to. Because their first kiss wouldn't be a possible goodbye. She'd forced away to make sure they got their time.

And because she'd been pushing aside all the things she truly wanted, her frustration ebbed to the top of her thoughts. "What do you want from me, Kai? What—"

"I'm not here to argue with you. I just need to ask you one thing," Kai grit through his teeth.

Camilla stared at him, afraid for the question she knew was coming.

He stepped forward, but miles still separated them. "Why not allow her the use of that name? It would be an honor to my brother for their son to hold his name."

When Camilla didn't answer, he visibly grew more frustrated.

"Tell me it's because it will be *our* son's name." After another bout of silence that Camilla could not get herself out of, he grit, "Tell me that's the life you see for us, Camilla."

Camilla swallowed back and raised a barely steady hand to show Kai the folded paper in her hands.

He stared down at it for a long moment before taking it and scoffing as he opened it. "What fucking excuse d—"

He stared down at the paper with furrowed brows, then up at her.

As nervous as she was, this time, Camilla would give him his answer. "I figured, he may get a bit bullied for it, but if his mother and father share the name, he should too."

Those beautiful hazel browns widened before he dropped the folded paper with the words *Nicolai Georgette Sinclair* to the ground and stalked toward her.

Before she could process his movements, he cradled her face between his hands and kissed her with a passion Camilla hadn't known until him. The same passion that fueled their arguments and kept them coming together time and again.

She kissed him back with every bit of herself, gave herself to him finally and fully.

They might not be demons, but this was their version of a mating.

When he pulled away, he just stared down at her for long moments. "I've been wanting to do that for a long time."

"I've wanted you to do that for a long time," she admitted against his mouth.

His lips tipped up into a smirk, and he leaned in again, opening her mouth for his tongue and giving her every ounce of himself.

## 50

There was a hope that by the time the babies came about, the family would be given the location of the second Delvaux Manor. They'd assumed since they were in it, that problem would have been taken care of.

What they hadn't accounted for was Hunter's spell around the property to wipe anyone's recollection of the location if he didn't change access restrictions. So they—everyone but the actual Delvauxs—continued to forget the location.

And Hunter was using it as a treat at the end of a stick, enjoying that they all wanted to know but couldn't. A real asshole.

Not like Maya helped. She only laughed when Hunter continued to play with them.

Loretta moved for her husband's lap as he and Augustine sat back in the pool room of Hunter and Maya's manor, watching the others in the water. It made Loretta imagine them as actual children splashing around rather than grown adults throwing each other about. Especially with Hunter's stolen water power and his annoyance at the lot, and Vera's levitating.

For the most part, Hunter tried to keep Maya in the corner of the pool as he caged her in, kissed her, and whispered against her lips. His hands played with her rounded belly, looking to have spurted overnight with how much larger it looked now compared to a week ago.

The others were more unruly, and that's when the demon would turn with his water power and tsunami them away from his little corner with his mate.

It was sweet, if not a bit too savage.

Again, though, Maya only laughed and pulled him in for another kiss.

In the meantime, Kai and Harry had their fun, allowing Camilla and Vera onto their shoulders for a chicken fight.

Loretta laughed as her hands settled around Bishop's neck. "They truly are children."

Augustine looked bored with the scene, not in the slightest affected by any of it. In fact, he continued to close his eyes for a nap rather than take any of it in. "Yes. Annoying, isn't it."

It wasn't a question. So completely demon of him.

Bishop laughed. "They will finally know a life in the supernatural that isn't plagued with attacks and mysteries. They will finally be able to enjoy this life of ours."

There was a fondness in the way he spoke, which made Loretta happy to hear as she responded, "We will finally know a life of being a family."

His eyes remained closed, but Augustine snickered at the comment, obviously not pleased by the fact that he was now part of this family. Because, though he loved and protected Maya, he truly didn't care for the rest of them.

It made both Loretta and Bishop laugh, though they tried to hide their amusement in one another's necks.

When they calmed down, they stared one another in the eyes, and Loretta whispered, "Thank you for choosing me, Bish. Thank you for this life we've lived and loved."

He shook his head. "Thank you, my love."

Warren had left the others in the pool room not long after they'd arrived. He'd needed to be alone, and what better chance than this to explore his brother's manor?

In reality, he'd only been looking for the library.

It was a grander room than their father's, but not as grand as Warren would have in his own manor. It was the one room he was ready to fill to the brim.

The library in Hunter and Maya's place was far away from the others within the manor, but in his current mental state, Warren needed to be away from them. Seeing the couples added to his wounds of desiring a mate. He wasn't envious in the way that he wished them to stop showing their love, but simply in wanting to show his own affection to his mate.

Ever since speaking with Maya and Hunter about their experiences, Warren hadn't been able to fight the undeniable—he may have bumped into his mate at the market all those weeks prior.

The more logical side of him said he was drawing circles where there were only squares. He was making this up because of his desire for a mate.

But something else within him, something almost primal, said it wasn't a lie. This was it.

Though not truly, since he had no idea who that girl had been or any way of ever finding her again.

As he played with the new ring on his finger, the picture of the girl was as clear as day in his mind. The way she looked up at him, just shy of Maya's height, but not quite Camilla's. The way those green eyes had shined up at him like *she* was *affected*. What had Maya said? Crazy turned on?

Warren laughed to himself as he stopped twisting the piece of jewelry, and his fingers skimmed the books within the library. It was amusing how horniness and wishful dreaming got him—thinking about a woman he didn't know and had no way of finding and imaging *her* affected by *him* rather than vice versa.

The way her lips had parted as she'd stared up at him, enticing Warren to lean down and taste them. Like he'd wanted to taste her name on his lips.

It still ate him up, the need to know her name.

*Then she said her name.*

If what his brother said applied to Warren as well, needing to taste her name was the only true evidence Warren had that this mystery girl was his mate.

But as he strolled the library and thought about it, he didn't want to bring his hope up. Not just because he didn't know how to find her again, but if he did find her, he wanted to learn her before knowing they were destined to be together in every life they lived.

It would be a difficult feat since he already wore his mated ring, which he'd made out of his own blood and the bit of hers the broken vase had collected. It would be impossible to forget about her as he wore her half of the rings on a chain around his neck, needing it to be close if it wasn't going to be on her finger. Whoever she was.

He knew it was ridiculous, but the same way Hunter said he couldn't explain his need to make the rings and officially make Maya his, Warren couldn't explain his need. All he knew was that he had to make the rings the moment he got home with the broken vase.

Warren tried to forget about her as he pulled a random book from the shelves.

As he flipped the pages, he couldn't help but think of the way her black hair had flowed around her shoulders as she'd turned away from him, almost like it was begging for his attention, for him to get a grip by her scalp and turn her back to him.

Warren closed his eyes and breathed out, whispering to himself, "She was just a beautiful girl, War, get yourself together."

As he looked down to the random page he'd flipped to, Warren stared into the eyes of a man behind a mirror. Another children's storybook—this one about a man who'd been sent to Hell's Gate, but instead of losing all his powers down below, he was still able to communicate to others above. The caveat—only his mate could respond.

This story always toyed with the fact that the man would live lifetimes, centuries, forever, never being able to find his mate.

The book ended with the man never finding said woman and stuck speaking to everyone through their dreams and mirrors and never getting any response back. Always searching.

Warren had always wondered if part of the reason had been in order to find his other half, or if it had fully been for the ability to have his mate help him out of the prison.

He scoffed and placed the book back. The story was a little too apt for his current situation—dreaming of his girl and never being able to see her again.

# EPILOGUE

*O*ne year ago today, her sister and the demon she hated most in the world had been sent to Hell's Gate by her boyfriend.

Camilla had been frantic and still arguing with her own feelings about who and what demons were. Because Hunter was a demon. But so was Warren. And she had thought them to be so very different.

Then he'd sent her sister down to Hell's Gate, and she'd been so angry. The idea of demons infuriated her.

Now, she would be an aunt to two little demons. And based on their annoying father, that was a figurative name along with a literal one. She could already see herself wrapped around both of their fingers.

Another scream echoed through the manor, and shivers ran down Camilla's spine as she looked up at Kai. "I lied. I don't ever want kids."

He laughed and took her face between his hands. "I'm a warlock, princess. The healing power will keep some of the pain off too. It's not our fault your sister refused it."

"Yeah, well, you know tough guy Maya." She smiled up at him.

He leaned down for a kiss that felt so right that every time he did it, it felt like her world was settling. She didn't know how else to explain it.

They broke apart as another cry shattered through the manor.

"You know, this big old manor we're finally allowed to, and we're standing right by the door that's freaking us all out of children," Vera said as she fell against the wall, making no moves to walk away.

Camilla laughed as she copied her sister. As much fun as this didn't sound, Maya was in the pushing stages and would soon deliver the babies. They weren't inside with her because she'd asked for it only to be her and Hunter with the birthing nurses—whose memories of this location Hunter's spell around the property was already ready to erase.

Even their mother hadn't been allowed in.

But Loretta hadn't been offended. She'd said she'd been the exact same way when she'd had all three of them—wanting only Bishop in the room, even if her mother had been an option.

So now, they all stood by the door to the room they were using as their birthings room—Vera, Harry, Warren, Augustine, Loretta, Bishop, Kai, and herself—with a ready Bridgers family a call away to introduce little Aurelia to the babies, and the Wittlieffs excited to port over as soon as possible. Adela had spoken of coming to the manor to wait along with them but had needed her rest, so they'd all insisted they would call when the babies were here. All of them—the Bridgers and Wittlieffs— were on Hunter's side and hoping for girls.

Camilla had a feeling, for this one thing, everyone was on Hunter's side.

"Hey." Bishop grinned at them. "It is Halloween. She's bringing a bit of fright into your lives."

They all laughed as her mother added, "Kind of apt, don't you think? A year after they were sent to Hell's Gate together, they're having their two babies."

Before they could answer, a cry rang through the manor, and they all held their breaths. A baby.

They had a baby!

Airy laughs fell out of all of them—even Augustine—as tears began to brittle at Camilla's waterline—her parents not far behind—and she turned to her man for a hug.

Kai held her tight, breathed in her scent at her neck, and brought Camilla to this reality of the two of them. Of the fact that she'd fallen in love with the man she hated. Because he was never the enemy, but damn, had he irked her to the core.

Still did, honestly. And she would never change that.

When they pulled away again, Kai leaned in so they were in their own little bubble and whispered, "Thank you, princess. For giving me this family."

At this point, Camilla didn't know if the watering in her eyes was for the crying baby in the other room or for her warlock. "Thank you for loving me despite my flaws."

"You make it quite impossible not to love you, Camilla Georgette Sinclair."

She laughed against his lips. "I'm not a Sinclair yet, remember, Kai Georgette Sinclair?"

Another cry popped through the rooms, and Camilla looked around to find everyone in accordance—there was baby number two. Her sister was officially a mom to twins.

When she turned to Kai for another hug, he kissed her tenderly and whispered, "You'll be one soon, princess. I don't want to wait for age to catch up. I don't care if people think you're too young."

She held him closer so their lips were basically molded as she said, "We're supernatural, Kai. No one's gonna care if I may seem a bit younger than the average human nowadays."

"So we don't care about the human life any longer?" He knew all about her desires to keep harmony between her old and new lives.

She shook her head, her fingers digging into the shirt at his back. "All I care about is this life. With you."

"So marry me. As soon as your sister feels up for participating in a small wedding."

Maya and Hunter had mated at the beginning of the year, and not long after had an official wedding to be both mates and husband and wife. Vera had married Harry over the summer.

She gave him a cocky smirk as she shrugged. "I guess it would be kind of funny if we all got married in the same year."

"Hilarious, princess." He was still looking down at her seriously. He truly wanted this.

She rose to the tips of her toes and whispered against those lips she'd become obsessed with. "I cannot wait to be a Sinclair, Kai. If she's up for it, I'd marry you tomorrow."

Tears bubbled to his eyes but didn't fall. "I think we can give her a little longer than a day to recover."

She laughed as she kissed him. "I love you, Kai. And I'm so glad you decided to follow me around even though you hated me too."

He shrugged. "I was always attracted to you, more than just physically. I didn't like it, but I needed to know more about you. There was nothing that could've stopped me from being at your side."

The door opened before she could get another word in, and the nursemaid smiled at them as she opened it wide to let them know they could come in. "Two boys."

They all caught each other's gazes and laughed. Hunter had been right—Maya always got what she wanted.

Her parents were the first to enter. Followed by her sister and new brother, then her ex—who coincidently was her sister's brother now—then herself with Kai, then the last grandparent.

They all moved for the bed Maya was now lying in, the pool for her water birth already getting cleaned by the nursemaids.

Maya held one baby in her arms as Hunter, who sat pressed up against her, held the other. They both stared down at the bundles with all their attention before looking to one another for a kiss, then back to the babies. Over and over.

Camilla's attention hovered over Hunter as he stared down at his babies, then looked over to his wife, and she knew of one thing in this life she was grateful for, it was that Maya had found Hunter. That he'd be the perfect father to those babies.

As they moved closer, all the warlocks froze and gasped down at them.

And all three Delvaux men acted accordingly, staring at them with hard edged gazes, stances hardening like they would attack if need be. Camilla's breath held, afraid for what could've possibly gotten all three men to react like that.

"What?" Hunter growled.

"They're..." Kai started.

"Warlocks," Harry finished in the silence of the room.

Now all eyes shot to the babies. It was a well-known fact that a baby boy born to a witch and demon, or warlock and demon, could only be a human demon, not inheriting any of the warlock features. It was only the girls who got both sides and were demon witches.

"That's impossible," Loretta gasped as she stared up to her husband.

Warlocks were the only ones who could tell when a baby had the warlock features. Other than that, the boy would have to wait until adolescence to see if the powers came in.

All Bishop did was shake his head. "It's meant to be. But this daughter of ours has made everything impossible seem the opposite."

They laughed as the new parents caught one another's gaze and kissed. Hunter whispered something against Maya's lips that wasn't heard by anyone else, but Camilla knew it was something to do with how much he loved her.

"Demon warlocks," Harry finally voiced.

Then Camilla turned to her man. "Looks like you can't hold that title anymore."

He huffed down at her with a smirk that held all the warmth in the world. "That makes me even more a part of the family. Someone's gotta teach 'em what it's like to be a demon warlock."

They all laughed again because though Kai wasn't a demon, his brotherhood with Nico and preference for demons inherited that title to him. And none of them, not even the uncaring Augustine or Hunter, would take that well-deserved title from the man.

Finally, Loretta moved to sit by Maya's side and stroked her hair back. "So do we have names for these impossible demon warlocks?"

Maya finally looked up at them and smiled. She pointed to the one in Hunter's arms. "That's Malachi Bishop." She handed her baby to their mother. "And this is Dmitri Augustine."

Bishop fell over his wife's shoulder as the first grandparent held a baby.

Then Augustine was at his son's side and Hunter was handing the baby over.

"I would give all our kids M names, but it wasn't even a consideration by my mate." Hunter teased his wife. "But Dmitri has a strong M in it, so it sounds just as perfect."

Camilla fell back into Kai as he held her tight and whispered down to her, a tear falling from his cheek to her shoulder. "Thank you, Camilla. So much for this family. For giving me a family."

***

Hunter stood off to the edge of the room and watched as the rest of the group fiddled over his family.

"Hard pressed to get a shit-eating grin on your face, brother. You have the perfect family now, what else could you possibly need for that smile to make an appearance?"

Hunter's eyes shined with his joy, and he'd worn a small, close-lipped smile, but as he turned to his brother, a smirk came about. "That shit-eating grin is reserved for my mate alone. And for when I get my daughter."

Warren shoved into his shoulder. "Always the asshole, brother."

They both turned to the others by the bed and watched as they all laughed. Watched as Augustine tried to hog both of his grandsons to himself, and Vera fought him for a nephew. Watched as Maya sent a glance toward Hunter every few seconds, not for help, but because she felt the constant need to do so.

Hunter loved seeing her equally as obsessed with him as he was with her.

Warren let out a breathy laugh. "I still can't believe you made an impossible happen, Hunt. Demon warlocks! Your swimmers really work, don't they?"

Hunter had to fight the shit-eating grin now as he shoved into his brother. Then they were both back to staring at their family.

"Thank you, brother," Hunter finally whispered the words he'd wished to tell his brother for months as he stared at his mate.

"For what?" Warren asked, his gaze burning into Hunter's profile.

Hunter finally pulled his eyes from his mate to his brother. "For sending us to Hell's Gate."

Warren's brows furrowed. "You two are mates. You would've gotten together whether I sent you or not."

"I know." Another small smile lifted Hunter's lips as he thought back to the year prior. "Down below is where we had our first kiss, so thank you. For giving us that time alone together. I have no doubts she would've tried to resist me a little longer had we not been forced to that cage."

Warren laughed. "Even though you two didn't speak the entire time you were down there."

Hunter smirked now, wicked and seductive. "Mates don't need to speak to understand one another."

Warren looked like he was having a flash of something but smirked back before Hunter could question it. "Well, then, you're welcome, brother. And while we're on thank yous, thank *you* for mating to the best sister a man could've asked for. For giving me two perfect little nephews."

A warmth settled into Hunter as he turned back to his family. "I thank Maya for those same things every night as she sleeps in my arms."

# DON'T FORGET TO REVIEW!

Thank you so much for finishing your read! Don't forget to leave a review or rating on all platforms as it helps me as an author more than you can ever imagine!

Amazon and Goodreads ratings help the most but feel free to talk about it everywhere else too—including social medias, blogs, Youtube reviews, and most importantly—word of mouth, and more.

# JOIN MY AUTHOR NEWSLETTER

Sign up for Nelly Alikyan's newsletter to be the first to know about new releases and cover reveals, receive exclusive content —like a special scene or two—and be up to date about any other exciting news, i.e. events, signed copies, etc.

www.nellyalikyan.com

# ABOUT THE AUTHOR

Nelly Alikyan is a girl from the Los Angeles Valley who's constantly on the move—from Boston to London to wherever she chooses next. She's the only reader in her family—not her only cause as the black sheep—and has dreamt of being a writer for as long as she can remember.

When she's not working on her books or in the real world, she's on Youtube at Nelly Alikyan!

For more books and updates:
www.nellyalikyan.com

instagram.com/authornellyalikyan
tiktok.com/@authornalikyan
youtube.com/NellyAlikyan
amazon.com/author/nellyalikyan
goodreads.com/nellyalikyan
facebook.com/authornellyalikyan
pinterest.com/insinpublishing

# ACKNOWLEDGMENTS

To the show Charmed for being the inspiration to book one and finally waking up the writer in me.

To all the readers who have read along the entire series and have fallen in love with Hunter and Warren and Kai and Harry and Augustine and the whole lot. To everyone who loves Maya and Camilla and Vera and the whole gang. Thank you for giving this series a chance.

Thank you, and I can't wait to see you in whatever I write next!